S0-BAM-561

THE WANTING OF LEVINE

MICHAEL HALBERSTAM

A BERKLEY BOOK
published by
BERKLEY PUBLISHING CORPORATION

Excerpts from this book have appeared in *Esquire* and the *Washington Post*.

FOR MY LATE FATHER,

CHARLES,

WHO, I HOPE, WOULD HAVE BEEN AMUSED,

AND FOR MY MOTHER,

BLANCHE,

WHO, I HOPE, WILL BE.

STATE OF THE UNION
SPRING, 1988

It was the worst of times, the worst of times, the worst of times. Everyone said so, though no one exactly knew why. The Mexicans were acting crazy, and the blacks wanted to turn the country back into some kind of prison, and the states were at each other's throats, and worst of all, the air conditioning was only on for two or three hours a day. A whole country was learning to do with less, and it was doing so with bad grace. Not that anyone ever learns to be happy when the party's over and the money tree stops yielding, but when 250 million people have to start learning it all at once, well, then you've got troubles.

Bad as it was, it wasn't like the Depression, the big one that the old people still remembered, because back then some rich people got by and stayed rich. Hell, a few did even better than before, what with prices down. But when the gas started to run out and the government came up with the energy coupons, no one escaped. You had to give the government credit—there wasn't much cheating that could be done with the coupons. The middle-class people, the ones who had hit it big in the fifties and sixties with their businesses and their professions, had it the worst. The nice things that went with their jobs were gone. There were no more easy trips to Las Vegas and Miami Beach for conventions. The American Bar Association met in Chicago instead of London. Everyone met in Chicago, now that gas was scarce.

One problem was there wasn't any fun to it. You had no feeling that everyone was struggling against the enemy, the way you felt when you collected milkweed to fill life jackets to keep the sailors floating in the war against the Japs. There was no enemy. There was no great hardship; there were just a lot of little hardships, and they, together, were the hardest kind to bear. In the winter there were

1

wood rustlers everywhere. You'd go to some back lot and find they'd been out in the night with their chain saws. And even honest folk—any time lightning knocked over a tree, people with saws would swarm all over it, like ants at a picnic.

How could you really complain about being hot and sticky in the summertime? People had always been hot and sticky in the summertime. Most everyone remembered being hot and sticky when they were young, and it was hard to work up a lot of anger and bad feeling because, after riding in air-conditioned cars for twenty years and finally feeling that it was your God-given right, you had to go back to a stuffy car and damp underarms and glasses that kept slipping off your nose from the sweat.

After all, in the old days people had complained about the air conditioning and the drive-ins and the supermarkets. Someone had written a book about an air-conditioned nightmare, and he was supposed to have been writing about America. People used to make fun of supermarkets all the time, but when they couldn't get the groceries any more, when the planes couldn't fly in the strawberries in December and the oranges in July, people didn't like it. The same ones who complained about markets that were too big, markets where you couldn't get a real neighborly feeling, began to complain that the new little neighborhood markets didn't have enough choices (they didn't) and had very high prices (they did).

There wasn't any war, which was a blessing, but you could never tell about the Mexicans. You'd always figured things were bad in Mexico—poverty and all that—and that they hated their rich neighbor, but you never thought they'd really *do* something about it. Now not a day went by without some kind of trouble—border incidents, kidnappings, trade embargoes, that kind of thing. The smoke that precedes fire.

Besides, the thing with the separate states was bad enough to be a war. Who would have believed when you read all the business about seperate and sovereign states back in high school civics that all *that* would come up again? Nobody was talking about secession yet, but matters on the edge were almost as bad. The troubles that had started with the little jealousies between states—the smuggling of cigarettes from North Carolina to New York, the lobster war between Maine and New Hampshire—had gotten ugly when the states, along with everyone else, began to run out of money. New York was losing $10 million every year in taxes from cigarettes trucked up from North Carolina, and if a state is going broke, $10 million looks like a lot of money. So when New York started inspecting all trucks coming up from the South, especially North Carolina, the people down south were not overjoyed, and it was not long before state policemen in North Carolina began stopping tourists with New York tags using up their precious coupons on their way to Florida, a duty the troopers did not particularly need to have urged on them. New York protested, but not much happened, so the state legislature in Albany passed a monstrously large sales tax on furniture made outside New York, a bill which happened to hit North Carolina right in the kishkes (as the chairman of the Joint Senate-Assembly Committee remarked joyfully). Too, it was a lot harder to smuggle sofas than cigarettes, though people tried.

This lesson was not ignored by Maine, which was having trouble with lobstermen from the strip of New Hampshire shoreline poaching in Maine waters. "Shit," said the mayor of Bangor, "give New Hampshire twenty miles of shore and they claim two hundred miles in every direction. Next to Chile, they think they're the world's leading fishing nation." Not that this trouble hadn't been going on for a hundred and fifty years, but lobsters were getting scarcer than snowballs in July, and expensive too. So, having tried to settle the matter in what was considered (by State-of-Mainers, anyway) a gentlemanly way, the Maine statehouse went ahead and slapped a tax on everything made in New Hampshire.

Up and down the country, states were snarling at each other. Oregon was trying to limit people moving up from the drought in California, Arizona was trying to lure old folks away from New Mexico, Idaho and Utah were trying to keep everyone out. The courts were busy night and day trying to sort out the constitutional issues, but the courts were having troubles of their own, what with the burnings, and people tended to pay them less attention than they used to. Violence was like chicken pox. Just as shootings would simmer down in one border area, they'd flare up in another. Of course, there'd always been trouble between the states—Maryland and Virginia oystermen had been shotgunning each other since George Washington's time—but this was something new. Before, the border troubles had always been unorganized. Now the raids and shooting were planned, and there was evidence that special units of state troopers were trained to carry them out.

Politics was getting all jumbled up in a way that no one expected. Of course, no one thought we'd go from hating the Japs in 1945 to loving them in 1955. The experts always say change is inevitable, but when it happens they're still just as surprised as anyone else.

Take what happened to the blacks. Still angry, almost bewildered, they'd gotten what they wanted, a middle-class, almost normal kind of life, and found out that people despised them for it. Young people especially. Oh, not all the young people, but certainly the radical ones—the hairs—and enough so that every time you saw a black cop stop a young white kid you could feel the tension, just like in the old days you could feel it when a black man walked into an Irish bar. In a way, you couldn't blame the hairs, those burnt-out exiles-in-their-own-country, like the hoboes of the Depression. Instead of wandering, they had found their hero in an ex-Harvard graduate student named Peter Caputo and taken to the hills. The blacks and the young people were squared off like boxers in a ring, always sparring, waiting for an opening to hurt someone.

On top of that were the Patrols. The Supreme Court set them up to get by the FBI's hiring system and provide more minority agents, but, ninety percent black, they had become the new vigilantes, more Catholic than the Pope, crusading against pornography and drugs. Theoretically, they were under the FBI. Practically, they answered to their own division chief—when they felt like it.

And those blacks who weren't desperately middle-class still formed a core of violence in the cities, so that, like the Irish before them, they simultaneously dominated both crime and punishment.

As bad as anything, though, was the sense of anger people felt, an anger that was totally real and yet had no direction. People had complained about "them" in the past, but the "them" had been vague—foreigners, bankers, Jews, capitalists, whatever—and the fear and hatred had been limited to a small part of society. America had been just what it felt itself to be: good-natured, a bit naïve, like a rich bartender anxious to show off his fancy new house to any passerby. Now the country's pride was hurt. Old friends deserted. New friends wandered away. What bothered people was that they seemed to lead decent lives and their friends seemed to be decent people, and yet everything they read or heard assumed as a matter of course their own venality and cruelty. Their experiences did not fit what they read about themselves, but the contrast, far from reassuring them or making them cast deeper into the causes of their disquiet, only unsettled them more, making them doubt the truth of their own senses. Not trusting themselves, they trusted few others.

And matters weren't helped by President Bigelow's decision. He had all the qualifications to be a great president except that he disliked the job—disliked it so much, in fact, that he wasn't even running for a second term, though the polls gave him every chance to win. "The burden of high office," Stephen Bigelow said in his official statement declining the candidacy, "has taken too great a toll of my family and of my own emotional and physical health." He was reported to have told his Secretary of State, "I can't stand the hours."

———————

All these things Levine knew. Sitting in the plane, scratching out lumpy sentences from a prepared speech, he felt the fears and hostilities of the nation. Knowing these things, he sometimes wondered how he could dart from one part of the country to another, talk to so many people, and have such a good time.

It's fun, Levine thought, as the plane banked steeply and headed toward Oregon. Only an idiot could complain about the hardships of campaigning. Years before, he had listened solemnly as some candidate or other had told a little group of worshipful supporters about the hardships and sacrifices of running for office, and even then Levine had thought, Nobody's forcing him to do it. Indeed not; and 15,000 feet above the irritations of Indiana, Levine remembered again that campaigning, difficult as it sometimes was, certainly beat working.

Ears plugged into an airliner's version of classical music, taste buds bristling from intermittent contact with highly chilled tequila, eyes skimming over *Playboy* cartoons, Levine felt wrapped in the best cocoon of all. Nothing was wasted. Every sense was present and accounted for. No phone calls. No questions to answer. No compromises to make. No one tugging at his sleeve or tap-tap-tapping on his shoulder. The songs that Bell sometimes played at night for the reporters came running through his mind, jumbled but just right: "Flying too high in the sky. . . . No dates that can't be broken, no words that can't be spoken. . . . Fancy free and free for anything fancy. . . . Thou swell. . . ."

Swell in fact, he thought, sipping the tequila. He thanked God he had lived through the Golden Age and had had sense enough to enjoy it while it was around. He had been in the middle of things when America had had all the confidence and all the money in the world, when the American tourist was the butt of jokes all through Europe. At a serious suburban cocktail party in 1962 a couple recently returned from Greece had complained to him because Athens was filled with Americans. Rejoice, Levine told them, when the world is filled with your countrymen and when bellboys complain about Americans, and second-rate comedians make second-rate jokes about American tourists, because it means we are the world's power, the successor to Great Britain and before that Spain and before that, who knows, Rome and Greece. And the serious suburban housewife protested that she did not want the United States to be a superpower, and Levine said, "Wait twenty years, and tell me how you like it when we're not."

He had never seen the suburban lady and her husband again, though their name and address were in his files and he sometimes thought of calling and asking how she liked living in a backwater of history. She probably hadn't been to Greece for five or ten years; if she had, she had gone with limited dollars and stayed at one of the frumpy houses where English schoolteachers used to cluster. The Hilton was filled with Arabs and Chinese, and there was an occasional rich American, just as in 1962 there had been one or two English industrialists, but the dollar didn't go very far in Greece or France or anywhere else, and people didn't harass you for your country's policy toward Greece because no one gave much of a damn what America did.

Not that the nation was powerless, of course. It had influence, just as France and East Germany had had influence in the fifties, but it was the influence of a follower, not a leader. Governments can respond only to one or two other countries at a time, and the United States was no longer one of them. Levine remembered being in Tokyo on business a couple of years ago, early '86 or late '85, and a Japanese friend had said, "Isn't your President Bigelow in Tokyo this week?" He *had* been, and there was a story on the third page of the Tokyo *Times* and there was a typed notice at the hotel inviting all Americans in town to a reception at the embassy, but Levine remembered when a visit by an American President would have turned the whole city upside down and where entire hotels would be taken over by American reporters.

People had been concerned, back in the fifties and sixties. Movie producers made films about atomic holocausts and the last families left on earth. Writers wrote about the future, with apocalyptic riots and famines. But when the change came, it hadn't come with riots and revolutions. It came with business phones that weren't answered until the fifteenth ring, with misspelled words in *The New Yorker*, with new cars that inexplicably lacked a spare tire, with sudden losses of sound on television. Nothing about it would have seemed unusual in 1952, in France.

Part I

ISLAMORADA, FEBRUARY 1, 1988

The men talked easily, openly. If anyone had overheard them—and, of course, no one could—their conversation would never have been described as a conspiracy or even a plot. They did not stop talking when the bar boy arrived to freshen their drinks, but perhaps their talk floated aimlessly for a moment. They had come to the club for years and they trusted the bar boy as they trusted each other, which was to say with everything except their weaknesses. Other members of the club strolled by their table on the way to the tennis courts or into the warm waters of the Keys. The other members nodded to them but did not interrupt the conversation, even to say hello. They assumed that the six men were trying to choose the next president of the United States and wished to be left alone.

Philip Bell, the youngest of the group, reached into his attaché case. He felt like a fool with the case, just as he would have felt arriving at Titmuss, Finberg and Stein in a bathing suit, but they couldn't expect him to carry reports in his back pocket.

"It looks okay," he said. "We got them to run through the Eighteenth Indiana—ninety percent Middies, by everyone's calculation—and it was Rackey fifty-four percent, Milwood twenty, Kennedy eight, Don't Knows the rest. We had them put it through a pure hair district—Second Vermont—and got the same order: Rackey thirty, Milwood fifteen, Kennedy twelve, all the rest DKs. Same thing as we got two weeks ago—solid strength, nothing spectacular. It fits with these early primaries. Nothing overwhelming, but can do. Definitely can do."

"Do you really trust those figures?" Levine asked. The only one in the group not dressed for the beach, he huddled in his dark suit under the tiny circle of shade the

11

beach umbrella yielded. A. L. Levine never wore a
bathing suit, never wore anything but dark, beautifully
tailored suits. In the old days when the Democratic party
had been in power, the White House photographers had
made a game of trying to get A.L. in some of those scenes
of presidential camaraderie, but he had always—or
almost always—ducked out of the way. Even if they had
caught him, what would have there been to show? The
president's group relaxing around the big fire at
Harriman Lodge at Sun Valley—A. L. Levine in a dark
suit smiling in an easy chair. The president's party with
snorkel masks and flippers easing themselves over the side
of the yacht *Athenian*—A. L. Levine in a dark suit, curled
happily in a deck chair. The president, lean and tan,
shaking hands with his partner and opponents after
friendly doubles on the White House courts—A. L.
Levine in a dark suit peering contentedly into the
noonday sun.

"Why not trust them?" Bell asked. They weren't his
figures, but he had paid for them.

"How can you believe what the hairs tell the polls?"
Levine said. "Their whole life is an act. Why should they
say anything at all? My guess is that any kid who would
talk to Harris's people is unrepresentative. Maybe we
should toss the whole Vermont thing out."

Curly McKelvin looked at A.L. and smiled. Damn,
that was what Levine was *for*, to look into the little chinks
of things. That's what the Hebrews were for, if it came to
that. They were not people to take things on faith. The
senior senator from Texas turned a smile of pure love
toward A.L.

"You're right, Mr. Levine, absolutely," said Bell. "In
fact, the first time they sent the interviewers up to the
heavy hair country that's exactly what happened. The
people who let them into their homes either deliberately
lied to them—'calculated dissimulation' is what they call
it—or they were about to leave the community and totally
unrepresentative. So they tried a new technique: Hire
hairs from other areas, ask them to find out who the most
disliked candidates are, and don't tell them anything

about tabulating the results or anything like that. Turned out that most of the hairs they sent up decided on their own to run sort of a poll, and because they thought of it themselves they were totally sincere and the other hairs leveled with them, and we got reproducible results."

"Nice," said Levine. McKelvin was blissful.

They all looked toward George Edwards, the Democratic National Chairman. They were grown men and their lives had been politics for as long as most remembered, but they had risen above their colleagues because they would not lose themselves to their emotions, would not accept one swallow as a sign of spring. They had seen trends come and go, they had seen men panic before alleged revolutions which had turned out to be merely twitches of the body politic, had seen other men wither because they refused to accept the computer. They had the evidence before them now, and because it jibed with their own intuitions and their own hopes they wanted to accept it, but they would wait for Edwards to declare himself first.

"Mah deah friends," Edwards began in his Roosevelt voice, "I think we better stop wondering about who it'll be and start working to get it for him."

The group smiled as one. If Edwards had had reservations about Rackey or asked for another week's sampling, they would have agreed with him. Now was not the time to cross him. His approval was like a papal sign, for he was respected not only as the master technician of the group but as the only one, except of course for Levine, who had not had or did not have political hopes of his own. He was, as much as any man could be, beyond personalities. He thought of himself that way. Not "above" personalities, for he was shrewd and realized that this implied saintliness. Edwards suffered from a lack of emotional response and knew it. He appreciated personalities in the same abstract way that he appreciated interesting primary figures, and as a result he could blend the two together and win elections. He loved his country and his party, but winning elections was what he lived for.

Spencer Cunningham hesitated before he spoke. They

were all friends, truly friends, but still Cunningham was a bit outside the circle. Very early in his career the senator had worked for the Kennedys, and the others sometimes thought that he might be tempted to report back to them from time to time. He had a hint of that group about him physically—he was tall, rich, a New Englander. He brought back memories.

"Are we that sure that Jim Rackey is the man? A few primaries, a few polls—that's all we have. God knows I'll fight for him myself, and I don't want us tearing ourselves to pieces in more primaries, but you know the reputation he has around the East. I know he's smart, you know he's smart, but he keeps pushing that logger bit. The days by himself on pack trips, the cougar skin on his cabin—Jesus Christ, in Massachusetts nowadays the UnGun people are so strong you can't even kill a deer."

"We'll get someone to hold him in on that during the campaign, Spence," Edwards said. "Rackey's said his piece; can't take back his past life. That was the way he was raised, that's the way he is. But you aren't going to get many other cougar-shooting economists from the Sorbonne running in this man's country, and you better start getting your people ready for him."

"And not many Caucs my people are going to stir for," said Jessington. Mayor of Chicago and the undisputed leader of the nation's blacks, Maceo Jessington held veto power over any major nominee. No Democrat could hope for office without the support of the blacks, and all candidates made the obligatory circuit of black shrines in Atlanta, Memphis, and Brooklyn. Rackey was a special favorite of the Negroes.

"He's not always going to do what your people say," Cunningham objected. "You can't control him in the Senate now."

"True," said Jessington. "That's why my people will stir for him. The way he got those hairs at the Malcolm Day service, us poor blacks will never forget—"

"The figures confirm that," interrupted Bell. "He runs eighty percent in black areas."

"Ninety-two," said Jessington.

"Eighty, almost exactly," said Bell. "There's a slight difference between New York and Washington-Baltimore, but—"

"Ninety-two," Jessington said.

"Well, I'll recheck with the Harris people. . . . Oh, I'm sorry. I didn't mean to sound—you know—"

"Bell, you are a darling man, what we used to call a honky, but you are beginning to learn." Jessington laughed and the tension was gone. "Let's say we go up to the clubhouse for some supper and then do a little swimming. What's the use of being important if you can't have some fun?"

Bell stuffed his papers in his case, A.L. stretched, the others shook the sand out of their swimsuits, and together they plodded slowly up the beach toward the simple white lodge. As they got closer Edwards noticed a green panel truck in the parking lot. That's the NBC people from Miami, he thought. How the hell did they get in? Then he saw Merlin, the Washinton political man, straining toward them, held back only by the cables connecting him to the sound truck. Trouble, awful trouble, thought Edwards.

The others saw Merlin too and tensed but kept walking. When they reached the patio alongside the lodge, Merlin came at them, pale, worried.

"Men, I know this is against our agreement, but I had to come down here. Senator Rackey has been arrested in Boise for murdering his wife. Stabbed her to death. He's been stabbed too, but he's okay. He's confessed, confession on tape. Blood-alcohol-test positive. Confirmed and reconfirmed. Can you comment for us?"

Cunningham swung easily, nicely, languidly, faster than the eye could follow, and abruptly Merlin's hand camera and mike were both wrapped in his bath towel. "You creep, you keep that fucking mike out of our faces. What sort of a ghoul are you? You come here with that news about our friend and expect us to dance for you?"

"Look, Senator, I don't like it any more than you do. You know I've been fair to you, been fair to the party. But the news has been out on the wire four hours now while you've been holed up down here. The country is frightened. It wants comment from the Democratic party, and this is where the party is, all together. I need something for the six o'clock news."

"He's right," said Edwards. "Poor Jim—God only knows. Someone's got to say something."

"We can't be interviewed looking like something out of Miami Beach," said Jessington.

"Gentlemen, I need something now," Merlin said. They hated him but respected him.

"A.L., say something for the networks," Edwards said. "You were Acting Chairman back in '80. Besides, you're dressed for it."

Cunningham handed the mike and camera back to Merlin. Levine stepped forward and took the microphone. He thought wryly of the absurdity of it all, the fat man playing in the sand, the wrench again from idle relaxation to tragedy ("What were you doing when you heard the news?"), decent Merlin with his indecent job. He thought of Jim Rackey, someone he had admired, someone in politics he could actually talk to; just what they said, a Sorbonne economist from Idaho, torn apart by too many contradictions.

He blinked into the setting sun and said, "I am horrified by the news about Senator Rackey, not because I wanted him as the party's nominee—which I did—not because of what he has done, drinking and murder—if these reports are correct—but because of what has been done to him and what again may be done to him. I have known Jim Rackey for twenty years and I love him as a friend. He is not a murderer, but he has, we are told, murdered. In our own families, in our own hearts, we have all experienced rages and lusts like the one which must have driven this wonderful man to attack his lovely wife. Let us forget politics. Let us pray for this man and for the soul of his wife."

Levine paused briefly, not knowing what to say next, but knowing there was something still to be said. Then the words came back to him, words heavy with the orphans' home and of old Teitelbaum, the Hebrew teacher, words that he never knew he had learned and yet were there. *"Yisgadal v'yiskadash,"* he began, and recited the Kaddish, the prayer for the dead.

They flew back to Washington that evening, seated apart and under assumed names. They were drained, sick of politics, but only by avoiding one another consciously could they keep from making plans when they were numbed, not sure of their own minds. Besides, traveling apart made them less conspicuous at the Washington airport. (Jessington was spotted anyway—his 280 pounds did not hide easily—but he brushed through the reporters.)

Edwards, able to drop his mask of importance instantly, looked like any government clerk back from an inspection trip as he was met quietly by his wife and driven home. She said nothing during the ride. It was just as well, because she had always distrusted Rackey— "That man's crazy when he drinks, George"—and anything she could say would be either insincere or mocking.

Edwards left his bags downstairs and went up to the bedroom. He'd bring the bags up later, when he had more energy. He'd been thinking on the plane and he knew he needed help, help from someone who was detached from the present. He called old Tom Ryan in New York. Tom Ryan had first been called "old" in his early forties, when he was working for Roosevelt. Now, somewhere in his eighties—or was he ninety?—he stayed barricaded in his New York suite, the decaying elegance of the Towers somehow just right for a man who had seemed elderly even in the prime of life. He lived alone surrounded by television sets that ran simultaneously and continuously. He hadn't been out of the Towers in ten years. Edwards, who called him rarely because the Old Man hated to be disturbed, thought he knew more about politics than anyone else alive.

The phone rang only once and was picked up. Edwards had been to the apartment as a young man; remembering the phone alongside the leather lounge chair, he decided nothing had changed.

"Ryan here." The voice was thinner than last time.

"Tom, it's Edwards, George Edwards. Tom, what do you think?"

"Get Levine."

Maybe the Old Man was cracked. Senile at last. He must have known that he'd be in touch with Levine.

"I'm meeting with him tomorrow."

"Don't mean meet him. Run him."

He *was* senile. At ninety, what could you expect?

"But Tom, Levine is—"

"Don't argue. You called, I answered. Besides, commercial's over. *Casablanca.* Thanks for calling." He hung up.

Edwards undressed and, exhausted, went to bed. His wife took his suitcase upstairs and unpacked for him.

Spencer Cunningham's chauffeur met him and drove him to the house along the river. You couldn't count on the cabs any more. His wife had the drinks ready. The children were muted somewhere upstairs. Sally Cunningham couldn't help talking about Rackey. She had always liked him, maybe because the hint of violence had always been there.

"Spence, it must be awful. What are you going to do now?"

"Christ knows. We thought we were set. I can't think about it now. How many of these things do we have to go through?"

"Hideous. You're right. You know what, dear?"

"What?"

"That Mr. Levine you talk about. I saw him on television tonight. He's really quite . . . darling."

"A.L.? Darling? He'd be thrilled to hear that. Though I don't know much that he'd do about it."

"You never take me seriously when I talk about politics, but you shouldn't make fun. Besides, he really is, you know."

"How do you mean?"

"Well, he's got a real nose, not one of those vestigial bumps stuck on him. His nose *means* something."

"It means he's Jewish."

"No, it's what people talk about when they say a face has character. And his eyes—they're smart and still, they're almost mischievous."

"Like a goddam Jewish Santa Claus," he said.

"You said it, not me." She was silent. "Let me fix you another drink."

Levine took a taxi from the airport. No one recognized him. The driver was a well-spoken black who rambled on about one-way streets, traffic patterns, and African trade. Probably a government employee driving part-time. Did they all drive cabs part-time?

When he got to the apartment overlooking the Potomac, Levine found his wife smiling. That was a relief.

"I saw you on television. It's not so bad, is it?"

"No."

"I always told you you'd look good on television. There's nothing to be frightened about. I told you that."

"You did."

"Next time you should wear the top button of your coat fastened. Otherwise you have a tendency to look stout."

They had been together almost forty years, and every once in a while Helen said something that reminded him of why he had married her.

They met the next morning at National Headquarters. First Bell brought the Rackey thing up to date. An autopsy had been ordered on Mrs. Rackey. Rackey himself was out of physical danger. He was still in jail and had refused to talk to the reporters. He had hired Quinlan of Chicago as his lawyer. The blood-alcohol levels had been confirmed at two separate laboratories.

Jessington sighed. "I guess that does it. I woke up last

night and couldn't see it all going down the drain like this.
Maybe, a sympathy campaign . . . like Curley running for
mayor from jail."

"Jesus, Jess, Curley was in jail for taking a Civil Service
exam for a voter, not for murdering his wife!"

McKelvin stirred. "Look, it's simple. Our man's gone,
we find a new man."

"What about Milwood or Kennedy?" Edwards said.
No faces lifted, no smiles broke.

"Of course, we know them, we're not going to drop
them. But we've got to run some more people through,"
Jessington said.

"Who?"

"How about Spence? We haven't talked about Spence
for a long time."

They hadn't talked about Spence because he had run
last time and done terribly. Lazy, the reporters said. Not
interested enough, was the politicians' judgment. Snobbish, said the crowds.

"Not me," Cunningham said. "I've done that. I'm not
one of your Stassens or Shrivers. When I've had it, I know
it."

"Don't blame you," McKelvin said. "But we can't send
up just two names. At this stage, people have got to
choose among, not between. Besides, I don't think you've
got too much to worry about." McKelvin was tactful, but
there was no tactful way of saying what had to be said.

"If you insist," said Cunningham. The others nodded.
He was a logical addition.

"We need someone else," said Edwards.

"Only one person dropped out," Bell murmured.

"One person, but he was clear in front. We're casting
around now."

"How about van Dillinham?" Levine asked. Governor
Dwayne van Dillinham was young, just above the
constitutional limit. He was a semi-Southerner from
Arkansas, a border state—charming, compelling, erratic.

They talked about van Dillinham warily. He was
young, but the party was committed to youth. The
platform said so. To ignore him would be to ignore their
own future. Reluctantly, they agreed.

"Anyone else?" asked Levine, who was keeping the minutes.

They were too depressed to dredge around for more names. Levine wrote something on a piece of paper and handed it to Bell.

"Take this up to Harris in person. It's a rush job. I think he ought to go back to the original mixed districts. You gentlemen agree?"

They nodded and the meeting broke up.

Jessington lived with his mother in a great mansion on Chicago's Lake Shore Drive. The first thing he had done as the city's mayor was to announce that the city needed a symbol of the mayor's presence, the mayor's concern. A pliable board of aldermen had instantly yielded to the idea that the city condemn and then buy the moldering home of a peripheral Swift. After spending a million and a half refitting it to his taste, Jessington had moved in. People, mostly blacks, drifted in and out of the twenty-two rooms, but Jess and his mother were the only permanent residents.

Jessington's lack of a wife was not held against him by his city constituency. There were rumors that he had been married once but had crushed his wife in a fit of passion. There were rumors that he had taken a vow of celibacy in order to pursue justice for his people, and it was in fact true that he was rarely seen officially or unofficially in the company of women. The only rumor that did not circulate was that he was a homosexual. Even if it had been true, no one would have believed it.

The truth was that after an early manhood spent making money and mounting women, Jessington had noted his sexual nature drifting away. Visits to various doctors confirmed what he already knew—that he had a bit of diabetes, a touch of alcoholism, and a bad case of fatness. After a furious and expensive bout with various injections, he had resigned himself with Aristotelian coldness to make the best of a bad situation. His political career had begun with his impotence.

"What do you think about it, Mama?" he shouted from

the pool toward the bar. The enclosed pool where the atrium had once been was one of Jessington's favorite spots. He loved to swim.

"Can't hear you, boy," she shouted back. The echoes were bad.

"Come in here, goddammit," he yelled.

She came in slowly, tiny and bent. She wore a tall plastic glass fastened to her left wrist, and from two plastic straws she slowly sipped a rum collins. Rheumatoid arthritis had made it impossible for her to grip a glass, but she refused to give up drinking.

"What do you think about Rackey, Mama?"

"Oh, I loved that man. Indeed I did. He was a man of fire, a man with real nature." She loved her son but never forgave the lack of grandchildren.

"You're a mean old bitch," Jessington said, and dove delicately to the bottom of the pool, practicing for his next trip to the Caribbean. Unless there was company in the mansion, he always wore a snorkel mask in the pool.

"Mean, but not stupid. No, sir!" she cackled back.

That was true enough. Jessington loved to tell visitors about his humble youth, the aching years in the ghetto, ending up, "Fact is, we were so poor my mother had to scrub white folks' floors. I remember having to go pick her up one day—streets weren't safe then—and coming to some fancy home—they wouldn't let me by the front door—and saying to myself, 'Someday I'm going to go in that house by the front door.' Of course I never figured I'd be living in it, but indeed I am. This very house is where my mama scrubbed floors."

It was, sadly, all untrue. No ghetto urchin but the stiffly proper child of stiffly proper parents was Maceo Jessington. His mother, far from being a domestic, had taught twenty-five years in the Chicago school system. One summer at normal school she had done some baby-sitting for a family her own mother had once worked for as a domestic; she might have scrubbed a floor then to help out, she wasn't sure. And the family, a drugstore owner and his wife, were so impressed by the quiet young woman who read Keats and went to lectures by Langston Hughes that they loaned her $500 so she could take a trip to Europe after graduation.

Jessington once knew all this, but the truth had been so long soaked in the colors of his campaign biographies that neither he nor his mother could recognize it any longer. For the usual visitor she would nod and smile as Mace told of their humble beginnings, and would nod "Amen" like a cleaning lady out of the Mount Gilead choir.

"But Mama, what do you think we ought to do now?" He floated face down, stirring his flippers faintly, raising his head, then staring through his mask at the deep blue bottom of the pool. His breath whistled through the snorkel tube.

"Son, I do like that Jew that was on television. He's got the most beautiful eyes."

That's funny, Maceo thought, I noticed that myself.

WASHINGTON, FEBRUARY 9, 1988

When they met one week later at National Headquarters, Bell was late. They talked idly, annoyed at Bell but not angry. They couldn't do anything without the figures, and Bell was bringing them down personally from New York. It made Bell look a bit like a courier, but it had to be done; the material couldn't be trusted to the mails or even private video transmission. Bell wasn't touchy about doing the traveling. After all, he was the youngest.

When he arrived, he looked pale and harried. He nodded briefly, sat down, and opened his briefcase. "Gentlemen," he said, "there's been a terrible, fascinating mistake. I've gone over it with Harris—he can explain it, but it's still a mistake. What I mean is that somehow Mr. Levine's name got added to the preference list along with van Dillinham and Cunningham. And he ran sixty to seventy percent. In all districts."

The eyebrows lifted and the eyes opened. Levine shuffled the note pad in front of him.

"Again," ordered Edwards.

"I've checked it all out with Harris," Bell said. "It was the printer's mistake. I took our memo up to Harris in person; he took it to their printer in person; the printer made a mistake. I brought back the original memo."

He passed it around. It was on the notepaper of the National Committee and in Levine's bookkeeper-clear handwriting read simply:

For: L. Harris
   On preferential poll omit Rackey and add the following.
      Dwayne van Dillinham
      Spencer Cunningham
                                    A. L. Levine

Levine glanced at it. "Crazy," he said. "I'm embarrassed. My name is off to the side the way it always is. It's obviously a signature, not another name."

McKelvin studied the memo. "No doubt about it. A.L. No one but a greenhorn or a damn fool would figure your name was part of the list."

"I discussed it with Harris," Bell said. "In retrospect we could see how a programmer who wasn't familiar with our procedures or who didn't know Mr. Levine's memo could make a mistake and set up the sample poll with his name on it."

"Just a little comedy of errors," said Jessington.

"Exactly," said Bell. "Nothing to worry about."

They all smiled and looked relieved. The next thought struck them all simultaneously.

"Jesus," McKelvin said. "We're all sitting pleased as little pink choirboys, and we've forgotten what those results were. What was that, Bell, sixty to seventy percent in all districts?"

"Except in the South," Bell said.

McKelvin smiled. "That figures," he said.

"It was forty-seven in urban South, forty-one in two representative rural counties. Still way ahead of Senator Milwood."

"I'll be goddamned," McKelvin said. "That about beats all."

Edwards looked baffled. "A.L., what do you make of this? I mean, aside from the fact you're involved."

"Taking first the fact that I'm involved, I want to say right now I'm embarrassed. I certainly had no intention of upsetting you gentlemen. Looking at it from the outside, it figures, in its own strange way. Remember what we've been saying and hearing the last few years, and what McLuhan wrote about the country's capacity to burn out its leaders, its tendency to get bored. Look what happened to poor Carter. I see this as an accelerating tendency. It used to be automatic for an incumbent president to get a second term; now it's the reverse. Politics is a kind of entertainment, and people want novelty in politics like they want it in anything else. Simultaneously, they want

continuity. They don't want to be wrenched totally from
the past. In a way the candidate we're talking about—
myself—is both those things. Politically, he's an unknown, a freak, a Jew, but he's a familiar freak—people
have read about him, known about him subliminally, for
years. I'm new, but not *too* new."

Edwards nodded. "You used the word candidate," he
said. "I mean, in talking of yourself."

"That was only in the context of analysis. I'm not a
politician. I have no intention of running."

"The hell you say!" roared Jessington. "Right now
you're our Number One Boy and you don't do any
backing out."

"It was a mistake," said Levine. "All a freak."

"Freak, my ass!" said McKelvin. "Nothing freaky
about it. First of all, you're right about what you said
about novelty. Surprised we didn't think of a Jew
candidate—a Jewish candidate—before."

"There was Thalmann," murmured Edwards.

"Thalmann! That constipated horse's ass. Just another
Lindsay with a big nose. Him and his fucking polo ponies!
No, I mean a real Jew like A.L. here. I'll tell you
something right now. I'll give you seven to five that when
Harris asked people what they liked about Levine, more
of them mentioned his looks than anything else.
Goddammit, he looks honest. He's so ugly he's
beautiful—'scuse me, A.L."

"No offense," said Levine, shrugging.

"You win your bet, Curly," Bell said. "Here's Harris's
report: 'Of those listing Levine as first choice, the
following qualities were checked by respondents (totals
greater than one hundred percent, since multiple reasons
were permitted): Intelligence, eighty-two percent; looks,
seventy-eight percent; strong family man, seventy-one
percent; honesty, sixty-eight percent; knows politics,
sixty-eight percent; strong leader, fifty-four percent;
leader of free world, thirty-five percent. Forty-two
percent wrote in "His eyes," and another forty-one
percent wrote in "They're smart" or a variant thereof.
This presumably refers to Jews.'"

"Presumably," said Cunningham.

"Harris also reported that respondents almost always mentioned that television statement you made about Rackey. I checked it out with the networks and they're still getting mail."

"Amazing," said Levine.

"There's nothing amazing about it," Cunningham said. "What's amazing is that it took us so long to see where people are going. I feel particularly foolish myself—my wife mentioned you as a candidate and I just dismissed it. I forget what I said. But it never occurred to me."

The others, remembering, said nothing.

Cunningham surged on. "What we've got now is a problem in surfacing you. You've got to come forward as a candidate spontaneously, not through any mistake on a secret poll."

"What about leaking the poll to a couple of columnists?" said Edwards.

"Won't work," Jessington said. "Too fantastic. Nobody believes them when they print something plausible."

"What about more TV time?" Bell asked. "He could go on *Out of the Frying Pan* or some show like that, to discuss the party's chances in light of the Rackey...er...thing."

Bell was learning all the time.

"I'll take care of it," he said. "We'll set it up for a week from Sunday."

Levine walked home to his apartment, a wispy smile on his face. His wife had the New York papers, *Variety*, and the *Guardian* by his luncheon plate. He read and ate slowly and then, when he was eating dessert, he said, "The people at the office are thinking of running me for president."

"Wouldn't your mother have been thrilled," she said.

"I mean it very seriously. Apparently a lot of people liked me on television."

"Didn't I tell you that already? You make a wonderful impression. And I meant it very seriously about your mother—if only she could have heard the news. I wish I could have known her."

"Me too," Levine said. "I mean, I wish *I* could have known her. Anyway, there's no news yet. There's nothing to talk about. It's just an idea."

"And a very good one, too. More fruit?"

"No, not right now."

NEW YORK, FEBRUARY 21, 1988

Levine, as directed, arrived at the studio a full two hours before the program. Greeted, welcomed, congratulated, flattered, he was led to the second-floor dressing room. The welcomer-flatterer-greeter showed him into the nicely decorated suite and said, "The shower is right through that door, Mr. Levine. We will wash all over, now, won't we?"

"We will," said Levine.

Dutifully, he shed his dark suit and his blue shirt and plodded into the shower stall. Images ran through his mind: his father in the steam bath when he was a boy, the bathroom at the Home where he had to shower with everyone else, Buchenwald. He washed himself vigorously. All over. It was rather fun. Not like Buchenwald at all. Every time someone took a shower, did it have to be Buchenwald? He made a note to speak about that someday. He lost himself in showering and writing speeches.

A voice rammed into his privacy. "Are we all finished now? We mustn't take too long in the shower."

Just like a mother, Levine thought. Maybe he thinks I'm playing with myself, too. In fact, in the steamy warmth of the shower, the idea had occurred to him, but he had rejected it—there were probably peepholes somewhere. He dried himself lovingly.

"Don't forget the Electrolux powder," the voice reminded him.

Levine dusted himself.

"All over," the voice urged.

All over.

Levine looked at the instructions pasted on the dressing-room mirror. "Frying Pan Guests: After shower, dry completely. Then dust—all over—with Electrolux powder. Do not neglect axillae (armpits) and inguinal area (crotch). After dusting, put on undershorts, ring for technician, and wait in the room."

Levine pulled on his shorts and rang. In a moment a white-suited technician knocked, entered, introduced herself, and placed small circular electrodes on Levine's palms, neck, axillae, and groin. "You may finish dressing, leave a urine specimen, and go outside to the lounge," she said, and left.

Levine dressed and peed briskly and walked outside. His guide was waiting there alongside a man of importance. The important man smiled and said, "Mr. Levine, glad to have you here. I'm Bill Chrisman. I'm just another of the vice-presidents around here, but *Frying Pan* is my special baby and I'm proud of it. Some of our first-time guests are a bit bothered by the special measures, but I'm sure you agree that they're necessary."

He didn't seem to want an answer, but Levine nodded anyway.

Out of the Frying Pan reached between 70 and 80 percent of set owners each Sunday noon. NBC called it a "revolutionary look into a man's soul" but it was, in fact, only a sophisticated variation of the interview shows which had been popular in the fifties and sixties. Audience participation had been added; in addition to the panel of newspapermen, anyone in the nation with a question to ask had only to press his "Send" button during the last half-hour and, if the computer and the newsmen monitors accepted it as an original, legitimate question, he was seen (after a seven-second lag) split-screen from the subject, interrogating him. The "Physiologic Response Scale," however, was the most popular feature of the show. As the celebrity faced the panel, the probes attached to his palms, soles, and armpits recorded changes in emotional perspiration. The "Sweat Meter" dial, superimposed on the side of the screen, gave silent witness as to how each question bothered the subject. Coupled with a pupillometer, which registered the pupil's dilation with pleasure and constriction with fear, it provided an extra dimension to otherwise routine interviews. A similar program, which had wired its subjects to a polygraph flashing "True" or "Doubtful" with each answer, had failed when it ran out of willing interviewees. Even on *Frying Pan,* guests had attempted to disguise their reactions by taking drugs that fixed the pupils or abolished sweating.

"The public believes in our program, Mr. Levine, and when the public believes, we just can't have any possibility of hanky-panky. Our staff may get a bit overcautious at times, but we can hardly blame them. You can't believe how devious some very famous people have been. Well, being in politics, perhaps you can. But I can assure you, if I weren't discreet, if I wanted to write a book, you'd hardly believe . . ."

Levine nodded again. The important man's talk slowed for a moment.

"Would you mind opening your mouth for a moment, Mr. Levine?" he said. Levine opened and the important man, who was taller (as most people were), bent over and ran his left index finger expertly under Levine's tongue, around his lower gums, past the bridgework that Dr. Brotman had cleverly fashioned in 1957, over the molar chipped in the auto accident in 1969, and out.

"All clear," he announced happily. "The way you were nodding without opening your mouth."

"It's a habit I have," said Levine. "One of my little habits."

"You might have had a little ampule hidden under there. You wouldn't believe. . . . Here, come and meet the questioners."

Levine knew most of them—Merlin, Coudert, Hampton—had given them background information in the past, liked them and respected them. He had never, however, met Francis Lasch, the permanent member of the panel. This was not unusual. Lasch refused to socialize with politicians or even other reporters. "I dislike the whole nasty bunch," Lasch said. "Politicians heaping up their own sand castles at the people's expense and the press trying to get a name for itself by knocking the sand castles down. Revolting people. Nonproducers.

Give me a man who makes things with his hands, and I'll show you a real man. Not these parasites."

Lasch's distaste for the guests he questioned and for his fellow questioners was genuine, but it was also commercially valuable. Along with the technical gimmicks it made the program.

"Five minutes to camera," someone said. Levine and the panel were ushered into the studio. Levine was fitted with the reflecting spectacles which mirrored his pupillary movements. He gazed impassively toward the panel of interviewers.

"Comfortable?" the technician asked. He had bad breath. Levine nodded. A tall brunette with delicately high cheekbones came over to Levine's desk with a pitcher of water. "In case you get thirsty." She smiled. Levine smiled back.

"Calibration perfect and normal," someone shouted from the background. Levine's eyes had constricted with the whiff of bad breath, had dilated with pleasure at the pretty girl.

The program began. Levine was nervous, for this was not his arena. His place was in the back of the plane or at a table after a political dinner, talking to reporters, giving them some historical background, putting in a little lecture now and then. Answering questions in public was something he had avoided all his life.

"How would you describe the state of the Democratic party?" Merlin began.

"We're in good shape, but no party that's out of power is ever as good as it should be."

"Could you elaborate on Senator Rackey's situation?" Hampton asked.

"How can you elaborate on a tragedy? You know what I've said about this before. The man has my prayers."

"Who do you expect to replace him as the party's candidate?" Lasch said. It was a typical Lasch question, reasonable until examined closely, when it would be found to be studded with barbs.

"He was never actually the party's candidate, so one could hardly place him as that. But as a leading contender, he will be missed, and we will, of course, continue to solicit the party leaders, the public—even the press—for their candidates."

"What about the Kennedy forces? How does the National Committee see Kennedy fitting in?"

"Of course, he's a very distinguished American, an excellent politician, from a famous family. And he has a very devoted organization. And so, speaking for myself and not for the committee, I am very glad to see him as one of the contenders."

"Mr. Levine, many people feel that the United States has been destroying itself over the past decade. We've grown fat, we've been destroying our own environment when we're not busy watching television. We need a return to fundamentals. Willard Rose, who's been out of politics a few years, has been a leading spokesman for this point. What do you say to it?"

Blaine Coudert had asked the question. Levine remembered him, somewhat rancidly, from 1980 and 1984.

"Well, I'm not sure how much of that was a question and how much a statement. Certainly, some people have grown fat. I've put on a few pounds myself, but them I'm a few years older. So is everyone else. So's the country. I don't think the Founding Fathers had a kind of Sparta in mind for the United States. I think they figured that if people wanted to get fat, God and nature gave them that right, and the United States could give them the opportunity. We shouldn't be too quick to fit people into our ideals, whether it's an ideal way to think or even an ideal way to look. And so far as watching too much television is concerned, I'm sure that the people who are watching this interesting program with you and your distinguished colleagues don't have to be told how much television they should watch."

Slowly the nervousness fell away. Levine realized he was enjoying himself. How long had it been since he had been up in front of the classroom and Mrs. Bentley had been asking him about the Constitution and he had been able to give her all the Amendments, even the Thirteenth, which she had forgotten? That must have been the seventh or eighth grade, P.S. 70, and here again was the warm feeling of *knowing*, of being the best in the class. I must have been a pain in the ass to the other kids, Levine thought, but that's the way I was. Maybe I was better for my honors orals—I knew that Blassingame didn't like Jews in general and me in particular, and yet we came out of that almost friends. I had suffered some by then. I wasn't so arrogant. Blassingame made a mistake in quoting Beard and I didn't correct him. You learn slowly that it's better for you to be wrong once in a while.

"I'm only a technician and not a politician, but my personal estimation is that our main problem is here at home and it's one of distrust. The separate states are moving further and further apart. The guerrilla raids are part of that. I'm afraid we're headed toward the kind of anarchy that existed under the Articles of Confederation, or whenever it was that the states issued their own money."

Lasch had been quiet a long time.

"You are said to be a very wealthy man, Mr. Levine. Is that correct?"

Levine nodded.

"Would you care to estimate your personal fortune?"

"If you don't mind, I'd rather not. My father taught me it was wrong to talk about one's income. I'd feel embarrassed. You can say that I have enough."

"Your biography indicates that in 1955 you were a salesman for an electronics firm, yet by 1974 you were one of the largest single givers to the Democratic party. Could you tell us how you made your money?"

"I was fortunate in some real-estate investments. Mostly recreational. Various parts of the country. It's all in the record."

Lasch paused for a moment. In the control booth Chrisman noticed that Lasch seemed to lack his usual bitterness. His questions were hostile, but his manner was not.

"Tell me, Mr. Levine, you've been close to politics for a number of years now. Have you ever felt like running for office yourself? Have you ever, to be specific, considered the presidency?"

The pupillometer twitched minutely. The skin galvanometer stood rock steady.

Levine smiled. "Oh, of course I've thought about running for the presidency. The last time I thought about it seriously, though, was in 1940. I was a senior in high school, and some friends had just nominated me for president of the G.O.—that was the student government. So I guess I had political ambitions then. Anyway, I lost. Then the war came along and I got married and then I had to earn a living and so I've been very fortunate to serve my party as a technician, an interested observer."

The announcer cut in. "Last question, gentlemen." The last question was traditionally reserved for Lasch. It was, after all, his ball park.

Lasch spoke slowly. "Mr. Levine, has anyone ever told you that you have the most extraordinary eyes?"

Levine nodded, and the commercial began.

———

They tried to sit on it for a while after that, but it was like sitting on an anthill. The station was snowed with mail. Levine hired an extra secretary at his office to handle the letters that came to him directly. Edwards received clandestine visits from the chairmen of two separate western states, both of whom began their conversations, "I know it sounds crazy, but have you ever thought of running A. L. Levine?" Someone soon would have to make an official move. Edwards called McKelvin in Texas.

McKelvin saw Levine come into the club and thought, Hot damn, I like that little Jew! He liked all small people, of course, liked bending over to whisper in their ears, liked the way they had to tippytoe up to reply. But there was something special about Levine. McKelvin liked Jews, too—they were like the blacks, knew how to laugh, not like the rest of those constipated East Coasters. Of course, even Southerners could be a pain in the ass. Like poor Carter. He'd gotten along with Carter, of course, but he'd never really enjoyed the man. Of all Southerners to be president, they had to pick someone who was still teaching Bible class. Carter always made him feel sinful in a way no Jew ever could.

He always remembered when his mother had first taken him into the store in Abilene—Friedman's, it was—and how she had said, "Now, son, we're going to meet Mr. Friedman, and he's a Jew. Goes to the Jewish church. Some people 'round here make fun of him, mock him for his religion. They're just ignorant. There isn't a finer man in all Abilene. Sells good merchandise, gives to the Chamber, supports his church, doesn't get drunk or hang around bad houses. Same as the rest of the Jews here—nothing beats them for being good to their wives and kiddies. 'Course, you don't want to get in any business deals with them, 'cause they'll skin you alive."

McKelvin never did, nor did he forget what his mother said. He could still remember the scent of lavender in the store as they walked toward the cashier's desk. Wasn't she the smart old lady, he thought.

"A.L., right over here," he said, and they began their meal.

McKelvin was proud of the Well and Wagon. People said there was no culture in Houston, but no one could deny there was money. Oak paneling, Sheraton highboy, Cruickshank prints. The air conditioning ran all the time. Like something out of London, all except for the men. This was second-and third-generation oil money now. No one except for a few old-timers in ten-gallon hats felt compelled to make a display of being oilmen, but neither did the younger members affect eastern accents or Irish tweeds. They knew what they were—rich Texans—and that was enough.

"Have a bit more wine, A.L.," McKelvin said. "You won't find a vintage like this very often. We're known for our wine cellar, if you'd like to take a look at it after dinner. It's down on the thirty-fifth floor."

"No thanks," Levine said. "But I will have another glass. Delicious bouquet."

McKelvin nodded and the wine waiter poured generously.

The dessert was a compote with crushed fresh raspberries. God alone knew where they got the berries; they were no longer cultivated in the United States. Didn't freeze well enough. Levine savored a spoonful. His mind drifted back to 1932. He was picking berries alongside the little summer house in the Catskills. His father was on the porch talking about Roosevelt. "At last, a mensch. Things may not get much better, but now I know they won't get worse."

"Dessert wine," McKelvin said. "Some Bernkasteler to settle your stomach." Another large glass. Were wineglasses larger in Houston than on the coasts?

They talked idly about the decline of oil in Texas's economy. The new fortunes were being made in farming with irrigation water pumped inland from the Galveston desalinization plant.

"Come into the reading room, A.L.," McKelvin suggested.

More oak paneling. More leather armchairs.

"Brandy and soda?"

"Don't mind if I do."

Glasses getting larger.

"Another?"

"Certainly. Lovely brandy." Levine noticed that McKelvin had developed a rather clipped accent. So had he.

"Thought you might be interested in a little game of chance. Usually a friendly poker game around here somewhere."

"Delighted."

Levine trotted behind as McKelvin lurched from room to room. He threw open a heavy door (walnut, this time) and peered in on five men seated at a round table. There was a rack of chips and a bottle of bourbon in the center of the table.

"Why, Senator McKelvin, it's sure a pleasure to see you again," a white-haired man said.

"Good to be here, good to be here. Mind if my friend and I sit in? This here's Mr. A. L. Levine from back East. Finer man never lived."

Five sets of weather-hardened Anglo-Saxon eyes focused on Levine. There was a chorus of five "Howdys," five names were offered, and the players' eyes returned to their cards. Levine sat down in a hard-backed chair. A tumbler filled with ice appeared at his side.

"You drink, Mr. Levine?" the white-haired man asked.

"I do."

The man nodded and the player next to Levine reached for the bottle. A torrent of bourbon filled Levine's glass. This was no place to do his tequila routine.

"Happy days," Levine said, and gulped down two massive swallows. He had never liked drinking.

The stakes were enormous, even by Levine's standards. Pots of five or ten thousand dollars were usual—big ones were twenty thousand. The players said little except for the rote responses of poker players everywhere: "Hit me," "Pass," "You're light," "Nice pot," "Goddamn." After every pot the glasses were ceremoniously refilled.

I have been here before, Levine thought. In a hundred grubby motel rooms, in the back rooms of a hundred seedy nightclubs, in a hundred tacky VFWs where you could get a drink after midnight. The traveling days again. The boys have captured a Jew and are trying to find out if he has horns. And to get him drunk.

Levine loved it. They will not get me drunk, he thought.

McKelvin looked across the table at A.L. and smiled. Levine was doing just fine. He wasn't losing, but he wasn't winning too much. He had a good game, playing percentages steadily except for unpredictable excursions into bluffing. But there was still something bothersome about him, and the more McKelvin looked and played and drank the more he resented it. Levine would not get drunk. That was the trouble with the whole bunch of them, when it came to that. They never lost control, never showed a weakness, and if a man doesn't trust you enough to get drunk and show you his weakness, then, by God, he doesn't really even trust himself. Because, by God, if a man really trusts himself, then he's prepared to show his weakness to his friends; he knows he's got enough strength so the weakness will be forgotten. It was a new thought to McKelvin, and he turned it around in his mind as he drank and played and shuffled the cards.

Occasionally a player would get up, stretch, and excuse himself to take a leak. Sometime past 2 A.M. one of the players, a man named Pitts, found himself unable to stay awake. Or conscious. McKelvin pressed a buzzer and a young attendant who looked like a hair (they weren't hiring Mexicans any more) entered, draped the man around his shoulders, and helped him to a room down the hall. At around 3 A.M. a player excused himself to urinate. Sounds of retching echoed from the bathroom. The player returned, paler and wearing a different shirt.

Levine did not move. He smiled, played his cards, stayed laconic. He would not get drunk. He would not urinate. Urination was a sign of weakness. He must write that down and use it in a speech sometime.

At 7 A.M. McKelvin looked out the window. The sun was rising. "Time, gentlemen," he said. The white-haired man was banker. Levine had won $27,000. Someone else had won $75,000. Someone was down $85,000. Levine never did get the names straight.

"A pleasure, gentlemen," Levine said. He and McKelvin walked through the empty clubrooms to the elevator. Levine was skipping like a child. He hadn't gotten drunk. He hated drunks. *"Shikker iz der goy,"* his father used to say. Why had God given man this marvelous brain if he was to poison it with alcohol? A little wine, certainly a couple of drinks—even rabbis drank—but drunkenness was disgusting.

They waited for the elevator. McKelvin looked mournful. He had lost. He was nauseated. Levine looked at him. McKelvin was a wonderful person. McKelvin was a mensch. He hated to see McKelvin sad.

"Curly, you're my best friend. I mean it. Really. You know, a man has lots of friends, but you I trust. You take this, for example. That printing place up in New York, where they do Harris's work. You remember, six years ago the party was looking for a printer in New York? Those are the people I suggested. My wife's brother-in-law. Wonderful people. But how could you tell someone like Edwards something like that? An Edwards wouldn't understand. But you're my friend."

McKelvin's nausea improved rapidly.

WASHINGTON, FEBRUARY 24, 1988

Edwards had moments of grandeur, dreams of a greater United States, but after a certain point was reached he became a pure mechanic. As National Chairman, he knew in his own mind what kind of candidate and what kind of party he wanted, but when the leaders and the polls indicated a different direction he submerged his own will to that of the party. When the party's new candidate or new policy had reached a certain momentum, Edwards had a hard time remembering that he had ever had any doubts about it. He had a talent for assimilating. The border between his ideas and party policies barely existed.

So it was that when the first hints of interest in Levine appeared, Edwards was interested but skeptical, but as the interest became more and more insistent, Edwards became more and more intrigued until still using his political experience but more and more impelled by a current of spontaneous popular interest, he began to think of Levine as "his" candidate and therefore the party's.

Levine's surfacing as an official candidate was not difficult. The impetus was taken away from the National Committee by the people. While the committee was worrying about the mechanics of bringing his name into the primaries, the press and television were doing the job themselves. It was, of course, in a gossip column that Levine's name was first connected to the nomination:

> And while we're thinking of politics—and when isn't today's modern woman thinking of politics?— what about charming A. L. Levine for the Democratic nomination? Insiders have long been impressed by his political savvy, but recent TV appearances have shown him to have political sex

appeal. Or is the National Committee afraid that Mr. Levine is too ... how shall we say ... different?

This was followed in a few days by a mention in a widely read entertainment column:

> Insiders are talking about New York's own A. L. Levine as a possible presidential candidate. Levine himself won't say nuthin', but his many years of experience—not to mention that fortune—make him a red-hot dark horse.

Circled in red by his efficient clipping service, these items turned up on Edwards's desk while he was still thinking of ways to uncover Levine. He decided to do nothing on the basis of the gossip column items. If there was anything substantial to the Levine business, one of the Washington columnists would fasten onto it. Two days later Frieda Kraft-Lawrence, the enfant terrible of the political writers, had the subject by the jugular.

> Reading is not particularly fashionable these days, and the reading of poetry assuredly not, and yet those planning the nation's political course might do well to return to Longfellow's simple tale, "The Courtship of Miles Standish." The story of John Alden's eloquent presentation on behalf of Standish, and Priscilla's gentle suggestion that he speak for himself, might ring a chord with the leaders of the disorganized Democratic Party, leaders who cannot seem to find a suitable presidential candidate and who in the very act of expressing puzzlement again and again bring before the nation one of the wisest and most self-effacing of modern political leaders, A. L. Levine.

In stately measures the column proceeded to its invariable literary conclusion.

> Those who remember the past, if I may coin a phrase, must remember it fully. I remind the

Democrats—and Mr. Levine particularly—that Longfellow's poem contains not only the famous injunction to "speak for yourself, John" but the less famous but equally cogent observation by Priscilla, "If I am not worth the wooing, I surely am not worth the winning." In other words, Mr. Levine must move and move swiftly.

Longfellow yet, Edwards thought as he called Levine. "A.L.? I know you've read it. What are we going to do?"

"I don't know, George. I'll have to talk it over with my family."

"Don't give me that crap, A.L. You know what you're going to do."

"It's not as simple as that. Really. We're close. This sort of thing has never come up before. I know what I think I want to do, but I can't do it without talking to my family. A campaign could be bitter—personal attacks, anti-Semitism, the whole bit. My family didn't sign up for that sort of thing."

Levine was not worried about anti-Semitism.

"I see your point," Edwards conceded. "Talk it over with them, make the right decision, and come see me. I'll give you a day to think it over."

"That's fair," Levine said. "It's getting late. Thanks."

In the chaos that had been Levine's childhood and young manhood one ambition had driven and haunted him, haunted because he was so sure that it was unreachable. To marry, to have a wife, to have children, to be normal seemed to Levine as elusive a goal as wealth was to most men. As a child he was a compulsive reader. Early on he felt an added irony: he was leading a nineteenth-century childhood in twentieth-century America. He was poor when Jews were rich, he was orphaned when orphanages were closing for lack of children, he was squat when everyone else was beautiful. His mother had died gasping of rheumatic heart disease when he was four ("It chokes, it chokes," he remembered her shouting from the bedroom he was not allowed to enter). His father had been cut down by the standard coronary six years later, and, incredible in a Jewish family, there was no one to take the child. Grandparents dead; most uncles missing and eventually dead in the Old World ("Hitler" the one-word cause of death); one spinster aunt, silly and penniless. Jewish charities took over. Three orphanages in a row, progressively shabbier as his father's small inheritance gave out. High school in secondhand clothes. Levine once thought that if there had been bottle-blacking factories in Manhattan in 1939, he would have worked in one.

Bent this way, Levine grew in curious curves. He loved the army, even loved being shot at in Italy, because it made him so *normal*. He barely minded being called a "dirty kike," for this lumped him in with the other Jews in his unit, the ones like Rubenfield who were rich, the ones—all the others—who had families. In college and graduate school after the war he did well, was brilliant, but trusted no one, loved no one, could not believe that he would be loved. And finally, in stumbling upon a woman whom he loved and who unreservedly loved him in return, in fathering a family, he first achieved ties to the rest of humanity and for the first time was able to turn his talents to the world at large. To risk his family for the nomination was to risk the foundation of his sanity. He phoned his children to come to the apartment.

"I've had an interesting proposition," Levine said after supper. "Some people are interested in my running for president."

"Who?" said Laura. Twenty-seven, married to an economist with the World Bank, she was bright and totally without imagination. She had always loved facts and had never been able to do anything with them except get good report cards in high school.

"For God's sake, who cares 'Who?'" Eli said. "That's great, great, great." He floated in euphoria. God alone knew what he took.

Samuel's eyes widened, and he smiled gently. This is the one to listen to, thought Levine. Oldest children were supposed to be the easiest to raise. They had brought Sam through the drug crisis and through the impotence crisis and through the work crisis and now at thirty-four he was a man, someone to talk to, to respect. He wasn't exactly fun, but he was nonetheless someone to be proud of.

"Why are you asking us about it, Dad? It's your work and your decision. It's a great honor. How could we object?"

"This is different. Up to now I've been in the back room. Even when I was Acting Chairman in 1980, everyone knew it was just temporary. No one cares about technicians except other technicians. When you run for office, you're everyone's target. Open season. And our family is included. It won't be pleasant."

"But, Dad, you've always told us to be honest and to help people. You've been honest. What do we have to be ashamed of?"

"No one lives a completely blameless life, Sam. Even if you always try to do right. It doesn't always look that way ten years later. There's always something."

"Do you want to be president?"

"Yes."

"Then you must do it."

Levine looked across the table to Helen. She nodded and smiled back at him. The decision was made.

In bed that night Levine for the last time raised objections.

"You know, Helen, political campaigns are not easy. They get bitter, personal. I'll be away a lot. Your privacy will not exist."

"I've been around campaigns, A.L. I know that. My privacy is important, but not that important. The country is important."

"Don't you have any doubts about my getting into all this?"

"I'd have more doubts if you didn't."

Then they made love, Levine fantasizing the red-haired stewardess he had had in Dallas in 1966, Helen fantasizing a younger Levine.

If you watch the Yankess long enough, even from the third tier above the first-base line, you might want to be Joe DiMaggio. If you watch politics long enough, the thought comes along: Why not me?

Levine had answered the political questions years ago, and in much the same way that he had resolved his desire to play center field in 1938. He wasn't the type. Quick and well-coordinated enough, he had no arm, could not hit a fast ball, much less a curve, and had a fatal inability to judge fly balls. He might make a great set-shot artist in basketball, but center field would have to remain the preserve of the Italians and Poles.

Little was different in politics. As he listened over the years to Kennedy, Johnson, Nixon, McGovern, Carter, and the others, it had been borne upon Levine that he was fully as intelligent and informed as they were. Privately—very privately—he considered himself their equal in charm as well. He could not match Kennedy's looks or Nixon's weasel-like relentlessness or Johnson's force, but there was no doubt that he was funnier than one, more honest than another. He was clearly luckier than poor Carter with his family problems. He wasn't, however, a politician. The more he watched and advised, the more he listened and observed, the more he was convinced that politicians, like albinos, were born different; one could no more become a politician than one could become an albino.

"You're going to have to run," Edwards said. "We can get you the nomination, but you're going to have to run."

Levine wandered around his office, glancing at the English hunting prints his assistant had bought to make the place more clublike. She had succeeded—Levine felt somewhat ill at ease in his own office.

"Why do I have to run? Where is it written?"

"You've got to run because you're all we've got. Because I think you can win. Because you love the party and owe it to the party."

Levine stopped. "Owe it to the party? The party has a couple million of my money and four-five years of my life. Maybe the party owes it to me, but the other way around—no, George, I won't buy it."

"I should have said you owe it to the country."

"The country's been rushing around, crying out for Levine, wanting Levine? Not that I notice. The country has gotten along without Levine for over two hundred years. It will survive another four."

"Sure it sounds pompous, but it's true. Who else do we have—Cunningham? A nebbish. Milwood? Another. Kennedy? We can't go through that again. For God's sake, A.L., you were the one who told us to hold our noses and vote for McGovern. You were the one who told us we couldn't duck out, that the elections really meant something, even if the choice was between a monster and a schmuck."

"That's a marvelous inducement for running."

"Okay, so it didn't come out too great. You know what I mean."

Levine knew, and it was hard to escape. There was no one else, really, and the polls after the Rackey thing could not be laughed off. After all those years in the background, Levine found himself with a following.

"It's one thing to say I should run, it's another to do it. I've never run for anything in my whole adult life. I've never been elected to anything, even in high school. I'm not a politician."

"Oh, for Christ's sake, was Wilson a politician? Wilkie? John Glenn? Reagan? What do you think—God comes down and puts some kind of mark on a baby when it's born?"

"That's exactly what I think. The other professors at Princeton knew that Wilson wasn't one of them, really. He was out of place as a professor, restless. Reagan was running for things in the Movie Guild or the Academy or whatever they called it from the time he got to Hollywood. I bet the astronauts felt the same way about Glenn, that he was different from the others. They were all just politicians who hadn't found themselves."

"That's crazy. People get interested in issues, they get involved, they find out that they're just as capable as the assholes who are running, and pretty soon they're running too."

"If they're politicians. If they've got that craziness that

politicians have. If they're normal, like me, they watch, they write a speech or two, they give some advice, they give some money—but they don't run. That's Bigelow's problem. He's president, but he's not really a politician. He doesn't have the craziness."

Edwards grunted. "What kind of craziness?"

"You know what I mean. The absolute conviction that you're the person to save the country, that idiotic blindness. There's nothing like it. In every other important field you have to have some kind of ability or record or intelligence to get ahead. In politics all you need is a sublime faith in yourself. No matter how many times you get knocked down, you keep coming back and eventually you may get somewhere. They despised Nixon, but in a way he's their hero: He came back. So they keep trying. Like Stassen. Or Shriver. If an athlete came to a pro try-out camp with as little equipment as some of those guys brought to politics, he'd be locked up for being crazy. But when a politician runs for president and gets money and people behind him and doesn't have a chance in hell of winning, people give him money and the newspapers interview him and all he's got going is nerve."

Levine paused. "Don't say it. Don't come on to me about whether or not I have nerve. For twenty years I schlepped around every little town in the country, knocking on politicians' doors, trying to sell myself and my product. You think it's easy being a salesman? I was no fucking Willy Loman, for God's sake. I read books, I knew there were other things in life besides Japanese radio transmitters. Worse, I knew that other people enjoyed their privacy. I knocked on their doors just the same."

Edwards got up. "Goddammit, you're a genius. I never knew you when you were selling radios, but you must have been some ticket. I keep thinking of you as I know you, a rich Jewish contributor, but, hell, you're a salesman. You could sell water wings to ducks. You're absolutely right. You don't belong in this. I'm convinced. Sorry to have bothered you. I'll be in touch soon to get together and try to pick someone else."

He headed toward the door.

Levine cleared his throat. "George?"

"Yes?"

"Don't you have any more arguments about why I *should* run?"

Edwards walked over to Levine's side of the desk and grabbed him by the arm. "Goddammit, I knew you'd say yes."

———

Well, why not, why not run the goddam country? Who better to sit in the pilot's seat than a ragtag Jewish kid from the Bronx, a wanderer in a nation of wanderers, a salesman in a nation of salesmen, an optimist in a nation of optimists? Who better to sit in the pilot's seat than a Jew? If a Jew could never define what being Jewish was, he was an expert on what being *not* Jewish was, and that was what the job called for. Who better to sit in the pilot's seat than someone who had been close to the great men of the time, who knew that their strengths were not that much greater than his strengths and their weaknesses no more appalling than his? Who better to sit in the pilot's seat of this vast and complex and amazing machine than someone who was convinced in his surest, deepest nerve fibers that ninety-five percent of the time the plane operated on automatic pilot?

———

The announcement was terse. "Because of my concern about the state of this country and at the urging of my friends and associates, I have decided to seek the presidential nomination of the Democratic party. My decision to enter this contest was made reluctantly and only after much personal examination. Having made the decision to run, I am in the contest completely and will not rest until I have earned the nomination."

Questions boiled up from the reporters. The *Times* transcript read:

Q. What are your immediate plans?

A. I will confer with various party leaders and meet groups of Democrats across the country.

Q. Do you plan to enter any primaries?

A. Yes.

Q. Which ones?

A. My campaign has a late start. It's too soon for us to announce which states we'll enter.

Q. Who will manage your campaign?

A. I don't know. We got our candidate only this morning.

Q. Have you discussed this decision with your wife?

A. Wouldn't you?

Q. What do you feel the major issues are in the campaign?

A. Maintaining a reasonable unity among the people. The end to guerrilla warfare, hair raids, state-line customs offices.

Q. What about persecutions by the Patrols?

A. Certainly they represent a major problem. Their response is understandable, but to understand it does not mean to excuse it. I will not ignore this problem.

Q. Can you tell us how you plan to deal with it?

A. No. In the course of my campaign I will speak on this and other matters, but right now is too early.

Q. You didn't answer my question about your wife.

A. Didn't I? Next question.

Q. Could you tell us something about your past history? The clippings are rather vague on your past, particularly the years 1945 to 1965.

A. They're vague because I was a rather ordinary sort of person in those years—not that I'm so extraordinary now—hardly the sort of person who would get mentioned in a newspaper. I worked at various jobs here and there. I sold radio equipment, as my résumé indicates. I assure you that I wasn't in jail, if that's what you're wondering *(laughter)*. A biography is being prepared.

Q. Do you think your religion will hurt you?

A. Only if I laugh *(laughter)*. Seriously, I do not think so. It did not hurt Mr. Goldwater in 1964. The

American people are fair. If I lose—and I don't expect to—it will not be because of my religion. I'm sorry, gentlemen, but I have to get back to my office.

Q. Thank you, Mr. Levine.

"I'll need an organization," Levine said.

"I'd be glad to help you at the National Committee," Edwards said, "but some of those pricks who work for me might think I was being unfair. We'll work out something."

The National Committee staff was as nonpartisan as a Boston primary. There was not a soul in the building, not even a clerk-typist, who wasn't there as the legacy of some politician somewhere in the country, not a soul who wasn't scheming and politicking every moment of the day to advance the cause of one person or another. Lawyers hired in 1968 as "Humphrey men" had been careful to have their options picked up by succeeding generations of politicians. The perky young receptionist at the front desk was the niece of a western governor. The switchboard operators were known Kennedy people and were suspected of keeping a log on the chairman's calls. The finance section had taken on a token Wallace woman in 1974, and when Wallace had begged off she had been sponsored by the Carter people. Nothing happened in the committee, not even the spring picnic, that the employees didn't see as the workings of national politics. Usually they were right.

Edwards called Jessington, who called Levine. Then Jessington called the congressman from the District of Columbia, who called his brother-in-law. The brother-in-law was a computer programmer at the committee. He was nonpolitical. As he used to say, "Hell, it doesn't matter to me whether we're counting up swimsuit inventories or convention delegates. Tell me what you want and I'll program it." He was apolitical, but he was a Jessington man, hired through Jess, dedicated to advancing whatever Jess wanted at the moment. He would do anything but fudge the figures for Jessington. Running a printout of active county and state chairmen state by state and then smuggling it out of the office wasn't unethical. Hell, a programmer was *supposed* to program. He gave the job of actually smuggling the data out of the building—the committee had gotten fussy about security—to a cleaning woman who had been hired at his suggestion.

Four days later they sat around the big table in McKelvin's dining room. Each man had a copy of the printout, sheets of blank paper with the names of the fifty-two states along the left margin, a Rand-McNally road atlas, and a copy of the county-by-county results in the previous two presidential elections.

Behind Levine's chair loomed his personal files, a triumph of the office manager's art. Semi-automatic, cross-indexed by state and by occupation, they were the culmination of Levine's years on the road.

"Lenin said that revolutions are won with filing cabinets," his friend Farbstein, the socialist, had told him years ago when he first got the job with Arco Electronics. "You might try using them as a capitalist."

"I'm not a capitalist. I'm a salesman. All I won is a mortgage."

"So? You're trying to be a capitalist. Take Lenin's advice. Get yourself some files."

"What for? I can remember who I talk to. I like meeting people. Names I can remember."

"Names you can remember, but what about addresses? Phone numbers? Take it from a socialist, there's nothing like files."

Levine had been skeptical. There was something too cold-blooded about writing down the names of people you met. People were to meet and to talk to, not to file away in metal drawers. Rushing home and writing down names and addresses missed the whole point of being a salesman. It was like the girls he dated in graduate school who underlined all their reading, transcribed their notes into beautifully kept typewritten summaries, and in the end still couldn't tell Turgenev from Tolstoy unless they were labeled.

Farbstein insisted. "Look, you write down the names and numbers of your suppliers, don't you? Already you keep a little notebook with addresses in it. So keeping notes doesn't mean you're a hypocrite. It just means you're systematic. For a salesman, every name is a potential sale."

Reluctantly Levine began to keep a record not only of the jobbers and wholesalers and politicians but of people he met socially. He'd chat with someone at a dinner or on a plane, get a business card or scribble down a name and address, and then, at his motel, jot down a one-man's *Who's Who*—"mar., epis, flying lessons, bro. surgeon N. Orleans." Back in New York he had the typist transcribe the notes onto 3-by-5 cards.

As the card file grew over the years, Levine became somewhat ashamed of it. Was he no more than a Jewish Babbitt, seeing nothing but sales prospects in the strangers who introduced themselves to him at bars and at parties? He took pride in not referring to his file system. He would rather memorize the names and occupations and personal habits in a bedtime litany than suffer the humiliation of seeking out human beings in a steel cabinet.

But the other people at Arco had no hesitation in using the file. "Hey, A.L.," Sid Hersch would yell, "what's the name of that wholesaler in Minneapolis, you know, the one with the redheaded wife who had the hospitality suite at the Carlton that year?"

Levine would dart into his files, check under Minnesota, and yell back, "Thorgenberg."

"Jesus, that's it. I knew it was some sort of crazy name. He Jewish?"

"God, no. Lutheran."

"How the fuck should I know? It sounds Jewish." To Hersch, who knew Chicago to be the only outpost of civilization between New York and Los Angeles, any name that ended in "berg" was Jewish until proven otherwise. Even then he suspected that its owner was trying to hide something, and he would artfully drop little Yiddish phrases into the conversation in hopes of unmasking the occasional Thorgenbergs and Stenbergs he met.

If not essential to Levine, the file was invaluable to Arco, and there was some bitterness when Levine quit and took it with him. Resettled in his own real-estate office, Levine pondered the file, which had some five thousand names, and decided that if it had been that important to Arco, it might be helpful to him in his career. He called in an office consultant and discussed the filing system. In the end, at the cost of $10,000, the names had been transferred to an automatic finding system, with duplicates on tape for eventual full computerization. It could present you, depending on your whim, with all of Minnesota, all police chiefs (past or present), all divorced men, all Harvard graduates—or any combination of the twenty categories each individual was typed for. For a time in the late 1960s Levine had kept his women catalogued too, with a code for their sexual preferences, but had hastily pulled the cards after reading a novel in which a widow figured out her late husband's appointment book. Sometimes he had erotic dreams about the lost cards.

"Shall we go alphabetically or by vote?" Jessington asked.

"By vote. Let's cut the trees and pick up the underbrush later."

"Okay. New York? California?"

Here at last was the smoke-filled room, the distillation of their combined years of brooding and planning. They were picking state campaign managers—suicide jobs with no money, no prestige, no advancement, endless opportunities to make enemies among your own neighbors, jobs with no potential at all, unless—unless Levine won, took the nomination and then the election, came up president, and could pass out thanks. Then the chairmen would be at the head of the line, and they themselves would have favors to pass back.

These were idiot jobs, and there was no lack of candidates. Some had already sniffed around, expressing benign approval of Levine's campaign, his wife, his

children, his religion. Others, the good ones, were waiting
to be asked. There were still good ones uncommitted—the
suddenness of Rackey's withdrawal had left a lot of
people stranded, and the new shortened primary season
gave them more time to decide—but they had conditions.
They wanted advance word on spending, control over
their own staff, promises of campaign visits, promises of
help for statewide candidates, promises of jobs in any new
administration.

"No promises," Levine said. "I don't care who we're
talking to, no promises."

"A.L., these people are pros. They expect something
back."

"They'll get it. The only promise I can make is I'll do
my best to take care of them. If they won't accept that, we
go to the next one on the list."

State by state, they argued the choices. In the big states
they all had favorites, and they fought them out until one
or another gave in. "Look, forget Cushman," McKelvin
said. "She's smart, but she's looking out for herself. She
double-crossed Jackson in 'seventy-six, she'll do the same
to you if she gets a chance."

"Get Cushman," Levine said. "She works like hell,
she's got the women with her, and she's smart."

"The woman thing is over," Bell said. "The polls show
no significant sex breakdown on any of the candidates.
They've had their own candidates, now they're just
looking for the best man."

"Or woman." Jessington grunted.

"Yeah. Or woman."

"I don't give a damn. It still counts for something.
Besides, she's the best person we've got there."

McKelvin shook his head again. "I don't trust her. I
remember that press conference in—"

"Look, I don't trust her either. We're going to choose
her and then we're going to watch her. And it'll be your
special responsibility to make sure she doesn't screw me.
Agreed?"

"Okay."

Levine nodded at Bell, who reached for the phone. The

phone rang and rang somewhere in New York until Cushman's answering service finally came on and said she was not available.

"She's not available," Bell whispered.

"Goddammit, she is too. Get her number from the service. Tell them it's the White House calling. Tell them it's an emergency. If the service won't come through, try her at what's-his-name's place. I want her on board tonight so that when we call the California people we can tell them we've got Cushman. They know her out there, they respect her. Let's get this goddam thing moving."

They found Cushman at what's-his-name's place; it was a dinner party and she was annoyed at being interrupted.

"I'll have to think about it," she told Bell.

"Let me take that phone," Levine said. "Mary, this is A.L. Mary, let me put it to you straight. We can't wait for you to think about it. You're a smart person, you've been thinking about it the last couple of weeks anyway. You've been thinking, 'Suppose Levine asks me, what should I do? Should I wait for the convention? Should I ask for something?' I know you've been thinking about it, Mary, and I want to level with you: We asked you because you're the best. But we got going late on this campaign, we're just starting on the soup and everyone else is ready for dessert, and we can't waste any time. So let me tell you, if you won't say 'Yes' we're right on the phone to someone else. Because we need you and we need New York, but we've got to have somebody big heading New York before we get someone in New Jersey. *Capisce?*"

"A.L., honey, it's too soon. I've got my commitments here. I—"

"Mary, come on. You know I'll give you a square deal. But you know I mean it; I'd like to come back to you later, but I can't. It's now or never. Say 'Now.'"

"Goddammit, okay. 'Now.' Are you happy?"

"Mary, you're a trooper. Thanks. We'll see you in Washington next week. Philip will talk to you again. Call me any time. You can always get through directly. That's a promise."

He hung up and smiled. "One down, fifty-one to go."

It was not as hard as Bell thought it would be. By the evening's end they had twenty-two definite and eight possibles who had to check with their wives or husbands or lawyers or accountants.

They were back to work the next morning at ten, poring over the lists, calling people, quarreling among themselves. They set up conference calls for some of the waverers.

"A.L., I just got to have more time to roll this thing over," Okimura said. Okimura was the mayor of Portland, an independent and the hottest thing going in Oregon politics.

"He told Jess at the Mayors' Conference that he wants to be an ambassador," Bell whispered to Levine.

Levine turned back to the phone. "Look, Oki. I told you last night we're in a hurry. We gave you time to talk to your wife. You can't caucus forever. We need to know today. I appreciate your problem, but it's the same for everyone. Mary Cushman came through for us in New York, Ludwig out in Minneapolis—we read you the list."

There was a pause. "It's a hell of a risk for me politically," Okimura said. "I'd like some kind of commitment for after the election. My wife still has family overseas. I've been thinking that because of my background—"

"I can't promise you anything, Oki," Levine said. "You've got my firm promise for nothing. Understand? That's all I can promise. You know I respect you, you know I'll try to find something you like, but there are no promises."

Another pause. "Are you taping this call?"

"For Christ's sake, of course I'm taping this call. All the conference calls. You wouldn't do it deliberately, no one that I'm calling on would do it deliberately, but it would be easy for someone to misunderstand what I'm saying on these calls. Someone else might get the idea that something—the cabinet, ambassador, regional programs administrator—had been promised. So everything's taped."

"Okay. I'll call back in exactly a half hour. Okay with you?"

"Hunky-dory," Levine said, and hung up.

"He's just keeping us on the hook a little longer," McKelvin said. "He knows goddam well he's going to accept. Just wants to make us sweat."

"He's not like that," Bell said. "He's a dealer. He's got a lot of hairs out in those mountains. 'Developer' is a bad word out there."

"Find me a place where it's a *nice* word and I'll build three hundred units with all utilities," Levine muttered.

"Two-to-one odds, my hundred bucks against your fifty, that he accepts," McKelvin said.

"Done."

"I'll hold the money," Levine said. "Where the hell are we now? Mississippi. I got two friends down there and they both turned Republican. Curly, what about Barry Reynolds? I get along with him all right, I see him over in the House from time to time. Doesn't he want to go upward and onward?"

"Shit, no. Ol' Boy had so much fun with the Kappa Sigs at Ol' Miss that all through law school he kept trying to find someplace that would keep him just as happy. Someone told him about Congress and he's been a congressman ever since. Closest thing to Kappa Sig a grown man can find. There's no way he's going to come in. Tell you what, though. I've got a friend over in Jackson, young lawyer by the name of Telfer. Not Jewish, if that's what you're thinking. Anyhow, he's smart and he's honest and he's got a good name for himself."

"Let's cross-file him right now. If he's as good as you say, I don't have any objections. Okay with the rest of you?"

They all nodded. While they were cross-checking Telfer, Okimura called from Portland, accepting.

Sturgis Hale spent a great deal of time reading the obituaries. He was young and in good health, and his preoccupation with the deaths of his elders was a matter of unease to his colleagues at the paper. Sitting at their desks, rereading their stories, checking to see what else had happened while they had swept their own little corner of the world, they would shout across the newsroom, "Where did Ettlinger get the money for a new house?" or "How come Wright never hits against left-handed pitchers?" The game was to read your own paper so thoroughly that you could pick up nuggets that everyone else—particularly the news editor—had missed. Arcane references from the competing papers were valuable, but a scandal or a possible story overlooked in the *Times* itself was the stopper.

Hale's specialty was obituaries. He covered national politics for the *Times*, but his small passion lay among the deaths of people he had never known, just as Jack Siegel, who had not been to a ball game in twenty years, glowed at finding errors of addition in the box-score totals. ("If Wills got three hits, and Singer two, how come we said DeMario pitched a four-hitter? Can't those assholes add?")

Hale would look up from his paper and say, "I didn't know Senator Wool had been married before. It says here that he is survived by his second wife, Elizabeth, and two children from a previous marriage. I bet the first wife's that old Mrs. Wool who's hot for dog-and-cat kindness."

"Who gives a shit?" Siegel said. "Wool's dead. And he's been out of Congress ten years."

"Still, it's interesting," Hale said.

It was more than interesting. It was, indeed, the secret of Hale's success. It was an unspectacular success, true, but it was real and still growing. His name was an elegant one, but his father had been an alcoholic millworker in Portland, Maine. "Three hundred years in this country and the only fucking thing I've gotten out of it is a job with a bunch of Canucks," he told his son. "You've got a distinguished name—it isn't worth shit. Get yourself an education." He died soon after, leaving neither the money nor the impetus for the education he had preached so loudly. Sturgis worked in the same mill for two years after high school and, his own experience having confirmed his father's distaste for blue-collar work, saved enough money to last him through four years at the state university. He was the first in his family in a hundred years to have finished college.

Hale had drifted naturally into journalism; it was literary without being faggy. Soon he had discovered a particular talent for newspaper work, and the obituaries had reinforced that talent.

"Weddings are okay," he told his wife, who brooded about his seeming obsession with death, "but they just give a peek. Obits open the whole door. In a marriage we'll tell you that the bride is the granddaughter of Commodore Vanderbilt and that the groom's father is a descendant of John Frémont, and that helps, but there's no hard news and no bad news in a wedding. In a good obit you get all the names: the clubs, the directorships, what the children's names are and where they live."

Facts from obits helped Hale, gave him connections that, stored away, came in handy a year later, two years later, when he interviewed a congressman or drank with a lobbyist. More than facts, he gathered the patterns, the rhythm of middle-class lives: a lawyer father, for example, an eastern prep school, ability *(Yale Law Review)*, discreet social climbing (an eastern wife, rich), power in the law (partner in Sullivan & Cromwell), government service (Secretary of the Navy in a Republican administration), and, after several foundation presidencies, death.

"There's a certainty to it that they don't even know themselves," he told his wife. "These people who keep coming down to save the country, these hot-shot lawyers, smart-ass professors, they're going to end up on that page sooner or later, and I can give you odds on what it'll say. I know the Roosevelt obits—for every Frankfurter, you've got fifty that say, 'Joe Blank Dies: Corporation Lawyer, Served Government.' They'll cling to those four years for the rest of their lives, and every time they defend an oil company or cheat some widow out of her farm, they'll tell their families, 'I worked for the president.' Creeps. The pattern's the same. The fun is sorting out the Frankfurters from the Kellys.

"These people dance and speak and screw and they're nothing. Last year I read an old obit on Mitchell Palmer. He was Wilson's Attorney General, tried to clear commies and anarchists out of the country. Most powerful man in Washington for two years, then completely forgotten."

There was another, bitterer lesson that Hale learned from the obits: that America was not so forgiving as it claimed, and that the press did not believe that *"De mortuis nil nisi bonum."* Once touched by scandal, you were followed by the scandal to the grave itself. "Figure in Teapot Dome...," "Indicated in Influence Case...," "Watergate Defendant...." All these followed men as inexorably as "Dropped Third Strike in Series Game." The American people allowed you no mistakes—in public.

And so, though his friends at the paper laughed and called him the Grim Reaper, Hale stuck with his obituaries and became a superior reporter. He was only thirty, but he seemed older. People he interviewed were struck by his depth, his sense of the past. He made connections no one else made, had facts that no one else remembered. Reporting in America was a young person's job, and Hale seemed wise beyond his years. It was not all obits, of course, for he worked his beat carefully and read American history when he had the time, but the added dimension came from a friendship with death.

Hale had watched Willard Rose for a long time, not with special knowledge of impending death—Rose was only forty-seven—but from curiosity about a career somehow out of phase. Rose had been a spectacular and even effective Republican congressman for four years, but his intensity had proved too much for the people of Vermont and he had withdrawn to his mountain home. He lectured, wrote occasional articles, and did the other things rejected politicians do while awaiting a chance to run again.

The judgment in Washington was that Rose was finished. "Too abrasive." He had had his chance and lost it. Last year's politician is as dead as last year's newspaper, and Rose was of the past. In twenty years he might be an official elder statesman, sought out for comment at times of national crisis, like a New England Alf Landon or George Wallace, but now he was too recently remembered even to qualify as colorful. He was ignored.

Except by Hale. Hale worked in Washington, read his obits, snuffled through back issues of the paper like a pig after truffles, and scented something different about Rose. There *were* second acts in American politics: Franklin Roosevelt was just another pretty young man in 1922, and Richard Nixon was a laughingstock in 1962. Literary careers rose and fell with the development of the writer's own talent, but political careers were the vectored outcome of both the politician and the forces that moved the country. Someone too abrasive one election year might crest on a wave of bitterness and disillusionment four years later. Hale looked at the country and thought about Rose.

He had Rose's phone number in his pocket directory, a directory he kept up to date by shamelessly stealing numbers from other reporters' scratch pads, address books, and kitchen wall lists.

Rose answered the phone himself.

"This is Sturgis Hale of the *Times.* I'd like to come up and talk with you for a couple of days if you can find the time. I'm doing a piece on you for the *Magazine.*"

Rose thought a moment and did his calculations.

"Come on up. I'll be glad to talk to you. I warn you, though, I'm outdoors a lot at this time of year, and I won't break up my routine for an interview. If you want to see me, you'll have to be ready to follow me around."

"I'll be ready."

"Bring hiking boots, then."

"I've got some old Peter Limmer boots that should be okay."

"They should be," Rose said curtly, and hung up.

Rose was elegant. His father had been a famous television reporter in Chicago, and Rose had grown up in a world of beautifully dressed men whose very handkerchiefs carried some subtle mark of prestige. He had forsaken the snobberies of the communications world and moved to the hills of Vermont, but he never shed the values of his earlier life. Reporters who had come to interview "the boy wonder of American politics" in his home near Plainfield wrote feelingly of its rustic simplicity. "Willard Rose has taken the Earth Movement as a personal credo," wrote *Time*'s correspondent. "Without martyring themselves, he and his wife have stripped the moss away from modern living, returned to the hard rock beneath." More observant reporters noted reminders of Rose's wealth all over the house—the sleeping bags stacked on the front porch bore the name of a world-famous Russian outfitter, the camping frames were made of custom-fitted titanium, the library held a first edition of Audubon's *Birds of America*. A woman reporter from Los Angeles once visited Rose, looked around knowingly, and muttered, "Brand-name simplicity." Her interview went poorly and she was not asked back.

Rose watched Levine's press conference with his press secretary, Elsworth Palmer. He considered Levine's candidacy a personal affront.

"Look at that midget sonofabitch," he said. "'The urging of my friends. . . .' 'Friends,' my ass. He doesn't have any friends. He takes over the National Committee and makes himself a candidate. Like a tennis umpire declaring that he's seeded number one. We can't let him do that. The goddam country won't stand for it. Goddammit, Els, I'm going after it. What do you say?"

Palmer was an appropriately tall, traditionally thin, reassuringly gray-haired Vermonter. He was a generous man, by nature gregarious and talkative, but he had learned in twenty years as a Washington correspondent that tall, thin New Englanders were supposed to be taciturn, and so he had adjusted his nature. He knew people said about him, "Why, Els Palmer—he won't talk any more than granite will," and as long as this reputation got him to important dinner parties as a typical Yankee, he cultivated silence. Besides, he learned a good deal, and when Rose needed a native Vermonter to manage his congressional campaign, he had been a natural choice. He had distrusted Rose at first but had learned to respect him for his manic energy, passion, and raw intelligence.

"If you say go, we'll go. You're the boss."

"Don't give me your rock-bound face. Tell me, do you think we can manage it?"

"I'm not sure. You're growing, I know. People are listening. They're tired of the old bunch. Bigelow's quitting and there's a vacuum. We could get New Mexico, California, Colorado, West Virginia for sure. The Midwest seems solid. And Vermont, of course. I wouldn't go after Levine personally if he gets it. Stay on a high plane, and all that."

"They're confused. Rackey is gone and they're desperate. Putting up Levine shows that. He has no feel, no charisma. He's old politics. People won't listen."

"I think we could get the money. Levine may be harder to beat than you think."

"He's weak, old. I'll run him into the ground. We'll get something on him. Where did he come from? Nobody knows. Where'd he get his money? Nobody knows. He must be vulnerable. Must be. I remember something I read in the *Times* in 'seventy or 'seventy-two. The first time his name came up with the old National Committee. I remember reading it and feeling something smelled. There was a word in it, a phrase, something that didn't ring right. Like when you read some guy has been stabbed to death in another man's apartment, the paper doesn't say they're fairies, you don't know they're fairies, but the odds are it's a lovers' quarrel. I just have that feeling. Who the hell does that little Jew think he is? This is *my* year."

BELVIDERE, MARCH 7, 1988

"Every country has its own ritual for reporters and important visitors," Jack Siegel told Hale. "The idea behind the ritual is to humiliate the visitor. In America we do it by showing them automated steel plants and tele-screen phones. We're not physical—we try to humble you financially. Of course, we're not as good at it as we used to be. Most countries hit you physically: the vodka thing or the ten-course dinner or the sheep's-eye stew. If they don't have vodka or food or sheep, they just walk your ass off, keep walking you until you say you're tired. When you do that, they've got the upper hand. You go back and write a story about the 'tireless Mexicans' or the 'indefatigable Iranians' or some such, and they've probably had their goddam Olympic squad escorting you and you never knew it. The first thing for any foreign trip: train like you would for a boxing match."

The advice was improbable coming from Siegel, whose jowls, belly, and half-lost biceps all wobbled as he moved, but he had once been a premier foreign correspondent, known for his ability to go anywhere for a story. Hale listened, and he jogged two miles a day before flying to Vermont.

After Rose's adolescent sons had put his bags away, Hale waited on the porch looking toward Montgomery Center.

"Let's take a look around," Rose said.

They plunged through a field, scrambled up a ledge, and started up a narrow path that went steadily higher. There were patches of snow everywhere. Rose talked steadily, identifying plants and trees, pointing out a pheasant half hidden in some brush.

"I grew up in Chicago," Rose said. "I lived for the summers. We had a place near Charlevoix and then at the

67

Huron Mountain Club, and we'd go up there for the whole summer. Life made sense there in a way it didn't in the city. Things you did with your hands counted—I learned how to change tires, then to fix an engine. We had our own boat. I could strip the outboard down and repair it while we were out fishing. I had friends there."

He paused, thinking. "In Chicago I was an Eagle scout. People make fun of that. It's become sort of a cliché, hasn't it—I mean, earning merit badges? People forget what merit badges are. I won't forget. You needed twenty-one for Eagle, and you had to have a theoretical knowledge of a subject and then apply it. Some creep could study the habits of birds until he knew Peterson backward and forward, but unless he went out in the field and identified thirty species, no badge. It's a nice system.

"Eagle scout! People make fun of it, but it was more important to me than college. Don't tell the people in New Haven that, though. Oh, hell—sure you can tell them. Yale was just like Chicago, in a funny way. I knew a lot of people already, and I never took hold of studying. I dropped out just in time to be drafted for Vietnam. I came back afterwards and graduated. You know the rest. Are you tired?" he added suddenly.

Hale had been scrambling, but scrambling adequately. He was not breathing hard, but he was sweating though the afternoon was cool.

"No, I'm fine. I'm anxious to see the view."

"We'll keep going, then," Rose said.

Rose talked their way to the crest of the hill. Hale found what he said and how he said it offensive—royalist views expressed in the nasal, cultured accent of a millionaire's son just back from Exeter—but he rather liked Rose just the same. This bothered him.

They came to a rocky clearing three quarters of the way up the hill. "This is the place," Rose said. "Look around." He waved toward the horizon. "That big one over there is Jay Peak. Used to be a ski center until the gasoline thing hit. Those are the Cold Hollow Mountains over there—nice name, isn't it? Way over there on the west, that's Lake Champlain. That smoke you see is coming from Canada. There's a refinery in Sutton, and their pollution laws are looser than ours."

"Beautiful," Hale said.

"I want to keep it that way. People don't understand about the land. The liberals used to blabber about conservation and ecology, but they didn't know what they were talking about. You can't be for ecology and be a liberal. You put the government into the land business and the National Park business and you get the notion that the land belongs to the people. As soon as it belongs to the people, it's gone. Something that belongs to everybody belongs to nobody. You think you're preserving something by making it a national park, but you're only destroying it. That's what happened to Yosemite."

"For the sake of argument, what do you say to the claim that private enterprise destroyed the land, that only public ownership and regulation saved it?"

"It's half true. That's why it's so dangerous. It wasn't private enterprise that destroyed the land, it was corporate enterprise. As long as the land belonged to one man or one family, the way we think it should, it was preserved. A man won't destroy the land he lives on or even the mine he gets his ore from. A corporation will, because it can go on to devour something else."

"You sound like a presidential candidate."

"Isn't that what you're up here about? You're not that interested in ex-congressmen. You're not even that interested in hiking. I had that checked out. Of course I'm going to announce. The *Times Magazine* is going to make a nice little springboard. I said 'little'—I'm not fooling myself about how the people in New York think about me. I'll take what I can get."

"People used to think of young people as liberal, of ecology as a liberal issue. What made the difference?"

"It was the food riots. When the government started issuing regulations on vitamins and then the FDA shut down the National Force food line, everything crystallized. Young people realized that you couldn't be for government regulation of the oil industry and oppose government regulation of health foods. They didn't mind the government running things so long as it just affected companies in Houston and Mexico City, but when the FDA cut off their wheat germ and honey bread, they saw they had Big Brother in the pantry. That's when they became conservatized."

"Conservatized?"

"Yes. It's a word. I just made it up. You can use it in the article. Let's go back. I have some serious talking I want to do."

——————

They ate well at Rose's. It was natural food but not vegetarian, and, because the wind had become chilly, the main course was roast haunch of venison. The venison was cooked over a great open fireplace in the kitchen.

"I hope you like the venison, Mr. Hale. The recipe comes from the *New York Times Cookbook*."

"It's excellent. I'll tell the New York office."

"I shot the deer in season. My neighbors find that a bit peculiar. I'm tempted to do as the Romans do, but it wouldn't look too good if I got caught."

"Yeah, I can see our headline now: 'Rose, Ex-Congressman, Arrested in Poaching Incident.'"

"No—it would be 'Conservative Ex-Congressman.'"

"Maybe. Anyway, we'd have a hell of an editorial."

Mrs. Rose, a trim, edgy woman with muscular calves, said, "It isn't fair. People around here shoot deer to live. The game laws don't make sense. We're being overrun by deer. They come into the vegetable garden and eat the lettuce. If we followed nature's laws, we'd kill enough for us and they'd be back in the forest."

Rose interrupted. "Susan feels strongly about this. Her family's from Vermont for generations. That's why we came here after Vietnam."

"Did you grow up here, Mrs. Rose?" Hale asked.

"Well, not exactly. We lived in Boston. This place belonged to my great-uncle. We bought it, restored it, and brought it back to the kind of life it provided before. We raise our food. The boys help harvest it. Maria and I do all the cooking."

Hale had noticed a swarthy, stumpy woman moving purposefully back and forth in the kitchen. He had watched her turn the spit the venison was on, baste it with dripping, and, sweating, bring it triumphantly to the table. He figured that if Mrs. Rose and Maria did all the cooking, Mrs. Rose's specialty was looking up recipes in the *Times Cookbook*.

"You see," Rose said, resuming the conversation he had ended on the mountain climb, "conservatives conserve. Literally. If you are a conservative, you must be a conservationist. The values we support—individual effort, the land, the family, honor—are traditional ones. We're not ashamed of that. It's part of the Republican tradition. President Bigelow came out of the corporation world, which is entirely different. I'm not sorry that he's not running again."

Hale had been saving his next question. Now was the time. "You get a lot of support from young people—the hairs—in New England and out West, and you also have strength among older people, the ones who used to go with Goldwater, the Westmoreland League. How do you explain that? And do you think you can keep that kind of coalition together?"

Rose stopped eating and stared at Hale. "You know, sometimes just as I'm beginning to like a newspaper man I realize all over again what bastards they are. My God, I've told you that three times over and still you come back to me with the same question, asked a different way. What do you think I'm going to do, change my philosophy between three o'clock and eight o'clock?"

"No, we—I'm just trying to get exactly the right phrasing, from you and for me. I sort of move around a subject, ask the same question in slightly different ways. I'm sorry if it bothers you."

Susan Rose interrupted. "I'm sure Willard wasn't upset at you personally, Mr. Hale."

"Look," Rose said, "I apologize. You're my guest and you're also doing your job. It's just that I've been away from interviews for a while and I forgot what they're like."

He paused for a moment.

"I apologize, and I'll answer the rest of your question. We have both ends of the age spectrum on our side because they both want a different America—the old ones, because they remember the way it used to be, the young ones because they have an idea of what it could be. They've gotten together because they're not locked into the corporate-liberal state. The old ones have been pushed out; the young ones haven't entered. And don't forget—there are enormous numbers of working people, middle-aged people, who agree with us too."

"How do you keep all that together?"

"How did Roosevelt keep the left-wing Democrats, almost socialists, with the southern Democrats? A certain community of philosophy, a certain practical advantage in banding together with other groups. I'll tell you one thing: my supporters have a hell of a lot more in common philosophically with each other than Roosevelt's coalition did. If you tell a seventy-year-old man that if you want to get the government out of regulating what kind of pills people take, you also have to get it out of telling what drugs people can take, he'll understand. At first he won't see the connection between legalizing cocaine and legalizing Pauling pills, but if you explain it enough, he'll go along. He may not like it, but he'll go along."

They talked about skiing and hiking the rest of the evening.

Levine thought about it for a week and then asked Philip Bell to run his campaign. Bell was young, but he was a professional. He was dedicated. He would stay in the background. He was conventionally Protestant. He knew some of the newer people in the party who Levine wasn't at ease with.

Together they scheduled the campaign. Levine would have to touch base with the ethnics, the chics in Texas and California, the blacks in the cities, the Irish in New Hampshire and Massachusetts. He didn't have to worry about the Jews. No need to campaign in Vermont and New Mexico—just getting election permits in those two centers of the hairs would be so difficult that the primaries would be over before he'd be eligible. Under the new law shortening the whole primary season, the New England primaries came together, but New Hampshire was still first. California would be hard, but it could be done. The South would be touchy. In the national election the South would probably go Republican anyway, but Levine needed those states for the nomination.

The immediate test would be the Black Mayors' Caucus, the "kink caucus" as distinguished from the "Cauc caucus." Protocol demanded that the candidate petition the caucus for a hearing. Bell sent off a properly humble telegram to Reginald Hollins of Cincinnati, the caucus's pro tem president, and, after a three-day wait, received an invitation for Levine to address "a small group of my friends" at the Alhambra in New York.

Levine had heard of the Alhambra, of course, but had never been there. It was closed to whites except on invitation. After waiting four hours for a glass of water in 1976, a fanatic seminarian named O'Rourke had brought suit in the New York courts against the restaurant's racial policy, and his right to service had been upheld by the State Supreme Court. It was a right he unfortunately was never able to exercise, since he disappeared on the afternoon of the decision. The policy had since been retested neither in the courts nor the restaurant itself. Whites ate there from time to time in the company of black hosts, and Levine knew that if he had mentioned it to Jessington, he would have long ago been invited. He was curious about the place, for the food and entertainment were famous, but he had been diffident about an invitation. "Don't go where they don't want you," his high school math teacher had said. The teacher had been talking about Levine's application to Princeton, but Levine fancied the principle still held.

Jessington met him at the airport and guided him to a limousine. On the way uptown he sketched the evening.

"Now, some of those old fellows will go right for your neck, A.L. You better be ready for it now. They'll want a promise of jobs for themselves, and they'll try to get it in writing. You can ignore 'em except for Harris and Stokes. The really important ones won't be so crude, and the unimportant ones you can just walk over. But Harris and Stokes—they're just crude enough to ask, just important enough so you gotta meet with them. Now you know the bunch of them like the palm of your hand, so I don't have to tell you much more. There may be some Jew-calling, but I'll step on that."

"Don't step on it, Jess. Let it come out. I'm not much worried about this bunch. Remember, half of them came up through the police department—the SWAT squads and the Special Operations divisions. Some of them I've known since they first made captain and I tried to sell them walkie-talkies. They're not going to like me any better if you fight my battles for me. Let it come. I've heard it before."

Jessington chuckled. "I bet, I bet. Anyway, you've never seen anything as good or eaten anything as good as Alhambra, so you might as well relax for a good time."

Levine was escorted in past cobra-lidded bouncers and loungers, along corridors muraled with protest art, down halls lavish with framed artifacts of black rebellion ("Bicycle chain used as weapon against oppressor, 1962, St. Louis") into a room in which fifty dark faces gleamed above fifty sets of Royal Worcester set evenly on an expanse of Irish linen tablecloth. There was polite clapping. Levine was shown to his place between Jessington and Hollins. He had met Reginald Hollins, the architect of the new black strategy, years ago, but he doubted if Hollins remembered it.

Levine had been still young enough or naïve enough then to offer up opinions when none had been asked. He hadn't yet learned to be still and just listen. So when he bumped into Hollins at the 1968 Democratic National Convention and suggested they have a drink together, he didn't let the black man get all his talking done.

He'd met Hollins a few years before, selling the Arco crime control system to the Cincinnati police. Hollins was just a lieutenant then, the first black police officer Levine had ever dealt with.

Had he liked Hollins when he first met him? He had almost loved him, loved his athlete's grace (he had played at Crispus Attucks before Oscar Robertson, had then been the first black to start for Ohio State), his deep, soft voice, his overwhelming dignity. They had talked some that first time and then, in Miami, trying to pick up the pieces after Bobby's death and Johnson's stepping aside, Levine was eager—too eager—to talk again.

They went to the Boom-Boom Room of the Fontainebleau, Levine taking a perverse pride in its garishness. Eyes locked on them as they were shown to a table. I've stayed here five times, I'm a millionaire, I'm one of *them*, Levine thought, and yet the people were staring at Hollins. Hollins looked as though he was somebody they should know—a singer or an athlete or even, by 1968, a famous politician. No one recognized Levine and no one wanted to.

"So," he said, "what do you think about what's going on?" Levine became perceptively more Jewish in Miami.

"Plain as wings on a pig," Hollins said. "We're going to nominate Humphrey and we're going to get our ass whipped."

"I thought you were for Humphrey," Levine said. He *knew* that Hollins was for Humphrey.

"Of course I am. That's no never mind. I'm not telling you what I want to happen, I'm telling you what will happen."

"How come you're so sure?"

"I can tell. We've got a lot of colleges in Ohio. You can't any more talk to those young people or those little professors with their fancy new mustaches than you can argue a Mormon out of Mormonism. They're for McCarthy or Bobby and Bobby's dead and McCarthy's about had it, so they'll kill Hubert too. Ain't no one goin' to come out of this alive." He shook his head.

Then Levine made his mistake. Thinking about it later, he tried to excuse himself by rationalizing it as an attempt to draw Hollins out, to get the black man talking about something that bothered them both. He knew this wasn't so. The truth was that he had been listening to his children, which was always a good thing to do, and taking them very seriously, which wasn't necessarily a good thing to do. He wasn't sounding out Hollins. He was, in fact, lecturing him.

Levine said, "Maybe the McCarthy people are right. After all, Humphrey is Johnson's man, and look what Johnson gave us."

"The Civil Rights Act."

"I was thinking of Vietnam."

"I figured you were. I think of it too, but there were lots of other people in on that. But when I think of Johnson I think of the Civil Rights Act and when I think of Humphrey I think of the convention back in 1948, and you can spread the blame for Vietnam around fifty different ways, but you can lay the Civil Rights Act right to Johnson and Humphrey, and I'm never going to be moved away from them. Not for a dozen Vietnams. Vietnam I just hear about. Civil rights I know."

Levine sailed on. "But the Civil Rights Act is just

frosting. Look at the way we've institutionalized racism in this country. It's just the way Bobby said it—what good does it do to sit at a lunchroom counter if you don't have the money to pay the bill? We've got to get to the root causes of poverty in this country."

Hollins looked at him, puzzled. "Levine, I never thought I'd hear that bullshit from you. You always seemed a smart man. You sound like someone who's been listening to a bunch of kids."

Levine kept still.

"Let me tell you," Hollins said. "That Public Accommodations bill was the most important law we're going to pass in our lifetime. You can have OEOs and job-training acts and income redistribution till they're coming out your nostrils, but they're not going to have the force of that one pen stroke."

He paused.

"You think you know something about discrimination because there were some clubs you couldn't get into and some places you couldn't live because you were a Jew. Now when I was coming up, we lived in Bowling Green, Kentucky. In Bowling Green, there wasn't *any* place I could go or my family could go. Kentucky was supposed to be a border state, but it was just as bad as Alabama back then. I'd go downtown on weekends, a nice, cleaned-up little kid, and I'd see the white kids having their ice creams at Stalvey's, where they wouldn't serve me, and the grown-ups coming out of Fran's Restaurant, where my mommy and daddy couldn't eat. They could shuffle around to the side and get a take-out order of ribs, their money was good, but they weren't good enough to sit down with some sweaty tomato farmer and his fat-ass wife.

"My father had men in his church, nice, sweet, gray-haired old men, men who'd worked thirty years at the country club or the Downtown Lunch Club. They used to talk about those places and those people the way the Greeks talked of their gods—it wasn't as though those white folk were all spotless, you know, 'cause we'd hear about who'd get drunk and who went off on the golf course with someone else's wife, but as though they even had the faults of the gods, faults of a higher scale than us just plain niggers. They'd talk about the richness of the food at the club and how much they drank and how they danced and what kind of fancy cars they had like a bunch of school kids marveling at the grown-ups.

"And it hurt every minute I lived in that goddam place. Not to be able to go where you wanted, places you'd always heard of. I wanted to know what a Stalvey soda tasted like. I wanted to see Marge Hooper do the Twist at the country club. I wanted to taste the lime rickey they made.

"After I made first string at State, I came back to Bowling Green to talk at the high school. They wanted to give me a banquet at Fran's. That was nice of them, not because I was black but because I'd played for State, even though they'd recruited me for Bowling Green. (At first they were pretty bitter about that, but my old coach was a pretty nice guy, and we made up.) But I still wasn't going to go to Fran's. Not if it was just for me. And I really wanted to see what it looked like inside.

"So when the public accommodations bill was passed, it took that whole layer of mystery off waiting rooms and restaurants. It liberated millions of little boys and girls. I went back to Bowling Green a couple years ago, walked into Fran's with my wife and kids, and nobody even looked up. I still don't guess I'd be a member of the country club, but at least I can go there like any other guest—not that I'd want to, but I like the feeling that I could. Do you see what I'm getting at?"

Levine nodded.

"What I'm telling you is that Kennedy and them had it all backwards. Black people never saw any reason to get ahead and make money. They could have all the money in the world and they'd still have to go to the side door at Fran's. But give them the legal right to eat and shop where they please, and then the economics improves. Not overnight, but eventually. So don't ever tell me that the Civil Rights Act was just symbolic. Don't ever tell me to turn my back on Johnson or Humphrey."

"I'm sorry."

"You don't have to be sorry. Now, why don't you tell me how I can get to be chief of police back home? I figure that's as good a stepping-stone to mayor as I know of. Trouble with black folk in Cincinnati, though, is they're just not as mean as your Cleveland nigger. If I was in Cleveland, the man would be begging me to be police chief and quiet down my people. You got any spare revolutionaries you could drop off in Cincinnati?"

———

Now, twenty years later, seated a foot away, Levine again felt humbled by Hollins's awesome dignity, the powerful athlete's body topped by a face carved of ebony, a face made magnetic by a scar, the reminder of a policeman's club, that ran from his forehead over his left cheek, a scar made more hypnotic by a heaping of pink keloid tissue like a makeup man's error.

Levine introduced himself.

"We met—what, twelve or so years ago?" Hollins said.

"That's right. And we'd talked in Miami back in 'sixty-eight. You were a consultant to the police commissioner then. Minority Relations, I think they called it."

Hollins laughed. "Boring from within, that's what I called it. Tell me, how's business?"

"Fine. How is your movement going?"

"We are inevitable. I say inevitable, because we are throwing off the chains of separatism. When I tell my people, 'Reach in, take over,' they respond because they know in their bones it is correct. The police force and the courts and the schools are important to us. We were put in an incorrect position vis-à-vis separatism by the leaders of the sixties. They were misguided because they acted—or reacted—out of frustration. What else? Our leaders were ministers and lawyers. They saw our situation in either moral or legal terms. The reason that today's black leaders are behaviorists—psychologists, sociologists—is because that's what the times call for."

A magnificent shrimp gumbo was served.

"How do you feel about the older leaders?"

"That's one of the differences. In the old days when black leaders were bypassed by events, the new leaders would turn on them. Then the people would turn on them. They were called Toms or burners or militants or integrationists or separatists or whatever. Because we're behaviorists, we don't turn on our bypassed leaders. We understand them. We understand what made them. We understand they are no longer needed."

"What do you mean, acted out of frustration?"

"Frustration was the black man's emotion. It seeped into everything he did. Look at the Negro and his relation to the Jew. In the sixties our people, our leaders, were ambivalent about the Jew. Malcolm, Carmichael, Brown—they disavowed the Jew publicly even as they were fascinated by him secretly. They were not yet secure enough in themselves to admit their ambivalence. The Jew's success, his survival, was an affront. Now we know ourselves better. We know we can learn from you, we know you have learned from us. As a politician, I recognize this. We need the Jews, the Irish, the old liberals to help crush the hairs, the people like Caputo."

"Crush?"

A white waiter removed the shrimp and brought a roasted squab on a spit. The squab was listed on the banquet dinner among the hors d'oeuvres. The wine waiter poured a light Moselle.

"They must be crushed because my people have not come this far to be pushed back again. We have not fought our way out of dirt-floor cabins in the Carolinas to accept dirt-floor cabins in Vermont. We have not destroyed the viper heroin in our slums to have cocaine sold legally in state stores. We have not gone to college to read foul, filthy books. We have not established a stable family to have the state legalize plural marriage."

Hollins's voice took on the cadence of a political speech, but there was a haunting rhythm to it that, like a half-remembered aroma, eluded Levine.

"We did not give up razor fighting in the streets to be murdered in a duel somewhere in the mountains. We succeeded in confiscating the foul pornography that was turning children to sado-masochism at age twelve. We have not worked to educate our children to have the schools become playpens, the colleges opium dens. We remember what white America has forgotten. These horrors are only a few years in our past. We will not have them again. We are the cutting edge of morality in America. I say that proudly. Yes, the Patrols made mistakes, were excessive at times, but in the end they helped save America from herself."

"You sound like a preacher," Levine said, remembering.

"My father was a minister of an A.M.E. church in Cincinnati. I rejected his supernatural beliefs, but I will never reject him. I was trained as a psychologist. I know one can no more reject one's past than one can reject one's left arm. It is a part of one. Your people know that."

"Most of the time," said Levine.

Roast oysters followed the squab. Hollins watched Levine carefully.

"You don't keep kosher, I see. Not that I expected you would, but it would have been a bit more tactful if the caucus had asked about it in advance."

"If I'd been in your spot, it never would have occurred to me to ask."

"I suppose you're right. Still, it's a shame. The old ways are forgotten. Traditions go. We blur. Imagine the fuss there would have been fifty years ago if a Jewish politician had been seen eating oysters."

"I don't think of myself as a politician."

"Perhaps you aren't, but these are most certainly oysters. And maybe the oyster doesn't think of himself as an oyster, but that's what he is and that's what he's got to get used to being. And so do you."

On Levine's left Jessington made a strangled noise halfway between a belch and a laugh. He had already finished his oysters and had gestured for another serving. His face glistened lightly with sweat.

A steaming dark soup was ladled out. Levine tasted sherry and something rich and deep, a mahogany flavor.

"Terrapin soup," Hollins explained. "Alex Williams, who owns this place, is the son of a man who was a waiter at the Maryland Club. His dad used to tell him about terrapin soup, how they used to raise terrapins in pens commercially all up and down the Eastern Shore. Alex never forgot. Always wanted to serve something that noplace else had. He's got some old darky down in Maryland who raises them for him, sends them up by truck fresh."

"Delicious," said Levine.

"So it is," said Hollins. "Also *treyfe*, if I remember correctly."

Jessington chuckled. The soup was removed, a new wine poured, fifty dark faces grew brigher, fifty dark laughs grew louder. The next item on the engraved menu was "Chateaubriand for Two for One." Great sizzling steaks were unloaded before each diner. Platters of halved Belgian mushrooms were passed. Burgundy sloshed in the glasses, was spilled on the tablecloths.

Levine carved his steak, A dying odor assaulted his nose. He bit cautiously into a piece of meat. Rotten! The taste of death itself. He looked down the length of the table. Silverware flashed, red-blooded meat disappeared into black, pink, sweating, happy mouths. They could eat this carrion? They liked it?

Levine swallowed heroically and tried another piece. Rotten.

He turned to Hollins. "I'm sorry, I think my meat is spoiled."

Hollins's eyes froze. His lids came together. The face which had been dignified in its majesty turned menacing.

"What's that you say?"

"My meat. It's rotten."

"I don't believe you. Not here."

"Don't believe me. Taste a piece. Here, try some. It tastes rotten. Like horseshit."

"Don't whisper at me." Hollins's voice rose above the talking and grunting and chewing from the long table. "You got anything to say, you can say it to my brothers."

"Look, I don't want to create a scene. They needn't know. We can just get another piece."

Hollins pounded his fist on the table. "No secrets at this table. What you told me, you tell the others."

The talking stopped. Fifty faces turned toward Levine.

"Get up and talk to them," Hollins said. "Tell them what you told me."

Levine bumped his knees against the table, stood up. The room wobbled indifferently before his eyes. There was the silence of total hostility.

"Look," he said, "I'm sorry to interrupt, but Mr. Hollins insists we can't keep any secrets. The only thing I mentioned to him was that my meat was rotten."

"What else?" said Hollins.

Levine halted for a moment. "That it tasted like horseshit."

The silence continued. It seemed to Levine that the room was growing darker imperceptibly. He wondered if he was going to faint. There was a rumbling in the room. The other fifty men of the caucus were getting up from their seats. They stood staring at Levine. Their faces were closed, unsmiling. Hollins nodded abruptly.

Fifty bright, gleaming smiles appeared. Fifty voices sang, "For He's a Jolly Good Fellow." Hollins slapped Levine on the back. Jessington leaned over and kissed his cheek. The diners sang and stamped and clapped their hands.

Hollins shouted in his ear, "It's a little crude, perhaps, but it's effective. There's an old saying in the South, 'If a man don't know horeshit, what do he know?' That serving of steak has been a tradition in our group since I was a young fellow just coming up. You see, if a man doesn't trust himself enough to tell us the truth, why, we don't trust him enough to work with him."

"I see," said Levine. "It makes sense."

"Of course it does," said Hollins. "Besides, it gives the men a little fun. You'd be surprised to see how many people we've had here who've swallowed the whole thing down. Afraid to hurt our feelings, you see."

"Yes," said Levine. "By the way, what—what was it that I was eating?"

"Don't you mind that," said Hollins. "That's one of the

secrets of the club. All you have to worry about is that we are ready to listen to you after dessert."

"Well, I'm glad I came through that all right."

"You most certainly did. They'll bring you another steak in a moment. Now I want to get back to talking about how we're going to crush the hairs."

WASHINGTON, MARCH 20, 1988

Spread out on the floor of Levine's office was a 36-foot-long scroll divided into sections for each of the hundred-odd days until the convention. On Levine's desk was a mimeographed ledger with five pages for each of those days, and next to the ledger was an enormous map of the country.

"Coming in so late, we're still scrambling for appearance dates. We have you on two TV shows this week, but no personal appearances until next week. You talk to the union people out in Kansas City."

"What about the stock-car races?"

"What races?"

"The stock-car races at Greenville," Levine said. "NASCAR. They're always the first week in April. Today's March twentieth. Get me down there. Call up Governor Brandon. He owes me a favor. Tell him I'm coming down to Greenville. I'll ride around the infield with him. I'll say a little hello to the people."

"Suppose he doesn't want to?"

"He'll want to. Give him the poll results. Tell him I'm going to get the nomination and then I'm going to be president. Remind him that I've got a long memory and that a small favor done now won't be forgotten. If he doesn't believe the polls, tell him to phone McKelvin."

"Okay. But why go to Greenville?"

"Jesus, that's where the people are. There'll be two-three hundred thousand of them."

"People don't like politicians popping up at sports events," Bell said. "They boo you even if they're going to vote for you. Besides, at Greenville everyone will hate your guts."

"You do the people an injustice," Levine said.

Always the jokester, Bell thought, as he phoned to make arrangements.

Bell, McKelvin, and Levine flew to South Carolina in a jet allotted by the Campaign Commission. As the reporters drank and argued in the back of the plane, McKelvin read to Levine from a pile of papers.

"We got them to run a one-day phone sample in South Carolina. Forty-one percent of voting age recognize your name; of those, forty-five percent respond favorably. Of that same forty-five percent, when asked if they would vote for a Jewish president, three quarters said yes."

"That doesn't make sense," said Levine.

"Harris explains it. He did it deliberately. He says that in rural South not everyone identifies you as being Jewish. Some people will vote for you on the basis of your TV appearances, but they wouldn't knowingly vote for a Jew."

"Fascinating," said Levine. "People don't identify me as Jewish?"

"This is rural South," said McKelvin. "And, of course, even a majority of them correctly identify you as Jewish. But there is a sizable group that does not. Therefore, the advice of the research people is to play down your Jewishness in the South. Maybe not in Atlanta, say, but particularly at the stock-car races."

"Play down my Jewishness? Do they want me to change my name? Have my nose fixed?" Levine spread his arms.

"Nothing like that, A.L. They mean, just don't play it up."

"I see," said Levine. "By the way, did Harris ask the people who wouldn't vote for me if they would vote for a Jew?"

McKelvin and Bell shuffled through the papers. "I don't believe so," said Bell.

"How come you're so sure this stock-car thing will go okay?" Bell persisted. "No Northerner ever campaigned there before."

"That's one reason it's going to go well," Levine said. "Those people are left out of politics now, always have been. People who go to those races may not have that much money, but they've got acres of pride. They need to be noticed. They'd cheer for the Archbishop of Canterbury if he made him a visit. I know that country."

"From what?" Bell asked.

"I used to travel a lot," Levine said.

Part **II**

SOUTH CAROLINA, SPRING, 1956

It didn't matter much what the name of the town was. Alfred Levine, traveling sales representative of Arco Electronics, Garden City, New York, remembered the names of the towns only so long as he was in them. The people were different. He had a system, right after he'd been introduced to a group of skeptical, yes, hostile, Anglo-Saxon faces seated around a table. He'd run their names back and forth, left to right, right to left, then at random, repeating them so he had them all perfectly, doing it while the mayor or sheriff introduced him. He didn't have to listen to the introduction, which always went the same way.

"Now this here's Mr. Levine of New York City," the sheriff would say. "He's got some sytem or other that he's interested in selling us and, 'cause he's got some real good recommendations from our friends over in Greenville, I thought it would be a good idea to hear him out."

They always pronounced his name "Lay-veen" and they always came down heavy on the "New Yawk" part.

"Thank you, Mr. Mayor," Levine would say. "Glad to meet you, Mr. Moomaw, Mr. Coates, Mr. Ruffin, Mr. Sullivan, Mr. Lagrange." He wouldn't miss a name, and he'd have their attention already.

"You know, of course, I'm a long way from home"—Lord God, wasn't that the truth!—"but I wouldn't be so far if I didn't have something worthwhile, something I believe in myself. We're all of us in business, gentlemen. I'm in the business of selling; you're in the business of good government, of keeping down crime." He would not add that he was well aware that some of the city managers or county board were also in the business of prostitution, bribery, gambling, and extortion.

"You've got a problem of crime here in Sedotalia. I've

seen the newspaper reports, I know about the house-breakings that are going on, I know that some people are looking to make political capital out of this, trying to accuse you gentlemen of inefficiency or indifference. Well, of course I know that's"—he'd hesitate a moment here—"hog-wash. They've got a problem over in Athens, they've got year-round guards at those fancy vacation places up in the mountains. And I'll tell you a secret. We've got crime up in New York. We've got enough of it so we could export it to the rest of the world and still not be safe in our own homes. I'm a liberal man, perhaps you may not agree with my politics, but I don't mind saying that we've got a terrible crime problem in the city, and it's the same sort of people up there as are causing you all this trouble down here. If you know what I mean."

Six faces would nod knowingly.

"Well, I may be a liberal, but I feel a man has a right to feel secure in his own home. Robbery and rape aren't liberalism. No, sir." By this time Levine would notice that his voice had a southern inflection. It wasn't exactly an accent, but it was a rhythm that he couldn't keep out of his speech even if he had wanted to. He did not want to. The men were leaning forward to hear him, bobbing their heads like so many corks floating on a lake.

"What I have to sell you, gentlemen," he would whisper, "is what Arco calls its Unified Crime Control Attack. They used to call it their Integrated system, but I suggested that that might get people off the subject of crime control and thinking about other things."

A few chuckles.

"Right now you folks have two patrol cars, each with a Collins two-way radio set. You've got four foot officers downtown with no radio equipment, just corner call boxes. You've got Sheriff Watson over in the jail. He's got a telephone. You've got Mr. Matthews out there at the road-gang base, and he's surrounded by a group of vicious criminals and a couple of trusties who can't run any faster than I can. All he's got is a telephone, and he's got to put his call through that little switchboard in Rivens, and you all know Miss Royce out there and how long it takes to get her attention."

Know your territory, the old salesmen used to say. Levine sounded as though he knew his better than the men around the table. He knew all the important facts, and he knew enough of the little ones to give an air of complete authority, to speak with an air of complete authority, almost as though he had grown up in Sedotalia himself.

"I have, gentlemen, the first complete communications system designed exclusively for crime control. It's specially designed for medium-sized cities like your own"—Levine avoided the word "smaller" like the plague—"not that the big cities couldn't use it, but they're too tied up in what they've already bought. And graft, too. Here we can deal out in the open.

"With our system each one of the units in your Police and Corrections departments is tied to the other with instant radio-band communication. Mr. Matthews out there can get to you, Sheriff, faster than he can dial long distance. Chief, you can reach your patrolmen, your men on the streets, immediately. They can reach the patrol cars soon as they see something going wrong downtown, a store being robbed, maybe, or a woman getting yoked. And, Chief, you can tell, with the special Directional Beam on our master transmitter, where each of your patrolmen or patrol cars is at any moment. You don't have to wait for the car to tell you where it is, you don't get an NA if the man has stopped by the side of the road to chat with some little lady he may have seen, and it goes without saying that no patrolman will be able to call in and say he's down at Main and Bedford when he's actually fishing at Niggerhead Pond. I don't say that your men lie to you, but I know it's happened elsewhere."

Another little chuckle.

"Now because our system is a unified system, everything works together. That makes it a lot less expensive than it would otherwise be, because the equipment is made to be compatible. I don't say that it's a cheap system, because it isn't—anything that's good isn't cheap—but it's a lot less expensive than it should be."

"'Zactly how much in real money do you figure this all would cost us, Mr. Levine?" someone said.

"I've taken the liberty of costing it out for you on the basis of what our consultants feel is the best number of units for a city your size. It would cost you twenty-five thousand dollars. Of course, this means that we install a complete new unit at police headquarters, replace the Collins sets in the cars, equip each patrolman, and have extra units available for deputies, in case of a manhunt for a murderer, for example. I've got it all down on this estimate we've prepared. Now I know that's a lot of money—that's half of what was appropriated for the new grandstands at Central High School—but you've got to remember what you're buying. You're buying safety from crime. You're buying quality. And you're buying yourself something that the voters in this town will be remembering—and thanking you for—for a long time."

That got them. Levine's eyes sparkled, darting from one man to another. God, how he loved that last part. He loved it mostly because he believed it, or at least he believed it by the time he got to the end of his talk. Arco's equipment was quality. In 1952, when people were still talking about "cheap Japanese imports," Sid Hersch had seen his first Nikon camera. Hersch, who ran a radio-TV business in Long Island with a specialty in ship-to-shore radios, figured that if the Japs could do that with a camera, God alone could tell what they might make with a radio. And so, before they had put up Sony Square in New York or the Mitsubishi complex in Chicago, Hersch was off to Japan in person to line up a deal. And it was a lovely deal, with a lovely short-wave radio as the result.

But it wasn't just that Levine believed in Arco. He knew that Sedotalia probably had more important things to spend its money on, that half the foot patrolmen would smash or lose their units and claim it was an accident, that Matthews probably wouldn't be able to figure out the "receiver-transmit" switch and would revert to telephoning Miss Royce the first time one of his work gang escaped. He knew all this, but he loved talking to the men, feeling their hostility, smoothing it out, turning it around so that it came out almost as love. Respect, anyway.

"Now I'm not the kind of salesman who runs in and runs out. I know you gentlemen won't be able to decide on a purchase like this overnight. I'm going to be in town a few more days to be available to answer any questions and take advantage of your lovely countryside for a rest. Maybe do some fishing. I'll be at the Quality Courts. If I may, let me leave now so you can discuss the proposal and have a chance to look over some of these brochures. Notice, by the way, that we've arranged for Travis Electronics in Anderson to handle all service problems. Not a finer outfit in the state. Good day, gentlemen."

And then he went around the table, shaking hands, addressing each man by name, and left.

A. L. Levine, traveling representative of Arco sales, gloried in his job, radiated enthusiasm every moment of the day. He had to, because otherwise he would have gone mad from depression. All his life he had longed for a family of his own, and as soon as he had one, he was forced to spend most of his time wandering through nameless towns talking to nameless people. On the road Levine ached for his family, for the simple faith of his children, for what he believed was the simpler faith of his wife.

But in 1950 there had been little work for ambitious young electrical engineers with undergraduate work in American history, and so Levine had bounced from one job to another, his savings growing smaller as his family got larger. Finally, he connected with Hersch, saw with clarity that Hersch had the vision and balls to do something big, and had gone to work for him. He was given a salary, a commission, a small block of stock, and a territory—the South. All the others were taken.

So Levine wandered half the year, first by company car and back-breaking two-lane roads, later by jet and rental car. It was torture of the most exquisite kind, Levine thought, as though someone had decided to find the most vulnerable spot in his psyche. It reminded him of Winston and the rats in *1984*. And so, with his absent family always on his mind, Levine set out to eliminate the pain of that absence.

Given his natural energy, the key was learning. If he

had to go to Sedotalia, he would learn about it. He learned his territory, not from the names of the other companies he was competing with or the men he would have to bargain with, but from the history books and John Gunther and the WPA guides and the Rivers of America series and the roadside stands and the local papers. At first he learned in order to fight off depression; later the learning built on itself, one fact suggesting another, so that eventually this foreign land was no longer foreign and he was, to his surprise, enjoying himself.

In Sedotalia the signs read, "Eat Catfish." That evening Levine drove around town until he found the best restaurant, or the one which seemed least bad. It was not a difficult task—places on the main street were almost always bad in towns over 50,000; places that had enormous signs were traps designed for tourists. Levine looked in the Yellow Pages, then worked the side streets and the outskirts of town. On the old road, the one before the highway, he found the place. The sign said MARTIN'S and underneath someone had stenciled in, OUR SPECIALITY—CATFISH. Another sign said BEER. There were a lot of cars.

Levine found a seat facing the bar. The waitress was attractive but not for him. Probably divorced, the town's classic easy lay.

"You a stranger?" she asked.

"Not for long, I hope," he said. "Tell me, where do the catfish come from?"

"The Long River. They catch 'em in nets. Use only the small ones. The big are too tough. They put them back for breeding. But Bob Johnson—guess you don't know him—he's got this idea of raising 'em in his farm pond. A 'catfish ranch,' he says he's going to call it. 'Bout the only kind of ranch they'll ever have around this dump," she added.

She was interested, Levine knew. She was waiting for him to ask why she called it a dump, to ask her something about herself, for him to say something about himself. People wanted this of him. Tonight he was all business.

"I'll have the Catfish Special and a beer. Make it a Miller's."

It was one of the many summers of "Your Cheatin' Heart." There had been silence when Levine walked in, but in a moment Hank Williams was telling the other diners—twenty or so of them—that they'd cry and cry the whole night through, but their cheatin' hearts would tell on them. Levine loved the song, but he had heard too much of it. Sometimes a drunken farmer or mill worker would put in a half dollar's worth of coins and play it again and again and again. He was relieved when the next song was something called, "When You're Cheating on Me, I'll Be Cheating on You." Nice sentiment, Levine thought.

He sipped his beer slowly. Of all the torments of his job, the worst was eating alone. The jukebox shut off. Eating alone was bad, but eating alone in silence was unbearable. Levine went over to the machine. There were a couple of good Hank Snows and, unexpectedly, Piaf with both "La Vie en Rose" and "Milord." Levine punched the buttons for the Hank Snows, in part because he liked them, in part because he knew people were noticing him and looking at his clothes, his face, his almost palpable Jewishness. Then he played the Piafs, each one twice. The car salesmen might not like it, but fuck the car salesmen.

He had another beer and started on the catfish. It was surprisingly good. Levine had expected it to be bad, almost evil, but he ordered it anyway because it was something new. He remembered fishing with his father on the lake they went to for a couple of summers when he was little. The lake, fished out and polluted, had been abandoned by the bewildered local residents, who sold or rented their homes to New York Jews, otherwise shrewd people who appeared grateful to pay high prices for beaverboard cottages and leaky rowboats. Why not? thought Levine. Those were the only moments of peace we ever had.

There were still some bass left in the lake, but no one Levine knew ever caught one, and for Levine and his father the harvest of an afternoon's fishing was usually a couple of perch and a few small catfish. He could remember his father's disgust with the bullheads. "*Treyfe*, they're scavengers, feeding off dead things. That's why the rabbis won't let us eat them. People think the dietary laws are superstition. They're science, that's what they are, science. Ignorant people." And his father would smash the catfish against the side of the boat to kill it and prevent it from propagating its unclean kind. How his father would have rebelled at the idea of raising these beasts for food, much less to be eaten by his own son. Times change, Levine thought.

The door opened and five men walked in and went over to the bar. Levine recognized two from the morning's meeting. He continued to eat slowly and sip his beer. He couldn't get up from his table now except to pay and leave. Anything else—going to the men's room, playing the jukebox—would be asking the men to notice him. They had already seen him; now they would have to come to him.

Levine ate slowly. The pie was terrible. About twenty minutes after they had come in, after they had finished their first drink, one of the men at the bar came over to Levine's table. It was Ruffin.

"Mr. Levine?" the man said.

"Good evening, Mr. Ruffin."

"Mr. Levine, I sure hate to see a man eating and drinking by himself. I'm over there at the bar with Mr. Moomaw and a couple other gentlemen. We'd sure be pleased if you could join us."

"Why, thank you. I'd be delighted."

Ruffin introduced him to the three other men. One of them struck Levine as interesting. He had the local accent, all right, and there was nothing unusual about his seersucker suit, but his shirt was the button-down kind that you didn't see very often down South. Besides, even though he was just in his early thirties and the other men were all older, they all seemed to defer to him.

Ruffin introduced him. "And this is Garrett Brandon, our new state representative."

Brandon smiled. It was a pleasant, open smile. "Actually, Mr. Levine, I'm just a small-town lawyer trying to get started. 'Round here just about anyone who's not on welfare is in the legislature instead."

"Gar's just funning you, Mr. Levine," Moomaw said. "Really, now, he's about the smartest little ol' boy that's come out of here in a long time. He was Boys State. Went to college up north but came right on back home."

"Glad to meet you, Mr. Brandon," Levine said. "Did you come back to law school here at the university?" That was the pattern.

"That's right. Just let me out a few years ago."

"Hate to interrupt this socializing," Ruffin said, "but we've got some serious business before us. Do you drink, Mr. Levine?"

Here we go again, Levine thought.

At first he hadn't been able to understand about the drinking. In the army he had watched with horror as his friends barreled off to Fayetteville and came back, vomiting and slobbering, three hours later. On the rare occasions in New York when distant relatives had given a party or Bar Mitzvah, Levine, invited as a charity case, sipped a few glasses of Scotch along with his third cousins and awakened the next day with a vicious hangover. Nobody drank in graduate school except a few rich gentiles somehow caught in the Jewish matrix of CCNY. But when he became a salesman, Levine discovered that drinking was part of the job, and so, conscientiously, he learned it along with the rest of the territory.

He found that it was a good idea to have a favorite drink, and he found his own. A friend had once come back from Mexico with a divorce and a bottle of good tequila. Levine sipped it. "This is good tequila," the friend said. The stuff tasted like the sweat of hell. Levine's eyes watered. His throat burned.

"If this is good tequila, then what is bad?" asked Levine, his stomach aching in an abrupt, unexpected manner.

"Don't ask," said the friend.

Levine bought a bottle of the good tequila and experimented with it at home. He found that if the stuff were ice cold and he sipped it slowly, sucking a lemon or a lime, he could finish a third of a bottle in an evening and wake up almost normal the next morning.

A nice thing about the tequila was that once they had tasted it, nobody else wanted it. "You actually drink that stuff regularly?" his friend of the Mexican divorce asked him a few months later. Levine nodded. The friend shook his head, but strangers who tried the drink looked at Levine in awe as much as amazement. Another nice thing about tequila was that a lot of bars didn't stock it, so Levine could make a small point of ordering it, grimace in slight annoyance when it wasn't available, and then settle down with a weak Scotch and water.

Increasingly, a final thing about tequila was the way it made him feel. Alone in an unfamiliar bar, he would bolt down a single shot of tequila (like Uncle Moishe downing slivovitz), and then wait as a warm, friendly feeling suffused him. The goyim had something, after all.

"What would you want?" Ruffin asked.

Levine glanced at the bartender. "Do you have tequila?"

The man nodded.

"Would you please bring me two shot glasses, some cut-up lime or lemon, a tray of salt, and the bottle? And might you have one of those appetizer bowls, the kind they use for shrimp cocktail, filled with crushed ice?"

The bartender arranged Levine's setting before him. "I apologize, gentlemen. I like the drink, but I like it ice cold. Back home with my family, I keep the bottle in the freezer. Can't expect bars to do that, so I try to make do as best I can."

The men watched as Levine filled one shot glass with tequila and jammed it into the nest of crushed ice. Then he filled the other glass, nodded to them, said, "'Scuse me, but I have a bit of catching up to do," and downed it in one gulp.

Established as a family man, drinker, and potential good ol' boy with just a hint of a southern accent, Levine smiled amiably as the warm flush of the tequila suffused him. Somehow Moomaw, Brandon, and the others had been transformed into his guests and, a little band of brothers, they were soon into the business of business.

"Town's coming right along."

"Never thought it'd happen."

"...had to sell the whole damn farm. Never made much but next year's chewin' tobacco, anyway."

"All those new people..."

"...jobs."

"...niggers working there, now."

"...hear the new Interstate might come by."

The town was floating on a wave of prosperity brought on when the textile mills that everyone said would never leave New England left New England. The first mills were marginal operations with little capital.

"Nylon tricot..."

"Cotton's still best."

"Hear the Japs might be exporting soon...."

"...new plant opened up just north of Simmonsville."

"...owner's someone named Friedman, from New York."

"Maybe you know him?"

Levine disclaimed any knowledge of textile manufacturers, sipped his cooling tequila, found it cold enough to swallow without wincing.

"Might I have a taste of that?" Brandon asked. "I've heard about it for a long time."

"Certainly." Levine offered him the glass. Brandon swallowed, spluttered, coughed.

"Great God a-mighty, I was raised on white lightning, but that's sure the strongest drink I ever did taste. How do you do it?"

"An acquired habit," Levine confessed.

"Hope I never have to acquire it," Brandon said. "Sure chews your guts out."

More liquor. Discussion of local real-estate deals. Discussion of local weather. Discussion of local fishing conditions. Discussion of women, nonlocal, women in nearby towns who were stepping out, cheating, round-heeled, and otherwise available. Good taste forbade discussion of local women with the same proclivities.

Levine listened to the nonlocal names. He could never tell when he might visit Simmonsville.

Levine told two dirty stories, carefully chosen to be only moderately dirty—nothing to offend permanently a hard-shell Baptist. Like all Levine's jokes, they had originated in the nexus of New York—Las Vegas—Los Angeles salesmen and high-rollers and were brand new. Cleaner versions would be on TV shows in a month or two. The men laughed, slammed the bar, slapped each other.

Levine told a third story, revolving about the sexual inadequacies of a black man faced, so to speak, with an actress famous (according to Levine) for her unslakable appetite. The story was funny and the men filed away for future use their inside knowledge of Hollywood, but the real work of the story was different. Levine had raised The Issue, and he had done it in a way that encouraged the men to talk.

"'Course, I know you're only funning, Mr. Levine," Moomaw said, "but down here we sure worry a lot about our nigras. Seems like the whole world's picking on us, but I'll be damned if I can find out what everyone's so excited about. Our local colored folks—why, I don't think there's a happier bunch of people around. We know them, they know us. Why can't you folks up north understand that?"

What lovely thin ice he now glided upon! That "you folks up north"! Certainly it was a general sort of "you folks," but only an idiot would miss that it was addressed to Mr. A. L. Levine of New York City, and all the tequila and dirty stories in the world would not permanently dissolve the fear and resentment of the Jew and the Negro in the eyes of the South.

"Why, one reason people up north don't understand is just what you said, Bill. They don't live directly with the problem, most of them. But you've got to realize that there are other issues involved. Take me—I'm a Jew. For years my people were told they couldn't eat at this restaurant or stay at that hotel or belong to that club, not because they weren't dressed right or made too much noise but because of their religion. Now, that's just not right in America. So we've been in the same place as the Negro, we understand how they feel. And, besides, we figure if people can do it to the Negro, they can start doing it to the Jew again. Or the Irish. Or the Chinese."

Moomaw was not stupid, but he was stubborn.

"Well, I see that, but how come people are always picking on us? God damn, but I can't pick up that *Life* magazine or *Look* without finding some sonofabitch or other telling us we should have the nigras in our schools. I been to New York. I been to Harlem. Didn't see many white kids coming out of *them* schools."

"Couldn't agree with you more. Most people up north think of the South as a foreign country. The way some people down here think about New York. You know, people say, 'New York's not America.' Everybody gets to thinking his own little part of America is the only real part. Those writers and intellectuals in New York—some of them are just as ignorant about the country as some redneck farmer who's never left McCall County. Happens that my job takes me all over the country. I've got friends down here. I know they don't have horns. They're fine people, loyal to the grave. So I can sympathize with the Negro—and, to be honest, I do—without hating the Southerner. Hell, I sympathize with the Southerner too. You didn't ask for all this."

"Still, seems like our nigras are the ones that are happy, and yours the ones that are stirring up all the fuss."

Levine grunted. "Maybe it's because the ones that don't like the old ways headed north. Could be that they're troublemakers. Or it could be that they're the most ambitious of the young folk, the best ones. And I've got another secret. Just the way the people up north think they know all about the South, it may be that some white people down here don't really know what the colored people are thinking. I wouldn't put it past some of those black folk to smile at you all day and hate your guts at night."

Moomaw started to answer, but Brandon interrupted. His voice was easy, but there was a precision to it that was hard to forget. "Bill, I'd think on what Mr. Levine's saying. You know that ol' Hattie Briggs, the one who used to clean for my wife's family? She's the one that had that real smart boy, Lucious. Well, he's up at Fisk now, and I saw him back at Christmastime, and that boy's changed. There's something different in the way he talks and the way he looks at me. Hell, even his hair looks different. And Hattie, *she's* different. She's getting *Ebony* magazine now—she reads right well—and the other day she asked me what did I think of this Reverend Martin Luther King. Well, I sort of backed and filled and said he seemed like an honorable man, and Hattie—you know her, she's never been rude or pushy in her life—Hattie says, 'Well, I think he's a good man. I don't see how we can't sit down to lunch at the Whelan's store just the same's anyone else who got the money. Some of the white trash they lets in there!' And she walked off."

"God damn!"

"That's right. And she ain't been talking to any northern agitators. Just her son. I tell you, there's something else moving out there. I don't rightly know what it is or even if it's good or bad, but it's new, that's for sure."

Levine kept quiet, merely noting that Brandon, too, became more countrified the more he talked. He means business, Levine thought.

The talk broke up in a jumble of incidents, recollections, and speculation. Brandon turned to Levine.

"Do you like to fish, Mr. Levine?"

Bred and born in a briàr patch, Levine thought.

"Yes, I do. I have, ever since I was a little kid."

"We've got some extra-fine bass fishing around here. If you're going to be around a couple more days, I'd be pleased if you could join me. I was fixing to go sometime this week, and I'd like the company. I could rustle up an extra rod for sure."

"That's fine. I really appreciate it. What about Thursday?" He had a couple of days. The waitress might be worth looking into, after all.

"Perfect. I'll pick you up at six o'clock."

"I'll be ready. Don't bother about a rod. I always bring one on trips. You never can tell when you might run across some nice water."

Born and bred in a briar patch, Brandon thought.

———————

The waitress had slipped out of his bed around two o'clock, leaving a note which said, *Goodby to my BIG friend from New York. You know what I mean.* The alarm clock rang at five forty-five and he fought awake. Something was wrong. Then he remembered agreeing to fish with Brandon. He looked out the window and there was a cold mist everywhere. He could call Brandon and tell him he was sick or had forgotten or had had a heart attack. Anything. He went back under the covers. Christ, how could the farmers do this every day!

The phone rang. A happy southern voice said, "Mr. Levine, it's five forty-five. You asked to be called." Levine grunted and hung up. It would get better, he knew. Fishing and screwing were the only two things he ever got up early for, and fishing was the only one where you had to be exactly on time. You couldn't keep another man waiting, not at 6:00 A.M. He rolled out of bed, picked his underwear up from the floor, and slowly dressed.

Brandon was exactly on time. He was wearing khaki pants and a tattered blue button-down shirt underneath a thin windbreaker. He smiled, said, "Hate to disturb you so early," and showed Levine into an old International pickup truck. They stopped briefly at a bus-station diner, where Levine endured the cruious stares of country boys about to rejoin their army units and Negroes heading north. The coffee cream was rancid and the hash-brown potatoes soggy, but the two of them ate mechanically until the food was gone. They got back into the pickup and Brandon hurtled along the main road for a quarter of an hour, turned onto a side road that wound between increasingly hilly farmlands, and then bounced onto a dirt road. From time to time Levine caught glimpses of a river, not the placid red-clay river of the rural South but a rushing torrent like something out of the Catskills. They jounced down a long hill, turned a sharp corner, and were confronted by a vast inland lake, sprinkled with islands. The woods and hills came down to the water's edge. No boats moved on the lake. There were no cottages. In the distance Levine heard some kind of bird singing.

"Stony Lake," said Brandon. "That's a whippoorwill. He must think it's still evening."

The sun was just coming up. Brandon let down the back of the pickup truck and handed down a small Johnson outboard motor to Levine. They they unloaded a tackle box, oars, a gasoline can, and a bait box filled with minnows. Brandon turned into the underbrush at the edge of the lake and dragged out a solid-looking rowboat. Levine rolled up his pants and waded gingerly into the cold morning water to help get the boat afloat. Brandon clamped the motor to the stern, handed the supplies to Levine, and pushed off.

"You left your key in the truck," Levine said.

"Yup. I'm awful afraid we might tip over and I'd have to strip off my pants to swim and the keys would come out. Happened once when I was a kid fishing with my father. He lost the keys that way. We had the car, all right, but we had to walk five miles out to the main road for a hitch to town. It was hot, too. Never will forget that."

"You left them in the ignition."

"That's what I mean. I'm forgetful. I'd hide the keys under the dash or someplace and then forget them. It's not safe."

"But is it safe to leave the keys like that? Suppose someone comes along and decides to steal your truck?"

"Why, hell, who'd come up here in the middle of the week? On Sunday there might be a few people from town fishing, but not on a Thursday. Besides, everyone knows it's my truck."

Brandon started the motor and they chugged slowly across the lake toward a small cove. Levine checked the drag on his spinning reel.

"What'll I use?" he asked.

"This time of year they're deep, even in the morning. There's a drop-off right near that cove, water goes from twelve feet to around twenty-five. There's an old stone wall under the water. Used to be Moomaw's grandfather's farm before they put in the big dam. Moomaw's father helped repair that wall. The bass like it. 'Round here we use these new plastic worms. You fish 'em real slow along the bottom. Bass takes it and you let him run with it. Then hit real hard—you have to drive the hook through their jaw. It's not like a surface plug when the bass does the hitting. If the worms don't work, we'll try the minnows." Brandon demonstrated.

A million lakes and streams in the country, Levine thought, and a million different ways to fish them. He had read about plastic worms in *Field and Stream* but never used one. He stared at the garish yellow worm. When I was a kid, he thought, my father used to say that the fish wouldn't bite if one bit of the hook showed. Levine had spent hours folding ragged worms over hook tips. The plastic worm, however, sported a gleaming unconcealed hook that looked to be about the size of a whaling harpoon. Either we knew less then, Levine thought, or today's fish are careless.

"Tell you what," Brandon said. "Let's try the lily pads awhile. If nothing's moving, we'll go over to the wall. Use a surface frog."

Brandon cut the motor, and in the windless morning they drifted slowly toward the cove. Brandon opened the tackle box and handed Levine a green and white spotted frog. It looked like a one-ounce lure and had a metal paddle in front like the old-fashioned Jitterbugs. Levine tied his on with a blood knot.

"Go ahead," Brandon said.

Levine brought the rod up to 90 degrees and snapped his wrist. The lure shot out twenty or twenty-five yards and splashed ten feet from a clump of lily pads. The ripples from the splash died down. Levine twitched the lure a couple times. The water was absolutely still except for the vibrations from Levine's green and white plastic frog. There was a bass under there, Levine knew. He twitched the lure again. Nothing happened. He began the retrieve, reeling in three or four feet, letting the lure wait, reeling again, occasionally lifting the rod tip to make the frog slurp noisily. Nothing hit. He brought the lure back to the side of the boat, reeled in, turned down the bail of his reel, and cast again. This time the frog landed about five feet from the lily pads.

Brandon, who had watched during Levine's first cast and retrieve, picked up his own rod and started casting toward a different clump of lily pads. They fished continually that way, alternating their casts about twenty seconds apart, saying nothing. Then Levine saw a swirl of water, like a bass coming to the surface, right at the edge of the pads. He overcast and his plastic frog hit in the midst of the plants. He tried to skitter the lure out of the tangle of green, but it caught on a flowered stem and held fast.

"Shit," said Levine. "I'm hung up."

"Wait a minute. I'll paddle us over."

Brandon paddled as Levine reeled in.

"I'm sorry," Levine said.

"Hell, that's okay. Happens all the time. I was beginning to think you couldn't miss." Levine smiled, reached over, and disengaged his lure from the lily pad. He relaxed. The testing part was over.

They started fishing again. On Brandon's third cast there was an enormous splash, a *thunk*, and then Brandon's lure came whistling at Levine's head.

"Shit," Brandon said. He gave an eloquent Hebraic shrug, lifted his eyes toward the sky, and said, "Shit."

Levine shrugged. "Happens all the time."

"Not to me," Brandon said, and laughed. It was going to be a good day.

Nothing much happened with the surface lures, and they began to fish over the sunken wall. Using the plastic worm was new to Levine, and holding the delicate monofilament between his fingers, feeling the early sun warm his shoulders, he noticed that he was sitting with his entire body tensed.

"Wonder what it is about fishing," Brandon murmured. He, too, sat statuelike, holding the line delicately between his fingers like the Muse with the thread of life. Even his voice was soft.

"It's focus," Levine said.

"Focus?"

"That's right. Everything, the whole world, is focused right down at the end of the simple string. Nothing else counts, not if you've got any imagination."

"To just see that ol' bass nosing back and forth, getting ready to pick it up and run."

"Yeah. That's why you can fish if you're very smart or very stupid. The in-betweens have trouble."

"Watch out now." Brandon's voice rose slightly. "Something's taking yours."

The line was softly slipping between Levine's fingers. It was like nothing he had ever felt fishing before, not a strike, not a bite, but as though an underwater butterfly were gently moving off with his lure.

The movement stopped. "He's swallowing it now," Brandon said. "Count to three and then hit."

Levine counted and hit. The line hit back, pulled away. Line, rod, and Levine became one. The boat, the lake, the sun disappeared. The bass attached himself to Levine's spinal cord. Levine kept pressure on the fish. The fish kept pressure on Levine. The fish yanked; Levine resisted the temptation to yank back. He reeled steadily, kept the rod tip up, prayed. The fish tired, swirled to the surface. Brandon netted him gracefully. A two-pound large-mouth. It was amazing how something so stupid could be so exciting.

"Nice work," Brandon said. He used a pair of pliers to release the hook. "That's a nice fish. They're some mighty big ones in here."

Over the next hour they each caught two more. Then the action slowed. The sun was hot. "They're out deeper," Brandon said. They moved toward the middle of the lake.

Brandon reached in one of the bait buckets. There was a six-pack of beer. He broke off a beer, reached back into the bucket, and brought out a bottle of tequila. "Brought this along especially for you," he said.

Oh, shit, Levine thought. The heat of the sun and the tequila would give him a headache to last a week.

"Thanks," he said. "I don't mind a sip or two."

They drank and fished. Conversation warmed with the sun and the alcohol.

"Mr. Levine, you get around a good deal. You know, I'm just a small-town lawyer, but I'm interested in politics, like everyone else. The problem is, I don't really see how to handle this new Supreme Court decision, the integration one. If there's anything I know, it's that we treat the nigras wrong. Segregation is wrong. I know it's the right decision, but I don't see how we can handle it or what to say about it."

"Don't say anything," Levine said. "Lie low. When people ask you, tell them it's the law of the land; but keep as quiet as you can. You're not the kind to go off shouting 'Nigger, nigger, nigger,' but even those who do, they're going to end up frozen out. And if you speak your mind, you're going to win a lot of friends up north and some paper or other will come down and do an article on 'The New Breed of Southern Politicians,' and you'll never be able to get elected dogcatcher. Now's the time to keep quiet, unless you want to be an unemployed martyr. The people who talk about how politicians always have to lead, they're people who've never run for office."

"You sound like you've done a lot of running yourself."

"Me? God, no. I read a bit, and I listen to people. I don't care what the *New York Times* says. People down here—white people—aren't ready for that decision. They're going to have to accept it, but they're never going to warm up to the people who tell them it's the right thing to do. Lie low. Keep quiet. Move in when tempers have settled down. Make the thing work."

"My friends back at Yale won't think all that much of me."

"Fuck 'em. They don't live here. You come out as a flaming liberal and your friends'll send you a hundred bucks for your campaign and you'll lose and they'll forget about you. They won't recognize your name. Hold off awhile, win, and they might even be in a position to do you some good. And you'll be able to do the Negroes some good."

"My wife keeps telling me I should speak out."

"She doesn't have to run either. Tell her what I said."

"I'll do that. You married, Mr. Levine?" Brandon's voice was quizzical, almost, Levine thought, accusatory. Maybe he had heard something.

"Oh, yes, very much so. Lovely wife and one little boy. Don't wear a ring, of course. Not part of Jewish tradition, you know."

That might be a mistake, Levine thought, as soon as he said it. Brandon was the sort of person who asked about things like that and might even know some Jews to ask. It wasn't like talking to shopgirls and small-town school-teachers.

"Must be mighty lonely, traveling so much."

"A man's got to live. Besides, I stay busy fishing and reading."

Brandon smiled again. The boat rocked gently. Butterflies darted over the water's surface. A small plane droned overhead, the only sound in a world that seemed to have moved back to 1935. What was it that Brandon had said? "Everyone knows it's my truck." What were these people going to do when the world hit them?

"Jesus Christ," Brandon said. He was lifting his red tip and tensing to strike. "This fish didn't just pick it up—he's scooting off like a possum up a tree. Just wait, just wait."

The line stopped. Brandon counted under his breath, "One, two, three," and hit. The fish moved off. "Lord, it's a big one," Brandon said. "Can't afford to lose this one. Don't let me be impatient, Lord, let me take my time."

He took his time and played the fish slowly. He used only the slightest pressure to move the bass toward the boat and did not resist when the bass headed deep. They were in deep water and there were no logs or weeds where the fish could entangle itself.

Twenty minutes later the exhausted bass fluttered feebly alongside the boat. Brandon netted it cautiously. "Jesus Christ," Levine said. "Largemouth. That must go ten pounds."

Brandon was smiling and talking to himself. "Lord, lord, lord, look at that fish." He took out a small spring scales from the tackle box. "These are accurate—got them from Abercrombie by mail. Let's see what he'll go." Holding the bass gently through the gills, he slipped the point of the scale under the fish's jaw. The bass flopped once, then dangled motionless. "Ten pounds, eight ounces," Brandon said. "Let's make sure we get a chance to catch him again,"

"Let me take a picture of him," Levine said.

"Oh, we don't need that," Brandon replied.

"People will never believe me," Levine said. Reluctantly Brandon nodded and Levine took a Polaroid shot of Brandon holding the fish.

Then Brandon threaded a long stringer through the fish's gills and watched him swim weakly alongside the boat for a moment. Satisfied, he paddled the boat toward a rocky point jutting out from shore. He paddled slowly.

"Got to go easy with these fish. You go too fast, you can drown them."

Levine nodded.

About twenty feet from the rocky point, Brandon picked up a heavy line with a three-pronged grappling hook at the end. He lowered the hook over the side and swept it back and forth. "Got it," he said. He pulled hand over hand on the rope and a large wire basket, like an overgrown birdcage, floated into sight. Brandon opened a trapdoor arrangement in the top of the basket and slipped the bass in. He looked at the shore markings once or twice and then lowered the basket to the bottom.

Levine raised his eyebrows.

"'Round here we like to keep these big breeder bass. Some of the meat fishermen, they'll take a bass like that home and cut it up and fry it like it was an ordinary catfish, and those ol' boys down at the VFW, half of them would take it to Atlanta and get it mounted to put up in their barber shops or dry-goods stores. More and more, though, the real sportsmen down here like to release the big bass. But if you release 'em outright just after you catch them, they're in a weakened condition, and the muskrats and other fish will tear them to pieces. So you let them rest up in the baskets, keep them safe from predators, let them feed up on the little fish that can swim through the mesh, and come back in a week or so and set them free."

Levine nodded. He never had seen the point in putting a plastic coating over a lovely fish and tacking it up on a basement wall. People were coming to their senses.

The rest of the fishing was anticlimactic. Their conversation ambled easily. On the drive back to town in the late afternoon Levine dozed in the truck. At the motel he thanked Brandon profusely, took a long tub bath to wash off the smell of fish, and then slept twelve hours, straight through breakfast.

The contract for the equipment was signed the next morning. Everyone smiled. Levine's commission was $5,000, his biggest yet. He made a few exploratory phone calls to local farmers and then left for Atlanta.

He brooded a long time about his trip with Brandon and his fishing with his own father. He thought about catfish and bass and about the sparkling new office buildings in Atlanta. These things were all linked together, and slowly he realized that beautiful land which had been so rare and so expensive around New York lay close to Atlanta—and was cheap. He saw that the locals were still fixed on land as being valuable for farming or subdivisions and did not see that the prosperity growing in their city would bring more and more people to vacation homes. But Levine remembered fishing on a polluted lake in Connecticut and being grateful for it. That afternoon he arranged the first of his land deals.

Four weeks later, he picked up the Charleston paper. He always read the local sections first; the world and national news was always a puny distillation of wire-service stories. The second section led with a two-column headline: "Lawyer-Sportsman Wins Sedotalia Bass Jamboree." The story was interesting. "Garrett Brandon, well-known local lawyer and sportsman, took first place in the annual Sedotalia Fourth of July Bass Jamboree by weighing in at the judge's station with a ten-pound nine-ounce bronzeback. First prize, consisting of $500 cash and a brand new camping trailer, was awarded by Judy Lee Smullens, this year's Miss Sedotalia."

Must have put on another ounce in the cage, Levine thought, clipping out the article and folding it in his briefcase. He thought awhile, bought a postcard of Stone Mountain, and sent it to Brandon. It read: *Congratulations. Sincerely, A. L. Levine.*

GREENVILLE, APRIL 3, 1988

The South Carolina State Police met them at the airport and gave them a screaming eighty-mile-an-hour escort to the raceway. Bell clutched his briefcase anxiously while Levine smiled and puffed on his cigar. There was a fair amount of traffic on the highway, people using their energy coupons to get to the races, and their driver wove in and out among the cars with easy skill, staying just the right distance between the police cycles in front and the patrol cars in back.

Levine leaned forward. "Driver, you do a nice job of getting us there. What's your name?"

"Pettiford, sir."

"You used to race yourself, maybe?"

"Some."

"That was after you got picked up for bringing in moonshine."

It was a statement, not a question.

Pettiford laughed. "Yeah, it was after they stopped me the *second* time. Couldn't see no future in it. 'Course, there wasn't much future in race driving, neither. Wife didn't think so, anyway. She kept after me to quit, and I wasn't winning all that much, so I did."

"Wasn't there a sheriff named Pettiford around here?" Levine asked.

"Sure, my uncle. Over in Henderson. He helped get me this job with the state. You figured that, didn't you?"

"Guessed it, maybe," Levine said. There was an economy to life, and there were fewer coincidences than one would suspect.

Bell clutched the briefcase until his thumb went numb. The cavalcade swung off the throughway and to the spur leading to the track. Without a perceptible slowing, Pettiford brought them from 80 to a dead stop in front of the governor. The door was opened by a state trooper.

Brandon stepped forward. He was a short man, not much bigger than Levine, red-faced, dressed in a white suit.

"God damn, A.L., it's good to see you. How long has it been now?"

"Thirty and two. That is, thirty or so since we first met, two since I last saw you."

"Well, that's too long both ways. Makes me feel old. Here, let's get in the official car and let the people see a real candidate, not some shit-lick old governor. We'll ride around a couple times, let 'em kind of say hello, then get up to our box. I've got a little stash of your favorite drink up there. Not so easy to get these days, with the border war and all that."

"That's right considerate of you, Governor," Levine said, "but before we get in the car I want to introduce you to Philip Bell from the National Committee. He's going to be running my campaign, but he's also here representing the committee."

"Hell, A.L., any friend of yours is a friend of mine. Glad to meet you, Mr. Bell. You just hop up in front with the trooper, and Mr. Levine and I will get ourselves settled in back."

The open car nosed along the ramp to the track, past the open sheds where the pit crews were still making adjustments on their cars, out onto the track itself. There were more people than Bell had ever seen before in one place: people jammed into a gigantic grandstand that ringed the entire five-mile oval, people and cars in one dense mass packing the infield, people screaming and shouting and waving as their driver slowly took them by. Somewhere in the grandstand a band was playing "Dixie."

A loudspeaker system boomed with the voice of God, a voice that was meant shortly to carry over the engines of fifty high-powered racing machines, a voice that would announce penalties, disqualifications, and the results of the inevitable accidents, a loudspeaker which seemed located in Bell's left ear. It told him and two hundred thousand other citizens, predominantly white and over twenty-one, "Ladies and gentlemen, we are honored to have the presence today of our honored governor, Garrett Brandon, and of a distinguished statesman, Mr. A. L. Levine. Let's give them a big hand."

The crowd roared and shouted. Lay-veen, Bell noticed, seemed to be the locally accepted way of pronouncing A.L.'s name. They circled the track once amid wild cheering, Levine and Brandon standing, smiling, waving their hands.

"They're enthusiastic," Bell said.

Levine didn't stop waving but said to him, "You'd be enthusiastic too if you'd been driving to get here four hours, sitting on your ass three, drinking beer and bourbon two, with nothing but a little band to entertain you. Remember what I told you about cheering the Archbishop of Canterbury."

Brandon didn't stop waving. "Archbishop, nothing. They'd cheer that goddam Rose. Anything to break the boredom. Anything to be noticed."

They went around the track another time. The cheering was more subdued but still powerful, like the first curtain call after a very good play. A tall red-haired woman leaning on the infield fence screamed at them, "Honey, it's me! It's me!" Levine smiled at her and kept on waving.

"She seemed to know you," Bell said.

"Wish she did," Levine said. "Garrett here is the one she must have been yelling at. All I know here is a couple of broken-down politicians like the governor and some senators. Maybe she's some of Garrett's home folks."

"She seemed to be pointing at you," Bell said.

"Have it your way. We'll drink to her when we get up in the stands."

The race was awful. Bell had heard of stock-car racing, had glimpsed it from time to time as he switched television channels, but he had never had the slightest desire to go to a race. Now he knew why. For the first two laps the roar of the cars really did send a deep tremor into his spine and made him excited and happy in a way that came only rarely. After that, nothing developed but monotony. The soul-stirring sound became a steady drone, the amazing speed of the cars seemed trivial—after all, what was so marvelous about a car's going 150 miles an hour if twenty other cars were doing the same?—and whatever tactics were involved in the race seemed crude and infantile.

Levine and Brandon and the other people in the box didn't pay much attention either, recognizing the race only to the extent of raising their voices when the pack of cars came by. People, mostly minor state politicians and major manufacturers, drifted in and out of the box and were introduced to Levine by Brandon. They chatted about the election, the hairs, the trouble with Mexico, and state politics.

Levine didn't say much about how he felt about these things; mostly he was listening, and every so often he'd glance toward the track and make a little comment on the race that seemed knowledgeable to Bell. The visitors would nod, but then they'd come back to the political topics.

"You're a smart man, Mr. Levine. You're up there in Washington with the president and all that. Tell me, how do you figure we're going to get out of this mess? The way I see it, the harder we try, the worse off we get."

"I've got some ideas on these things, of course, but I want to wait a bit before the convention before making them definite. But I'd like to hear more of what you think, Jim. What do you mean by saying, 'The harder we try, the worse off we get'?"

And the man would tell him, and Levine would nod and thank him, and the man and his group would go on to the next box.

As the afternoon wore on, their guests all seemed a little bit drunk, some of them very much drunk. Levine had a bottle of tequila in front of him, a small silver shot glass, some cut limes, and a tray of salt. He drank the tequila, which was hard to get, in his old-fashioned way, keeping a little pile of salt on the back of his hand, sucking at the lime, sipping the tequila, licking the salt. He poured small amounts steadily from the bottle into the little shot glass. When he finished a drink, he would toss the glass into a bucket of chipped ice that was kept at his side. The bottle of tequila was about half gone, Bell noticed, but Levine seemed sober, perhaps slightly red in the face.

Finally the race ended and someone was the winner and the governor and A.L. went out and congratulated him and gave him a trophy and were photographed smiling and shaking hands, and it was over. Brandon walked them back to their car.

"A.L., a lovely day. Great seeing you again."

"Thanks, Garrett, I enjoyed it. Give my regards to the family. Remember what I said about Rose and the blacks. Come look me up in Washington."

"Sure will. I guess things haven't changed that much after all."

"Except that I can't drink that stuff the way I used to," Levine said, and they both laughed.

"That ain't all I can't handle the way I used to," Brandon said, and they laughed again. Levine wondered if Brandon had heard anything about him.

They got back in the car. "Mr. Pettiford, tell the boys up front to really move, would you please?" Levine said. "We've got to get back to Washington just as soon as possible." Pettiford and the motorcycle escort, their brains on fire after four hours of stock-car racing, got them back to the airplane at ninety-five miles an hour instead of the conventional eighty. This could be dangerous, thought Bell, but he had had enough of Levine's tequila to feel, unaccountably, that he was very safe and that somehow Pettiford and Levine would take care of him. He fell asleep, still holding his briefcase, well before they got to the plane and had to be shaken awake to get on board.

Bell stationed himself under a Japanese maple and surveyed the party. The unseasonably warm weather had brought the azaleas out, and the lawn, which stretched down toward the Potomac, was dotted with clusters of people, rarely more than five in a group, almost never just two. As soon as two important people got together and began talking intently, a third person, drink in hand, introduced himself. Bell imagined the intruders at their jobs or their own cocktail parties later that week. "I was talking to Senator Dunlop and Secretary Miller, and Miller said..."

The bartenders were busy, but there were no lines. Bell edged himself behind one bar and asked for two rum collinses. He would be goddamned if he'd wait in line twice, and, besides, he had to avoid people. His job was to see how Levine worked this routine and help him do it better.

First of all, he had to find the sonofabitch. That was the trouble with a five-foot-six candidate (Levine said five-seven, but Bell knew better). Levine was lost in a forest of rich Wasps, all guaranteed to be six feet two inches tall. Bell looked from left to right, hoping to find his man from the people around him.

I hope that's him, Bell thought, noticing a group of six. There were four men, including the chairman of Ways and Means and the publisher of *New Day* magazine, and two pretty women. They all seemed to be laughing and listening together. Bell edged closer and heard Levine's voice, quiet and confident: "... not proud to be a Jew—I never was part of that Jewish Power movement—but happy. After all, did I have much choice? You are what you are. So I can't say that I feel grateful that I'm what is called a serious candidate. Maybe it should have happened some time ago. How should I describe what I feel?" he asked one of the women.

It was clearly not a rhetorical question. "Maybe you're pleased," the woman suggested.

"Honored," chimed in the publisher.

"Yes, that's it," said Levine. "That's what all candidates say, but that's what it is. There's no reason I should feel differently than if I were some third-generation Protestant. By the way, I enjoy the magazine very much, and I wonder why you don't add a section of new industrial technology. We used to be a nation of inventors, but we seem to have forgotten about that. We read a great deal about new discoveries in medicine, new types of music, but no one tells us about practical technology."

The publisher beamed. "We're a step ahead of you, Mr. Levine, and I can see that that doesn't happen often. In fact, we've been working on a mock-up of just that sort of section. We're going to call it New Things. Of course, that's just a working title."

Nice, Bell thought, but if he's really a pro he'll get out now. Maybe he's already talked to the Ways and Means chairman, but even if he hasn't he should cut out now. Let them talk about him after he's gone. Go on to meet someone else. There were another hundred people who had paid $500 a person for the privilege of talking to him.

"Excuse me," said Levine. "I see our lovely hostess over there, and I've been neglecting her all afternoon."

I'm supposed to be advising this guy on how to work these benefits? Bell asked himself. He remembered a friend whose first job in Washington had been as a special assistant and ghostwriter to a cabinet officer who in turn wrote speeches for Adlai Stevenson: he was a ghost for a ghost for the most literate man in politics. Levine looked as though he had worked the lawn-party circuit all his life. The part about the hostess—maybe it was pure instinct, but the one way a politician could disengage himself without implying that he had more important fish to fry was to invoke the hostess, and Levine did it at just the right time.

Indeed, Levine was peering up at the hostess. Margy

Scanlon, the widow of a senator more noted for his wealth than his statesmanship, had refused to go back to Montana after her husband's coronary. She had become a Hostess, with a sub-specialty in politics. There were always a few diplomats and socialites at her gatherings, but her original contacts had been in senatorial power, and she had cagily preserved them. Right now she was pointing Levine at a group of lobbyists and then introducing them. Bless her, Bell thought.

"Your man is doing very nicely," someone whispered behind him. "Why don't you relax and share a few of your rum collinses?" Bell turned and saw Sally Cunningham smiling at him. She wore a simple yellow dress. Her hair was cut in a pageboy. Her face was as open and ingenuous as a twelve-year-old's.

"You're the only person here I'd give one of these to," he said.

"What about our charming hostess?"

"Our charming hostess is getting just what she wants from this party. She was on the outside of things for, say, two months; now she's right back at the head of the parade. We don't owe her any special thanks. Besides, she made a semi-decent proposition to me two years ago and I pretended to misunderstand, so we're just good friends."

"I'll remember to keep my semi-decent propositions to myself, if you're one of those refuse-and-run men." She sipped her drink and giggled.

Bell looked at her steadily. The conversation had changed, shutting them off from the rest of the party. Bell sexualized many of his political relationships, but Sally Cunningham had always been just another senator's wife. A young one, a pleasant one, but one who seemed happy in her marriage and her children. Bell knew all the political gossip, and there was none about Sally and Spence Cunningham.

She giggled again. "You're working your computer," she said. "Trying to think what you've heard about Spence and me. Figuring out what would happen if you made a move. Working out the angles if we got caught or if I talked."

He nodded.

"That's too bad," she said. "I heard from the newspaper people that you're a man of action. That's why I talked to you." She turned and walked away.

Bell went after her. "You heard right. Let me bring you another drink from the collection of our fabulous hostess. By the way, where's Spence?"

"Off campaigning someplace. California, I think. Returning Habib's favor from 1976. That was a rum collins, remember?"

"I remember."

They stood together watching the clumps of people form and re-form. "Do you enjoy this sort of thing?" she said.

He looked surprised. "Of course. It's my job—a part of the job. Anyway, it sure beats waiting at airports for the high school band to finish playing and the mayor to stop talking so that your man can say enough to make the people remember him and say it short enough so he can keep the plane just four hours late for the next two speeches. Yeah, this is better."

"But what do you get out of it? You don't need the free meals."

"Sure—the 'How awful these cocktail parties are' thing. But how else can you run through a whole bunch of new people and get some sort of line on them?"

"What kind of a line can you get on people at something like this? They're all prettied up, all acting. Look at the way they try to get to Levine. They don't even have the nerve to walk up to him. They just sort of get in his way so they meet accidentally."

He laughed. "Yeah, I prefer the ones who barge right in. But even that teaches you something about people. Maybe they're putting on an act, but some acts are better than others. You learn about as much about someone in the first five minutes you talk to them as in the next twenty years. It's like the difference between just reading about Paris and having been there overnight. Something that's just been words becomes something you've had personal contact with. It doesn't need much contact."

"It's not the same with people," she said.

"Yes, it is," he said quietly. "I've seen you before, but I've never talked to you. Now you're a real person to me. A special person."

She was quiet a moment. "You're right about that, anyway. You can tell a lot in a few minutes." She paused. "Do you think we could find a place to be alone inside?"

"It's got twenty-two rooms," he said.

"You go now," she said. "I'll follow in about five minutes. There's a bathroom on the hall to the right on the first landing. There's a door from the bathroom that goes to one of the guest bedrooms. Go in there and lock the doors. I'll knock twice."

He smiled. "Why don't we just go back to my place?"

She giggled. "It's sexier doing it in someone else's house. Weren't you ever a kid?"

On the lawn Levine turned to follow Margy Scanlon but found his way blocked by a tall, important-looking man wearing an old-fashioned button-down shirt.

"Excuse Me," he said. "My name's Levine."

"Yes, certainly, Mr. Levine," the man said. "I'm Max Fineberg. One of your co-religionists."

"You're Jewish?"

"That's right. You may have heard of me—I'm on the board of the Jewish Political Advisory Board. We're very interested in your candidacy."

"Of course I know of you, Mr. Fineberg. My old friend Sam Tallus in Denver has told me of you. And I'm glad JPAB is interested in me. There's been some talk that the board wasn't too happy about my candidacy."

"Quite frankly, Mr. Levine, you are correct. I think some members of the board—not that I count myself among them—would have been happier if you had discussed your plans with them before your announcement."

Levine smiled amiably. "I've heard something along those lines. I'm sure that the board realizes that my candidacy was as unexpected for me as it was for the people around me. I barely had time to tell my wife."

Fineberg was insistent. "But you did consult with your wife, Mr. Levine, and you realize that there are some people on the board—not necessarily myself—who feel that consulting with the board is just as important as seeking the counsel of one's loved ones."

This fuckhead sounds like a funeral director, Levine said to himself. Maybe that's how he got rich. No, it was wholesale groceries in the Toledo area. Levine knew the background of all the board's members, though he stayed away from them personally as much as he could. Don't be angry, he told himself. Don't call him a fuckhead. For a moment Levine flushed. Maybe he had called him that out loud, which was why Fineberg was looking more and more distressed.

"Look, Mr. Fineberg—may I call you Max?—Max, I've never personally been involved in a campaign before. In the past I gave money, came to the same sort of fund-raiser that I'm giving today. So I'm not too familiar with what an actual candidate does. I was rushed for time. I discussed meeting with the board with my advisers. They're practical men, Max, very practical, and a majority were for my going to the board before I announced. But as I listened to the discussion, I more and more got the feeling that it was not wise. Do you know what I mean?"

Fineberg was becoming more interested in listening than in moralizing.

"I don't want to give away political secrets," Levine said, noticing Fineberg bend over more attentively, "but I know you can keep something confidential."

Fineberg nodded majestically. He had the bait and now was the time to set the hook.

"Because as I listened to my advisers—and most of them, in the political business, are gentiles—they were talking about how much an endorsement from the board would help my candidacy, how much early money we'd be able to raise when the other candidates were still schlepping around looking for a lousy ten grand here or twenty there, how we'd be off and running. But as I heard them, I noticed one thing. They were talking about what was good for Levine, not what was good for the country. Especially they weren't talking about what was good for the Jews."

"Still, the board thinks about what's good for the Jews."

"That's true, Max, but they've never had to face this particular problem before. They've endorsed candidates on the state level, they've mediated disputes between two people running in a Jewish district, they've put out Jewish viewpoints on political issues. But they've never had to think of a Jew running for president before. And that kind of appraisal or consultation before I announced my candidacy would have been bad—bad for the Jews. Think of what people would have said: 'Jews never do anything in politics without the approval of the board.'

"Now, of course, I'd be delighted to meet you—just have your people set up a time that's mutually agreeable. But as a practical matter, for me to consult with the board before I announced would have been bad for the Jews."

Fineberg nodded. "There are angles that I forget about."

"Thank you, Mr. Fineberg. And, please, you'll help me set up that meeting?"

"Of course. I'd be honored."

May God forgive me, Levine thought.

"What about another one?" Bell said.

"No. That was yummy, but I don't want to set records. Not now, anyway. I've got to be getting back to the party."

"And leave this romantic spot?"

They were propped up on the floor of a children's playroom. A four-story dollhouse dominated the room. Shelves were stacked with Monopoly, Clue, Three on a Match, and half-forgotten board games. A toy chest stood in one corner, incompletely closed because of baseball bats and hockey sticks poking out. A pair of pants hung from one hockey stick.

"You didn't take off your shirt," she said.

"Of course not. If someone had come in, it would have looked suspicious."

"I see. On the other hand, with your pants off and your shirt on, everything would have been fine."

"Yeah, I could just have been overheated or something."

She got up, slipped on her panties, straightened her dress. She picked up a pillow she had been lying on, inspected it, and tossed it back on the crib. Then she fluffed the pillow.

"Don't your knees hurt?" she said.

"No. I've got calluses on my knees. The way surfers get them."

"You ought to try it in a bed sometime."

"Can't. Not in my life. If you go upstairs, there's always some kid you'll wake. Lots of silent screwing in my life."

She giggled again. "I'm not used to all this, but I can see where it might be fun. Do you think anyone's missed us down there?"

He looked at his watch. "Fifteen minutes. There are a hundred or so people. Lots of wandering around. Lots of people going in and out the first floor of the house. We weren't talking together for more than four minutes, and we left separately. So I figure Levine noticed."

"Why Levine?"

"Because he always does."

———————

Levine looked around for Bell. He was going to have to make a short speech, but he wasn't sure of the best time to interrupt the drinking and gossiping. Not everyone had come, but if he waited too much longer people would be too tired and too high to respond. Bell knew which people should hear the speech, which ones were late, and which just weren't going to come at all. By now Levine had a pretty good idea of where to find Bell at fund-raisers and receptions. He glanced at the fringes of the crowd and in back of the bar. No Bell. He looked at the benches under the great oak trees. No Bell. He checked out various women.

Sally Cunningham wasn't around. He had noticed her

earlier, with her yellow dress and her long legs. For a politician's wife she was, Levine decided, very nice. Not just her looks, because politicians tended to have high-standard, good-looking wives, but her voice. None of that throaty, lacquered "How glad to meet you!" crap. None of that professional look-them-in-the-eye stare that they must teach in Politician's School. Sally looked at you as though you were a person, not a voter or a contributor.

Another long glance, 360 degrees, through groups of pretty people talking pretty talk. Sally wasn't there and neither was Bell. If Bell is screwing her, Levine thought, there is going to be trouble and not the kind of trouble I need. Spence Cunningham's ties to the Sierra Club and the other deep-breathing conservationist groups were too important to jeopardize. Bell should be too smart to get involved with her. Still, Levine thought, she was a fine, healthy hunk of woman. He wouldn't have minded that himself.

Sally appeared in the doorway of the big house. She was talking eagerly with old Senator Sellers. Sellers came from a chicken-raising state and thought of all national problems in terms of how they affected chickens. His conversation was limited to details of scratch foods, incubators, and automated sexing devices, and even connoiseurs of monomaniacal bores avoided him. Yet Sally Cunningham wouldn't let go of his shoulder. Framed in the doorway she talked to Sellers, lectured to him, giggled loudly, gestured extravagantly. It was hard to miss the pair of them.

Levine looked toward the side entrance of the home. Bell came strolling out of it with Margy Scanlon. Bell was holding her arm in a protective but faintly intimate way. They stood at the edge of the swimming pool for a moment and then, still arm in arm, walked down toward the rest of the party.

That son of a bitch, Levine thought. I couldn't have managed it better myself. Still, if Bell were shtupping Sally Cunningham—and it was a damn good bet he was—something would have to be done about it. Bad enough that the candidate might have troubles like that. Someone had to keep his eye on the ball.

Bell came over to him.

"I think it's about time to start the spiel," Bell said.

"You're sure it's okay? You're sure I won't be inconveniencing you? After all, we can all have another drink and you could go back inside."

Bell almost blushed. "Was it that obvious?"

"To me it was obvious. To other people, I don't think so. Yet."

"We'll talk about it later, if that's okay with you."

"It's okay. Now, let's start."

Bell went back to Margy Scanlon and whispered in her ear. She nodded, stepped gingerly up on a picnic table made from a single slab of redwood, and clapped her hands together.

"I hate to interrupt your good time—I hope it *is* a good time—but I know you are all anxious to meet our guest of honor. It's my pleasure to be able to invite you all out to Twin Oaks today, but an even greater pleasure to be able to introduce A. L. Levine. I have known A.L. for ten years in party politics, and I am honored he..."

Levine finished his speech, waited for the polite applause to disappear into the lovely Potomac evening, and then asked if there were any questions. This was the part he dreaded. He did not mind giving the same speech again and again, because each time there was a new audience and he could gain enthusiasm from their naïve interest. But when the questions were asked, he was an audience of one, and it was hard to appear interested by the repetition of questions so obvious, so familiar, so banal to him, and yet so daringly clever to the questioner. He wondered if anyone ever asked questions in genuine search of answers. If there were no one else around to impress with a "searching" question, would questions exist? If a tree fell in a forest with no one to hear it, would there be a noise?

"Do you feel your... religion... will be a handicap in the campaigning?" an earnest young woman asked. She had a broad, sweet face and a horsy accent. Levine knew her, or at least her type. Her parents were rich, vacuous, and mildly anti-Semitic. She was rich, vacuous, and confused. She felt that there was something she should do about the state of the nation, but she was not quite bright enough to figure out what it was. A nonviolent Patty Hearst. She would have made a good cocktail-lounge waitress, with her affability, decent looks, and I.Q. of exactly 100. People from her family did not become cocktail hostesses, and politics was one field in which the need for earnest, vacuous women—and men—with lots of money would never be exhausted. You did not have to learn anything to be accepted on the fringes of the political world.

Levine, of course, had covered the question in his talk. He answered her politely, thanking her for "allowing me to expand on what I could barely touch on in my speech." He mentioned again the maturity of America, the historical tradition of acceptance, the particular place of the Jews in the mosaic which was American society. Then he answered the expected questions about Mexico, the Patrols, the Arabs, and the border fights and tried to appear interested. When the question period was over, he circulated again among the small groups, and watched Bell carefully avoiding Sally Cunningham. He had spent his adult life meeting strangers on their home grounds and, if his antennae had taught him anything, it was the difference between coincidence and calculation.

EN ROUTE, WINTER, 1960

Traveling, listening, snooping, sniffing, eavesdropping, Levine added to his knowledge. If there were no women available, he could read books. It there were no books, he could talk to people. For reasons that he was only too aware of—he was short, his face lacked guile, he was a stranger—people seemed to want to talk to him. If not too tired or absorbed in his own thoughts, he obliged. You could always learn.

One night in 1960 he had to get from Atlanta to Columbus for an early meeting the next day. There were no planes, and he felt too tired to drive. He'd catch a bus, get some sleep, and try to be fresh the next morning. He settled down in a back seat, curled up, and started to doze. When the bus stopped in Covington, an old black man carrying a cardboard suitcase came on. He looked up and down the half-empty bus and sat next to Levine. The bus started.

Levine glanced at his neighbor. The man was old—seventy or seventy-five—country, and scrubbed fresh. Probably on the way to visit a child in Augusta. He had the kind of beautiful brooding face that made you wonder how anyone could have ever held slaves.

Levine nodded to the black man. The man nodded back.

"Nice night," Levine ventured. The man nodded.

"Going to visit family?" he asked.

"Got me a daughter in Augusta. I stays some time with her, some with my son. My wife, she's been dead twenty years now."

"Sorry to hear that."

"That's okay. We didn't get on any too good, at that. Still, I miss her. You get to be my age, you miss *anybody.*"

"You must have seen a lot in your lifetime."

The man looked quizzically at Levine, judging him coolly. "You from up north?"

"That's right."

"I thought so."

There was a pause. Levine offered the chance again.

"You must have seen a lot of changes in the way people live."

"That I have, that I have. I'll tell you what I remember the most."

"What's that?"

"First time I ever saw that Ford automobile. It was in 1910. You see, they didn't start making that T Ford until 1908, and in Newton County, hell, nobody had money except a few of the planters. It was Mr. George Stavens who bought that first Ford. Yes, indeed, I can remember it like it was today. I was driving my daddy's mules to town and I hears this terrible noise behind us and it's Mr. Stavens in that Ford. I'd *heard* about it, but I ain't never seen it before. Lord, the mules picked up and was ready to float to town, they was so scared. Was all I could do to hold them down when, normal, I had to beat them just to raise their feet. That sure was a day."

"You must have seen a lot of changes since then."

"Indeed I have. I remember when the first six-cylinder car came along, must have been 1922 or '24 and I was doing part-time work at the sawmill and part-time at the livery. But I could tell the livery wasn't going to last much longer. Not with six-cylinder cars. And I remember when he brought that A Ford out in 1928. How could I forget that? I'll tell you, mister"—he poked his finger into Levine's chest—"I was the first colored man in Newton County to buy hisself his own car. They was some talk about it, but since I worked at the livery, there wasn't no fuss. And I'll tell you something else."

Levine was expectant. "What?"

"I got me an A Ford and it never did hold a candle to the T. No, sir. People who complained about it, they was right. Those Ts, they lasted all through the Depression, when the As was dropping like flies. It was the frame and the universal that went. Of course, modern times, everything's changed."

"How?"

"Power brakes, air conditioning. Everything's changed."

There was a pause. Finally Levine ventured, "You must have seen a lot of difference between whites and Negroes in that time."

"That too," the man said, and went to sleep.

Outside it was 97—a very humid 97. God had turned off the cooling Gulf breezes that were said to refresh the city from time to time. Levine hunkered down in the comparative safety of the Red Snapper Lounge of the Red Snapper Motel. Galveston was another sector of hell, and the Red Snapper was only a nasty trick, designed to keep wayfarers from collapsing completely before they had suffered enough.

"What do visitors around here do for fun?" Levine asked the bartender. There was no one else to ask, it being dead 3:00 P.M. on a Tuesday afternoon, and honest and even dishonest Texans were getting and spending.

"Mostly they fish and fuck," the bartender said. He was the first bearded bartender Levine had ever seen and, besides, he was young. He looked like what the papers had been calling hippies, but he spoke with a whanging Texas accent.

"I'm a married man," Levine said.

"Mostly they fish and fuck," the bartender repeated.

"Where do they fish?"

"Beats me, mister. Cain't stand it, myself. My uncle, he goes. In the Gulf, ah suppose."

Levine nodded. "I've never seen a bartender with a beard before."

"You intend to make something of it?" The bartender asked this in a mildly solicitous manner. He was very big.

"No, no. I was wondering if any of the customers bother you about it."

"Oh, every so often one of them oil-rig roughnecks makes a remark or passes something. Says something foolish, you know."

"What happens?"

"Well, ah usually cold-cocks the sonofabitch. 'Course,

sometimes ah lose. Not often, though. Ah'm a big sonofabitch myself."

"I noticed."

There was a prolonged, unpainful silence, and Levine asked if the bartender's uncle was around.

"Shit, yes. Ah cain't get him out of here. Thinks just 'cause ah'm working here he can get his drinks cheap."

"He can, can't he?"

"Sure, but he takes on so 'bout it that pretty soon the manager's gonna be firing mah ass. Not mah uncle's. Mine."

A half hour later the uncle came in and began drinking. He was a quick lively fellow, small as his nephew was large. Levine introduced himself.

"Jew, ain'tcha?" the little man said.

Levine nodded modestly.

"Knew it right off," the little man said. "Big nose and all that. Knew you weren't from around here. Hey, nephew, this here man's a Jew." The nephew kept wiping his beer glasses—ethnology was not one of his interests.

"Me and the boy, we're from Arkansas. Used to be Jews there coming to Hot Springs. Hell, when I was a kid, they'd used to stop us on the road and ask directions. Arkansas warn't much on road signs in them days. Other kids and me, we'd always give 'em fuck-up directions." Suddenly conscious of the proprieties, he added, "Nothing personal, though."

Levine shrugged.

"Well, shit, don't take on like that about it," the bantam replied. "Not like I was cussin' out your mother or somethin'. Here, let me buy you a drink."

"He don't pay anyway," the bartender muttered.

"Don't mind him," the little man said. "Nephew, I'll have another fuzzy-wuzzy and Mr. Levine here will have—what you drinking?"

"Tequila. On the rocks."

"Jesus. You drink that stuff? Worst thing about Mexicans is their liquor. Next is their food. After that, it's the flies. Then, there's their women. Jesus, when I was merchant shipping I caught me a dose in Tampico that lasted me nigh a half year. Could have made a fortune out of that drip. Just like cream, it was. Drink up!"

Levine sipped warily. The little man seemed harmless, but who could tell? Maybe he was just a barroom loudmouth; maybe he was an anti-Semite with a revolver tucked away in some back pocket. Levine felt no inclination to argue with him.

"Don't worry about me, I'm harmless," the man proclaimed. "I'm not half so crazy as I seem, either. Been all over the world, I have. I was never one to stay on ship and play with myself and get drunk. I drank a little, but I always got ashore. Always learned something. Used to read something awful when I was on the ship."

"That's true," the bartender said. "This here's my Uncle Bushrod," he added.

"That's a biblical name," Levine said.

"Well, shit, you think I need any goddam Jew to tell me about the fucking Bible?" the little man said belligerently.

"No, no, I was just making conversation."

"Make it someplace else, for Christ's sake. Hell, I don't mean that. Have another drink of that Mexican Drano."

Levine drank rapidly. Fears melted. "Mr. Levine here is interested in fishing," the nephew said.

The little man looked up. His facial expression changed, became alert, almost predatory. "That so?" he asked.

"Right."

"Where you staying?"

"Here. Upstairs."

"Go get your things. I'll be ready for you in ten minutes. We can still get there in plenty of time."

Levine needed no explanation. Amplification would help, though.

"Do I need waders? What sort of rod? I just have a couple..."

"Waders? Shit, you're in Texas, not Minnesota. I got the rods. You just get on some old fishing pants and some sneakers."

Levine hurried to his room, changed, and returned to the bar.

"Jesus Christ," Uncle Bushrod said. "I ain't never seen a Jew in a jump suit before. You get that at Sears?" Levine nodded. "Well, it fits real nice. Let's have a drink and go."

Ten minutes later Busrod aimed his fish-stinking old pickup down the center of the road and headed out toward the Gulf of Mexico. There was a brief stop for bait, a bumpy ride over some dunes and, fifteen minutes later Levine walked behind him along a deserted strip of beach.

"Waders! Jesus! Even an Arkie like me'd fry to death out here if it warn't for that Gulf water up 'round my armpits. You just follow along and do what I do, mister."

Levine watched with some anxiety as Bushrod turned from the beach and began a steady march into the water, a gnome intent on suicide. Levine followed. The farther Uncle Bushrod advanced into the Gulf waters, the more the junk he had bedecked himself with made sense. Nipple high in water, he was surrounded by a collection of boxes, empty Chlorox bottles, plastic coolers, and tin buckets, all of which, attached by snaps to his belt, bobbed cheerily in his wake. He turned back toward Levine.

"When you walk along, shuffle your feet," he yelled. "That's to scare off them stingrays. Hurt like hell if you step on 'em. This here's how you do it."

He reached in one bucket, attached a live shrimp to his hook, and cast his rig fifty feet farther into deeper water. From another bobbing chest he pulled open a beer, snapped open the top, and sucked noisily.

"That's better," Bushrod said. "Just don't cast off the fucking shrimp. I can't be bothered running back every hour or so and getting more bait."

"I'll be careful. How far should I set the float from the bait?"

"'Bout four feet."

"What are we fishing for?"

"Sea trout, o' course."

Levine had never seen a sea trout before, but in the course of the next two hours he caught a dozen of them, beautiful lithe fish that truly looked and fought like trout. The sun, reflected off the water, gradually baked his face

deep red. In the distance behind them he could see faintly
the buildings of Galveston. There were no boats, no other
fishermen. Occasionally, like some relic of the 1930s, a
single-engine plane chugged slowly across the horizon,
holding their attention until it disappeared.

"You ready to go home?" the little man asked.

"Whenever you are."

"I'd just as soon stay, but it'll be getting dark in a half
hour and we won't catch shit. Let's pack up."

They waded back to the shore, Levine shuffling with
religious intensity. Bushrod talked constantly. He was,
Levine thought, just as he had described himself—a
shrewd, grotesquely self-educated man, lumpy with
semi-assimilated knowledge.

"Hey, Levine, you never once cast them shrimp off.
Not bad."

"I've fished before."

"I know now. Shit, I hate people who say they fish and
the next thing you've got 'em in your boat and they're
puking all over your lunch box or they get their line so
tangled with yours ain't neither one of you going to fish
for a half hour. I like a person who says he don't know shit
about fishing, and that's the truth. You hungry?"

"God, yes."

"There's a juke joint back 'long the road to the city
where they can take care of these trout for us. Let's go."

The restaurant was run by a man named Minelli whose
grandfather apparently had lost the way to Brooklyn.
Bushrod dumped the fish on the back landing, told a
black man, "Fillet 'em all and tell Sam to cook us four,"
and gave him a dollar. Inside, the restaurant was clean
and simple. Bushrod nodded to several men. They sat
down and ordered cracked crab and creole shrimp as
appetizers. Then they ate the fish they had just caught.
Nothing was ever better.

"Who lives out here?" Levine asked, waving his hand in
the direction of the beach. They had driven past a few
tottering frame houses on the way.

"Out here on the island? No one but a bunch of dirt
diggers and crabbers."

"It's pretty. You'd think there'd be more people here."

"Pretty? Shit, Texans are afraid of the water. They don't think nothing's pretty unless they can get oil or pussy out of it."

The island was ten minutes from Galveston, a hour from Houston. Levine didn't know much about Texas, but he knew what was happening to Houston.

Buying the land was heartbreakingly easy. There was no need for straw men or bribes. People wanted to give it away. The coast was littered with For Sale signs—on the finest, cleanest beach he had seen since the Caribbean! It was like coming to Miami Beach before Flagler. For two days Levine bought feverishly. On the third he worried that he had overcommitted himself, worried about the lack of an access road, and on the fourth he began buying again.

He held on to the land. In the next ten years Texans overcame their fear of the water, and in every tiny town within two hundred miles of the Gulf anyone who could swim and many who could not bought themselves a first boat after their second car and headed toward the water where Levine was waiting. The lack of an access road never bothered them. They just put low-pressure tires on their cars and turned the beach into a freeway.

He never could remember when he decided to leave Arco. It was like so much of life: the business lunches, the office conferences, the executive sessions, all combined to decide something important, and in all of them the substance melted away until you were at home trying to remember what had been said, what decided, and there was nothing there. Thinking back, Levine remembered discussing the decision with his wife, could almost recall the place—a Chinese restaurant in Bayshore—where they had talked about it, but he had no idea of what he had said or how she had responded.

The decision had evolved. The thrill had gone out of selling equipment, though the magnet of new women remained. There wasn't enough money in radio systems, even selling them to entire states and bigger and bigger cities, not compared to land development. What had begun as a sideline was making him rich. He had asked Sid Hersch to let him buy in, reduce his selling, and put him on the board. Hersch had laughed. "You're a salesman, A.L. You're the best we ever had. You'd be out of your element in a boardroom. Believe me, it's for your own good."

Levine did not want to be impolite, but he was irritated. "Look, concede that maybe I know something about what's for my own good. Okay?"

Hersch wouldn't budge. "You're making good money on sales. Since we gave you the Southwest along with the South, you're making twice anyone else. We've given you bonuses every year. What else do you want?"

"Just what I asked for."

"You have my answer."

"So you know what's good for me? Let me ask you a question. Roughly how much are you worth? Don't bother lying; I can find out for myself."

Hersch shrugged. "I'm sure you can. I'm worth about four hundred thousand, most of it in company stock."

Levine thought. He had just netted half a million on a land deal in the Sandia mountains. He had assets of two million. He was making $75,000 a year from Arco. Arco had been a good entry, but it was costing him money.

"That's the way it is, Sid?"

"That's the way it is."

"Okay. I quit. No hard feelings. You and Shirley feel free to visit us any time."

"A.L., I want you to reconsider."

"No chance. You know me enough for that."

"I guess I do. Well, good-bye. Thanks for the invitation. Shirley and I, we don't get out to Long Island very often."

"No, I was thinking you should stop by in the summer."

"I didn't know you had a summer place. Where is it?"

Levine was still irritated. "Actually, we've got a couple. Punta Roja—west coast of Florida—a little place near Myrtle Beach—and a place in the Smokies. I like to fish, you know."

Hersch said nothing.

"Look, if you're near any of those places, just call. If we're not in, there's always a housekeeper to answer the phone. The housekeeper will have your name. Just make yourself at home."

"I don't see why you want to move to Washington," his wife said.

"I didn't say we'd move to Washington. I said we ought to try living there awhile to see if we like it."

"How can we move just for a while? The kids are in school. We can't just pick them up and put them down like lumps of sugar." She stirred her coffee furiously.

"Other families do. Besides, you always say you have no friends out here."

"Sure, but I *know* I have no friends out here. In Washington, I wouldn't know where anything was—the stores, the doctors, everything. Besides, I don't see the point of it."

"The point is that it's the same as a business. If you have a business with three branches and one branch is getting all the action, you shut the others down. It's the same with me. I'm shutting down electronics. Someday I'll be shutting down land development. Who needs them? We have enough money for the rest of our lives. For the rest of the children's lives, if you want to know. Now my business is politics. I keep investing my money in politics and my candidates keep losing. I like the excitement, but I want to win. If you're going to win, you have to do it from Washington."

"You want to go down there so all those senators and congressmen and reporters can come buzzing around and take you to lunch. For them you're nothing but a Golden Fleece."

"A what?"

"You heard me. Someone who gives them money."

"I don't deny that. I like the attention. I know I'm being flattered. I was a salesman for twenty years, remember? I know there's a lot of ass-kissing going on, but I think I know the difference between love and seduction."

"Have it your own way, then. Just don't expect me to like it."

They rented a suite at the Watergate for a month, and she liked it. Loved it. Her husband was an important man, and in the political community she was automatically an important woman. On Long Island her neighbors had been vaguely aware that Levine was interested in politics, just as she was vaguely aware that one neighbor was a lawyer and another made armatures. At the synagogue men were pointed out who were rich from textiles or plastics and she was impressed, but she knew that no one else in the whole world cared if she knew Merrill Lichtman, the plastics man, or not. How could she visit her sister and say, "I sat next to Merrill Lichtman yesterday in temple?" But the people she met in Washington—even the people in the elevator—were people she had heard of all her life. Merrill Lichtman was never going to be on the seven o'clock news. But even her sister had heard of Senator Anderson, who lived down the hall.

They made a desultory attempt to look for other places to live and ended up buying their own place in the complex. "Why move," she said, "when we're already here?"

Farbstein the socialist was skeptical about the move, too.

"You'll die away from the city. That I know."

"Farbstein, for twenty years I lived half my life outside New York. All of a sudden, I'm going to shrivel up and die?"

"There's no culture there, no art, no theater."

"Farbstein, when's the last time you went to the theater?"

"That's immaterial. It's knowing that it's here, that I *could* go if I wanted."

"When was the last time you went to the theater?"

"Pins and Needles."

"So that was, what, thirty years ago? You'd die of culture shock if you moved away from your precious theater? Come on."

"You'll see," Farbstein warned ominously, but Levine moved anyway. He had felt the time coming. The involvement with McCarthy in 1968 had been fun, but the loss too stunning to forget. The candidate might depreciate his candidacy; not so Levine. He had smelled power and wanted—needed—to make it his own. What was the use of being a Jew named Levine with $30 million from real estate if people got you confused with another Jew named Levine who had $30 million from shopping centers in Chicago? What was the use of having $30 million if, somehow, you couldn't make things better for other people? His life had led him into politics; politics led him to Washington.

He treated Washington like any other place he had ever lived. He listened a great deal, read compulsively, said little. Helen enjoyed going to the congressional and diplomatic receptions. He used them as strainers, sifting out people he might want to talk to later, seeing those same people at other receptions and greeting them again, talking idly, but measuring. For the first time Helen wanted to give a series of dinner parties herself.

"I think we ought to wait," he said.

"We owe a lot of people. I'd like to get to know the Andersons better. And that TV woman, Sue Dempsey. We've got a nice place here. I'd like to show it off."

"Wait a bit longer, dear. We owe for cocktail parties, not dinners. People are nice to us because they read about us in the paper, because you're pretty and I'm rich, because I'm supposed to be powerful. Let's see who invites us to *their* dinner parties."

Their novelty peaked and then died. They were not mentioned among the guests at diplomatic receptions, even when they were invited. Invitations kept coming, but they were for fund-raising dinners at $150 a couple. The excitement sugared down, leaving behind a residue of people who seemed genuinely interested in them. They were asked to dinner by party people, lawyers, some journalists, a couple of historians. They entertained in return. Levine began to form a little circle of friends. For the first time in his life he felt as though he were dealing with equals. Selling, he had encountered shrewd, sometimes brilliant men, but men of little learning. In New York, after his first tentative involvement with politics, he met brilliant men with what appeared to be very little knowledge of the real world. Washington was a mixing bowl of practice and theory, a place where people sold ideas (sometimes their own) with the vigor with which he once sold radio systems.

He took the land-development business with him when he moved. He was not interested in new deals, but he had to keep an eye on some of the old ones. The money had to be invested and reinvested. He had to have a place to go after breakfast.

It was as natural as the sun's rising that he should outfit his office in shag rugs and Naugahyde and that he should hire a well-spoken, pretty black secretary. He told the employment bureau, "I deal with a lot of people from the South. I need a secretary who can run the office while I'm away. I have a prejudice against bad English and sloppy accents. I want someone who is crisp, efficient, and black. I'll pay the right person twice the standard starting salary."

The employment service sent over a succession of pleasant young women who made most of the same grammatical errors as pleasant young high school girls from Long Island, along with some which seemed indigenous to Washington. If their spoken English was clear, their memos were disasters. "Your wife called and said never mine about the groceries" was usual. Levine called the employment people and told them to stop bothering him until they found someone who could do just exactly what he had asked for.

Miss Simpkins was tall, cool, and amused. "I understand you're looking for a super-nigger," she said. Her accent, if any, was faintly midwestern. She had been brought up in Pennsylvania.

"That's more or less it, I guess." He was blushing.

"Do you always blush like that?" she said.

"I'm not used to that word."

"You will be. Oh, don't worry. I promise not to use it in

front of your clients, Mr. Levine. I just like to feel at home with my boss. Not familiar, you understand, but at home."

"Am I interviewing you or are you interviewing me?"

"Both. You want a woman with a list of qualifications that would fit a Ph.D. Give you credit, you're willing to pay for it. I've got those qualifications. I got my M.A. in Special Education, taught high school, speak passable French, and haven't made a mistake in English since I was four years old. I got sick of trying to teach kids who didn't want to learn, especially in school districts where they didn't want to pay me. My sister was working in Washington, and I decided to come and take a look around. I was making twelve thousand five in McKeesport breaking my ass teaching, and I found out that I could make twenty thousand in Washington just looking and talking nice. IBM has been after me for two weeks now. They'll put a black lady like me out in front of the reception room, and all I have to do is give my nice cultured, 'Mr. Williams is with a client, but he'll be out just as soon as possible' fifty times a day and I'll be taking home twenty-two thousand. 'Chief receptionist,' they call it."

"So why don't you take it?"

"I might, I might. As I said, I'm interviewing, too. Tell me, what's a land developer like you doing in Washington?"

Levine told her and she was interested and she took the job. Three weeks later he was screwing her.

"My momma won't never believe this," she said afterward.

"You're not planning to write her, are you?"

"Sure. Momma and me are *tight*. Not like my skinny-leg sister. Can't tell her *shit*."

"How come you're talking this way?"

"The accent? Oh, I save it for special times. Watch out for my earrings, okay? That's better. No, I mean it. Momma'll get a real laugh out of this."

They were on the office couch. The Naugahyde was cold against Levine's legs.

"Do you want a blanket or something?" he asked.

"No, I'm fine. Too tired to roll over. You're okay. I mean, I don't go around comparing people, but that was fun. Look—my scalp's still wet and my hair's getting straightened out. That's a good sign. I'm surprised."

"You mean, because I'm white."

"Hell, baby, that's not it. You don't think I believe all that shit about black men being better, do you? You're not the first, you know. Lord, I've had black men, white men, a couple of Japanese. If anyone knows, I do, and I can tell you a lady never knows until the action starts."

"So why were you surprised?"

She took his head between her hands and looked at him. It was the kind of look that Levine had forgotten, a tender, gentle, loving motion. She smiled.

"You've got to be about the ugliest man I ever went for," she said. "I'm a very pretty lady, and I've known it since I was twelve years old. I had the football players and the doctors' sons and, in college, I had a couple of white boys who were crazy to marry me. I could pick and choose, and I always chose the prettiest man I could find. Always have. And you're short and you don't have much hair and you wouldn't win any special prizes with that face, and I went for you. And I don't usually fuck my bosses."

"Usually?"

"In graduate school I had something with one of my professors, but I wouldn't exactly call him a boss."

"So why me?"

"I thought you were kind. I felt you care about people. And I'd never screwed a Jew before."

"So?" He lifted his palms before her.

She slapped his palms and laughed. "So—so not bad. Not bad at all. Momma won't have that letter but ten minutes before she'll be calling, asking all about it."

"How come?"

"She's got a thing about Jews. All niggers have. That's one thing I'm going to do for you—teach you about niggers—and that's the way we talk about each other. You know damn well ain't nobody else can use that word, but we feel that we, like, have a patent on it. Get me a cigarette, honey."

He padded over to the desk and pulled out a pack he kept for visitors.

"What sort of thing about Jews?"

"Love-hate. You'll see all these street dudes talking about how the Jew oppresses them and the Jew's the landlord or the storekeeper or the lawyer or the agent, and how the Jew lives off the sweat of the nigger's brow, and as soon as you hear that, you figure, there's one nigger who wants to live off the sweat of other niggers' brows, so he lays it on the Jews. It goes beyond envy, see, because the nigger, even the street nigger, knows that he and the Jew are still in it together. That the rest of society don't like 'em even when they *are* rich, and so together they've got a thing going, laughing at the real lames."

"The lames?"

"Right! The turkeys. The ones who stopped learning in third grade. Nixon. The ones who listen to Lawrence Welk. The Jews, they're the comedians, and the niggers, they're the musicians, and they're both sticking sand in the white man's ass."

"Did you think that up yourself?"

"That's a dumb fucking question. If you hadn't just screwed me, I'd be insulted. Of course I thought it up myself. What do you think I did—read it somewhere?"

"Well, yes."

"People don't write shit like that. All they write is wars and poetry. Which I don't read, anyway."

"People do so write that. You ever heard of Norman Mailer? Lenny Bruce? James Baldwin?"

"We read Baldwin in college. How come you know him—he's black, isn't he?"

"Sure. But everyone reads black authors."

"Not me. I read Ann Landers and the ads for Woodies. And *Five Smooth Stones*—that's a real book."

"Okay. Let's make a deal."

"Very Jewish," she murmured.

"Let's make a deal. You say you're going to teach me about blacks. I say I'm going to teach you about Jews. But except for screwing, all my teaching begins and ends right now. And I'll do it in one word."

"What's that?"

"Read."

One thing Levine had found in twenty years of traveling was that there were few if any mute, inglorious Miltons in the United States. No society had ever pushed talent so relentlessly to the top, had propelled strong-armed boys or strong-voiced men from high school festivals in the hills to national prominence. Part of the talent machine was television, and part was a system of colleges that needed an unending supply of new brains to remain self-perpetuating. Talent rose. Not always to the top. At a certain level luck and publicity played their parts, sending one first-rate woman singer from the local night clubs to national television, leaving another equally talented to play out her life as Shreveport's Own Lady of Song.

But once major-league baseball was integrated, if there was any vein of talent left unexplored in America it was among those blacks who were just what the standard liberals said they were: victims of an educational system designed to shove them out as maids and day laborers. Tutoring Simpkins (as she liked to be called—"Like one of those English movies, you know"), Levine was astonished as much by the depth of her ignorance as by her ability to learn. She was as smart as any of the corporate directors he met, and she was a college graduate, and yet she knew nothing of black history, much less white. He shoved *The Lives of Black Folk* at her, fed her Frederick Douglass, gave her a biography of Paul Robeson. She was not a fast reader, but she forgot nothing and made connections that would have made a Ph.D. supervisor jump with surprise and delight.

"What I'd like to know," she said one day in her apartment, "is how come I never learned this before?"

"Two guesses."

"You think it's racism, don't you, Levine?"

"I do."

"But most of my teachers were black, right through teacher's college."

"Victims take on the ways of their oppressors," he said.

"That's too easy. Levine, I think it was just plain meanness. I think back on those teachers, and some of them could have pushed me along a bit. Miss Simmons, the one I told you about, she must have known I was smart. She knew something about writing. She could have encouraged me. Instead she treated me like shit. She was afraid someone in the whole school would know a little bit more than she did. 'Stead of being proud that she could help me along, she held me back. They all did. They weren't even scared for their jobs. They were set."

"Don't be too hard on them. They were a minority, marginal people with marginal jobs."

"Don't tell me not to be hard on them niggers. I went to their goddam school, not you. There wasn't anything marginal about them, not in our part of town. I tell you what the matter was. They were Negro intellectuals, back in McKeesport, and a Negro intellectual is like a Jewish general. He's always scared he's going to be found out."

"Maybe that's what I meant by marginal?"

"Don't you people ever give up arguing?"

"Never, except to screw. Turn the stereo a little higher."

Her apartment was in a quasi-fashionable building on 17th Street, gleaming on the outside, already run-down and peeling inside. The residents were a mélange of elderly white widows, black secretaries, African graduate students, prostitutes of various colors, and harried white men in the throes of alcoholism or divorce. Drug dealers and pimps gathered in the lobby. Hurrying on his way to an interlude with Simpkins, Levine swaggered through the lobby, his hands (he hoped) dangling ominously at his side, step (he believed) hinting of panther-like grace and menace.

"Who that dude?" one idler asked another as Levine fled into the elevator one Saturday afternoon.

"That the Jew who's fucking that nice lady in six fifteen. Her boss, I think."

"That's some fine split, that lady. How come she won't play with the brother?"

"She do, man, she do. She got some big motherfucker spends the night with her Mondays and Tuesdays. She just stringing this Jew along. The money, man, the money."

"So how come we don't take care of him?"

"She like him, that's why. And she got the man at the desk and the manager, they're her friends, and she got that big mother on Mondays and Tuesdays, and she got some other niggers who come up and visit, and they big, too. And she know everything that go on down here, man. So you just keep hands off the little honky and try 'n' hustle some other dude. She making money from the white man, and, like I say, anything you bring into the community, it's okay with me."

———————

Levine wasn't paying for sex, and the sex itself had faded into the background. They were no longer teacher and student, they were students together and, cautiously, they began to appear together. He took her to a couple of cocktail parties when Helen was out of town and, although one or two of his friends joked about wanting to have a secretary as beautiful as Simpkins, none suspected that their relationship was anything other than plain friendship. The contrast between her youth and beauty and his age and ugliness made the racial difference irrelevant. Sex between Levine and Simpkins required a leap of imagination foreign to Washington. A New York imagination, accustomed to bald Jewish garment manufacturers who attached themselves to beautiful showgirl types, might have made the connection, but in Washington it was assumed that Levine was a nice liberal talent scout who had made a discovery. Simpkins was usually taken for a black attorney or politician, and she did nothing to weaken the illusion. People didn't ask many questions. It was a time when blacks were very scarce at cocktail parties, and no one wanted to frighten them away.

Not so at black parties. He went, at first reluctantly,

with Simpkins, who was always being invited to "cabarets," get-togethers, and just plain cocktail parties. She was on the reception list for several African countries, black ambassadors being as anxious to have beautiful ladies around them as their white counterparts. Besides, polygamy was traditional, and many a wife was left at home, too provincial to be brought to America. Levine was not the only white at most of these parties, but he was usually the only white man with a black woman, and he learned to take the stares and hostility that he had never felt as a Jew among gentiles. He was playing in a tougher league.

"I don't want to go," he said. "I know Levoy Williams, I think he's a nasty racist, and I don't want to go to his house."

"Baby, he invited me. He knows I go with you. I want you both to talk."

"What the fuck do you think I'm going to do, convert him?"

"No, but you might make him listen."

"He wouldn't listen if Joshua shoved a trumpet down his throat."

"Just try to be polite."

"Polite! What am I, a Hitler? A Bilbo? Of course I'll be polite. That's my problem."

He had no chance to be polite to Levoy Williams, a Washington lawyer who had made a career of television appearances. Whenever a reporter needed an outrageous statement, Williams could be counted on to provide one. Knowledgeable blacks and whites alike considered him an idiot, but he could not be ignored. He was believed to be a "civil rights leader." He had won a string of monumentally counterproductive legal victories against racism. Charging that the city discriminated against black alcoholics in its health program, he had convinced a local judge that all alcoholics were entitled to psychiatric treatment comparable to private therapy. The city figured out that one fourth of its entire budget would have to be devoted to psychiatric services, and so it abandoned whatever services it had offered in the first place. Williams's victories usually turned out this way.

Levine had no chance to be polite. Introduced by Simpkins, Williams merely stared at Levine, shook hands grudgingly, and said not a word. An old anger welled up in Levine, a desire to knock his famous host on his famous shag rug, but he had promised Simpkins to be polite, and starting a cocktail party with a fight was hardly good behavior. Besides, there were enough movers and shakers at this particular party that word might in fact get out to bigger Washington.

The only other white present was a radical Jewish lawyer, whose eyes met Levine's briefly and darted away just as fast. Jerry Wachtman wasn't going to be seen seeking out other white folk at a black man's house, no, sir! Neither was Levine. They avoided each other like ex-husband and wife.

"I want another drink," Levine told Simpkins. "Just bring me a bottle of tequila and some ice."

He sat on an overstuffed couch, pouring and sipping.

"That's a solid woman I see you with." The speaker was a young black man, quite drunk, slightly midwestern in accent. "You fucking her?"

Levine shrugged.

"Man, I'm asking you for a serious reason. If you ain't fucking her, you got to be crazy, and I get nervous around crazy white folk."

Levine poured himself another drink. "You want some tequila?"

"No, man, I got my own." He took a pint of brandy from his back pocket. "Levoy Williams never will have more than one bar at his parties, and I get tired of waiting just so I can drink bar bourbon. You dig?"

Levine nodded.

"My name's Arthur France, like the country. I'm pleased to meet you."

France was drunk, vulgar, and possibly threatening, but he was the first person at the party who had been halfway civil.

"Levine's my name. A. L. Levine. That's what they call me—A.L."

"Well, I'm glad to meet you. I'm glad to meet anybody who knows that foxy Simpkins lady. You rich?"

Levine shrugged again.

"No, man, I'm serious."

"I've got enough for the moment."

"Shit, you got to be rich. Why else would Simpkins go out with you?"

Enough was enough. Levine leaned over to France. "She goes out with me because Jews are famous for being good lays, and I've got a big cock. That's why."

France was, for the moment, surprised. After a pause he looked up and said, clearer and more intent than before, "You're putting me on."

"No, I'm not. Here—Simpkins, come here a moment."

Simpkins turned and came over to the couch.

"Dear, this is Mr. France. Tell him why you go out with me."

Simpkins shook hands graciously and whispered, "He's the best fuck in town."

Levine smiled triumphantly.

France shook his head. "I don't believe it."

"Oh, I don't blame you for not believing it. I'll tell you what—I'll bet you a hundred bucks that I'm better hung than you. Here's the money. I can tell you carry a lot of cash on you. Let's make it simple. One on one. Sight unseen I'm willing to bet."

France looked at him carefully and began to laugh. "Man, you're one crazy Jew. You almost had ol' Arthur France going for a moment." He turned to a fat, brocaded man who had just come into the room. "Hey, Jess, come here. I got one crazy Jew for you to meet."

Jessington was the first black politician Levine was to meet through Simpkins, but not the last. Her beauty kept her part of the network of talented and ambitious blacks who came to Washington. Through her Levine became not part of the network but aware of it. They were all politicians, whether they were congressmen or tennis players or movie stars, and if some were bombastic and ugly in public, others were curiously shy and, like Simpkins, eager to learn. Publicly they had to keep at arm's length from the white man. Privately, they were as anxious to find out about whites as Levine was about blacks.

"What are we doing about the conventions?" Lee asked.

"Jesus," Lafferty said. He was the network's vice-president for programming.

"It could have been settled," Lee said, "if we hadn't fought that Public Information Bill." Lee was one of the vice-presidents for public affairs. He was the smart one.

"We couldn't let them pass that. Christ, you let the government tell you that you have to televise all the conventions, and next thing you know they're telling you that you have to do the Federal Trade Commission live. I mean, we went to the wall on that one, and we were right."

"I know, schmuck," Lafferty said, "but it would have made things so goddam easy. No more decisions. We could just let them flick those cameras on for two days, go off to the beach, and come back and collect ten million from Uncle. Now we have to start thinking all over again. I'm tired of thinking. I'm too old for it."

"People still watch them," Miller said. He was sales, and he could tell you how many people were watching bowling on Friday night, what the leading brand of snuff was. Miller went on. "Interest is going up. Last convention all networks together had thirty-five percent of audience at peak viewing time. That was up three point six percent of audience from the peak eight years ago. At this exact instant seventy-two percent of Americans say they intend to watch part of the conventions. Extrapolated falloffs would place the actual peak viewing audience at forty-one percent. Give or take one standard deviation."

"That's still not the Super-fucking-Bowl," Lee said, "especially when you've got it spread over three days."

"Nonetheless, advertiser interest is up. At this exact instant sixty-five percent of major accounts have expressed interest in commercial purchase during convention time. That, too, is up significantly from four years ago. Given extrapolated fall-throughs—"

"Oh, shit," Lafferty said. "Next you'll be telling us how many people are picking their noses at this exact instant. We get the picture. It's a matter of practicality. If we do spot coverage, we can hold on to our best programs and view around them. If we cancel out the Monday night bullfight, we lose five hundred thousand dollars."

Goldberg said, tentatively, "There is a Jewish candidate."

"Levine?"

"Yeah, Levine."

"Holy Mother of God," Lafferty said.

They were talking about the unmentionable, discussing shovels in the home of the corpse. They were powerful men and nothing was sacred to them. They could watch a world-famous woman sociologist interviewed on a talk show and outdo each other in the unnatural acts they planned for her. They could—and did—tell powerful politicians to go away. They had even on occasion rejected big advertisers who had infringed upon what they believed was their integrity. But they worked for a network whose president was Jewish, whose board of directors was Jewish, and whose founder had been Jewish. No one joked about this. The network thus had no Jewish religious hour, never interviewed rabbis, always hired news reporters with Anglo-Saxon features and southern accents, and rarely covered events in Israel. It was, of course, still known as the Jewish network.

Horace Friedman, the president of the network, grunted. "What's so bad about a Jewish candidate?" he asked.

The others were silent. Friedman was not only president of the network, he *ran* the goddam place. He had been in the business since college and he was president because he was the best. He had instinctive judgment of talent, a glutton's appetite for facts, and an ability to remember every program and personality that any of the networks had featured for so much as a single half-hour. He interfered in the prerogative of all his vice-presidents and was always better than they were. When the network needed someone to host its series on Decline and Fall of the American Automobile, Friedman had remembered a funny West Texas car racer he had once seen interviewed after a crash. In two months Sam Appleman had become the most popular commentator in America. "The Will Rogers of the Automobile," *The New Yorker* had called him.

And so the other men listened carefully to Friedman. He did not want yes-men around him, but he did not want people who were wrong either. If you made too many errors, if you did not understand television or the audience, there must be someone around who did. Someone who could do your job better than you did. It was okay to disagree with Friedman, if you were right.

So no one spoke.

Friedman grunted again. "After all, what's the problem with a Jewish candidate? We've got the tube filled with blacks and spics, don't we?"

"Sure," said Lee, "but this is different."

"How?" said Friedman.

Lee had launched himself into the deep water. The others waited to see if he'd make it back to shore.

"Christ, Horace, you know as well as I do. Old Man Plotzki and the board of directors, they're not going to want us giving three straight days to a Jew. Shit, we didn't cover the president of Israel when he came here."

"We made a mistake," Friedman said. "What's the matter with covering a Jewish politician? He's probably an asshole like the rest of them."

Lee couldn't back out. "Christ, Horace, you know the way the board is. Afraid the public is going to think we're too Jewish. You know how they do things, I mean—"

"We'll do them a favor," Friedman said. "We'll cover the convention. We'll show the people a Jewish politician. If he's an asshole, we'll show the people a Jewish asshole. It will be just what the board wants. Maybe we could run a series, Famous Jewish Assholes."

Lafferty and Goldberg laughed. Miller was silent. Lee was sweating.

"You know, Horace," Lee said. "I've heard this Levine,

and by no means is he an asshole. He's really pretty good. And he's got a lot of southern connections."

"So what? If he's different, the ratings will be up. The board may not like too many noses on the tube, but they'll like those ratings. A Jewish candidate. It's new, it's different. I'll buy it. We go for around-the-clock coverage. Understand?"

"Vershtannen," said Lafferty. They understood.

Part **III**

WASHINGTON, APRIL 21, 1988

There's no honor, Eli Levine thought on the way to the Potomac jogging path. People don't value themselves. Slaves to machines, to plastic. He remembered a television show he had seen once when he was a kid, sick at home, propped up on the pillows, drinking ginger ale his mother fetched him. On television a fat-assed master of ceremonies led shrieking women to an enormous plastic Christmas tree, hung with packages. The point of the program was for the women to get a package from the tree. Like crazed monkeys they shook the tree, pushed each other, scrambled to climb the polyurethane trunk, and jumped up and down, while the stupid audience matched them scream for scream. The program, *Christmas Every Day*, was still on daytime television.

If any woman I knew did that, Eli thought, I'd kill her. Literally. The stink of it all, the exposure of greed, the willingness to look awkward or ugly or half naked, just for an electric toenail clipper. People like that demean us all.

But how were they different from the rest of the masses, other than in their stupidity in letting their greed be televised to make the network money? How were they different from the corporations that sucked the land dry or the smiling lawyers who justified A one day and B the next, Left on Monday and Right Tuesday, God now and Mammon next?

How were they different from his father? Didn't his father see what had happened, how he had made his money to change things and then been changed to an alloy, something unnatural, not himself?

From his childhood he remembered a father who came home. Every few weeks, anyway. That's what his father did, mostly—come home. He knew his father worked,

161

sold things, and traveled a lot, but the reality was coming home, and the A. L. Levine who came home then was different from the one who lived now. He was a simpler man then. He liked toys a lot and used to bring them home with him. Eli remembered a beautiful silver model of a jet plane that his father had brought him once. It hadn't been his birthday or anything, his father had just loved that plane.

The house on Long Island was simpler, too, more like nature. There were, he remembered, trees and bushes. Places to hide. They knew the people on the street—the Corbettes, who were old and used to call him "Sonny"; Mr. Pearland, who had an accent; Mr. Russo, who parked his plumbing supply truck in front of his house every night. He used to envy Jimmy Russo, who had a father who was home every night and who had his own truck. His mother used to fuss about the Russos' truck in front of the house and say that it looked bad for the neighborhood, but he had wished his own father had a truck with his name on it. Grown-ups were hard to understand.

I was right when I was a little kid, he thought. Mr. Russo did honest work. He was proud of it. If you do honest work and are proud of it, you put your name on your truck and you park the truck in front of the house and you don't give a fuck about what the neighbors think. Just the name itself made Mr. Russo real: RUSSO BRS. PLUMBING SUPPLIES. Today it would be called "United Home Furnishings" or something even grander but vaguer: "Unitex" or "Rusco International."

People don't honor their work, David thought, so they don't put their names onto it. If they don't honor their work, how can they honor themselves? Crawling and groveling, they were nothing. Only a new spirit of personality would free them. Peter Caputo was right. Modern sociology and psychiatry were just excuses for creeps and fuck-ups. People had to cut their way through a lot of sentimental crap to see it, but it was true.

Ahead of him the path curved gently to follow the bank of the Potomac. He looked at his stopwatch and began to run. He'd run fifteen minutes, jog fifteen, and run another fifteen. He had to work himself up to thirty minutes of straight running, then an hour. You had to be hard. He was proud of his body—that was part of honor, too—but he hadn't disciplined it enough.

He was moving nicely, easily, when he came around a bend and saw two black kids with their bikes blocking the running path. He waved his hand, motioning them to clear the way. They didn't move. Fucking leroys, he thought, not slowing down.

He came closer and still they blocked the path. He wouldn't move around them. Fuck them. His father would move around them, any politician would move around them, would pretend they weren't there like you pretend a drunk on the subway isn't there, but they *were* there, two of them, not kids but hulking young men, fifteen or sixteen or eighteen, out of school, probably never in, not going to move, and neither was he.

He stopped two feet away from them.

"You're blocking the path," he said.

"No shit?" one of them said.

"No shit," he replied. "Move 'em."

"Hey, sweeties, you some kind of famous athalete or something?" the other kid said. "You aim to be the fastest man in the world?" He paused. "Fastest white man, maybe."

The other one laughed. "That's right, Tab. Worl's fastes' white man." They laughed together.

He hadn't gone looking for it. He was no Westie, no Avenger. He had just wanted to go running. But the challenge had come to him, and he knew that he must act. He knew how his father would react. He knew his father's stories of the separate bus sections when he traveled in the South. But then he remembered his own time at Stanton School in Washington and Berthelle. He knew what his father would have done, and he knew what he must do.

He looked up and down the pathway. Nobody in sight.

"Hey, ain't nobody coming along to save your ass, worl's fastes' white man," the first one said. There was one on each side of him now.

"No, bubbie, I'm not the world's fastest white man, I'm the world's meanest." It was a textbook situation, one that he had worked a hundred times. Simultaneous foot smash and hand chop. The blacks couldn't have positioned themselves any better if they had been working from one of Rhee's diagrams on his *Full-Kontact Karate* television series.

It was as nice as he had thought it would be. He saw the one he chopped drop to the ground as he heard the sound of the other's ribs breaking. He spun to see the one in back of him on the ground, too, vomiting through his nose. He kicked out the front wheels of both bikes and then stomped the toes of both blacks. He didn't want anyone following in too big a hurry. Then he chopped them both across the Adam's apple. He didn't want anyone yelling, either.

He turned around and jogged back toward the apartment complex. He wondered about identification. Shit, we probably all look alike to them anyway. Maybe he ought to call the police and tell them what he had done. He had done it and he wasn't ashamed. Christ, he was proud.

It would mess up his parents, he thought, but he could take that. His father's fucking politics weren't anything to begin with, and his mother would be after him for something else, anyway. No, he wouldn't tell the police. Aggravated assault was a mandatory first conviction. He knew that from the group's magazines. There was no use spending two years in jail just for shit-kicking a couple of wise-ass blacks. No use in going to the mattresses, either, for a street fight. He'd keep shut, make sure he wasn't identified, and save himself. If he were going to go underground, it would be for something better than this.

Barnes, the shuffly old black who had run the security system ever since they moved to Washington, looked at him through the closed-circuit TV and turned the switch that unlocked the outer doors. He stopped by Barnes's glassed-in control center to chat. Might as well let him remember that I'm nice and calm and not a scratch on me. Ten to one those kids will tell the police they put up a great fight, beat me all over, but I got out a club or something.

"Nice day, Mr. Levine."

"It's really lovely, Barnes." His father called him "Mr. Barnes," but it sounded foolish. None of the other tenants did. Barnes wanted to be called Barnes. That's the way it was. Of course, when he had been younger, he had said, "Mr. Barnes." That was one thing he agreed with his parents about: respect. Respect for the adult by the child. He wasn't a child any longer.

"Good to see young people taking exercise. So many people nowadays, all they do is just lump around."

"Oh, I just like to keep in shape running."

"That I know, that I know. I see you most every day. You sure look good running along there."

"Thanks, Barnes. I better be getting on up for breakfast."

"You do that, Mr. Eli, you do that. Your folks sure are proud of you. 'Course, we're all real proud of your daddy." Barnes's voice changed subtly. His accent faded and his eyes focused. "What do you think about this president business? You think the country's ready to have a Jewish man for president? I've worked with all sorts of people—white, black, purple, you name it—but your father's about the straightest person I've ever known. Real likable, if you know what I mean."

Eli knew. He knew that his father had the magic talent for being liked which everyone else in the family lacked, almost as though he had stolen it from the others in their sleep and accumulated it for himself. Eli almost liked the little shit himself.

"I think he'd be a fine president, Barnes," he said.

"Don't we all," said Barnes, waving him toward the open elevator door.

In the apartment he showered, watched TV while he dried, changed, and sat down for breakfast.

His father was studying the *New York Times*. Not reading, studying.

"Good morning, Eli."

"Good morning, Dad."

"Have a good run?"

"Yeah."

"What happened to your hand?"

He glanced at his hand. There was a red swelling over his chopping edge and a purple-blue color was beginning to creep into it. Must have broken a little capillary, he thought. Sonofabitch!

"Oh, that. I stumbled and landed on it."

"Funny way to stumble, no scratches or anything. Have some more eggs, okay?"

He was still reading the breakfast mail when old Barnes buzzed him from the security desk.

"'Scuse me, Mr. Levine, but there's a couple of Patrols here who'd like to speak to your boy."

"Send them up, Mr. Barnes," he said. He knew Barnes wanted to be called Barnes, but he couldn't leave off the "Mr." If Barnes needed to be servile, to play out some part in a plantation drama, that was Barnes's problem, not his.

There was a knock at the door and he opened it to find two Patrols standing there, crisp in their khakis and Sam Browne belts. He peered up at their handsome, sullen black faces and asked, "Would you please come in?" They nodded together and, almost elbowing him to the side in his own hallway, strolled into the living room and sat down on the sofa.

"I'm A. L. Levine. Perhaps you might tell me what this is about?"

The older Patrol, whose name tag read Gaithers, said, "We'd like to talk to your son."

"Yes. But about what?"

"There's been an incident."

"Oh. Could you tell me what sort?"

Hostility smoldered, but civility was maintained. "I'm sorry, but this is part of an investigation. We'd like to speak to the boy."

Levine sensed danger and, quickly, a way to deflect it. He turned and headed toward the bedrooms, saying over his shoulder, "I'll get him now." The younger Patrol started to say something, but Gaithers gave a grunt heavy with menace.

He knocked on Eli's door and then went in. The boy was lying on his bed, listening to something on television through his stereo headset. He motioned his father to go away. Levine closed the bedroom door behind him.

"Eli," he shouted over the earphones, "there are some Patrols to talk to you."

The boy shook his head, put his finger to his lip, and motioned to the TV set.

Levine went over and snatched the headset off.

"My Italian lessons—" Eli started to say.

"Listen quickly," his father interrupted. "There are two Patrols out there to ask questions about something they call an incident. They want to talk to you. They haven't asked me any questions yet. Whatever you say, don't worry about my backing you up. If you went out, you went out. If you stayed home, you stayed home. Understand?"

"Capisce," the boy said. He straightened his shirt and pants and went out to the living room.

"Are you Eli Levine?" Gaithers asked.

"That's right." No "sir," no smile, no hint of accommodation. Levine marveled at his son. Eli went beyond the usual hostility between young people and blacks. There was a coldness, a fierceness about him that instantly matched Gaithers's dislike, matched it and somehow overcame it. Perhaps it was so common for people to be fawning in the presence of the Patrols that any sort of defiance, no matter how subtle, was twice magnified.

Gaithers hesitated, plunged ahead. "There was an incident on the jogging path this morning. Two young citizens were assaulted by a Caucasian youth and their bicycles destroyed. One youth is seriously ill. You are known to frequent that path. We haven't been able to get any identification from the citizens—they are too badly hurt to help—but it appears as how you might be about the same age and type as the person who hurt them."

"Now just a minute," Levine said. "Is this an official investigation?"

"You guessed it," Gaithers said, his contempt reestablished.

"Then I think my son should have advice of counsel before he answers any questions. Furthermore, I think that under the Miranda ruling you are required to—"

"Oh, Dad, forget it," Eli broke in. "I didn't do anything. I don't need a lawyer." Then he half turned toward Gaithers, nodded toward him, turned back to his father, and said, *"Non voglio un avvocato. Tutto va bene."*

Gaithers looked puzzled. "What's he say?" he asked Levine.

"The same thing as in English. He doesn't want a lawyer. Go ahead with your questions. May I stay?"

Gaithers turned to the other Patrol. They huddled for a moment, and Gaithers shook his head no. Levine excused himself and went into the study, where he pressed his ear against the air duct and listened to the questioning.

Sure, Eli said, he had been on the jogging path that morning. He went daily, rain or shine. Everyone in the apartment complex and along the river knew it. No, he hadn't see the two young citizens. It was early. He had met one other runner he knew, an old man with an old sweat shirt that said *U. S. Marines—The Finest.* He didn't know the old man's name or where he came from. No, he hadn't been in any fights. Look, he said, look at my face, my chest, my hands. No marks. I couldn't have been in an incident like that. Gaithers and the other seemed satisfied. They asked a few more halfhearted questions and left.

Levine went back into the living room.

"You didn't spend a lot of time showing them your hands, I noticed," he said.

"D'accordo," Eli said.

"Goddammit, stop that. Your older brother spent four years trying to be a black, now you're trying to be an Italian. Why don't you play at being a Jew for once?"

"Like you, Dad?"

The urge to hit was very strong, but the truth was stronger. Why argue?

"Okay, you have a point. I'm not the most perfect example. I don't want to get sidetracked onto that. The important thing is those Patrols. You were lucky you didn't have smarter ones. If they'd questioned me first, alone, I might have been tricked into something. You were lucky."

"Kunz."

"What?"

"Coons. Dumb coons. What do you expect?"

It was early in the day and he still had his mail to do. There had been a thousand fights with Eli, and this was not the time for the thousand and first. He shrugged his shoulders. "Why don't you go back to your tapes? I have some work to do at the desk. If I were you, I would still think about a lawyer. Those Patrols might be back." Eli said nothing but went back to his own room.

Levine sat on the sofa, thinking again of the irony of it all, the lectures he had absorbed from his older son on his own racism, his guilt, his ineffectuality. Samuel had been drawn to every vanished interracial organization, each one proclaimed as "the new wave," each one gathering, cresting, and disappearing like the waves themselves—CORE, People Against Racism, Snick, SCOPE, DUPE. All gone. But bad as it had been to be lectured by a self-righteous radical of a son, it was worse to be lectured by a little racist and have him set up housekeeping in the spare room.

Whatever Eli had against blacks his father could not overcome. Maybe it had something to do with Stanton School, but that had just been a little name calling. The pressure from Eli's own friends was too great. Their horror stories of having been frightened in schools, of having jobs shut out during the frenzy of affirmative action, of insults received daily may have been true, but, like Samuel's recitation of the evil he—A. L. Levine himself—had done blacks, it lacked ultimate conviction. Blacks were merely a focus around which young people played out their feelings about themselves and their families. Looking back, Levine was faintly nostalgic for Sam and his lectures. The choice was a narrow one, but he still preferred a sanctimonious radical to a sanctimonious bigot.

He went back to the study and, still worried, shuffled through the personal mail. There in the middle of the pile, all pink borders and little smiling faces, was a letter in Sheila Jo's unmistakable adolescent script. She would be around forty-five now, he thought, opening the letter. How the fuck did she get my address?

ALABAMA, AUTUMN, 1955

In 1955 Levine had for the first time violated whatever commandment it was about adultery. When, six months after their marriage, Helen had said, "My mother has always thought you were wonderful—when we were first going out, she told me, 'A fine person, you'll never have to wonder where he is,'" she, an innocent, had thought it a compliment, but Levine even then knew its cruelty. The old lady knows I'm a nebbish. I'm short, but my face isn't much. The old lady was right, too. What Levine knew about sex he had learned from Helen. Helen did not know much.

He had been willing to accept the world's judgment on his attractiveness until October 18, 1955. He would have been willing to accept it then, too, but the lady in question, the owner of a lending library in Anniston, Alabama, was not. An invitation to discuss recent novels over coffee in her walk-up apartment, made and accepted in all innocence (never again!), turned into an orgy of brushing, touching, glancing, and leering. All hers. Levine plunged stolidly on, talking of Saul Bellow and James Gould Cozzens. Finally, grasping his thigh, she turned off the light and said, "Kiss me."

Levine was surprised. "Here?"

"It's my apartment. Why not?"

"I'm married."

"Don't you think I'm pretty? Don't you even like me?"

"Don't be foolish. Of course I do. I just—"

"Then kiss me."

Levine did. He dimly realized that a woman was seducing him, something he had read about but which, like x-ray vision, he had believed limited to fiction. Her feelings will be hurt if I don't, he rationalized as she unbuckled his belt. Reluctantly, gallantly, ineptly, he screwed her. When this brief encounter (two minutes?) seemed to leave her unfulfilled, he reconsidered his options. He had broken his word to God, Helen, and the children. There was no turning back. Rested, he screwed her again, less reluctantly, less ineptly. This time they both slept. In the morning, pursuant upon some variation which he learned from her, he managed again. He ate an enormous breakfast, sold the Arco system to three small towns, drove his car up to 110 miles per hour on a deserted back road just to see what 110 was like, and drove back to New York happy as a clam. He had discovered sex.

As it turned out, a great many other people made the same discovery at about the same time. Over the next decade many of them wrote about it, talked about it, worried about it. Levine lived it. God had put him down with unlimited travel and an ample expense account at the very time that American men were discovering *Playboy* and women the birth control pill. It was a marvelous time to be an American. Levine learned that women thought him handsome, fascinating. Each conquest swelled his tiny ego and, like coral, built something of nothing. Believing himself to be handsome, he was.

"You're looking good," his old friend Farbstein the socialist said after one of his trips to the South. Farbstein had a run-down two-family house in Brooklyn that was a convenient stopping place between the office and Levine's house on the island.

"I can't complain."

"Tell me," said Farbstein, who had a goatee and looked like Trotsky because he wanted to look like Trotsky, "tell me, are you getting any ass on those trips?"

Usually they talked politics. In fact, they had always talked politics or the city or Jews until now. Farbstein's interest in personal affairs had been limited to the obligatory, "How's the family?" before getting down to interesting topics. He had met Helen once and had not liked her.

"Any ass?"

"That's right. You heard me. I'm not a saint, just because I have this little beard. You know what Trotsky said about women: I'm interested, like anyone else. So?"

Levine shrugged. "What can I say? It's marvelous. You can't get away from it."

Farbstein's eyes sparkled as they did when he talked of Lenin's trip back to Russia from Switzerland. "A lot, eh?"

"Everywhere. Everywhere and everyone."

"That's what I was afraid of," Farbstein said, shaking his gentle, saintly head so his beard twitched ever so slightly. "That's the one thing I was afraid I was missing."

"I'm sorry, but it's true."

"I believe. Tell me, aside from the numbers, is it any different? Are women any ... better ... than they used to be?"

"Saul, remember when we watched basketball and Cousy was the first one in the country in a regular game to dribble behind his back? Remember, his own teammates couldn't tell what was happening. Now you go down to the playground, every fifteen-year-old *Schwartzer* is dribbling behind his back. Saul, it's the same with fucking."

"Better?"

"A quantum jump."

They both sipped their slivovitz and thought long thoughts. From that time on, after every trip Farbstein asked about the women, and Levine would tell him a little. The older man wasn't dirty in the way he asked, and there was no cheap hard-on in his curiosity. He wanted to know more about America, and to remember his own youth on the East Side.

For himself, Levine had to have someone to tell about his adventures. After his first encounter with the lending librarian in Anniston he had hardly been able to keep from telling Helen the good news. He couldn't tell Helen, and, if not Helen, who? His few friends on the island were also friends of hers. His friends at work were mostly cheap-shot salesmen, good enough for the moment but not men to share reflections with. Besides, given a little edge on his personal life, they wouldn't have been above using it to screw him at the company. He laughed when they told dirty jokes and exchanged stories of the women they had had, but he kept silent. For them he was still the nebbish, the scholar who blushed when anyone farted.

Someone had to know that he once screwed three women in one day, that he had humped the daughter of Biloxi's Irv Zeitzman in the family's greenhouse, that he had committed acts natural and unnatural with the black receptionist of an Atlanta law firm. Farbstein knew and believed. He prided himself that he never lied to Farbstein or had to. He barely believed his own life.

Sales trips which once had ended up with Levine back in his motel room, indolently beating off to the accompaniment of *Playboy* or the latest Updike, now were stalking games. Preternaturally alert, Levine scented out new women everywhere he went. He developed his own sexual constituency. He avoided married women, no matter how tempting. Who needed it? His women didn't have as many adjectives as Updike's, but they enjoyed screwing more. Women in their thirties or even late twenties, sometimes single, often divorced, women with intellects or pretensions or politics slightly too lofty for their quiet southern cities were drawn to him. For them Jews were exotic, a little daring. Sometimes, Levine suspected, he was a hidden charity case for a pretty shiksa working out her father's anti-Semitism. It was ludicrous that women should feel guilty about Jews—blacks, maybe—but if they were pretty, why spoil their pleasure?

He did not lie to the women, did not pretend to be in love with them or to be single. Lying would have made sex even easier, like shooting fish in a barrel, but then he would have had to live in the barrel.

So, too, Levine read less about America and saw more of it. Rather than hole up in his room reading the Rivers of America series he sallied out, dapper in his Haspel cord suit, to escort a lady to dinner, a show, and bed. Local lore now came firsthand, often with the monotonous insistence of February rain. You couldn't always tell from a

five-minute chat at the bank or the library or city hall or
the airport if a woman were as smart as you thought.
There had been the teller in Columbus who began every
sentence, "Maybe you won't believe me, but..." There
was the waitress in Jackson City who followed him to the
airport and tried to get on the plane with him.

Mostly, though, there were the awful lives of
semiabandoned women. Single women, their coffee
tables and bureaus festooned with Plasti-frame photographs of nieces and nephews. Divorced women, jammed
in too-small apartments with sullen children. Smart
women, who sensed that early marriage had robbed them
of dazzling careers. Dumb women, who believed exactly
the same thing.

They were marked by bitterness, that fine Middle-
American female bitterness which could not be dissolved
in the masculine solvents of alcohol or deer-hunting or
Saturday night fights or business competition but which
festered until, later, it became a Cause.

"If it weren't for that kid, I'd clear out of this damn
place so fast all you'd see would be a bitty puff of smoke,"
a girl in Macon said.

"He wasn't a bad man as men around here go," the
display girl in St. Louis said. "'Course, men around here
don't go very far."

"'Bout the only time he ever got it up was the time I got
pregnant," a widow in Nashville said. "When he died,
what was the difference? Nothing before, nothing after."

"Court ordered him to pay a hundred bucks a month. I
get it about three times a year. No use in going back to the
court—you can't get blood out of a stone. He never was
much and he won't ever be much." Levine couldn't
remember who said that. Lots of women.

The bitterness would have been impossible to endure if
he had not realized that what had attracted him initially to
these women was a certain sense of capability, of laughter,
of resilience, and that these qualities did in fact exist. They
rushed home from duty-smiling low-paid jobs to take care
of the kids coming back from school, tidy up the house,

do the shopping, change, look pretty, and vanish off into the night with Levine or the night's suitor.

"How does she manage?" the neighbors asked themselves, and Levine learned how she managed. She managed by always smiling, by always looking well-dressed (the happily married could show up at the supermarket in curlers, not the divorcees), and by never complaining. Except to Levine. He had become, he discovered, the instant psychoanalyst of dozens of women.

They told him their troubles for the same reason they screwed. He was sympathetic, intelligent, and he would never, never, tell anyone else in town. To admit troubles in America was as disgraceful as admitting a blow job.

Along with the women Levine met their children. Everybody's poppa. Levine liked children, though some on his Tour tried his patience. Those were the ones who screamed as their mothers tried to edge out the door with their "date," who begged Mommy to read one more story or fetch one more glass of water before leaving, who pinioned Levine to keep him from coming in. Levine became an expert in the psychopathology of early childhood, gauging the year of the divorce or separation from the degree of the kid's neurosis. There were dozens of little Lo's, eight-year-old seductresses who cuddled up to him, grazed his thigh, and asked plaintively if he was going to be their new daddy. Levine was not fooled—they didn't want a daddy, they wanted men. Among the little boys there were cadres of potential gay decorators and curators, too sensitive for noisy mill towns, up in their rooms playing with their home-made theaters. Levine could see them twenty years later, in Greenwich Village, a trace of the South still in their speech. There was a handful of outright psychopaths, little Specks and Whitmores, flaring up in such hatred of their mothers, their mothers' boyfriends, and themselves that the disaster headlines of the future already hung over them.

Mostly, of course, the children were pleasant, a legion of well-scrubbed, slightly curious, slightly indifferent kids, looking up from their television with practiced quick glances to see who Mommy had brought home tonight. There were kids desperate to be loved, their desperation making them all the more unlovable, and there were kids so open, so decent that Levine longed again for his own family and wondered what bizarre force of nature had him courting a hard-shell Baptist schoolteacher in North Carolina. He knew the answer, but every so often he asked the question anyway.

GEORGIA, AUTUMN, 1961

Levine did not allow himself comparisons, but, indeed, Sheila Jo was different. She had been working in the Deeds and Properties Division of the Madison County (Georgia) Department of Courts when he met her. Levine was then hot on the track of a 200-acre woodland property alongside one of the finest bass rivers he had ever fished. Discreet inquiries locally had brought nothing. He journeyed on to the county seat, to the basement, to stacks of files and plats smelling of long-dead arguments, to dust-covered books and records and even dust-covered toilet seats. But behind the desk, smiling up as though she had just emerged from a brisk morning shower, was a young woman whose desk plate proclaimed her to be Sheila Jo Williams.

"'Scuse me, Miss Williams, I wonder if I might have plats one eighty-six through one ninety. That's near Pells Falls, I think."

"You think right." She shook red hair that flashed like a warning blinker. "You from around here?"

"No. It's one eighty-six through ninety I need."

"Just wait a minute, now. I'm still drying my hair. Where y'all from?"

"I'm just a visitor. I'm just curious."

"Maybe your folks grew up on that land and you're doing some—what do they call it?—genealogic research."

"That's about it."

Miss Williams laughed. "Now Mr. Levine, I know you're staying at the Quality Court off the Interstate, and I know you're selling, but what you want with those plats is surely your own business. Will you come with me, please?"

Down rows of record books, stacked high on both sides, down a tiny flight of circular stairs to an even more

stygian level. "Let me turn on the lights," Sheila Jo
Williams said. She flicked a switch, which activated not
bank on bank of cheerless fluorescent spotlights but a
single 50-watt bulb.

"Down here," Sheila Jo Williams said, motioning him
toward the darkest of the catacombs. A dim reflection
shone off her red hair. Levine was suddenly reminded of
Miss Nelligan, who had done the cleaning at the Jewish
Home.

"Now let me see," she said, pulling down Volume 3435
and blowing the dust off. "I think this one right here has
those Pells Falls plats."

She handed it over to Levine, who opened it at
random. At random his left elbow connected with Sheila
Jo Williams's right breast. Sheila Jo did not flinch.

"Let me see now," Levine said, peering toward the page
and increasing the pressure on Miss Williams's breast by 6
pounds per square inch. Miss Williams pushed back,
gently. Levine moved his elbow slowly up and down. Miss
Williams leaned harder. "It's not the volume," Levine
said.

"Leave me get the right one," Miss Williams said,
edging her way back between Levine and the stacks.
Levine stood his ground. Miss Williams's gently arched
buttocks glided in front of Levine. Miss Williams bent
over. Contact! Very gently, Miss Williams pushed
backward, backward against an ever-expanding erection.
Levine slipped his legs apart slightly. Miss Williams
murmured, "Oh," and bent over more. "This may be the
one," she said, spreading her own legs slightly. Levine was
in full, magnificent flight, on takeoff. He leaned a bit
farther forward; she leaned a bit back. All systems go.
Lift-off near. "Oh, please," said Sheila Jo Williams and
hiked up her skirt and, back still to Levine, pulled down
her panties. Levine fumbled, emerged, himself triumphant. Sheila Jo reached behind, grabbed, said, "Oh,
God," bent forward, pushed back, wrong place for a
moment (nothing kinky about Levine), felt Levine slip in,
and began rocking back and forth. She began a
long-drawn-out "Ahaaaa," went rigid, turned pink.

Levine came with an extra thrust, knocking her head against Volume 3421, which popped out the other side of the stack and slammed to the floor. Miss Williams did not move. They stayed joined until she looked over her shoulder, whispered, "Sweet man," and straightened her skirt.

"Nice," he said, kissing her gently on the lips.

"Yes. Wouldn't you like it in a nice, comfortable, private place?"

A soft just-right bed. "God, yes."

"Wait a minute, honey." She disappeared up the steps. He busied himself with plats 186–190. The land was locally owned, and there were just two big parcels he'd have to put together. Nothing to it. After they'd been over to her place and he'd had a chance to tidy up, he'd check out the owners of those parcels with her. If she knew that much about him, she'd know every landowner within a hundred miles. A gold mine. And a great fuck, too. He brushed off his pants.

A moment later he heard her back on the stairs. She came over, smiled, and said, "Let's go."

"Home or my motel?"

"Silly boy. Right in the middle of the day? People wouldn't talk about anything else till Christmas. You come right with me."

He followed her through the half-lit stacks to a door that had been stenciled W. W. HEMPSTONE. She took out a key and they entered a tiny room with an old desk, an old rug, and two bookshelves filled with county agricultural bulletins.

"Here?" he said.

"Here."

"What about Mr. Hempstone?"

"Been dead five years. I'm the only one who has a key, besides Otis, the nigra."

"Right now?" ·

"Right now. The sign on my desk says Miss Williams will be back in fifteen minutes."

Too soon, Levine thought. I'm not old, but I'm not seventeen, either. Give me a twenty-minute intermission, for God's sake.

He started to tell her that he needed more time when she began to kiss his open mouth and kiss and kiss and move against him and slip down her panties. And Levine caught a glimpse of that golden-red snatch, and it was Miss Nelligan all over again, Miss Nelligan who he had once spied on when she took a leak in the dormitory bathroom (strictly forbidden to her, so who was to say spying on her was wrong?), Miss Nelligan whose briefly glimpsed pubic hair dominated his erotic imaginings for five lonely adolescent years, Miss Nelligan who he had dreamed of screwing one thousand, two thousand times, and now he was, and there was no more hesitation about his response to Sheila Jo Williams and he had her down on the rug and her legs were wide apart and he was screwing her and would be able to screw her forever and he jammed it home harder and faster and she began to wail and turn purple and Levine let loose.

When he looked up from her shoulder, they were still on the floor but her head was, unaccountably, under the desk.

"You screwed me under the desk," she said.

"Unintentional."

"I don't see how we could start out in the middle of the floor and end up under the desk," she said. "Were you creeping up ever so little?"

"Not me."

"Maybe the earth moved," she said.

"You know that?" He was surprised.

"Sure. Ingrid Bergman and Gary Cooper."

"It was a book."

"Well, I know that. I finished high school. I read that book too, Mr. Smart-Ass. Any time there's a good movie around here, I look up to see if there's a book of it. We can read and write right well around here."

"I'm sorry."

"I'd be a lot angrier if you weren't such a tally-whacking fool. Now, get yourself together and scoot out the back door."

"Yes, ma'am."

"And come by for dinner tonight. I could show you some of my other books."

"I'd love to."

"Don't be too sure. I'm a good cook, but there's a little boy and a crazy old man at home. You afraid of little boys and crazy old men?"

"Not if you're around."

"It's Fifteen eleven Mason Street. Out toward the city line. Old house, all by itself. Six o'clock. Okay?"

"Okay." He went that night and, over the next several years, many more nights. The little boy grew up and the old man got crazier, but Sheila Jo stayed the same. He never could tell where she began and Miss Nelligan left off. He took an innocent delight in introducing her to Chinese food and Mozart, but in the end, as usual, he learned more than he taught. She was the first to take him to church.

————————

The congregation blasted into the last verse of "Amazing Grace" and Levine, now secure in the words, joined in full throat. Sheila Jo nudged him with her elbow as they sat down.

"See, honey, I told you you'd feel right at home. And you have a real sweet voice, too."

Levine's reply was lost as the minister spread his arms, nodded, and spoke.

"Fellow soldiers in Christ, friends, neighbors, how fine it is to hear those mighty chords again. And how good it is to gather again to praise Christ Jesus. This Sunday, as you must have seen in the Bulletin, we have a special treat. I'm going to get out of your way and let our own Reverend Bill and Nancy Dowthey preach their ministry, the amazing story of their missionary work among the savage natives of the Congo."

There was no applause, but there was a pulse of reverence as Reverend Bill took the pulpit. He was a small missionary, going about five feet six inches, and his voice was high and nasal. Levine reflected that the savage natives of the Congo were hardly getting the pick of missionaryhood.

Reverend Bill was modest about his work, but it was a modesty just barely concealed. He approached missionary work in that same manner that Hersch approached the Arco system. "When we first came to Alfredville, what our local natives call Lomongomala, we had a Sunday school class of seven boys and girls. Today, a mere five years later, we have a hundred and twenty-five children from our village and the surrounding area. When we first arrived, the dispensary treated an average of twenty adults a week. Today we treat twenty adults each day. When we first arrived, average attendance at Sabbath service was . . ."

The figures were impressive. Levine wondered if Reverend Bill worked on commission. Bill droned on, telling of how "our lovely Nancy" with her nurse's training was curing leprosy right and left, while he introduced the natives first to their ABCs and then to Christ.

Then the lights dimmed and a series of color slides, their jungle hues broken regularly by someone's fingerprints, flashed before the awe-stricken Christians. There were shots of children lined up at the dispensary, of Reverend Bill leading the choir ("They sure love to sing; 'Abide with Me' is their favorite"), and of Bill and Nancy sitting for dinner at home, patches of sun coming through the Quonset's tin roof.

The slides ended, a special collection was taken (Levine slipped in a fiver), and, with the minister's blessing upon them, the congregation filed slowly out.

"What'd you think, honey?" Sheila Joe asked in the sanctuary of the great outdoors.

"It was fine. Very interesting."

Sheila Jo laughed her open, solid laugh. "Honey, it was no more fine than a J. C. Penney bridal suite is fine. All those awful hypocrites, sitting there and telling us about the poor heathen Africans, and if a black man ever showed up in that church they'd every one of them fall out in conniptions. Not that I'm for the colored in our churches, but it sure seems funny to go halfway across the world converting them into the Four Corners Methodist Church when your own cleaning lady can't come in to tell you the toilet's overflowing."

Levine was surprised. He had not known her long, but

her political views had always seemed as commonplace as
her accent.

"Honey, you don't believe me, do you? You think I'm
exactly the same as every other little girl around here,
'cept maybe a bit prettier. But if I was the same, I'd hardly
be keeping a little Jew salesman in my bedroom, now,
would I?" She wanted an answer.

"No, I suppose not. Actually, the word is 'Jewish.'"

"Around here it's usually 'kike.' You listen to me, Mr.
Levine. You think it's all a piece here, but I tell you that
when a lady is left by her husband and has to raise a child
by herself and tend after a crazy old man, she sees a
different side of folks than when she's a member of the
Methodist Youth Fellowship or the Young Married
Circle. People just melt away when you're on your own,
and you can't help but think of the people who used to call
themselves your friends. When I saw what happened to
me, that old song came into my head and never went
away."

"What old song?"

"'Jesus Loves the Little Children.' You know—'Jesus
loves the little children,/The little children of the
world,/Yellow, brown, and black and white,/All are
precious in his sight,/Jesus loves the little children of the
world.' We sang it, and the Baptist GAs and RAs sang it,
too." She sang it nicely.

"Why that song?"

"Because I sang it when I was a girl and I knew it was
wrong then and I know why it's wrong now. I don't see
how they can still sing it—'All are precious in his
sight'—and talk about niggers the way they do. Either
treat 'em the same and keep singing the song, or shut up
with the song. You hear?"

Levine heard, and for years the little verse would run
through his mind when he thought of the South and the
blacks. The Movement was just a ripple in the South in
1961, but Sheila Jo knew the contradiction, a contradiction felt by others who had seen the struggle between the
South's ardent Christianity and its ardent racism but
who, perhaps, had never sung that little hymn in Sunday

school. In the hymn the message was not oblique but
direct—"All are precious in his sight"— and from those
whites who had sung the song there would come an
eventual acceptance of the Movement which would end in
ten years a system of segregation that had persisted for a
hundred.

Over the years Levine would think of that Sunday
service as a model for the America which died with Nixon
and Vietnam. When he had first traveled around the
country, there had been a very simple reaction from the
people he met. They were sure of themselves—sure of
their Catholicism or Methodism or Americanism—but
suspicious of him. But after America lost its innocence,
the people lost their confidence. They were unsure of
themselves and sought advice from him. From him—a
Jew, an outsider.

He couldn't count the number of strangers he had met
on planes or in bars who had looked him up and down,
introduced themselves, and said, "Now about this
abortion business. I'm not sure. I'm a Methodist, but..."
In the old days the Methodists *would* have been sure.
The Catholics too. Now they were all gun-shy, like kids
whose homework has been ridiculed in class.

At the church service he had seen actual missionaries, a
breed once as common in America as streetcar conduc-
tors and as rapidly extinct. True, in the last spasms of the
wars in the Congo and in Bolivia and in Vietnam, a few
American missionaries were always flushed out just as the
insurgents took over. They would turn up on the
television news shows, curiously archaic, photographed
at some godforsaken airstrip, saying something about
"leaving behind our life's work." How strange that they
had been there at all, all that time, like the Japanese
soldiers emerging into the sunlight on Okinawa every five
years after the war ended. Didn't the missionaries know
that their war had ended years ago?

It was a dirty word by the late sixties: missionary. But
only a country supremely and naïvely sure of itself could
have sent those waves of pink-cheeked country boys to
teach the Asians about religion. As he grew older, Levine

thought of that innocence and confidence and wished he had been more charitable, somehow, toward the Reverend Bill. The missionary spirit lived on in America, but it survived in men and women who were far too sophisticated to realize what it was or call it by its real name. The more Levine lived in politics, the more often he would find it.

OHIO, AUTUMN, 1974

There were many bad places to be in October, 1974, and Sandusky was among the worst. The downtown that had lured farmers and apple growers every Friday and Saturday night for fifty years was already a frightening mix of abandoned stores and massage parlors. Driving in from the airport, Levine caught a glimpse of an alcoholic Negro propped up against an empty building. Like the man, the building was devastated but had an air of lingering authority. On the lawn, the glass broken and the letters missing, was the ecclesiastic signpost:

> AME Methodist C ur h
> Rev L st r Willia
> unday Tex

The building had a round dome, a funny shape for a church. From the corner of his eye Levine saw a great six-pointed star in stained glass and felt a deep chill. Maybe because it was almost dark and it was another strange city and he was by himself again, or maybe because of the abandoned synagogue, he felt it all coming to an end. He had never been to Sandusky before, but he knew of the great ore boats and grain loaders and he knew that people had lived and loved in that city, and that Jews had huddled there and started shops and gone to school and sent their kids to the University of Chicago or Northwestern, and that the kids had become lawyers or programmers and hadn't come back. Even to run the stores, they hadn't come back. He knew that the blacks had come, first before Emancipation, when Ohio was red-hot New England Abolitionist, and then in the 1930s when the mills and the mud trades opened up just a bit more, and then even more during the war, when the mills would take anyone, especially a two-hundred-pound black with an eighth-grade Louisiana education who couldn't pass the army's SPA Basic Literary Test but who could help empty a boxcar in half an hour. He knew that in the fifties the hillbillies had come up from Kentucky, even cruder and more frightened than the blacks, no city smarts at all, driving back the 600 miles every weekend so they could sit on the front steps of dirty shacks with shit-stinking backyards, hunt squirrels with their sons and brothers, screw their wives, get drunk in town, and drive back to Sandusky. Worse off than the blacks, Levine thought. Like the Puerto Ricans, shuttling back and forth from San Juan, never making it the way they should in New York because San Juan was too close.

All those people into this city, Levine thought, and now even the blacks and the hillbillies are gone and it's a shell. In October of 1974 there had already been one fuel crisis and the auto people were beginning to catch on to the fact that, no, they would not be able to sell four cars to every family, indeed they might no longer be able to sell even one, and the mills were slowing down and where had all the blacks and hillbillies gone?

They certainly had not gone to the Holiday Inn, where the president of the United States was speaking that night. Levine parallel-parked his rented Firebird and, edging his way past several blank-eyed Secret Servicemen, peeked in at the grand ballroom. Table after table of good-natured, white-haired, slightly plethoric, stroke-prone Republicans and their pompadoured women stretched before him. Though the meal was well under way and the Republicans were eating with admirable vigor, many of the places were empty and some tables were completely vacant. Levine turned and headed toward the bar. It was your average Holiday Inn bar, but it hummed with a special presidential hum.

Levine decided to sit at the bar. He figured there'd be someone in the bar he knew and, perhaps, someone he'd like to talk to. On the other hand, he might be cornered by some nasty little slob with a bitch about the 1968 campaign, and if you were at a table or a booth you couldn't walk out on them as easily as at the bar.

"Tequila on the rocks, please, and a glass of crushed ice on the side."

He said it softly, like a gentle cast upstream on a nice pool where you know—know!—that the big trout lie hungry and where they can be spooked by the whip of the line or a fleeting shadow. It was a gentle cast, and it worked.

"Levine, what in God's name brings you here?"

He turned around to encounter the truest, dullest face in Christendom. It was a face of memorable mediocrity, the face of a thousand security guards and desk clerks and bookkeepers, a face wiped clean of any curiosity or experience or longing. It was a face you could meet every day for 364 days and not recognize on the 365th. Levine remembered it instantly.

"Arthur Jones! Good to see you." They shook.

"You didn't answer my question."

Arthur Jones covered state politics for the *Plain Dealer*. He was as ordinary as his name or his face. He had an ordinary Ohio background, had gone to the ordinary university, graduated just in time to fumble his way through World War II as an ordinary private, and had entered civilian life as a copyboy for the *Plain Dealer*. He had never worked for anyone else. He had left the state four times in twenty-five years, twice for his children's weddings, twice for political campaigns. He kept close counsel and knew everything worth knowing about Ohio politics.

"Look, Arthur, I just happened to be driving by and I saw all those helicopters and television vans, so I asked myself, What's going on that I should know about? And here I am."

"Tell me the truth."

"The truth—so help me—is that I was in Cleveland on business and I read that Ford would be campaigning here for what's-his-name, and I thought, I've never seen this president, maybe it would be a good idea to take a look. They come and go so fast these days."

"That they do."

"So I thought I'd take a look at this one. Listen a bit."

"Good idea. What were you doing in Cleveland?"

"That was a business trip. Electronics."

"Come on, A.L., I know you sold your last bit of Arco years ago. You're living off your income, for God's sake. You were in Cleveland for Strauss, I know that. You talked to Stokes, you talked to Harper, you tried to deal for some quiet at that Kansas City convention. Tried to keep them in their place."

"If you know all that, how did I do?"

Jones leaned forward. "I'll tell you how you did. You got nowhere. You people are trying to keep the blacks in line for Kansas City and you've got nothing to offer, not when you don't have any poverty money to hand them or an air base or a federal judge. You're dealing with super-coons, now. They don't roll over for a little bit of rewording of the charter or some nice promises about being first in line the next time you people elect a president. Lord knows, the next time you people elect a president could be 1992."

Levine shrugged. "So?"

"So? So I'm right, aren't I?"

"A lucky guess. Come, it looks like the guest of honor is about to deliver himself."

They went back upstairs and edged into the balcony press section. Levine was with Jones, and even the officious hangers-on at the press gate didn't challenge Jones. Sitting row after row in the balcony, smoking, reading the sports pages, sometimes glancing again through the advance text of the president's speech, were a hundred or more reporters. There was a sprinkling of editors and a handful of Washington columnists, taking their obligatory dip in mainstream America. Most of the columnists were bright, small-town boys themselves, and their nostalgia for the simpler past usually lasted only three days out of Georgetown. They used the travel time wisely. If they spent a whole day in Cleveland, with a half-hour trip to Strongsville, the story would be datelined "Strongsville." More authentic, somehow.

Levine recognized some of the press from 1968 and

1964, others from Washington parties and conferences. He nodded to friends but kept his eyes low. He didn't want to turn this into some kind of reunion and start greeting every hack he had ever shared a drink with. He wanted to talk to Jones and to listen to the president.

Ford talked in an easy, jovial way. It was, Levine thought, almost foolish. The self-deprecatory jokes, the football references, the homilies about hard work. The president started to sweat, became emotional. He roared clumsily into a commercial for the party's candidate for the House from the Sandusky district. Commercial, Levine thought. That's the problem. He knew all the crap about the president's being the leader of his party, and he knew the political history of the country as well as any other journeyman party worker, but, still, there was something offensive about what he was hearing, the president's shilling for a second-rate congressman. A president should work for his party, surely, but for such a schmuck, such a nonentity? Maybe Sir Laurence Olivier has the right to do commercials, but should he? Just for the money? If the president gets so worked up for such an asshole, such a nothing, what emotion is he going to have left over for the Russians, the Arabs? Did he have to sweat for a second-term congressman?

The audience liked it, though. They clapped and cheered, and the reporters annotated their copies of the speech, indicating which lines had brought applause. There was nothing the matter with the people in the audience, and Levine knew that in small numbers he would find them decent people, some with unexpected flashes of humor and esoteric passions like Chinese jade or antique barbed wire or baroque music, and yet, seeing them all together, all white, all middle-aged or elderly, he felt the same creeping despair that had swept him in Sandusky itself, the sense that these people lived in a dream world, that they had seen their city and their past vanish and they had no idea, not even a hint, that their future was about to go under too. They were not bigots, they were too decent to be bigots; they were the kind of people who, as tourists, came to Washington during

Abernathy's awful Resurrection City and pressed their noses against the fences and asked the hostile, angry blacks, tell us what we can do, in voices so innocent that even the blacks said, Oh, shit, come in and we'll rap. They were true innocents still, wrapped in layers of unconcern, and the president was spinning another layer around them even now. Thinking of the chill of downtown Sandusky, the smell of a dying town, Levine remembered the family drunk who shows up at every wedding bringing with him the curse of ultimate failure. No wonder the people in the grand ballroom did not want to look back at Sandusky. They had failure just over their shoulders, like everyone else.

The speech ended, the reporters made dirty jokes, pulled out their typewriters, or hurried toward the phones, and Jones and Levine went back to the bar.

"What was the most interesting thing about the speech?" Jones asked.

"To me the most interesting thing was that there were two hundred empty seats."

For a moment something rippled across Jones's face. Surprise.

"You know, I was thinking the same thing. Here he is, president by a fluke, in power just a few months, the most important man in the world, and they couldn't get five hundred people to come and hear him."

"Maybe it was the tab. What was it, fifty bucks a plate?"

"It was twenty-five, but A.L., you know that doesn't mean beans. They give those tickets away. Always have. They find they have an extra two hundred or so, they call up their friends, they call up precinct workers, they call anyone and tell them, 'Here, you and your wife have a fifty-dollar dinner on me. It's all paid for, and you can get to hear the president and meet a lot of important people at the same time.'"

"And so?"

"So! So! Don't give me the Hebrew thing again, A.L. You know what the 'so' is. The 'so' is that they couldn't give tickets away. What's today, anyway?"

"Wednesday."

"So it's 'Kojak.' That's what the so is. If it was Monday it would be football and if it was Tuesday it would be M*A*S*H and you name it."

"That's too bad."

"Too bad." Jones's face was suddenly suffused with passion. "A.L., I don't have to bull you like I bull my editors. Nothing's too bad about it. Tell me, did you learn anything tonight? Were you inspired tonight? Did you have some good laughs tonight—more than you'd get with Johnny Carson or Archie Bunker?"

"No."

"Of course not. What makes you think the American people are dumber than you, that they have some hard instinct that makes them love being bored in one seat, a bad seat at that, for three straight hours, when they could be home watching what is called high-priced talent on TV or making cider or jumping their wives. Nothing is too bad about it at all. The people are just too smart."

Levine nodded. "It's more than that, though."

"Like?"

"Like people don't care. Too many presidents dead or resigned. We've gone through five presidents since 1959. Look, in 1960 I was just an amateur in politics. Had done nothing, given nothing. But I was interested in Kennedy. He was different, so I got interested. I didn't fall in love with him, understand, I didn't mortgage my house and march off to Washington. But I got interested and I helped. And, back then, I knew people, forty-five-year-old men, who gave up their jobs and went to Washington. They didn't hold out for the cabinet, they didn't have lots of money socked away, they just thought they could help. Then in 1968 I saw a lot of young people with McCarthy. Frankly, they were mostly jerks, but they tried hard and they thought they could help. First we burned out the middle-aged people, then the young people. Then we had Nixon. Jesus, if you were Pavlov and trying to find a way to condition people to hate politics, you'd invent Nixon. Does anyone care any more?"

Jones drank slowly. "That's what I can't tell my

editors. I'm a political reporter, they're political editors. How can I tell them people don't care, that my job is like reporting soccer to the people in Massillon. They don't want to hear about it. They want football. In Rio people kill over soccer, but in Massillon they don't. For politics, my editors live in Rio and the readers are in Massillon."

Levine shook his head. "I see that, just like I see the closed-up stores and the empty restaurants, and it scares me. I see the same thing in Washington now. There's no young people coming up."

Jones was a contained man, not given to affection. Still, he put his arm around Levine's shoulder and almost hugged him. "Look, A.L., don't worry. All this moves in cycles. For a while, with Kennedy, McCarthy, people expected too much of politics. They expected too much of politicians—they wanted people who weren't just good men but great men, handsome men, rich men, amusing men, brilliant men. It didn't work out, and people backed away. There's a whole group of people, the ones who were young between 1960 and 1970, who will never get hot for politics again. But that leaves a hole, and after a while people are going to start to move into that hole."

"Who? When?"

"You know, A.L., I don't know why I'm bothering to give all this wisdom to some little Jew who's supposed to know all the answers anyway."

Levine smiled. "It's because you like to show off that you're smarter than me."

"That's just part of it."

"It's because I buy you drinks."

A little smile worked across Jones's face. "That's funny. No, I think maybe it's because I trust you and I think you'll use what I tell you intelligently."

"So?"

"So look around again. We've burned up the young people, the cause people, the coast people. Kennedy used up the East Coast, Nixon killed the West. On the coasts there's too much to do besides politics. But you take the cities out here, say a hundred to five hundred thousand people. Or in the South—the South would be good too.

Watch this Jimmy Carter—he's on to it. The cities are all filled with hotshot forty-five-year-old lawyers who are tired of being on local TV, who are getting sick of the country club. They all have forty-year-old wives who've never met an ambassador or Walter Cronkite. The husband and the wife, maybe they'd both like something on the side. If you're that kind of successful forty-five-year-old guy, you don't pick up and go to New York or join the Peace Corps or quit the firm to weave belts in San Diego. You don't become a missionary and go off to Africa to convert the heathen. You go to Washington. That is, you go if you're asked. It used to be a New York–Boston thing. Yale University, Harvard Law, ten years in a good New York firm, then serve your country for four years as an assistant secretary of something or other in Washington. Usually you went back to New York or Boston; sometimes you stayed. People really did that. But that well's dried up. You just have to find other wells."

"When?" Levine asked.

"Hell, some of them are ready now. Like the lady schoolteacher from Akron, the one my brother spent a week with at the Ohio Dental Convention in 'fifty-eight, they've never been asked before. But if I had to guess, I'd say the crop'll really be ready in another eight to twelve years. Let this guy"—he gestured toward the grand ballroom—"let him bore them another couple of years, and let things get worse a bit with the next guy, and pretty soon people will be interested in politics again."

"I'll remember that," Levine said.

The meeting ended just before midnight. Edwards had dropped by just for a moment; the National Chairman was supposed to appear neutral before the convention. McKelvin and Jessington had done most of the talking. McKelvin had agreed to be the up-front man and convention floor manager. Frank Sweeney, a ferret-faced corporation lawyer from Buffalo, agreed to take the job of campaign treasurer. His father had been an alderman for thirty years. He was honest, knowledgeable, and totally Irish. He knew the Jewish and Wasp big money but wasn't part of it.

Sweeney listened while McKelvin urged the job on him. He was the only one they all could trust, McKelvin said. He had good contacts in the big states and with the older party leaders. People trusted him. They respected him. Besides, the treasurer's job would give him a chance to build a national reputation, break out of Buffalo, make his law firm a national influence. It was his great chance to serve his nation.

"In other words," Sweeney said, his narrow face expressionless, "you want a token Irishman. That right?"

"Now just a minute, son," McKelvin began.

"You're right," Levine said. "Do you have any objections?"

"No," Sweeney said. "I just wanted to get it straight and to get the ground rules."

"Let's hear your side," Bell suggested.

"It's easy. I don't wany anyone jerking me off. I don't want anyone promising things to people if they come across with money and then not being able to deliver. I'm not going to make promises to people, if that's the rule, but no one makes promises without checking them with me. That goes for Mr. Levine too. Okay for you guys to make promises you can't keep, you'll all find something else to do, but if this campaign comes apart, I'm the one has to go back to Buffalo and practice law. People think I'm a liar, I'm lost. Agreed?"

Jessington muttered, "Fair enough."

"That's not all. I know the campaign finance law backwards and forwards. I know the amendments. I know what parts you can and what parts you can't. I know the in-between, too. I know the parts where, if you play around the edges, take money that a guy gave to his friends just so they could give it to the campaign just so he could exceed the individual level, I know the parts where some wise-ass kid in the Justice Department could maybe want to indict and where some old judge who's trying to make a track record with God because he's already had one heart attack, where some old judge might convict. I remember all those Nixon people going off to jail in their striped ties and imitation Ivy Leagues suits. And I don't want any part of them. I spent too much of my childhood at Danbury and Lewisburg, going down with my father for weekends, visiting his friends who got picked up on one thing or another.

"My father was always very loyal to his friends in the slammer. We visited Curley. On the way down he told me, 'Francis'—he was formal about my name—'Francis, to tell the truth I was never much friends with the governor and, indeed, I never carried much admiration for him. To my mind the man has been painted as a rogue-saint when, if the truth be told, he was not much more than a larcenous politician with an extravagant vocabulary. But all that is beside the point—the *point* is that I did work with him, I did know him, and he did do some favors for me, little favors that have long been paid back. But when a man is incarcerated, Francis, things prey on his mind. He tends to forget what he has been paid back and to believe that people are avoiding him because he happens to be on the wrong side of the steel bars. And rather than have a man think that about me—or about himself—I feel I should go an extra step. It's a kind of blessing, I hope."

"He said that, did he?" Levine asked.

"Indeed he did. And it made a fearful impression in my mind," Sweeney added. "Being a lawyer, as you others know, one has the occasion to spend some business time with the incarcerated, and it is a pitiful condition. When friends of mine from the Assembly or the Council have been put away, I have gone the extra step to visit them. But I will be goddamned if my friends will ever have to spend their Sunday afternoons trekking out to see me, nor will I have my own dear children, dressed up like it was Easter, come to me sniveling through the bars. Never. No edges, gentlemen, no edges."

"Eloquent," Jessington said, taking up the cadence that rose and fell through Sweeney's outburst. "And might you be running for office yourself one day?"

Sweeney blinked and halted. "Yes, perhaps I did go on a bit. But I'm deadly serious, gentlemen. I take the fall for no one."

Levine waved his hand. "Look, that's just what we wanted to hear. For my own part, who needs it? Was I sitting around for years trying to become president? Let me tell you, the answer is no. And so now I have a chance, it's a quirk, I've got to live with myself and my family afterwards."

"And your God," Sweeney added.

"That too," Levine said.

Bell surreptitiously crossed himself, whispered *"Olav shalom,"* and winked at Levine. Levine gazed furiously at the ceiling. "Well, now that we've established that we're all incorruptible," Bell said, "could we get along to the primary schedule?"

The others nodded, and Bell dragged over a blackboard-sized calendar. They worked back and forth, filling in dates, arguing about priorities, until the meeting ended.

———————

"We got a lot done," Levine said, as Bell picked up the piles of paper and pushed the blackboard calendar to the side of the room. He looked at the calendar and carefully erased all names of cities, mayors, and governors. You could never tell about the cleaning people.

"I suppose so," Bell said.

"How do you mean, 'suppose'?"

"I don't know. I guess I think your time is too important to be used working out scheduling and all that crap."

"Look, I know scheduling. I helped with it on McCarthy, McGovern."

"I know that. You were scheduling when I was in law school. It's different now. You're not a technician, you're the candidate."

"And so I'm supposed to give up everything I know, become some kind of puppet that my friends move across the country the way they see fit? No, thanks, mister. I know something, I'm going to use it."

Bell was irritated. "Sure, sure, but don't use it the way you did tonight. Stay away from the fine print. Let them sweat over the schedule. They bring it to you, you check it out, add, subtract, change it around. Let's face it, ninety percent of it is mechanical: how many days you can spend in one part of the country, how to connect with the big local events, what the fuel allotment is going to be. Have them work out the ninety percent, you save yourself for the other ten."

Levine nodded. "You make sense. I was foolish."

"No, you weren't. It's just that you've never run for president before."

Levine laughed. "President, schmesident. I haven't even run for Congress. Come, let's have a drink."

———

They took a cab to a flat, modern hotel in the reconstructed section of downtown Washington. Vast acres of concrete lay on either side of them. Monumental streetlights glared down on pedestrian arcades empty of pedestrians.

"Mussolini architecture," Levine said. Bell smiled.

In the hotel they took the elevator downstairs, walked

through empty corridors past empty conference rooms
with empty names—the Madison Room, the Jefferson
Room—and toward a faint murmur of voices and music.
At the end of a corridor a sign above two imitation-brass
doors proclaimed THE PRESIDENTIAL LOUNGE. Levine
opened the door, nodded to the hostess, and was shown to
a table in the corner.

Bell looked around. There were no imitation colonial
signs or seafaring artifacts on the wall. There was no
plastic. The walls were wood-paneled, the tables old
wooden desks with the drawers removed. The desks were
a gimmick, but they were big and solid and did not teeter
when you rested your elbows on them. A guitarist and a
flutist played back and forth to each other. The only
concession to the hotel's colonial theme was a large open
fireplace at one end of the room. A well-tended fire
burned with just the right amount of noise and warmth.

"This is fine, just fine," Bell said. "I didn't know it
existed."

"You're not supposed to. When they leased out the
franchise in this concrete desert, they had enough sense to
offer the bar to Walter, who used to be at the Hay-Adams.
Walter said he'd take it, but he had to have control of the
room."

"Another Sweeney!"

Levine laughed. "Right. You know how bartenders
are. They all want to be owners or managers. And you
know how hotel chains are. They tell you what kinds of
Scotch you buy, how big the shots should be, what the
decoration will be. They hire the music, move the
musicians from one of their places to the next. Walter said
no, if he was going to run it, it was going to be his place
from top to bottom. Someplace in their organization was
a someone smart enough to know a good thing. They got
Walter. Walter got his place. Nothing else in the hotel is
worth a damn. Walter brings in enough money, has
enough out-of-towners who actually stay at the hotel to
be close to his bar, to keep the whole place going. When I
get depressed about the country, I just think of Walter.

Somehow human beings still make their way through the cracks."

There was a lingering touch of winter in the springtime evening outside, and they both had hot rum drinks.

"Try the Old-Fashioned," Levine suggested, and when it was brought it tasted to Bell the way God had intended Old-Fashioneds to taste. It was not an old ladies' fruit punch but a solid belt of bourbon with a hint of sweetness and a true bitterness.

"Nice," Bell said.

"Everyone else in town uses a prepared mix," Levine said. "Walter fixes his own—every night. It's the little things that make a difference."

"Like in the campaign?"

"That's right, like in the campaign. Either a thing is genuine or it's not. People can spot it. Lincoln was right. One thing he didn't say, though, is what happens when some of the people find out that they've been fooled some of the time. When that happens, they won't believe you on anything. You've got three kids and a satisfied wife; they think you're a fag in disguise. You show them proof you graduated from college; they figure you quit in eighth grade and the FBI worked up a phony diploma for you. You can't lie to people. Exaggerate, yes, maybe they expect that. But no lies. In a way, we're still paying off Nixon's lies."

"You really believe that, don't you?" Bell said.

Startled. "Of course. Don't you?"

Bell shook his head.

"You're too young to be so cynical. An old person like me, it's okay. Why you?"

"I've been around politicians too long."

"And where have I been?"

"You know, A.L., this is ass-backward. I'm a clean-cut, middle-class young Wasp from the Midwest. You're an ugly old Jew. How is it that I'm corrupting you?"

"Maybe because you're so far ahead you've ended up behind. Every once in a while it pays to trust people."

"People, maybe, but politicians?"

Levine grunted. "You're beginning to sound like me already. Yes, politicians. In 'seventy-two I got a phone call from the other side, the Republicans. 'Levine,' this guy says, 'get rid of your office messenger.' I was astonished. The messenger was a drooling dunderhead— no education, no background, no nothing. He came through some employment agency. For all he knew he might just as well have been delivering coffee in the Agriculture Department as running memos for McGovern. So I ask this guy from the other side, an individual who was no particular friend of mine, why I should do this. And the individual, he puts on an accent and says, 'Dun't esk!' So I fired the messenger. Later it comes out that he had a photographic memory, he was part of that Operation Touchstone, whatever they called it—"

"Gemstone."

"That one. And the point of it was that the man who called me, he never could have been implicated in it. He wasn't trying to protect himself or make points with me. Because what I'm saying is that what this messenger, this Benedict Arnold, picked up, it wasn't only things that would hurt McGovern, it was things that could have been very damaging to me. Personally. Financially. There were things that could have made money for the individual who warned me. And so a couple of years later I see the individual who warned me, we're at a meeting together, and I ask him how come, and he told me. 'I'm a shit,' he said, 'but not that kind of a shit.'"

"Honor among thieves," Bell suggested.

Levine shook his head. "More than that. Honor among people. That person couldn't come out and tell me, 'I did it because I'm an honorable person.' That would have sounded foolish then. Now, too. So he made a joke of it. There are many other honorable people that I've met in politics. It's a shame they have to pretend they're crooks."

"Who's pretending?"

"Don't be a wise guy. It doesn't sit well with such a pretty face. Another round?"

Bell nodded. As the waiter left, Bell gestured around

them. "You really believe it matters, don't you? You really think it matters to these people who the president is, what laws get passed, what we do with Mexico?"

"It doesn't matter to you?"

"Christ, no. No more than it matters to a greyhound whether he's chasing a mechanical rabbit or a real live bunny. What matters is the chase. The greyhound lives for it."

Levine thought. He spoke very slowly. "No, you have it all wrong. Certainly the Jewish part. If you think, as you said, that you are corrupting me with cynicism, that somehow it *should* be the other way around, you are wrong. True, we Jews are wary people. We look at the rules of a game very cafefully. We look for the fine print, for ways that we might be dealt out, for ways, sometimes, where we might bend a rule to work our way in. But we always play. We do not sit the game out. And we do not play merely to pass the time. We play because the game itself is important. There may not be a God, but there is a purpose. Part of the purpose surely is for men to be better. Part of being president is to help them be better."

Bell shook his head. "Where did you get all that? From your father?"

"No, from an orphanage."

NEW YORK, SUMMER, 1935

Few adults ever saw the inside of the Jewish Home for Children. This was understandable; most of the children lacked not only parents but any other close relative. Jewish uncles or aunts or grandparents did not readily let strangers raise their children. Still, the Depression was the Depression, and the Home was crowded. When, in rare cases, relatives existed, they were poor and made the long drive out to White Plains with difficulty. The visit itself was never pleasant. As delightful as touring a home for incurables, as beautiful as a visit to a tire factory, was a trip to the Jewish Home for Children.

Yet visitors sometimes straggled in. Humble, accented, lumpy in winter coats worn all year round, they would come out on Sundays and, embarrassed, pick up an equally embarrassed child and drive him home for a hot meal and a trip to the Bronx Zoo.

Levine had his share of these distant relatives, and there would be Saturday afternoons when Mr. Ushofsky, the hairy, bow-legged math teacher who ran his cottage, would call him into the office.

"Albert, you're going to have visitors tomorrow."

"My name isn't Albert, Mr. Ushofsky. The records are wrong."

"So long as you're in my cottage your name is Albert. Did you hear me about the visitors?"

"Yes, sir. Who are they?"

"How should I know? They're your relatives, aren't they?"

Visiting hours on Sunday began at eleven. Levine, dressed in his best, least-smelly corduroy waited in the reception room with twenty other boys. There were 150 boys in the cottage, which looked like a textile mill. The twenty boys, all dressed in the secondhand clothes that labeled them "orphan kids" in White Plains as surely as a six-pointed star, waited for relatives they would rarely recognize. A shabby couple would come into the reception room and shout, "Moscovitz? Sheldon Moscovitz?" Moscovitz, shamefaced, runny-nosed, would shuffle forward. The couple would peer at him. The man would say, "That's him, that must be him," and the three of them would leave together.

Sometimes the visitors did not come. Levine would wait hours, looking up as each adult face appeared in the doorway. If the boy was popular or if, as rarely happened, he had attractive relatives, Mr. Ushofsky himself would escort the visitors to the reception room and point out the proper orphan. Levine did not care particularly about visitors, but when they were promised and did not come he would sit in an agony of shame as the other boys were led off around him. You were not permitted to go back to your bunk once a visitor had phoned. As the others left with their visitors, the rejects huddled together, playing gin, telling dirty jokes, laughing loudly. Once the reception room narrowed down to Levine and an evil child named Flegg. Then a young woman called for Flegg and Levine was alone in the reception room with the Chinese checker board without marbles and the deck of forty-seven cards and the old copies of *Liberty*. He cried.

One visitor was reliable. When Levine was twelve years old, Cousin Max had begun to visit. Max Lifstein was a distant relative of Levine's mother. He was married to a pleasant, fat woman who, childless, spent most of the day cleaning her three-room apartment on Chandler Street. Max was a cut above the other relatives who visited, certainly above those who visited Levine. He was, the boy realized, clean. The other visitors were not. Too, Max owned and drove a car. This was because he had no children to support.

Cousin Max worked in Metropolitan Hospital, and sometimes he would take Levine along to work.

"Are you a doctor?" the boy asked on their second trip to the hospital.

"Yes and no, yes and no," said Cousin Max. "When you grow up you will realize that the medical profession is very complex. There are doctors who take care of people, and there are other doctors that help the doctors that take care of people. I am one of those. Technically, however, I am not a doctor."

Levine understood. There were so many people working in Metropolitan Hospital they could not all be doctors. Cousin Max kept a clean white doctor's coat in the hospital. He would go to his locker room and change into the coat and come back to the lobby where the boy sat huddled under a great mural of Pasteur holding a test tube to the light.

"Wait here, boychik," Cousin Max said. "I have to finish some work. I'll be back. Be quiet."

You had to be quiet. The lobby of Metropolitan Hospital was hushed and solemn. Fearful, Levine waited, sometimes for two or three hours, until Cousin Max came back. He would be smiling and apologetic.

"Sorry to be late, boychik. He had an important case. Let's go get something to eat." Then they would have a sandwich in the cafeteria. Cousin Max nodded and smiled to the nurses and the doctors. Because Levine had been a good boy, he would be allowed coffee. At the orphanage coffee was forbidden.

After he had visited the hospital two or three times, Levine grew less frightened. The woman at the information desk, Miss Brindle, was nice to him. She had gray hair and glasses, and when she saw him waiting in the corner under the painting she would bring him magazines to read. *The New Yorker* had jokes.

"Do you want to be a doctor?" Miss Brindle said. She smiled.

"I don't know. I'm just a child."

"What an extraordinary thing to say. Of course, you're a child. That doesn't mean you can't think about what you want to do when you grow up. What do you want to do when you grow up?"

"First, I want to leave the Home." He told her about it.

He had never talked about it with anyone else, certainly not cheerful Cousin Max. She understood, a little.

"Besides, I'm poor," he said.

"Poor people can become doctors," Miss Brindle said angrily. "You must study very hard."

"I do. I don't think that boys...from where I live...are doctors."

"I can hardly believe that. Jewish people make excellent doctors. There are some on the staff of this hospital. Even if it were so about the Home, you might be the first. I will bring you some more magazines."

She did, and she brought books that he could keep. The books had her name in them, but she wrote below it, *To A. L. Levine—with best wishes for a fine future, Alice Brindle.* He was glad she used his initials and that she had not called him Master.

One day, waiting for Cousin Max to reappear, he was seized by great waves of nausea. He and Max had eaten eclairs from a sidewalk stand just outside the hospital. The nausea came and wouldn't go away. Then he felt diarrhea beginning. He was terrified and humiliated—he was going to be sick and he would embarrass Cousin Max. The hospital floor was marble and it was cleaned and waxed twice a day. He would ruin it. He tried to think the sickness away, but it stayed and got worse. He went over to Miss Brindle's information desk.

"I'm sick. I'm going to throw up. Please, please get my cousin." He started to cry.

"Poor dear, sit right down. What's your cousin's name again?"

"Max. Max Lifstein."

"Of course. Here, I'll put this wastepaper basket right alongside you until we get your cousin. Don't be frightened."

Miss Brindle walked across the lobby to the other corner, where the switchboard was. She spoke to the switchboard lady. The switchboard lady shook her head. Miss Brindle talked to her again and pointed at Levine. A moment later the public-address system boomed, "Max

Lifstein, emergency. Max Lifstein, please call the operator." Max's name echoed down the marble corridors.

A minute later Max hurried into the lobby. Miss Brindle explained. "I'll get him right over to Dr. Sterling in the OPD," Max said. He picked up the boy and carried him down the corridor. They went through swinging doors and into an area marked off by frosted glass. Max lay him down on an examining table and he vomited over his cousin's white jacket.

"That's all right, that's all right, you'll feel better now," Max said. Levine looked up at his cousin's face. Max was frightened. A young doctor with a red face came over.

"This is what you might call my nephew," Max said. "He just got sick. He vomited. It could be his appendix."

The doctor started asking Levine questions about how old he was and where he went to school. All the time he kept pushing on the boy's belly, flexing his knees back and forth, bending his neck.

"Look, Max," the doctor said. "His belly's as soft as a baby's bottom. No rebound. McBurney's point is negative. I'm surprised at you, Max; you don't usually miss a diagnosis. Tell me, young man, did you eat anything unusual today?"

"Not unusual. We had some eclairs."

"Eclairs!" The doctor was happy. "Max, acute staph enteritis. We're going to have to send you back to medical school. You lie down, young man. We're going to give you a shot. I hope that when you grow up you can make a better diagnosis than your cousin."

The shot made him sleepy. He vomited again and he had diarrhea and then he was better. In the car going back to the apartment, he looked up from the back seat where he was drowsing and asked, "Cousin Max, did you go to medical school?"

"Not exactly," Max said. "You might, though."

He fell asleep and never remembered arriving at the apartment. Back at the Home he read the books Miss Brindle gave him and studied hard. He never liked the sight of blood and forgot about going to medical school.

Years later, in college, talking to a friend, he realized that Max Lifstein had been a porter at the hospital. Usually Max cleaned the floors. When they were short of orderlies, he helped load patients on the stretchers. Jobs were scarce in the Depression.

"Okay, I can see that you've had a hard life," Bell said. "I knew from the bio data we've got. In fact, I'll admit I'm touched. You don't talk much about your childhood, and I guess I'm guilty of reading over the word 'orphanage' and thinking it's some kind of seedier St. Paul's or Exeter. The story hit me. But is it going to hit the public?"

Most of the other drinkers had left or settled into silence. The guitar of fatigue and boredom. Levine's angry whisper rose above them.

"Philip, Philip! You're not stupid. That story isn't for the public. Do you think I'm going to come along like some shuffling old Jew, asking people to feel sorry for him? Look, as soon as the blacks started asking people to feel sorry for what happened two hundred years ago, everyone got so mad they forgot what was happening right then. The same with the Indians, a bunch of fucking sore losers. I should feel sorry for Indians? My ancestors bought slaves, stole hunting grounds? Look, I'll tell you—not only did my ancestors not do such things, but until I was twenty I never met anyone whose ancestors had. In this country, as soon as you ask people to feel sorry for you, to be guilty for something that happened even two years ago, much less two hundred, you're dead. Americans don't go for losers. You should read history, Philip. We don't much go for the past, either. The country runs on the present and the future. You know that old Jewish joke?"

"Which one?"

"The one about the man who over the years had done everything for his partner: lent him money, lied to his wife, bailed out his children. Then he gets in some trouble of his own. The partner by now is doing well, so he asks to borrow money, the partner says no, the man recites all that he's done in the past, the partner says, 'But what have you done for me lately?' That story."

"I've heard it," Bell said.

"That's what it's about," Levine said. "This country—who gives a fuck what you've had, what good deeds you've done in the past? Maybe we should put it on the coins, make it the national motto: 'What have you done for us lately?'"

Bell laughed. "Yeah, it's a little better than that old Kennedy thing: 'Ask not what your country can do for you.' All that."

"Which is how you got me all wrong. I told the story about Max not to give you my troubles but to tell you why this thing is important to me. People like you—your father was a dentist, you played football in high school, you were an SAE at Bloomington—people like you don't think of the government when you've got troubles. You don't need the government, except maybe for a VA loan when you buy a house. You didn't grow up looking to the government for help, because your parents didn't. If your father needed to buy a new drill, he didn't look around for the Small Business Administration. He talked to the banker at Rotary or he asked his rich cousins. My people didn't have Rotary. We didn't have rich cousins. Everyone we knew was poor, different kinds of poor. The only thing that could save us—and believe me, we didn't depend on it—was the government. Maybe there'd be some kind of loan program. Scholarships. Subsidies. Housing projects. You must understand, people like us just barely kept their heads above water. A little wave, a recession, two months' unemployment, a cutback in some government program that no one ever heard of, and we drowned. I saw it happen. To me it matters what the government does. I hate to think of it."

"Of what?"

"Of children, kids being ashamed of their parents. Fathers with holes in their overcoats taking kids to buy cheap Christmas presents. Kids sense that kind of thing. No matter how much dignity the father has, that hole in his overcoat. Those kids in the Home, ashamed when their relatives would come to pick them up! It wasn't the actual life that was so bad, you must remember. We were warm, we were well fed, our clothes weren't bad. What was bad was what was inside our heads. We were 'kids from the Home,' nobody wanted us, nobody needed us. We figured the relatives who picked us up and visited with us were shit, too. We weren't grateful. We figured anyone who bothered with us must be nothing themselves."

"Your cousin too?"

"No. Not my cousin, not Miss Brindle, not some other people I could mention. But people like that were geniuses, heroes. You can't expect ordinary people to talk to an orphan kid, to visit with him, without condescending somehow. It doesn't take much, but an orphan kid can spot it in a minute. So can a black. So can anyone who's lived on the outs."

Walter came over from the entrance. "Good evening, Mr. Levine, good to see you again. It's going to be last call in a moment or two."

"Another round, thank you, Walter. This is my associate, Mr. Bell."

'Pleased to meet you, Mr. Bell. If I can ever be of help, just let me know."

He walked off and the two of them stared silently at their empty glasses.

"That's what it's all about, really," Levine said.

"What?"

"Politics. It's so kids shouldn't be ashamed of their parents or themselves. I know it doesn't sound very sophisticated, but that's why I'm in politics."

"You think government can do that?"

"No. It can help."

Bell thought for a while. "Maybe you *are* different."

Levine laughed. "That'th what they all thay," he lisped. "Look, Philip, I'd like to give you more authority. Campaign manager plus looking ahead to after the elections. We'll call you Special Assistant."

"Which means what?"

"Which means the whole works. You point me in the right direction, point other people at me. All major decisions are cleared with you."

"What about the press guy? I want control over him. I want to help choose him, and once we've got him I don't want him shooting off his mouth. They always do, but this one won't. As soon as you take some reporter and make him assistant press secretary in the State Department, he thinks he's John Foster Dulles. Find someone who can follow instructions."

"I was thinking of Alden from Chicago."

"No good. He's too young. He won't be able to take orders from me or anyone else his own age. Besides, he's ambitious. He'll keep getting his own face out on the screen."

"What about McDermott?"

"Never. Two kids in college, plus alimony. He's got a two-thousand-dollar monkey on his back every month. You might get him, but all the time he'd be playing footsie with the corporations, looking to get over to some corporation at a hundred thousand a year."

"The guy from *Time*. The one with the pretty wife."

"Horowitz? You've got to be kidding. Two Jews up front?"

"I forgot. It's just that I liked him."

"Sure, he's good. Do you know Zuidema at all?"

"I remember him from 1968. A fine man. Isn't he a little old?"

"No. He's sixty. He just looks eighty. It's that look us midwestern Protestants all get. He's in good health. Races his bicycle, jogs, all that. He's always been close but never inside. For him, this job would finish off a life's work. Especially if you won."

Levine thought another minute. "I'm just not sure I can work with him. What about the guy from Cleveland, what's-his-name with the *Plain Dealer?*"

"Arthur Jones?"

"Yeah, that's the one. What about him?"

Bell thought again. "Jesus, he sure is the dullest sonofabitch I've ever known. But it's like you said—he's honest and he wouldn't be angling for anything else. And I've got to give him credit: He's smart. He knows everything there is about midwest politics. The other reporters respect him."

"Could you work with him?" Levine asked.

"No problem. Jones could work with Attila the Hun."

"Then it's settled. That would be fine with me."

Bell paused. "Yeah. He'll be fine." He waited again. "Thanks for letting me pick the press secretary. Come on. Let's get out of here."

CALIFORNIA, SUMMER, 1968

It was during the Humphrey campaign in 1968, and he was out on the West Coast helping with a financial problem. It wasn't lack of money—it was the era of the real big hitters, and Shorenstein, Palevsky, Krim, and the others were people after his own heart—but how to distribute it. As usual the congressional people were complaining that the presidential campaign was siphoning off their money, and the presidential people claimed that they weren't going to be able to pay their phone bills if more money wasn't funneled their way. Levine was sent to investigate and arbitrate.

The problem was essentially a simple one, a clash of mega-egos, and was settled by a stern lecture ("We're on the *Titanic* and you're complaining about the quality of the hors d'oeuvres?") and some hand-holding. The candidate himself was going to have to knock a few heads together, and Levine waited an extra five days in Los Angeles for his man to arrive. It was not a long time to wait, and the days passed agreeably enough at the Beverly-Wilshire, and yet one experience crystallized his lifelong unease with the state of California.

It was a routine fund-raiser or, at least, routine by California standards. The house was a big house, with more sliding panels and glass partitions than doors. The party began in the late afternoon, with a set of standard Filipino waiters toting drinks and crabmeat by the side of a standard pool. After a few hours of casual drinking and gossip about the studios, the local candidates were languidly introduced and, after languid preambles ("I hate to intrude on your drinking for something as trivial as the U.S. Senate...") gave the authorized speeches. Then the guests, all of whom looked prettier or handsomer than regulation-issue Americans, drifted inside for a sit-down buffet. It was the year for Beef Wellington.

Levine was seated between a young actress noted for her interest in social justice and the wife of a Beverly Hills radiologist. The actress declared, "I've read everything there is about Vietnam" and demonstrated her social commitment by talking about the "fucking war," but she appeared under the impression that Ho Chi Minh was Chinese. The radiologist's wife made him uneasy by talking about her two children, both of whom were junior figure-skating champions. "I'm going out to visit them in Colorado Springs next month," she said.

"Colorado Springs?" he said.

"They live there," she answered.

"Does your . . . er . . . husband live out there?" he asked.

She laughed prettily. "Oh, heavens, no. We're not divorced. He's over at that table near the fireplace—the bald one with the Madras jacket."

"But your children are in Colorado?"

"They had to move out there to be with their coach."

"Oh. . . . But don't you miss them?"

"Well, actually we get to see more of them than ever before. You see, my husband's a very busy man, and I'm just overwhelmed with my welding classes and political work like this, and we just weren't spending much quality time with the children. But Colorado Springs is just three hours away by way of Denver, so they come home every weekend and we all get together."

"That's lovely. What do you do together?"

"Usually we go down to the Coliseum so the kids can practice with their old coach. They're really wonderful. Watch for their names—Scott and Bruce Epstein."

"I'll remember," he said. How could he forget?

After dinner the guests were shepherded back outside, where a five-piece rock combo had assembled its artillery. People began to dance. It was the only thing about the evening that was not languid. Middle-aged couples twisted and bobbed like teen-agers on *American Bandstand.* Levine watched, puzzled and a little envious, until the music made his sinuses ache. He retreated inside, glanced at his watch, and entered a small alcove. He switched on the television set and watched his party's candidate, the man to whom his fellow guests had pledged their fealty, make a major speech.

He had watched for about fifteen minutes before he felt the presence of someone else in the room. He glanced over his shoulder and saw his hostess, a striking woman of about forty who had been a noted dancer before she married a screenwriter famous for his liberalism. "Harvey always felt guilty it wasn't the Hollywood Eleven," she once said.

Levine smiled at her and nodded to the screen, where, over the noise of the rock group, Humphrey was happily painting a picture of full employment and racial justice. The woman smiled back and listened, still standing up.

Humphrey was still talking when she said, "What side are you?"

It was a puzzling question, but he answered it as reasonably as he could. "I'm a Democrat, of course. On his side." He gestured toward the screen.

"No. Damn that music. You can barely hold an intelligent conversation. No, I said what *sign* are you?"

It still made no sense. "Sign?"

"Sign of the zodiac."

It was the first time he had ever been asked. "I don't know."

"Of course you know. When were you born?"

"February fifteenth."

"I knew it. I knew it."

"Knew what?"

"That you'd be an Aquarius. You're so forceful and so intellectual. Do you read Camus?"

"Uh . . . not regularly."

"He was a Scorpio, you know. You can always tell."

The trouble was that Levine could not always tell. He was beginning to believe that his brain had been affected by the combination of sunshine, alcohol, and loud music. He went home early, slept late, and gave himself a day by the hotel pool to recover. Then, fulfilling an earlier pledge, he called Farbstein's brother.

"When you go out to the coast, call my brother," Farbstein had said. "Lives with his wife and daughter in Long Beach. That's my brother the furniture man. She's a lovely girl, the daughter, very interested in politics. I've been telling her about you for years. Take her to dinner. No funny stuff, though. She's still in high school."

Dutifully he called Morton Farbstein, doggedly he found his way to Long Beach, manfully he sat and talked with Mort and May while sneaking glances at young Shirley seated opposite him. Mort Farbstein owned a small chain of furniture stores, most of them in ghetto areas. His living was in dining room sets, his life in opera, which he loved with a passion all the more noble for its flowering on a dreary Long Beach side street.

"Do you like opera?" he had asked Levine when greetings were over, and, given a genuine though reserved affirmative, he had plunged forward like a dog set free from a chain. He played records on a massive stereo, he raced to show Levine a score autographed by Galli-Curci, he lovingly pulled out backbreaking sets of old 78s. When he finally wound down, Levine thanked him, waved at May, and gallantly escorted Shirley to his rented car.

"He's nuts about opera, isn't he?" she asked.

"He certainly enjoys it. How about you?"

"Are you kidding? It all sounds the same to me."

"What do you like?"

"Surfing, tennis—the usual."

The usual, indeed! Here were the Farbsteins with their generations of wandering Middle European ancestors, their half-instinctive voyage to America, their brief flowering in the gentle socialist Saul and the passionate opera lover Morton, and their crashing halt in the person of this Amazon, this Shirley.

Amazon! Rarely had he seen a woman, Jewish or gentile, so awesomely strong. She did not walk but swaggered. Her thighs were as the trunks of trees, and approximately the same color. She had fine square shoulders and prominent biceps. There was not a thought in her head.

"What are you doing next year?" he asked.

"I'm going to Stanford."

"Stanford?"

"Why, is there something the matter?"

"No, I just figured you'd be interested in something nearer the beach."

"Yeah, that's true. But they've got swell tennis there, and it's only a couple hours away by plane. Besides, I get good grades."

There was no doubt of that. She was, it turned out, in the top tenth of her high school class, and there was nothing innately stupid about her. Yet she knew little and had read nothing. The daily newspaper, such as it was, went unread. All books not assigned in class did not exist. The staples of late adolescent life among bright New Yorkers were not what she fed on. Cautiously he tested her out; she was ignorant of Humphrey Bogart, Willie Mays, Sylvia Plath, and Edith Piaf. Worse, unlike Simpkins, she was rather proud of her own ignorance, to the extent she was aware of it.

"I guess I must sound awfully dumb to someone like you," she said.

"No, not dumb, but—"

"But we're just not interested in that kind of old thing. I mean, it's like my father and his operas; you know what I mean. The way I see it, it's the things that are happening right now that are important. That's my philosophy."

Levine agreed that this was a profound way to approach life and, casting judgment aside, enjoyed the rest of the evening as Shirley crunched her way through a Surf 'n' Turf Special with a monstrous Caesar salad on the side. Watching her eat, he recognized the feeling that had clung to her parents as they talked to her at home, a sense that they had brought forth a new species altogether. Levine prided himself on his ethnic sensitivity, but there was nothing about this girl—nothing in her gestures, her inflections, her movements, her attitudes—that was remotely Jewish.

In the car going home she rambled engagingly on about tennis, school, dates, and her parents. She was, he suddenly sensed, like the average thirteen-year-old in

Westchester, and only the realization that she was seventeen and would be going on to the finest college in the state made the situation at all incongruous.

As they turned up the street to her house, he said, "Well, it's been a great pleasure meeting you. Give my regards to your parents, and I'll tell your uncle I saw you."

"It's been neat. You want a blow job?"

Farbstein's niece?

"No . . . er . . . I . . . no."

"No sweat. I mean, I'd just as soon not, but some of these older guys, they sort of expect it, you know. Bye-bye."

And she bounced out happily into the soft California evening.

He was never easy with California after that. He was not afraid of it, but he did not understand it, which of itself was frightening. He felt genuinely at ease with crazy backwoods farmers in the South, but he had no clue at all about what—if anything—motivated Farbstein's niece from Long Beach. The very skills and sensitivities that oriented him among the dispossessed of the nation abandoned him among people so near to him that they could be his own family. He had nothing against Californians, who were pleasant people except for occasional pretentiousness; San Francisco was a nice city, but its quest for artistic leadership seemed to have taken it no further than the artful stringing of Japanese fishing floats. What perhaps bothered him at the very core was his uneasiness about what would have happened to his own ambition and curiosity if God had happened to set him down in a state where factory workers smoked dope on their coffee breaks and teen-age girls offered blow jobs as a good-night courtesy.

Part **IV**

NORTH CONWAY, APRIL 29, 1988

"We're going to New Hampshire," Bell said. They were alone in Levine's office overlooking the Potomac.

"Why bother? I'd just as soon go to Vermont."

"New Hampshire expects candidates—even new ones—to visit. Even with the other New England primaries pushed together now, they're still the first."

"I know, I know."

"Then why in hell..."

Levine tossed him the *Times*. At the bottom of the front page a headline read, "Two Businessmen Missing in New Hampshire: Ransom Plot Feared."

"You creep, you," Bell said. "You make sure I don't get my paper and then you try to catch me on things like that. It could just as well have happened in Vermont. More likely, probably."

"I know. Still, make sure there's lots of protection when we go up. I've only got one life to lose for my country—I'd like to save it for the election."

"You'll be safe. Christ, you won't be able to pee without a Secret Serviceman on either side. You don't think we're scared of those places? It makes me nervous just to think of it."

"Relax," Levine said. "Nobody's ever assassinated an advance man. Yet."

"I'm relaxed, okay. I still want the charter. The jet. We've got the money, we've got the energy allowance, and it makes sense. Your time's too valuable to hang around airports. The press—they'll be, you know, angry to start with. Like wolves. They're used to those jets."

"Fuck 'em. I tell you, Philip, this is one thing we don't change. I'll let you do the schedules, I'll talk to the people you want me to talk to, but no more of the empire. No hired jets, no fancy suites, none of that."

"You'll kill yourself that way, A.L., it'll tire you out. You need the rest."

Levine walked over to the window facing toward Arlington Cemetery and shrugged. "For twenty years I traveled every ass-backward little road, every one-plane airport, every Pick-Lee-Manger-Hyatt-Sheraton-Quality Court-Hilton there ever was, and this person is telling me how I'll be comfortable on the road. He's telling me how to take care of myself." He turned back toward Bell. "So maybe you have some tips on how to fold a jacket in an overnight bag?"

"Okay, I was out of line. Maybe you know what's best for you. But I've advanced for candidates before. I know what the people out there expect. They want some glamour, some class from the candidate. Get caught in their minds with anything shabby, second-rate, and you might just as well pack your bags."

"Mark Cross, I suppose."

"Huh?"

"Before your time."

"Be serious a minute. The people up there expect a first-class operation. The press expects it."

Levine suddenly had a glimpse of his future, and it was not joyous. If it was taking so much to educate Bell, who was bright and available all the time, how long, through how many repetitions, would it take to educate another 250 million?

"Philip, you think you understand me, we think we know each other, and sometimes you miss the whole point. Philip, the local officials and the press, they don't expect all that, they *want* it. They want to get in on it, the shrimp, the Scotch. Maybe they don't buy a meal for days. But that's not what I am. I'm not running a campaign for the benefit of the mayor of Laconia and the correspondent from the L.A. *Times*. I'm trying to get votes. And people remember. The people are wise to that crap. They don't get to fly on the plane. No shrimp. No drinks. But they got the idea they pay for it, and they're right. We're not rich the way we used to be. Nobody is.

"But you're right. They want some class. Class and free drinks aren't the same thing. Even in New Hampshire everyone's been to a hospitality suite at some die-workers' convention. They're not impressed. Maybe I could impress them with ideas?"

Bell grunted.

"So, I can't impress them with ideas. What about my tailoring?" Levine pirouetted before the window, displayed his dapper, finely-cut glen plaid to the world at large, and sat down.

———————

They flew commercial to Concord. First class, though, and Levine worked on his speech notes and talked to Bell and Jones.

"Funny thing about New Hampshire," Bell said. "It doesn't have nearly so many hairs and Caputos as Vermont. It's almost safe. Strange."

"You ever live there?" Levine asked.

"No. Traveled through when I was in college, but never really stayed."

"Well, I did some business in New England years ago. You'll see the difference. New Hampshire has too many factories, too many French Canadians, to attract the amateurs, the dime-store revolutionaries. It's too real. If you're going to be Peter Pan, generally you move to Vermont."

Jones leaned over from across the aisle. "New Hampshire was electing Catholic senators when Vermont was still trying to decide whether to let 'em vote."

Levine touched Bell, gently but intently. "You must learn the differences. People talk of New England. There *is* a New England, but there are separate states. New Hampshire was settled through Boston, but Vermont came up the river from Connecticut. New Hampshire's still fifty miles from Boston—it has the Irish thing, the factories, the gambling. Different watersheds. It's in the way kids divide when they leave high school. From little towns in New Hampshire, they drift down to Boston. From Vermont, they end up in Hartford or New York or Albany or even Montreal. Watch the land when we fly over."

The last hour of the trip was lost in a cloud bank.

They landed in Concord and were met by Landis, their man in the state. "Smart, but lazy," Bell had said, after spending a week with him earlier. He was a manufacturer, a liberal, a majority leader in the statehouse. They hadn't been able to shake loose any more prominent endorsements.

The press contingent trooped grudgingly toward its bus. Landis chatted on.

". . . apologize for the weather. One of those late April storms. Should be warming up soon. I've made sure your rooms are in order. 'Course I don't have anything against the Queen City Motel, but usually the people from Washington stay at—"

Levine clutched his arm. "Mr. Landis—may I call you Sam?—Sam, that's a good point you just made. Usually people from Washington stay at the Inn. But we're not the usual people. That's the point of the campaign. Now, I'm not a saint. I like a nice meal, good clothes, as much as the next man. Who knows? Maybe more. But you know, Sam, the people are tired of politicians living like movie stars. You ask people to accept energy rationing, you've got to do some of your own."

"I see your point, Mr. Levine. Still, most regular politicians—"

Jones broke in. "Mr. Levine, when shall we say you'll have your press conference for the local papers?"

"Just before dinner. They'll be too hungry to hang around with a lot of extra questions."

———

Solemnly shaking hands, lifting babies, greeting half-remembered "old buddies," Levine moved up and down the state for three days. Bell and Landis had worked well, but still there were screw-ups. Levine turned up for a Rotary breakfast in Wolfeboro—but the Rotarians did not, having canceled the meeting and informed everyone but the guest speaker. Then the press bus took a wrong interchange on the route to Berlin, and the reporters arrived hours late at their motel. The result was twenty-four hours of bitchy coverage, plus grist for two oracular columnists ("Amateurism and bad planning have already begun to plague the unprecedented primary campaign.... A small but significant portent was found in the campaign's inability to manage even so simple a procedure as bus schedules for the press").

"What did you think about Markson's column?" Jones asked in the fully plasticized bar of the North Conway Marriott.

"Asshole," Levine said.

"Still, that stuff hurts. The professionals read it, they back off."

"The professionals don't run things any more. Remember, I'm one of them. I know. Maybe in 'sixty-eight a column like that would have hurt. Some businessman in Los Angeles, someone with too much money and a little conscience, he wants to give to McCarthy, he reads that kind of column and no, thanks, he's not going to waste fifty thousand on a born loser—a man who can't even keep inventories straight, for Christ's sake. So McCarthy's out fifty thousand. But today, there's no fifty thou from anyone. There's the limit."

"Yeah," said Jones, "they just donate people instead of money."

"Okay, the law gives an advantage to people who can organize volunteer workers. The unions, they can get their people out. But not like before. There's no Lewis, no Dubinsky. Believe me already. Don't brood about such things. You piss off a couple of important people every day. Every day! If you lose you can go back and look over the campaign and say, This I should have done, that I shouldn't have done. I listened to the McGovern people after 1972: We shouldn't have had Eagleton to begin with, we should have dropped him sooner, we should have worked Watergate harder, Nixon played dirty. The McGovern people worked it both ways: They blamed dirty politics for beating them, but they forgot that it was dirty politics—the Canuck thing—that helped beat Muskie and give them the nomination in the first place. They complained that Nixon did all that crap when he was so far ahead anyway, and then they forgot what that meant about their own campaign. Little things don't win elections. Big ones do."

"The analysts don't agree."

"Political analysts? What do they know of fancy fucking?"

Jones looked puzzled. "What?"

"I forget. It's not that you're from Ohio, it's that you never left home for so long. That was the tag line on a joke we used to tell. You know, salesmen always had to have a new joke for the people out in the sticks. When I traveled, I'd talk to my friends in textiles and get the new jokes from them. You could almost feel them spread across the country. Forget it. What I meant is that the analysts, most of them, don't know. They're like the sportswriters. They tell you that so-and-so's injured ankle, so-and-so's fumble, so-and-so's last-minute penalty, all that crap lost the game. They forget all the other injuries, all the fumbles by the other side, all the penalties that went the wrong way for the team that won. In every campaign there's a hundred fuck-ups. If you win, no one ever remembers them. Believe me."

———————

Some burst of corporate genius had located the North Conway Marriott in the center of the village rather than on the franchise belt of highway just outside of town. It was, therefore, possible to walk from the front entrance of the motel's harmoniously designed New England portico down the street to other centers of life. Levine recklessly sloshed through mounds of still-melting late-spring snow to explore.

His years on the road came back, the sense of excitement, even half-felt danger in a new town, the presence Levine had that other salesmen called instinct but which, in truth, was the systematic analysis of carefully observed detail. It did you no good to drive past the beautiful homes of southern Vermont if you did not see the names on the mailboxes—Shapiro, Doukis, Edelman, Longworth; and it did no good to remember the names on the mailboxes if you did not put together a pattern, a pattern that told you "outside money," whenever you saw a house or a farm that was newly painted and had a fine picket fence or well-kept stone wall around it; and it was this kind of observation that saved you from thinking "Vermont is prosperous" and made you suspect that New York was prosperous and Vermont was becoming its colony.

And if you had asked Levine why he walked past the Yankee Peddler and the Schussboomer Lounge and Al's before entering the Conway Tavern, he might have said instinct, but he could have said, No, the first place seemed too well lit from the outside and must be after tourists, and the next was too cutesy for the people he half hoped to meet, and Al's was too genuinely authentic and would hold the town's truly serious drinkers, which he did not need, and there was a subdued quiet about the Conway Tavern that seemed pleasant and would attract people he might like.

Inside, the right kind of feeling held. There were local people, middle-aged people with pale faces, not skiers and not drunks, people who had to be local couples out for a quiet drink; and there were some backpacking, late-spring skiing couples, young but not aggressively so; and there was one probably illicit affair working in a corner booth (they were talking too intently to be married to each other but were trying, unsuccessfully, to be discreet about their affection); and there were the reporters.

The reporters, too, had a way of scenting out the best local places—the good reporters, anyway. There were others, like young Blaine Coudert, who were good but were part of the invisible network of the rich. Levine knew that there was no town so small that a traveling Jew couldn't find another Jew nearby, and there was no place in America where Coudert couldn't find a friend of his mother's or his stepfather's or someone he had gone to prep school with. Coudert was probably in a restored farmhouse a couple of miles out of town, drinking and talking with some old friend from Yale, someone who had moved to New Hampshire to escape the rat race. He and his friends would be telling Coudert about New

Hampshire, and Coudert would write a feature piece on the state filled with inside information and then would be surprised when the election didn't go the way his friends expected. No, Levine thought, he won't be surprised. He'll have forgotten it by the time the election comes along. People like that don't learn. They think that by playing at being just plain folks, by eating lunch in McDonald's or going to Disneyland, they can escape their backgrounds. They escape it for everything but the important things.

"Have a drink?" It was the young fellow from the *Times*, Hale, who asked. There was a reporter from *New Day* and a dramatically handsome photographer from the *Sun-Times* and Sue Dempsey, a pretty, aggressive television woman, at the table. They were nice people, but Levine had not spent the morning answering reporters' questions, and lunchtime hopping from one table of reporters to another, and the shank of the afternoon smoosing with the reporters in their bus to run through that stretch of highway again.

"Thank you, no. I'm exhausted and might say something foolish, and it wouldn't be beyond you people to quote me on it. I would if I were you. Besides, I just want a quick quiet drink by myself."

He had been taking in the room as he spoke. In a concession to its name, the Tavern had six long wooden colonial tables set down its middle. The tables seated fourteen and clearly were open to anyone. There was an empty seat on the end of the bench nearest Levine.

"Thanks again," he said to Hale, and sat down on the bench.

"May I?" he asked the person next to him, a young woman with an unpretentious New England face. Her skin had the dark, almost black tan of midseason Miami.

"Sure. Move over, Billy." A boy of about twenty next to her hunched his shoulders together.

"Nice place," Levine offered.

"Yeah," the girl said. "Especially after you've been climbing on skins all day long."

The offering. The response.

"Skiing? This late in the year? Skins?"

"Yup. At Tuckerman's. No lifts, so you have to walk back up to the top. You walk uphill with your skis on. You put a covering on your skis—skins—to keep from sliding back. You're not a skier?"

The question in that was minimal. Levine laughed. "No, I never learned. It looks like fun, though."

"It is. What are you doing around here?"

No need to spoil the innocence of the politically unaware. "I'm sort of a salesman. I'm just traveling through."

She looked at him closely. "Say, aren't you that candidate? You know...the one from New York?"

Anonymity would be harder and harder to come by. He smiled. "Yes. A. L. Levine is my name. People call me A.L."

"Glad to meet you. I'm Kathy Derrick. This is Billy Remson. Over there"—she pointed across the table to an equally tanned, open youth—"is his little brother, Charles."

They nodded, smiled, raised glasses.

"I've never met a famous person before," Kathy said.

"I'm not famous."

"You've been on TV all this week."

"Next week I'll be gone. There'll be no sign of me."

"Melted," said Billy unexpectedly. It was funny and apt, and Levine liked it.

"Like the old Ray Charles song," Levine said. "'Busted.' Maybe they could have a skier's song called 'Melted.'"

They knew the Ray Charles, which was surprising for young people, and they were surprised to find that a really old person knew it too and that Levine had met Ray Charles and had known people who had played with him and had stories of the tensions and the drugs on the tours.

"How can you do it?" said Kathy.

"What?"

"Travel like you're doing. Every day saying the same thing over and over again. Answering the same questions. Kissing ass when you have to."

"That's funny. When I was part of the McCarthy campaign—just a small part—I used to look at that man, so smart, so ironic, a true Catholic intellectual, you know, and wonder how he could go through what you're talking about: the master of ceremonies who gets your name wrong or who makes his own speech—in Concord one guy spoke for fifteen minutes on snowmobiles—"

"They're awful," Billy said.

"No, let me continue." Levine held on. "You listen to old ideas, badly expressed, by people who think they're discovering them for the first time. I used to wonder how McCarthy could stand it. The secret was, he couldn't. He saw it all ironically. He was displaced. He knew that it was absurd."

"And you think the same thing?"

"No, that's the difference. I'm a smart man, but I never had a taste for meditation. There's no place for irony in politics. You're a skier, right?" She nodded. "You've raced." Nodded again. "Now, it's exciting to race—I haven't skied, but I've played other sports—but it's more exciting to win, to do your best. I go all out. I can't take that extra step of detachment to the side. Not that I'll commit suicide if I lose, but I'll be disappointed. So I try to learn all the time. Even at Rotary breakfasts, while someone else is talking, there's something you can learn. You can tell I'm always learning, because I haven't let you say a word since I sat down. But please, tell me—what's with the snowmobiles?"

Kathy took up where the young man had interrupted. "Billy said it. They're awful. The noise, the stink. Cutting trails through the woods. They tried to stop them in the statehouse several years ago, but the lobby, all the salesmen, got together. They've got limits on them, certain places they can't go, like in the state forests, but mostly they're all over the place."

"You didn't grow up around here?" Levine said.

"No. I was born in Dedham. Outside of Boston. I moved up here a couple of years ago. Substitute teach. Mostly I ski and pack."

"Do me a favor?" Levine said.

"What?"

"Early tomorrow, before my first speech, come with me and my assistant, show us some of the people around here. Maybe you'd introduce us to some—I don't want to use the word natives—you know."

She looked uneasy. "I'm not sure..."

"Go ahead and do it, Kathy," Billy said. "You can take him over to Simpson's place."

"Oh, powerful! Yeah, that'd be fine. You see, there's this old man Simpson Oxenbridge and he lives all alone—"

"Any place you want to show us."

The boys looked at each other and nodded. "Look," Billy said. "We'll be around in the morning if you need any help. We're falling in now."

"Okay, kids." Kathy nodded. "See ya."

They walked off, young, confident, clean. Tall. Levine watched them half enviously. They could still stir that faint unease in him. The rich ones couldn't do that, the Spence Cunninghams, even with their good looks piled on top of the money, because they were in his own game and he was better than they were. It was the uncomplicated decency of the Remsons, the absence of posturing, that made him see what his childhood had lacked.

Kathy was not watching the boys. Her eyes were intent. She wanted to know about campaigning—what did he learn, how did he decide where to go, how much did it cost? Had he known John Kennedy? And what about his wife, did she go with him on campaigns, was it hard to be married to a politican? The questions continued, and Levine felt her lean gently against him on the hard bench as they had another round of drinks, and then the reporters nodded and went home, and they had another round, and she yawned and said, "I guess I better be going back to my place."

Gallantly he escorted her through the slush back to her rooming house—"The boys are staying over at the Ski-mor"—stood on the front steps trembling like any virginal adolescent, kissed her gently, slid his hands down to her delightfully taut little bottom, and waited.

"Come up, why don't you?" she whispered.

It wouldn't do. Not fear of the reporters, not worry about Helen, not any sticky problem of whose room or whose bed, but just a feeling that she was testing him. She would screw and be delighted to do it, but left behind would be a new coat of cynicism. Even the old ones, especially the old ones, she'd think, all they want when it comes down to it is screwing. He had an obligation to the rest of the grown-up world.

He squeezed her tight, let her know he wanted her. "No. I've got speeches to work on still. And besides, you're going to be helping me tomorrow. A politician can't get too involved with the people who're helping him."

"Sure."

Maybe she believed him.

———

By eight o'clock the next morning Levine was drinking his third cup of peppermint tea. His host, Simpson Oxenbridge, sat in front of the kitchen fireplace and told them—no, lectured them—about how the country had gone wrong. Kathy was rapt.

"First they stink up the rivers so's the salmon die. Then they cut off the trees so there's nothing but third-growth birch. You can't build a decent barn because there ain't no trees left big enough to give you solid beams. Then they build the goddam roads. If that ain't enough they sell those fearsome Sno-Cats. Then they run out of gas, for everything but the Sno-Cats. Then wood rustlers come out from the city and cut down your trees for firewood. I don't hold with any of that. Grow my own food, do my own trapping. I'm learning to sew, finally, so's I can make my own clothes."

"Admirable," Levine said. "You were born up here?"

"No. Actually, I grew up in New York. Used to come up here skiing. After my wife died twenty years ago I moved up by myself."

"Remarkable. I congratulate you, Mr. Oxenbridge. Frankly, an inspiration. Now, I'm afraid we've got to be going. Politics, you know."

Oxenbridge smiled complicitly, gave them each a tin of maple sugar, and sent them on their way.

"Isn't he a beautiful man?" Kathy said. "I mean, when you consider the independence he has. At his age, too."

"He's only seventy," Levine said snappishly. He himself was sixty-five. If he stayed slim, he'd still be brisk at seventy. It wasn't as though seventy were synonymous with feeble. Besides, he suspected that a lot of that independence came in the form of quarterly divided checks.

On the way out from Conway, Levine had noticed a prosperous-looking farm with two snowmobiles set in a shed near the barn. Passing it on the way home, he saw a sturdy man coming out toward the mailbox. "Pull in here," he told Bell. The name on the mailbox was LeMaire.

The car stopped and Levine stepped nimbly out, pulling Kathy after him. The farmer looked puzzled.

"Mr. LeMaire?"

"That's right."

"I'm A. L. Levine. I'm running in the—"

"Seen you on television. Know all about it. Sorry I can't chitchat now. Got to get the mail for the wife."

"Those are nice snowmobiles you've got. What are they, Suzukis?"

The man looked up with an expression of mild pleasure.

"That's right. Best there is. Can't beat 'em for deep powder."

"Who uses them?"

"The wife and me. Who else? The kids are all grown and in the city."

"What do you use them for?"

LeMaire smiled. "Hell, I use 'em for everything. Cow gets stuck in a fence, I cat right down to drag her out. Long as the snow holds, I use 'em to check my sugar maples. Mostly the wife and I just use 'em for helling around. Midwinter, we'll bundle up and take along a bottle and go down to the road to the Grille. Lot of others'll be there. We'll have something to eat, drink some, have some races. Right down the middle of the road, if the snow's right. Or we'll chase off across Thompson's fields. Ain't nothing like it."

"You do much skiing, Mr. LeMaire?"

He snorted. "Hell, I ain't been up a pair of skis since I was six years old. Fact is, you ain't seen anyone the likes of me near any of them ski places. We ain't wanted around there, if you know what I mean. It costs you an arm and a leg, besides."

"Tell me, what did people around here, people like you, do in the winters before the snowmobiles?"

LeMaire paused. "Well, a lot of people shot themselves." He paused again. "That's just a joke, you understand."

"Sure. It's been good talking to you. Mr. LeMaire. Do me a favor. Look at the six o'clock TV news tonight. I can't promise you I'll be on, but I think I might be."

"Sure will. 'Bye."

In the car Levine glittered with the early morning cold. "What's the matter with you people that you don't see?" he shouted, a shout directed not only to Kathy but to most of New England. "You talk about noise and pollution and scenic values, and what you're really talking about is putting the Catholics in their place. The French-Canadians. It's the same war you've been fighting here for two hundred years, but you're just calling it something else."

"But, I don't—"

"Kathy, darling, I'm not blaming you. Not personally, if you see what I mean. But you're smart, you should be able to see all this crap. Look, would you believe I know something about the ski business?"

"You?"

"Me. A. L. Levine. I was what you might call a land developer. If you don't like me, you call me a speculator. If you're my friend, you call me a developer. Mostly in the South, but there was land up here too. I could feel it coming. So I was up here already with my family one summer, there was some land for sale, a mountain all ready, they said it was ideal for skiing. What did I know about skiing? I came back in the winter and looked around. I found many interesting things, but one thing I discovered—they were all talking about skiing being a sport for everyone, but there weren't any local farmers or factory workers on those mountains. It wasn't just the money. Times were good. The workers had the money. If you want to know the truth, the truth was that they felt it was a Protestant thing. Even a Jewish thing. A Boston thing. But not a Manchester thing. Not a French-Canadian thing. A girl who was a nurse in Manchester, she wouldn't ski much because the other nurses would think she was snobbish. The same girl, if she went down to Boston, would be driving up every weekend to learn. Because in Boston it was okay for Irish and French-Canadian nurses and teachers to ski. Up here, it was pushy. But the people had the money just the same, and when snowmobiles came along they bought them, and then the Protestants tried to take them away, too. That's what all the fighting is about. You see, you see?"

The noon speech was at a factory rally in Nashua. It was raining in the parking lot, but when Levine came up, manic with enthusiasm, prancing back and forth, and began his speech by saying, "Let me tell you about skis and snowmobiles and Catholics and Jews," no one moved from the audience and the workers whooped and yelled, and for all intents and purposes he won New Hampshire that afternoon.

That evening he slipped away from Bell and over to Kathy's room. He had given her time to get over the father-figure infatuation, and after all there was no use in holding out forever. Nowadays, twenty-four hours was plenty for a girl to get her head straight.

"I just love Jewish men," Kathy said, several days later.
"Uh-huh." Levine was hoping for a little sleep.
"You're so sensitive."
"Uh-huh."
"I mean, not like sensitive in any faggy way, but truly

sensitive. Like, for instance, you like music and writing, but you like sex, too. A lot of people think that if you like music and writing you have to be gay or faggy, but Jewish people aren't."

"Some of us are."

"What do you mean?"

"I mean there are lots of Jewish men who are fags."

"I haven't met any."

"You wouldn't."

"I'm serious. I think you are beautiful people. It's awful what people say about you."

"What do they say?"

"Oh, you know...." Her voice trailed off. She was twenty-two years old and on their first night together she coolly explained that he'd have to keep a finger in her ass if she was going to come, but she couldn't quite bring herself to utter the anti-Semitic clichés. He knew that the liberals regarded this as a triumph, that bigotry and violence had now become literal obscenities and sex natural, yet somehow he wished that Kathy weren't so matter-of-fact about one and so terrified of the other. He had wished that many times before, with other women.

"What sort of things?" he repeated.

"Well, that you stick together and you cheat in business and that you hate gentiles and that you always protect your own kind."

Now that the cap was off the gusher was flowing. It was just the way it had been in the old days with sex—get by the initial inhibitions and in a few nights they were screaming obscenities with the best of them.

"How did you hear those things?"

She blushed prettily. "My parents used to talk that way."

Levine was surprised. Overt anti-Semitism always surprised him, more so when it came from the nice, clean educated people Kathy's parents must be. Twenty years ago, maybe, but in the 1980s it seemed so foolish and old-fashioned.

Kathy rushed on. "I mean, not that my parents would ever hold anything against you, but, you know, if they knew I were seeing you like this . . . I'd be in trouble. I had enough of a time when I told them I was going to work on your campaign."

Kathy had been hired as a press assistant.

"Just working with you has taught me a lot about Jewish people. Like the way you're so close to your family."

Levine glanced slyly across the pillow to see if she was joking. She was staring at the ceiling and had on her puzzled, serious expression. She wasn't joking.

"I mean I think it's wonderful that you and your family are all so close. My family . . ." She waved her arms vaguely.

Levine was depressed. He had been tricked again by the wisdom she affected and which some of her contemporaries truly had, having lived twenty lives in the same number of years it had taken Levine to get his first apartment as a graduate student. Her own wisdom had worn thin in forty-eight hours.

"Still, you don't seem that different," she said.

Kathy wasn't listening for his answers, when there were any.

"Like what?"

"Well, you know."

"I don't know. Tell me."

"Well, your religion doesn't seem much different from anyone else. You eat the same foods. You're supposed to eat different foods. You're pretty much the same as everyone else. How come?"

He didn't feel much like giving a crash course in modern Judaism. Not at 2:00 A.M. Not with the Massachusetts commuters waiting.

"It's a long story," he said.

Kathy had a relentless New England manner. She had an insight by the scruff of the neck. She wasn't going to let it go.

"Can't you make it short?"

"Look, I'm the wrong person to ask. I'm just a twentieth-century American Jew. That's the last person you ought to ask to explain Judaism."

"What do you mean?"

"I mean that we were taught that we were the same as everyone else at the same time we were being taught that we were different from everyone else. We had a history of always being strangers in whatever country we were living, but America stumped us. We didn't know what to make of it. After all, if you're a Jew in France, ninety-five percent of the rest of the people have the same religion and the same national background, they've lived in the same province for hundreds of years. They're French—you're a Jew. The same in Germany or England. Not that they don't have subdivisions of French, but it's the same as with the Masons; they've got different degrees, but they all belong to the same outfit. But America was different from the start. Everyone was a stranger. There wasn't any American religion or racial type. The only thing people had in common was their differences. So you couldn't maintain a religious community merely on the basis that you were different. It made it very hard for the Jews."

"It should have made it easy."

"No, hard, because they had to choose. Say, in Poland, in the old days, a Jew didn't have much big choosing to do. He had his place set in the universe. There were only certain people he could work with, certain people he was allowed to marry, certain jobs he was allowed to do, certain places he was permitted to live. In America Jews could do anything. Choosing is always harder. What made it even tougher, the Jews had to ask themselves what part of being Jewish was really truly Jewish and what part came from having been perennial strangers."

"What part *was* truly Jewish?"

"Don't ask."

"Now you're making fun of me."

"No, I'm making fun of the Jews."

"Maybe that's the part that's truly Jewish?"

"You're learning," he said, and fell asleep.

"You'll get shot," Bell said. He was practicing chords on a Baldwin the management had sent up to the suite.

"No one's going to shoot me," Levine said.

Bell ran off another chord series. He was working on progressions for Strayhorn's arrangement of "Lush Life."

"You're going to get shot and your wife's going to be hysterical and I'm going to be out of a job. So forget about it."

"Jews don't get shot. They have heart attacks, mostly."

Bell slammed down the keyboard cover. "I'm not fooling, for Christ's sake. You're not going to start wandering around this city like some goddam Arab tourist with a big nose and a little camera. This isn't New Hampshire. This is Indiana. My state. There's every kind of nut running around on the streets. From now on, I don't care if it's Indiana or California or wherever, you stay with the security people."

Levine didn't feel like arguing any longer. He had a speech in the Civic Center at 8:00 P.M. and it was 2:00 P.M. and he had spent all morning in the suite talking to local leaders, and he was tired of being in one place.

"Okay, okay. Is it all right if I go back to my room and take a leak?"

"Funny. Sure, so long as you don't get lost."

Levine went back to his room, scribbled a note that read, "I got lost," slipped it under the door, and took the elevator to the lobby. He wandered past a couple of curious reporters and out onto the street. Great glass storefronts, coffee shops and travel agencies, lined the downtown. Levine followed the scent away from the hotel. In the cities there was almost never anything worthwhile within two blocks of a big chain hotel. In small towns sometimes the Holiday Inn or the Ramada was the place to go, but in cities the only people you'd meet within three blocks of the Hilton were more refugees from the hotel, just like yourself.

Levine steered away from the main streets, heading toward the side streets. He passed a tall old building that proclaimed itself "The Executive." Alongside the entrance were the plaques of some law firms and brokerage houses. The plaques were tarnished, but the names were good. Around the corner was a small diner, old-fashioned, with stools along the counter and booths on the side. A few people were still eating. They looked like businessmen. The diner was called the Olympia. Levine went in and sat at the counter.

"I'd like a grilled Western and a coffee, please."

The man behind the counter nodded. "Any dessert? We've got fresh rhubarb pie."

"Sure."

The man cracked three eggs, whipped them, folded in some onion and chopped ham, poured it on the grill.

"You want your coffee now?"

"Thanks."

The man stared at him a moment. "You look like that guy, you know, the one in the primary."

"Levine?"

"Yeah, that one."

"That's me."

The chef was grizzled, gray, hawk-nosed. He had the air of a man who had been running either a diner or an ocean liner for many years. He gave orders, never took them.

"I don't care for what I see of you, to tell the truth. You talk about justice, and I know about justice. I'm an expert on justice. And who the hell can get justice when these blacks or Negroes or whatever they call themselves this year are running the police and the courts and the city hall? Where is there justice for a white man? What kind of justice is it when a man can't gamble a little in his own house or see the kind of movies he wants? You talk about understanding, but who has time to understand when he's always looking out for Patrols and nigger judges? And those goddam Vietnamese and their restaurants—they work for nothing, like slaves." The man waved his arms eloquently and in the same motion bent over the grill, scooped up the Western, slid it between two extra-large slices of toast, cut the sandwich in half with a razor-sharp bread knife, and offered it up to Levine.

Levine took a bite. "Marvelous Western!"

The man nodded. "You like it?"

"I've never had a better one."

"I wonder how come you don't eat at your hotel?"

"You know food, don't you? Try living a month on banquet food. Every night, almost every noon, I eat at banquets. You know what they'd do with the Western you just served me? They'd crack two thousand eggs and cut up five hundred onions and slice twenty hams, and by the time they'd finished doing all that the onions would be limp and the ham would be dried out, but they'd make a thousand Westerns and then they'd keep them waiting on a steam pan for half an hour while some coconut made a speech welcoming me. Then I'd have to eat that Western. You eat food like that for a month, and you'll start looking for something good on the side."

"The rhubarb pie is homemade."

"I can barely wait to start it. I'm just making this Western last longer." Levine paused. "You Greek?"

The man looked angry. "My English isn't good enough for you?"

He'd stepped into that one.

"No, not at all. I never would have thought of that. It's just the way you spoke of justice. I had the feeling that I was speaking to a man who knew about democracy."

The man shook his fist at Levine. "We invented democracy, we Greeks. I was born on Crete, came here as a little boy. Seven years old. Sold papers. Sold ice cream. Bought my own ice cream. Bought my own candy store. Then, the restaurant." He waved about him. His gesture included most of downtown Indianapolis.

"Magnificent. So if you're Greek, you know the struggle between the oligarchy and the democracy. Pericles said that if men were destroyed it was not easy to get them whole again. May I have the pie now?"

The pie was placed in front of him. It was all it should have been.

"A noble pie. Noble! So, as I was saying, if we destroyed the blacks, not destroyed them so much as warped them, it follows that they will have to work that warp out. We gave them no power for two hundred years. Now they have power and sometimes they abuse it. But you remember the Klan in Indiana?"

The man nodded.

"So you know what we did to them was worse than picking up someone for reading dirty books. Much worse. I know, it wasn't you. It wasn't me either, but they weren't north long enough to know that. All they saw was the white man. So now they have power and they don't always use it correctly. Quite frankly, I think they use it better than we deserve. Still, they're not perfect. But that's what the Greeks knew about democracy: the people weren't always right, but you had to trust them anyway. Think about that, Mr.—"

"Contas."

"Think about it." Levine shook his hand, paid, turned and said, "The best restaurant in Indianapolis," and left.

Levine wandered around town for three more hours. He ate Westerns at a small café near the bus station and at a sleepy neighborhood restaurant on the edge of downtown. He had pork barbecue at a gleaming rib shop on the edge of the black neighborhood. In midafternoon none of the places was crowded, and at each he was recognized, he chatted with the chef about politics, praised the food, and left. When he came back to the hotel he was full but bouncy.

"Where the fuck have you been?" Bell asked. "I don't care who you are, don't play this kind of trick again."

"You saw the note," Levine said.

"Goddammit, I was about to call the Secret Service and the FBI. Sure, I saw the note. What good does that do me? We've got a thousand people at that banquet tonight, we've got to tour the housing projects, and you're off getting laid or window-shopping. No more!"

"Okay, we will get it straight," Levine said. "Until—unless—I'm nominated, I'm not the property of the Secret Service. I'm not your property either. I'm still my own man and I make my own rules. The campaign's not a baseball spring training camp; no one has a bed check. Everyone's an adult. It's not a democracy either; I'm the boss. So—"

"If you're shot—"

"Let me continue. I'm just as much against getting myself shot as you are. More, if you want to know the truth. Ever since the army, I've been afraid of guns. I want to stay alive. But I also want to be president and I want to be president not just for the hell of it, but to help this country." He paused a minute. "Did you read Bellosi's study of presidential assassins?"

"I did. But that was years ago, after the Wallace thing."

"If you read it you remember what he said. Assassins are drawn to power and the *circumstance* of power the way hornets are drawn to sugar. The more Secret Service you have around you, the more security, the more they want to assassinate you. Sure they'll get caught, but they don't mind being caught—they want to get caught. If they don't get caught, they never get famous. They're all the same: homeless, fatherless, half in, half out of being crazy. Just sane enough to want to kill the king. Or kill the father they never had."

"Where do you come off with the psychological bullshit?"

"It's not me, it's Bellosi. But, if you want to know the truth, I was in analysis for a few years back in the sixties. When I had the time and the money for the first time. Nothing serious, I had a few little problems I wanted to talk to a psychiatrist about. If you're raised in an orphanage, you always have some problems. It was interesting, helpful. So I know something about psychology. But no one has to be an expert to see that assassins don't kill Coolidges and Hoovers. They go after the imperial presidents."

"They tried to kill Truman, for Christ's sake."

"Sure, but that was different. That was a real South American assassination, a political plot. That's not what you worry about. You worry about the one guy with the gun."

"Johnson. We never had anyone as imperial as Johnson. We never had such a bad time with demonstrations, Black Power, Stop the War, and nobody ever even tried to kill him."

"That's what I mean. He couldn't leave the White House without a battalion of Secret Service. He couldn't give a commencement address without sweeping the whole campus first. He was a prisoner in his own White House. I'm not going to let that happen to me, and the time to prevent it is now. We downplay the candidacy, the presidency. I want to be alone, for God's sake. I don't want that swarm of people around me all the time. I don't mean just the Secret Service. I mean the TV people and my advisers and even my friends. I just need to be alone in public awhile. Talk to people. Eat at a diner. Scratch my ass without someone doing it for me. When was the last time you ever saw a governor or a senator walking by himself? Nowadays they've all got hangers-on. They never meet anyone new. Everyone gets filtered through that swarm of disciples. You watch Senator Milwood walk down Connecticut Avenue and it's like Jesus and the goddam disciples, all nipping at his heels."

"So?"

"So people are tired of seeing that. They see these little packs of men moving up and down their streets and they think, 'There's someone important,' and they don't like it. They react against it. And the crazy ones, they want to kill."

"You want to be some kind of Jessington, slipping and sliding among your people, disguised as a humble beggar?"

"Maybe I will. Mostly I want to be by myself some of the time. Let me tell you why. First, because I might learn something. Second, because it will get me votes—every one of those short-order cooks I talked to today is going to tell a hundred people about meeting me, and every one of the hundred is going to tell another fifty, and you'll be able to find the districts I visited by myself just from the percentages when the votes come in. Third, because there's no point in being president of a country where everything the president does hinges on his chance for assassination. And last, because when you strip all the crap and the chrome away from the presidency and get down to just another elected official who can go around the corner for a piss when he wants, then he's less likely to get assassinated in the first place."

"But if anyone does want to assassinate him, the chances they'll succeed are a hell of a lot better," Bell argued.

Levine shrugged. "You can't win 'em all."

———————————

"Where was he this afternoon?" Jack Siegel asked at the press briefing. Jones was explaining what the evening schedule would be, and a pretty young man was handing out mimeographed schedules.

"This afternoon? This afternoon"—Jones hesitated—"this afternoon the candidate conferred with his advisers. Privately."

"I got some guy who swears he saw Levine coming out of a rib place this afternoon," Siegel went on.

"The candidate went out for a snack by himself. The candidate often has a bite in midafternoon."

"So I went around town and I found some guy who swears he saw Levine eating at some hash house near the bus station."

"The candidate has a hearty appetite," Jones said.

"I'm not sure about all this," Coudert said. "You mean he wanders around the city by himself?"

"Yeah," said Siegel, "like some kind of fucking Arab."

"Nothing so dramatic as that," Jones said. "Mr. Levine just likes to be by himself sometimes. He feels that not everything in life can be scheduled."

Coudert looked unhappy. "Has the Secret Service advised him about this?"

"Naturally. I wish you guys wouldn't make too much

of this. It's not anything that the candidate wants to play up. I mean, you can tell that he'd prefer the opposite. He's no Greta Garbo, he just likes to be alone some of the time. The security people don't like it, but he's the candidate. It's a free country."

"I could argue that," a young kid from one of the radical papers said, and the other reporters groaned.

"What's with these people?" Bell asked Levine.

"The Jewish Political Advisory Board? It's a whole bunch of Jews looking for something to do. It's like with the infantile paralysis thing. When the scientists finally discovered a vaccine, there were a couple hundred people, fund raisers, publicity men, who used to work for the Polio Foundation, suddenly out of work. Technologically obsolete."

"That was before my time. Must have been quite a kick in the nuts."

"Yeah. No one likes to think he has a vested interest in cancer or paralysis. But those guys were smart. They said, 'We did such a good job combating polio that now we will go out and combat some new disease.' So they changed their name and went out combating birth defects and everyone kept his job and the public was happy too."

"And with the Jews?"

"The B'nai B'rith was founded to fight anti-Semitism. There was a famous incident in the nineteenth century when a Jew couldn't get into a resort hotel. At first the B'nai B'rith was sort of snobbish itself, mostly German Jews. That changed in the 1930s, and they started letting in immigrants who had made money, guys who were influential in local Jewish affairs. There was Hitler in Germany, discrimination in America; they had lots to do. After World War Two, there wasn't so much anti-Semitism. Israel was the hot ticket item. The same people who had been active in B'nai B'rith moved into Israel Bonds, fund-raisers, all that. All during the sixties there were rallies, resolutions to protect Israel. Then when the Russians had their troubles and everyone put the squeeze on the Arabs, the heat went off the Middle East and the people needed a new cause. There were beginning to be more and more Jewish candidates here in the States, so someone figured that there should be a national board to advise them and to get some kind of Jewish consensus on domestic issues, the way there had been a coalition of groups working for Jewish interests in the Middle East and in Russia."

"You sound like you don't like them."

"Oh, I like them in a way. It's just that they're mostly such second-rate assholes. They're professional Jews and amateur politicians. The people in the Washington office aren't bad, but the board itself—God save me. Political groupies. People who got touched by Roosevelt or Kennedy or McCarthy and got the excitement of the campaigns without the hard work and decided to believe the newspapers that called them 'influential liberal figures.'"

"People like you."

Levine laughed. "People enough like me to make me think, 'There but for the grace of God.' Sure they're people like me. People like you are always the ones that bother you the most. You see your own faults quickest. You think, 'Am I really as much of an asshole as Max Fineberg?' After all, I'm not going to look at Jessington or Cunningham and see myself, but these people are too close for comfort. Come on, let's go. We're already late."

In the cab Bell asked again, "Are you sure it's okay for me to come?"

"They understand. I told them you go where I go."

"Am I your Shabbas goy?"

"God damn, you're learning, Philip, you're learning. No, the Shabbas goy is the one in the old days who would run the store or do the household jobs on Saturday, when the Orthodox couldn't light fires or deal with money. It became an expression for an up-front gentile, someone who gave a touch of class to a Jewish law firm or brokerage house. Window dressing."

"Isn't that what I'm doing at this meeting? Being your house gentile?"

"You've still got a long way to go. The board is pompous, but it isn't stupid. They know the National

Committee isn't a Jewish operation. They don't need any token gentiles to remind them of that. No, you're along for two reasons. Make it three. First, to learn. Second, to help me if I need help. Third, to bring those creeps back to earth. Remind them that there are other people in the world besides Jews. They'll complain that you put a constraint on things, that they can't talk as easily with you there, but that means that they can't put themselves into an entire fantasy world where the United States government rises and falls on whether or not there are enough Jewish policemen. It's the same thing I did when they used to trot me out to meetings at the Grosse Point Country Club—I'd just sit there, smoking my cigar, looking Jewish, reminding those sons of bitches that there were other people in the world besides automotive engineers. It wasn't just that they couldn't say things about 'Jews and niggers,' it was that they had to force their thinking back to the real world. The people today, they'll feel uneasy that they can't use the word goyim without apologizing to you, but the real thing is that you're going to remind them every minute that there's a bigger world."

Bell reflected that as duties went in the universe, this was one he'd just as soon skip. Even if Levine said he wasn't going to be a token Protestant, that was what he felt like, and he was quite sure it was not what God had destined him for. As he and Levine entered the hotel lobby to be met by Max Fineberg, the feeling became more acute. Fineberg greeted him politely, all right, but the greeting was followed by a long silent stare, and Bell suddenly felt a flash of identity with all the Jews and blacks in history who had walked into schools, stores, concert halls, or clubs and were greeted with one silent, deafening chorus of "We have to take you, but we don't have to like it."

Truthfully, the other men in the private dining room were much friendlier. They had had about an hour's head start in drinking, and, though Bell's mother had told him of Jewish sobriety and distaste for alcohol, the distinguished members of the board seemed as well oiled as the

Muncie Elks on Veteran's Day. Voices were loud, laughter was uninhibited, and the firing point for laughter seemed low indeed.

"You know, Mort, I've had some trouble with that Kingston supplier. The one you told me about."

"Frankly, Bill, so have I."

Enormous guffaws for this flash of legendary Jewish wit.

And while Fineberg steered him around the room, making sure his glass was filled, introducing him to various manufacturers and lawyers and professors, Bell began to feel a specific unease. It was, after all, the first time he had been the only gentile—only!—in a Jewish gathering, and he began to be embarrassed by the fact that his hosts did, in fact, all look alike, that for the first time he was absolutely, he thought, able to separate out a specific "Jewish" look, "Jewish" mannerism. The faces were such solid faces, he thought, such lived-in faces, that he was sure his own pale blue eyes and minimal nose must mark him as an irredeemable innocent. He felt intimidated, the way he had the first time at the university in Professor Bering's seminar on Statistical Probability and Politics, a small-town innocent among a gang of ruthless, whip-sharp graduate students, most of them Jewish. He had heard of Roger Shapiro before, just as he had heard of the captain of the football team, but it was an unnerving experience to sit silent as Shapiro, hands and hair flopping about wildly, stumbled to the blackboard to amend Bering's equations.

Bell wasn't prepared for this, any more than he would have been prepared to find himself guarding a first-string forward in an intramural basketball game. He had no inclination to go one-on-one with Roger Shapiro and his friends, much less with Professor Bering, and he had stayed silent for two months until he had begun to realize that he was as smart as the teachers in Muncie had always told him, that all he lacked was big-league experience, and that he was getting that experience right now. There were books that Shapiro had read in high school that he had only heard of and there were things that Shapiro had discussed with his parents that his own father would never hear of, but once Bell began to catch up on his reading the distance narrowed between him and the others in the seminar, and by spring he was one of the leaders in the class, a late-hours beer buddy of Shapiro's group, pleased, then, when Shapiro called him "our honorary Jew," though later he would find this irritating, with its assumption that only Jews were clever and intellectual. At the time, in Bloomington, it had certainly seemed so.

Now, in the Madison's dining room, he was experiencing a sense of déjà vu. He had been at ease with individual Jews since college—they were interesting but not frightening. Now he felt locked out, by their looks, the assumptions and friends they shared in common, the unspoken knowledge that now they were insiders and he was an outsider.

Holding his bourbon and water tensely, listening to three men argue heatedly about the effect of the Mexican affair on the transistor business, he felt a light tap on his shoulder. He looked around to see a tall, distinguished looking man with his hand held put.

"I'm Sam Tallus. Glad to meet you, Mr. Bell."

They shook and Bell felt there was something familiar in Tallus's deep eyes and narrow lips and realized that Tallus looked like *him,* that Tallus could be a Protestant too.

"Don't take it so hard, Bell," Tallus was saying.

"What?"

"The sense of being an outsider. It's not just that you're not Jewish, it's that most of these people have known each other for years. It would be the same if you dropped into somebody else's family reunion back in your home state—you're from Indiana, aren't you?"

"That's right."

"Well, you'd feel awkward at first. But if you kept going back to that reunion every spring, you'd start to see familiar faces and it wouldn't be half so hard. I assure you, the first time I came to a meeting like this I knew only one or two other people, I had heard of only another two or three, and I stuck like glue to the people I knew."

"I guess you're right. Still, I can't help but feel like a third wheel."

"Forget it. If A.L. wanted you along, you can't be a third wheel. There's a reason for everything, as God told us."

The reference to God startled. What the hell was going on?

"Don't mind when I talk about God. I'm a little out of place in this company—I'm what they call a religious Jew. I studied for the rabbinate before I got interested in computers. I still officiate at some ceremonies. People think that's odd, but if you know anything about Jewish tradition, what is really odd is to have people who do nothing but conduct religious ceremonies. In the era of the Temple, even the priests had what you and I would call other jobs; they were farmers or goldsmiths or merchants. The idea of a full-time rabbi is something we copied from the gentiles. I still think—"

Tallus was getting warmed up, and his flat Rocky Mountain accent was developing hints of a hebraic cadence, but the conversation was interrupted by the call to dinner. As they ate, Bell was entertained by the man on his right, a gentle dove-eyed film producer named Jack Lee who explained why drive-in theaters would be making a come-back, and Tallus, who explained the scientific rationale for the kosher dietary laws. The explanations were equally Talmudic. Lee predicted that, faced with the choice of using energy coupons for gasoline or for home air-conditioning hours, people would choose the former because "Travel is a natural thing for humans. So is sweating. It's unnatural to be at home, cool, all the time." This somehow struck Bell as convoluted. So did Tallus's dissertation on the dangers of trichinosis and hepatitis, topics which, no matter how kosher the dinner, did not fan his appetite.

He was relieved, then, when Fineberg struck his wineglass promptly as the coffee (no cream—Tallus started to explain) was served.

Fineberg was surprisingly succinct. "A.L. Levine needs no introduction to this audience, so I won't introduce him. And, since anyone who can count up to twenty knows that he's running for the presidency, I won't talk about that either. Here is Mr. A.L. Levine to tell you about his candidacy as it affects the Jews."

The applause was less than wild. Bell felt the ambivalence Levine had predicted, the wariness of men who had made it to the top by not making waves, a wariness mingled with grudging envy for the man who had stepped out in front in the political area they had considered their own. Levine was not content to be a water boy or a coach or a manager or even a franchise owner, he wanted to be a player, and for men who had wistfully wanted to be players all their lives, it was hard to accept someone as ugly, as unassimilated, as *Jewish* as themselves as a candidate without at least a tinge of regret.

"Thank you, Max. It's a pleasure. We're all among friends, now, so I'm going to skip the bullshit and get right down to cases. I'm running for the presidency and I need your support as individuals and as a group. I want your support, your endorsement, and your contributions. The reasons are obvious—basically, I endorse the same kind of social justice that you have supported in previous campaigns. I'm not going to give you a whole megilla as to the specifics. Rather than that, since I think my policy has been pretty well outlined in broad terms, I'd like to talk to you individually, answering the questions I know you must have. Just go ahead, raise your hands like back in school, and let me talk to you. . . . Over there." He pointed to the back of the room.

"Bob Goodman from West Hartford. I—"

"You don't have to introduce yourself to me, Bob. It would be like my own brother, if I ever had one, introducing himself. Nobody in this group has to introduce himself."

"A.L., I didn't hear you address yourself to the question Max raised—your candidacy as it affects the Jews."

"I'm glad you asked that, Bob. My candidacy will be good for the Jews because I am convinced I will be a good president. My candidacy will be a Jewish one to the extent that I was raised as a Jew, with the perceptions that

many—not all—of us share. I'm what used to be called a
liberal, but as you know, despite what many people, both
Jew and gentile, think, there is nothing intrinsically
liberal in Judaism. When abortion was an issue in New
York in the old days, most liberal Jews were in favor of
making abortions easier, despite the fact that, from a
Talmudic viewpoint, abortion is evil. So my views on
issues will be formulated primarily from the perceptions
of A. L. Levine, not because there is any kind of Jewish
viewpoint on them."

"I'm Irv Zeitzman from Biloxi. What about relations
with Israel? The Middle East could give us trouble again,
you know."

"Irv, I'm aware of that. My duty in relationship to
Israel is clear. As president of the United States, my sworn
duty is to preserve and protect those states. That comes
first. That's been my primary interest all my life. As a Jew,
I want to see Israel survive. Fortunately, the U.S. has a
mutual defense treaty with Israel. I can, unlike some
people, see instances where the interests of the U.S. and
Israel would diverge. In that case I would have no
problem. I have lived all my life in this country, my
parents lived here, my children live here, I would have a
duty to the people of this country. However, if it ever
came to the absolute case in which an action I might take
would destroy Israel, rather than merely weaken it, I
could not take that action. I do not foresee that
happening, ever, but if the situation arose I would resign."

"That's the same answer you gave to the Episcopal
bishops last week."

"Would you want me to give different answers to
different people?"

The man who asked the question seemed puzzled. "No,
but still, I think you have a special obligation to your own
people."

Bell was startled to see Levine gesture to him to come
to the head of the table. "Philip, go downstairs to the
lobby. Get me a copy of last week's *Times* of Israel. I
know they have it here; they have a big international
newsstand. Okay?"

As Bell left the room he heard Levine saying, "I don't know how to answer that any more explicitly than I already have, but..."

The *Times* of Israel was available, just as Levine said it would be, and Bell hurried back to the room to hear Levine say, "...keep the United States healthy, then Israel will be healthy too. But if I get distracted, think first of Israel's health, then we're in trouble back here. The prime minister of Israel is paid to look after Israel first, and he does a pretty good job."

There was a murmur of approval as Bell slipped the paper to Levine. "Thanks, Philip. Let me read to you gentlemen what the leading Israeli newspaper said about that statement to the bishops: 'Mr. Levine's position does credit to himself and to the maturity of the Jewish community in the United States. It should end once and for all the insinuations of dual loyalty.' I don't think I have to add anything more."

There was a long pause and then a few desultory questions about Mexico, the Patrols, and the border problems. Bell sensed that there was a hidden agenda, which perhaps was about to be revealed.

"If there are no more questions," Max Fineberg said, "I think it's appropriate for me to make a few remarks. The executive committee has, of course, been very interested in A.L.'s candidacy. I think it's fair to say that, while we agree it's a great honor for a fellow Jew to be considered for the presidency, we have reservations about his running at this time." He paused and repeated, "At this time."

"I'm not sure what you mean," Levine said.

"The board feels—and I think I can safely speak for the majority—given the historic place of the Jews in this country, given the ever-present possibility of a reemergence of anti-Semitism, that a candidacy such as yours would only tend to focus people's resentments on the Jews *as* Jews. Historically, we have worked behind the scenes in politics, kept a low profile. While we hope that this will change, today is not the time for it. Those of you who are a bit older may remember a somewhat similar problem we had with Arthur Goldberg, when he wanted to be governor of New York."

Levine half rose from his chair. "Well, suppose the campaign goes along and I get elected? Wouldn't that square it?"

Fineberg smiled. "We considered the possibility. Again, while it would be a great tribute to the American Jewish community to have one of our leaders elected president, it would still be a great danger to the community at large. As opposed to a candidate whom people fear because of what he *might* do, a president can become hated for what he *does* do. That hatred would inevitably reflect onto other Jews."

"Jesus Christ," Levine said. "You mean you think that a Jewish president would be *bad* for the Jews?"

Fineberg spread his hands eloquently. "A.L., that's what I'm saying. That's what our leading sociologists have agreed. Please don't take it personally."

Levine bounced up and down, half in, half out of his chair. "Don't take it personally? Of course I take it personally! Let's get some things straight. You men are practical people. You know that if I get elected president, it won't be a great tribute to the American Jewish community. It will be a great tribute to me and to the people who believe in me. And if I muck it up, it won't be any reflection on the American Jewish community, it will be a reflection on me. Oh, sure, it will be mentioned, but don't you see that the same people who hated Jews before will hate them still and use me as an excuse? No one's going to become an anti-Semite because his taxes go up. Christ, people hated Catholics, and when Kennedy was president you didn't see them going out burning churches after the Bay of Pigs."

Sam Tallus stood up. "If I may interject, I would agree with A.L. that his candidacy has a larger purpose than nurturing the Jews. It's a simple matter: This board should be for the candidate who is best for America. It's a marvelous thing, really, that that person is a Jew."

Fineberg smiled again. He was, Bell thought, the kind of man who smiled as he told you that he, personally, was very sorry but your child was not bright enough for his school, and you knew that he was not sorry and that one of the major pleasures of his life was telling his social and intellectual superiors that somehow they or their children did not quite measure up. Every time Fineberg said he was sorry, he smiled, and the smiles looked less and less genuine.

"I'm sorry," Fineberg said, smiling, "but the matter is pretty well settled, as I think you know, Sam."

Levine stood up. "Does this mean I cannot expect the board's endorsement?"

Fineberg hesitated. "The board this year will take a policy of endorsing no candidates in the presidential race. We certainly would not endorse another candidate over you."

"Thanks. Let me say this. Naturally I'm disappointed that you cannot find yourselves able to endorse me. I know that many of you would like to and perhaps voted to do so in the early sessions. I'm not going to try to find out who voted how. I'm going to assume that everyone here voted for me, and somehow got outvoted. There will be no retribution on my part. I assume goodwill on yours. While I'm disappointed that the board cannot give its official recommendation, I know that as individuals you can endorse and work for candidates, and as my campaign goes along I am confident that each and every one of you will do so. Thank you again for taking the time to listen."

In the cab back home Bell said, "That was sweet."

"What do you mean?"

"You could have gotten their endorsement if you had worked for it. I can't believe that you and Tallus couldn't have gotten a majority to go along with supporting you."

"Well, true, we didn't buttonhole them personally, but I don't think that's dignified among people you know—"

"Bullshit. You didn't buttonhole them because you didn't want to win."

"And why, please tell, would that be?"

"Because you've got the Jewish vote, whatever it is, sewed up. And because you figure that whatever uncommitted, unsure anti-Semites are around, and that may be twenty million votes, they're not going to be overjoyed if the board endorses you. You want a little distance between you and the board, and you want it to seem like genuine distance."

Levine smiled. "That would seem to be reasonable, but I'm hardly as Machiavellian as that, Philip. Hardly."

"Do it in the studio," Bell said. "It'll be more dignified, we'll have a prepared script, and there won't be any audience to rattle you or get your timing off. We can use that backdrop they have in New York—it makes you look like you're sitting right inside the Oval Office."

"What do you think, Garrett?" Levine asked.

"I'm not so sure. From what I've seen, ol' A.L. is better before live people than a couple of cameramen and a lot of lights. I don't ever remember you being rattled, and that's the truth."

"Arthur?"

Jones shook his head. "Do it live. Do it extra-live. Not in front of one of those fund-raising dinners but out in the open. Get some shouting and hollering out in the audience. Be yourself."

Levine nodded. "Philip, I asked the others for their opinions because I'd checked them out before. To tell you the truth, I haven't been a public person long enough to get bored speaking to an audience. I like it—okay, maybe not five times a day, but once a day. It's a funny thing, but while I'm talking I get new ideas."

"One new idea in a campaign can kill the whole thing," Bell said. "Remember Goldwater and Social Security, McGovern and his income allowance, Cabot Lodge and his black vice-president? If you want to be spontaneous, be a night-club comedian. If you want to be president, stick to the script."

"Suppose you want to be a night-club comedian *and* president?" Levine asked.

"That's just the sort of wise-ass remark that you're going to make some day and kill the whole thing off."

"I'll try to stick to my notes. But it's decided. We'll do it live, from an outdoor rally. If you can promise me the people."

"Don't worry about the people. Worry about the speech."

They found the place and the people, all right. The poll outfit found that Paterson, New Jersey, fitted Levine's demographics exactly: lots of middle-class, older whites, enough blacks to make it realistic, enough unemployed to make jobs an issue (and be available to go to political rallies), and not many young people. A Democratic mayor, who could be counted on to close off a main plaza for the rally. Enough Jews nearby so they could be carted in by the busload if the crowd seemed disappointing.

It wasn't. The advance people had done just what was needed. There was plenty of newspaper and TV talk in advance, there was a high school band for the old people and a funk band for whichever kids showed up. The unions got their people out, and no one had to cart in Jews by the busload; they came on their own.

"Jesus Christ," Bell said, looking out over the square. "There must be five thousand people out there."

"The police figure is ten thousand," Jones said.

"That's right, there must be five thousand people out there," Bell repeated. "I haven't seen a crowd like that since Kennedy ran."

"When you were ten years old," Jones added.

"I can remember, for Christ's sake, from the time I was two. Anyway, what are they doing here?"

"It's a way for some people to be alive. Old people, people without jobs, kids dropped out of school. They can be busy doing nothing and feel that they're helping the country. If you're not busy making money you have time to think about politics."

"Here comes the boss."

Levine suddenly emerged from the crowd and ascended to the platform. The crowd cheered. The mayor introduced him. The crowd cheered again. Levine smiled, waved at the crowd, and began.

"What nice people you all are! I'm grateful that you all came to hear me, and proud that you would want to listen. You notice that I walked from the back of the crowd to the front by myself to get up on this platform. The Secret

Service want me to pop right out from behind the platform, but I'm not a tall person and, quite frankly, with my looks I can walk through any crowd of people and not create a commotion. In fact, people don't notice me. And so I worked my way through the crowd and listened to you talk, as you waited for the figure to pop out on the platform, and I heard you speak and I was proud and thought, What good people you are! It was almost like being present at my own funeral service. The people in the crowd who were talking about me were saying nice things, saying that they had heard good things about me. Many people were skeptical—that's the way it should be. Many people weren't talking about politics at all; they were talking about the basketball game, and the weather, and the hiring down at the Balmore mill—that's the way it should be. The world will go on whether I'm elected or not. I heard a lot of different languages—Spanish, Italian, Hungarian, Yiddish, Vietnamese—and of the people speaking English I heard many different accents—rich people's accents, hill country accents, North Carolina accents, southern accents.

"And I thought what a fine people we are, we Americans. I think this often, but especially during political campaigns when people get so angry at each other and with what's wrong with the country that we forget more and more our noble qualities. I would not bother to run for office did I not feel that our people deserve much better officials than they have been getting. I do not use the word 'leaders'—if anyone out there is looking for a president who will lead us away from crime and unemployment and border wars, he should not look at me. In our country it is truly the people who lead, and it is the president's job to sense the mood of the people, to genuinely believe in its concerns, and to help translate those concerns into action. A candidate can pretend that he or she shares the concern of the people, and may even get elected. But you can't read polls, find out what the people are supposed to be thinking, and then claim that you've been thinking that all along. You'll be found out.

"Now, what gives me the right to say that I think I truly

feel what America wants and needs? First, I am not a politician, though I have been interested in politics. This is the first time I have run for office. It's an advantage not to be a politician, because, like all occupations, politics puts a mark on a man. Politics is a worthy, noble profession, but a lifetime in it requires so much compromise, so much dealing, that a person tends to forget what his real principles were in the first place. After a while a politician can justify almost anything if he believes the majority of people in his district or city or state are in favor of it, or if another politician who's in a place to do him a favor is in favor of it. Compromise is necessary, but a lifetime of it leaves a mark. It is fine for a career in the Senate, but not necessary or even desirable in a president. I am, I believe, experienced in politics, but not a politician.

"Why should an orphaned Jewish boy from New York grow up to think he can become president? Why not? In a sense, we are not only a nation of immigrants but a nation of orphans. Somewhere in the past, our parents, our grandparents, our great-grandparents, someone in our family cut himself or herself off from relatives, sailed across the ocean, or set out across America itself, looking west or heading north. In Europe, where my grandparents were born, it was almost sinful for a son to wish to be different or better than his father. If the father was a cobbler, the son must be a cobbler too. But in America we assume that children will get more education, more money than their parents, and so we have seen sons grow away from fathers, daughters drift away from mothers. Who better feels this than someone like me, secure today in my fine wife and children but raised among strangers, dreaming of parents of my own?"

He paused and looked out over the great mass of faces. It was the opposite of the French painting that, created out of thousands of almost identical dots, grew together into a scene of quiet beauty. Here the crowd was meaningless, and only by focusing on the separate dots could you get the scent of humanity. Levine saw a tall Puerto Rican man smiling up at him, clapping and nodding. The man looked as though he, too, had lost his parents as a child.

Levine felt a great wave of love pass from him out over the crowd to converge on the tall Puerto Rican. How hard it was to be alone, a young man, trying to make one's way among people speaking a language forever clumsy in your own mouth!

Levine fought back tears. He paused again and began to speak of the issues, and as he spoke he felt respect radiate back from the crowd—the Puerto Rican man—and in a way that neither he nor the reporters could ever explain, he became eloquent.

A convention is no more to be experienced from a hotel room than an opera from a phone booth. A convention is a college reunion for people who never went to college, an orgy for people who never go to orgies, a street fair for people who shop only at the A&P. To be real it must be experienced from the convention floor itself, where the faces and accents of fifty-two states, the sweats and passions of two thousand delegates, the ambitions of a dozen candidates all run together.

Levine watched the convention from his hotel room. Pacing back and forth, he stifled his need to be with his friends, his enemies—his people!—with a kind of indoor roadwork.

"We are still listening to the deliberations of the platform committee," the announcer said, "Speaking in favor of the resolution on Mexico will be Kansas delegate and state senator Willis Kimche, who—"

"Who hasn't drawn a sober breath in the past seventy-two hours," Levine interrupted. 'Not that I blame him. Having to defend that thing on Mexico and then go home to Wichita won't be easy. What the hell kind of a name is Kimche, anyway?"

"Hell, A.L.," Garrett Brandon said, "you're our resident ethnographer. If you can't tell us a name, us southern boys surely can't help. It took me twenty-five years to find out that Bernard Goldfine was Jewish."

Bell shouted in from the balcony, where he had been sunning himself,

"Kimche is a German name. I know, I used to date a girl named that once."

"Kimche is a Korean name," said Jessington. "It's something you eat."

"The same goes for that German girl I used to date," Bell yelled back.

Kimche spoke eagerly, ploddingly. The professionals in Levine's suite paid him about as much attention as people at a heavyweight fight give the first preliminary bout. Kimche was an amateur, a stumbler, far beneath their interest, and yet they couldn't quite ignore him completely. Who knew when the immortal spark might first be seen?

". . . once again siding with the repressive forces all over the world," Kimche said. "The gallant revolutionaries in Mexico are fighting, not against the United States government but against United States oil interests . . ."

"What's the difference?" Levine and Jessington shouted out simultaneously.

". . . and persistence in our neo-imperialist policy will only further the conviction of the Third World . . ."

"Third World," Jessington murmured. "I haven't heard that for years. Good to have the old Third World back again."

"Won't you come home again, won't you come home? Third World we missed you so," Bell sang as he darted to the piano.

Farbstein the socialist shushed them. "Quiet, I'm trying to hear."

"Farbstein, you're nothing but a fucking socialist," Dwayne van Dillinham roared. He was only mildly drunk, but since he was a governor he roared as a matter of course.

"I can't listen here," Farbstein said. He shuffled out of the living room into the balcony, where he turned on a portable set.

"It's Farbstein's first convention," Levine said. "He'll learn."

". . . that the Mexico C.D.F. presents no problems to the United States except in its own blindness. Rather than a threat . . ."

"Fucking Kimche wouldn't recognize a threat if one ran a bayonet up his ass," van Dillinham said. "Us Arkansans have seen agrarian reformers before, but he ain't never seen them with heat-sensing missiles. We want those fuckers *out*. I don't care how many sweet ol' peasants they've got signed up."

Kimche finished and was followed by Wormley, a stately black man who supported the other resolution on Mexico.

"...Indeed, was willing to take up arms when the threat to our sacred liberties was ninety miles from shore. How would we answer our great John F. Kennedy if we refuse to take notice of a serpent nestling against our very bosom, a serpent..."

"Hey, Jess, where do you get these people?" van Dillinham yelled.

"I don't get them, I merely sit by and watch their own sweet selves take over," Jessington said. "I think I'll go for a swim."

"...meet this threat with the utmost of sanctions," Wormley continued, "up to and including force of arms."

"How come you people are so warlike?" Levine said.

"We were peacelike for two hundred years and look what it got us," Jessington said.

Wormley finished. Phone calls came to Levine about the resolution. "Oh, shit," he said, "vote your conscience on that. I don't want to get boxed in on any policy in advance. Jesus, I start endorsing military action and I'll get every lady voter in America..."

"Not to mention Mexico," Bell shouted.

"...on my back. We can leave it blank for a while. Fill in the holes yourself. Tell them I'm studying the issue. The reason you tell them that is because I am." He hung up.

"I can't take this any more, Garrett. You watch awhile and make sure nothing awful happens. I'm going to call Helen."

She didn't like conventions, which was understandable. She didn't like noise, dirt, sweat, hard liquor, and bad language under any circumstances, and gathered together in one spot for a convention they horrified her. He had taken her down to Miami in '72 and she had gone back to Washington after two days. "What's happened to Miami?" she said, just before she had left.

"Hello, dear.... Fine, fine.... And you?... Just waiting around, watching television.... No, it's not very hot, Actually, I'm not sure—we stay in the hotel room all day.... I can't go down to the convention, I'm a candidate.... I know it's unfair, but it's a tradition. I don't know why.... I will, I will.... Stay well.... See you soon.... I'll tell him."

He hung up. "Garrett, Helen sends regards."

"Why, that's just fine. You going to watch awhile?"

"No, I think I'll go back to the bedroom and take a nap. If anyone wants me, just buzz me."

Arthur Jones came by and Levine talked to him about the press conferences. Sweeney came by and Levine talked to him about some maximum givers who were holding out until they had some more definite word on his Mexico policy. Kathy Derrick came by with a couple of press releases to check, and Levine, against his better judgment, screwed her. With women, his better judgment often wasn't very good. Kathy wasn't demanding and there was no reason to think that she wanted anything from him but a quick come and a brush with power, but she was young and he knew from experience that it was foolish to trust any woman under thirty. The young ones sometimes fell in love and called you at the office.

———————

In the evening, he received. Bell had set the schedule and he kept to it. No politician was going to complain that A. L. Levine had kept him cooling his heels for a couple of hours, waiting in a hotel suite with only a dead-ass television set for company. No one would be kept waiting, not before the balloting, anyway. Every fifteen minutes for three hours a new entourage was ushered into his presence. There were governors urging vice-presidential candidates and senators urging platform positions and big givers pushing themselves. Levine waited, listened, and nodded. He had been on the other side of the desk too many times to miss what was happening. The governors and the senators and the big givers smelled victory, smelled it like you could smell cantaloupe in the middle of the bay from a school of bluefish, smelled it the way you would smell sex on a woman who had had to dress too quickly for a shower. They smelled victory and they

wanted a piece of it. Levine doled out the pieces
grudgingly.

When the last of the supplicants was gone, Bell went to
the icebox, took out a beer, and walked out to the terrace.

"You're angry?" Levine asked.

"Of course, I'm angry."

"Then tell me. Don't walk out and slam the door, like
some society woman with cramps. Tell me, you didn't like
the way I handled Scuzarro?"

"No. Not him and not Fenn, either. Both of them could
help you."

"Both of them are going to help me."

"Bullshit. Scuzarro's got his hands out to the Kennedy
people. They'll know how to use him. They've always got
a place for someone with a hundred grand and a chain of
movie theaters and a few thousand employees who
wouldn't mind volunteering. I know Scuzarro and I know
the Kennedy people."

"You know him, but you don't know him enough.
You've never been there in his shoes, trying to make
something respectable for your grandchildren out of
some old-law dirty movies. I've been there. Scuzarro isn't
going to jump to Kennedy or Cunningham or anyone else.
He's been around. He knows I'm going to win. He'll be
back. So will Fenn. Philip, maybe being a politician is
being a whore, but the first thing you learn is not to sell it
cheap. Don't make it any more complicated than it has to
be."

"I'll bet," Bell said. "No, come to think of it, I won't."
He went over to the piano and began to work on
progressions.

"That's nice," Levine said, "but why do your
homework in public? Play something you like, something
quiet."

Bell began some variations by Gottschalk. Jessington
came in, plumped down on the sofa, closed his eyes. His
right little finger tapped gently with the music. A few
wire-service reporters wandered in, nodded to Levine,
and poured themselves drinks. Sturgis Hale threw open
the door, started to ask a question, heard the music, and

sat down on the floor. Bell played for an hour, then got up and stretched.

"That was great," Hale said. Bell nodded.

"Why don't you play those things you did back in Chicago, the ones we can sing with?" one of the reporters asked.

"I'm in my concert mood now," Bell said. "No sing-alongs. Anyway, this band's packed up for the night. It's time to hear the loyal opposition."

He switched on the television. Rose was getting ready to deliver an equal-time reply. He was speaking from the front porch of his place in Vermont.

"...amidst these green and ancient hills," Rose was saying.

"Oh, Jesus," one of the reporters muttered.

"...so prominent in our nation's heritage..."

"Which I bought into when I married a rich wife," Hale said.

"The priceless heritage of clean air, clean water, room for living, room which is about to be destroyed by the developers and exploiters who see America only as a business opportunity, not as an ideal..."

"And who had the bad taste to get here fifty years after the original exploiters and developers," Levine said.

Rose plunged on. He was good on television; his father's lessons were well remembered. He evoked a quiet, green America, a nation of happy yeomen, planting farms, raising cattle, working leather.

"Of course, we cannot retreat into the past," Rose said.

"Of course," chorused the group in Levine's suite.

"...mighty industrial power and continued advance in our standard of living. Yet we cannot allow ourselves the easy equation that any change is, by itself, progress, and that anything newer or bigger is necessarily better."

Levine grunted.

"...protect our national resources for the people themselves...a philosophy of government that is all of one piece, which says that we are a unique, sovereign nation, that we are not the world's policeman or even its traffic director, that we cannot involve ourselves in every little border struggle on the globe, but that when our own national integrity is threatened by a communist-led revolution on our very border we must reply immediately, with full military strength if necessary. We are not the world's policeman, but we are not its pushover, either."

The little band of Rose's neighbors that the television people had gathered for "A Front Porch Chat" nodded and clapped, and the program ended.

"He's a shrewd sonofabitch," Bell said.

"Sure. You don't get that far by being stupid. Usually."

The wire-service reporters were arguing with Hale. "How the hell can he live with himself? You can't fool all of the people all of the time."

Hale shook his head. "You guys have it wrong. You think it's an act, but no one like that is an actor. Rose believes all that. Some of it doesn't make sense, some of it's contradictory, but that's the way life is. So long as it seems to hang together, that's all you want. It's not a matter of fooling all of the people all of the time. You must have to fool fifty-one percent of them."

"Once every four years," Slaven from the AP said.

"You guys are up past your bedtime," Levine said. "Have a drink and clear out. Jessington's been down on the floor, and we've got some counting to do."

They were living by lists then, endless lists of the states in alphabetical order with the magic number of delegates alongside each state's name.

Jessington's figures were not encouraging. "I don't like it," he said. "I figured us to go over on the first ballot, but we're still about two hundred and fifty votes shy. The Illinois people are holding out. Hein's people in Colorado won't budge. I'm trying to shake them loose, but they're stubborn."

Bell looked over the lists. "Suppose we asked Hein to come up here and talk to A.L. tonight?"

"I hinted about that. They're not interested. They've got a lot of hairs and freaks out there. They don't like developers. They say they're going to argue it out among themselves some more. I believe them."

"Leave them alone," Levine said. "Don't try to hustle

them. Tell me, how many votes do we have for sure in Arkansas?"

Jessington looked at his list. "Twenty-two for sure, another ten possibles. Van Dillinham doesn't quite have a stranglehold on his own state."

"How many are we telling the press people we've got?"

"The same. Actually, for the press we've put two of the probables into the sures."

"Take them out. Get the word around that we've lost ten in Arkansas, but make sure that you tell them that we've picked up another twelve further down the road."

"Where?"

"Christ, how should I know? Oregon, maybe? Wherever you think it's plausible. Some from here, some from there. Play it by ear."

"You trying to sandbag them?" Bell asked.

Levine shrugged. "What else?"

"It won't work. People are wise to that."

"You're wise to it. You've been through this before. Forty-five percent of those delegates have never been to a convention before. The delegation leaders don't have the kind of control they used to. You've got thirty-five hundred amateur Jake Arveys milling around there, all thinking that they're red-hot politicians and most of them knowing nothing. You get them expecting twelve votes for Levine from Arkansas and all of a sudden there are twenty-two or twenty-five, and they all think they're geniuses—they've spotted a trend. Levine's moving! Some of them are going to jump. Not many. Maybe about two hundred and fifty altogether."

Jessington rolled his eyes. "Yeah, it worked once, for Stevenson. But look how many people got burned by it. When word gets out you're losing a few votes in Arkansas, those same geniuses will be figuring you're losing hold, and they're going to start looking someplace else."

"It's a risk, but if you're sure we're still short two fifty and we can't bargain any more, it's a risk worth taking. I feel the same way you do: if we don't make it on the first ballot, we may be in trouble. Some of the magic gets rubbed off. If they see I'm not Super Jew, they may start

to deal right there on the floor. I don't want it to get to
that. We take a risk with sandbagging, but there are two
things I'm sure of—we can get the governor of Arkansas
to back up whatever we say about that delegation, and A
comes before O in the alphabet."

In the end, of course, they didn't need the sandbagging.
The milling crowd of delegates, half mob, half congregation, was swept by tides of rumor and passion. Depending
on their own inner controls, the delegates either hunkered
down with their original choice or darted one way and
then the other, seeking a perfect candidate or a perfect
deal. But Jessington, Brandon, van Dillinham, and the
other floor leaders moved among them like mother hens.
The planning had been perfect, even down to Levine's
insistence that the managers had to be familiar, not to the
insiders or the delegation leaders but to the delegates
themselves. Confused, uncertain, they saw time and time
again faces that they knew from television—people they
recognized!—people who were the moving, cajoling
vanguard of Levine's candidacy.

They went over by 213 votes on the first ballot. When
the result was announced, the Arkansas delegation
started hollering and some of New York began to dance in
the aisles. A gray-haired woman waved a banner that read
"Israel Lives." And then, starting God knows where, but
moving down row after row of delegates, picking up
volume with every repetition, came the full-throated yell,
"We want Levine, We Want Levine."

Watching in his hotel room, Levine wept.

There was talk of getting someone great, someone
dramatic for vice-president, but Levine stopped it. "It's
going to be Senator Milwood. He's a good man, he can
run the country if he has to, but basically he's not a
president and he knows it. You can't have all-star politics
any more than you can have an all-star night-club act.
Someone has to be the topliner. Put someone great in as

vice-president, and he either gets bitter with hatred or he's always trying to push himself in front of the president. It's Milwood."

He was an ideal choice for vice-president. He was proud but had no pride. It was impossible to hurt his feelings, for a lifetime of politics had worn his sensibilities so smooth that nothing could engage them. When once a heckler shouted at him, "Shut your fat-assed mouth," he replied—gravely, "Thank you for your contribution. This is a free country, and freedom of expression is what made us great."

He came from Nevada and no crowd was too small for him to winnow for votes, an invaluable asset in a vice-presidential candidate. No one took his campaigning ideas or speeches seriously but Milwood himself. His personal staff begged for a plane, but often enough he was reduced to bus caravan sweeps through what were called "crucial districts." He visited Akron so many times that the mayor called Bell and said, "Jesus, keep that sonofabitch out of here. I trooped out all the Senior Citizens last week, but I can't get the City Hall people again or they'll call a strike. They won't go."

When he was permitted a jet, his enthusiasm invariably betrayed him. Like an Irish setter puppy he bounded into a waiting crowd at Hartford-Springfield Airport, shook hands enthusiastically, and was only slightly upset to find that he had greeted a large Italian family, waiting for their dying mother to arrive from Florida.

"Well, my sympathies are all with you fine folk," he said. "Remember us on election day."

"Fongul," someone muttered.

Once there was a kind of Fourth of July firework, considered safe even by anxious mothers in the Midwest, which consisted only of a faintly obscene gray pellet the size of a lima bean. Touched by a match, the pellet did not explode or sparkle but almost magically extruded a long, gray tail which went on endlessly until the tiny pellet had turned into something yards long.

As a boy Bell had disliked the pellets—they reminded him somehow of rabbit turds, and the material they extruded, when it did not appear fecal, was definitely snakelike. "Snakes," the other kids had called them. Bell had been fascinated by and afraid of snakes, and it was not until he was older, perhaps ten or eleven, that he dared touch the long tail that issued from the pellet. It had crumbled instantly under his fingers. Ashes, that's all that the snakes had been.

He told this to Sally Cunningham as they sipped Cokes and waited for the room to cool down. Spence Cunningham would be angry if his energy coupons were used up for air conditioning while he was campaigning for friends in California and Oregon.

"Why did I tell you that?" Bell asked.

"You told me that because you are going to tell me next that campaigning reminds you of that snake."

"Jesus, I guess we better get married. Two minds with but a single thought."

He was about to add something about "a single thought except for one other thing," but decided to let it go by. They were past the coy eroticism of early lovers.

"No, it's not that," she said. "It's just that I'm smart too. Don't you think that after all these years I haven't thought about how crazy campaigns are? It's a good simile, though, the magic appearance of something from nothing, the . . ."

"Actually it's a metaphor."

"I never could remember the difference, but I always knew a good one when I saw one. I'll tell you something else, Mr. Campaigner."

"What?"

"I know why you people love them so much. The campaigns. There are some people who love politics but not campaigning, and then there are other people who come out every four years or six years or two years and do your campaigning for you and never show up until the next election. They don't ask for anything, either."

"Yeah, I know. What's your theory?"

"It's easy. It's like somebody said, it's the moral equivalent of war. Men can get out of their homes, go off traveling, live together with other men, like boot camp, screw girls they'll never see again, and then come back home safe and be heroes to their wives."

Bell was hurt. "Women do that too."

"Oh, relax, I know that. My God, the women reporters and speechwriters. My God! The ones that traveled with Spence. I was at a party with him after the last presidential election, a stuffy party in Hartford, and some old guy, probably insurance, came up to Spence and chatted with him and said, 'By the way, I happened to have met a Polly Travis during your campaign,' and before he could say anything more, Spence said, 'Well, if you met her you screwed her,' and the man turned red and walked away. Spence was a little high."

"Sure, there's some of that," Bell said.

"Some! Don't be naïve. My God, you are naïve. You're still messing around with probies and married women. You've never been married. You've never felt that awful seven-year or one-year or two-month itch when any crumby semiliterate dropout waitress looks like a better screw than the magnificent woman you've got at home."

"I haven't had the pleasure," he said.

"Well, I have. For me the seven-year itch developed two months before we were married—people still got engaged back then—and it's lasted right on through. I wish we still had delivery boys instead of these damn girls in their little trucks."

"Those girls aren't bad. It's part of liberation that I'll go for. Think of all the pitiful fantasies that men had to build up about being traveling salesmen or icemen or delivery boys or something to get you into a strange woman's house. We never had fantasies about strange women coming to our houses or apartments, because they didn't."

"Poor babies!"

"Well, it's true. You people had all the fun of getting it right at home. We had to scrounge through bars and colleges and young adults meetings. Now, with those Serva-Girls, we get it delivered hot and steaming into our own rooms."

"You can't do anything with those Serva-Girls, though. They test them regularly."

"If you believe that, you believe in the Easter bunny. There's nothing in the world that can keep a lady from screwing if she wants to. I've had friends who've screwed Serva-Girls."

"What did they say?"

"Well, actually, it wasn't a they so much as a he."

"What did he say?"

"He said the pizza was better than the screw. Hotter and juicier."

She laughed. "Maybe they could use that in 'Life in These United States.' I wonder. Levine was a salesman; I wonder if he ever got much."

"Not Levine."

"Why not him?"

"He's shy. He's old-fashioned. What's the word they use? 'Courtly.' He's courtly around women."

"That doesn't mean he doesn't mess around."

"Yes, it does, in a way. It's a way of sending out signals, telling women you've got them up on a pedestal. If someone talks crudely, any woman who hangs around knows what he's interested in."

"Maybe Levine's interested in another kind of woman."

"Jesus, why don't we get off the subject of Levine? I spend all day with him, and as soon as I get into bed with a beautiful woman she starts cross-examining me about him."

"Don't blame me. I was ready for fun and games."

"It's still too hot for me. Let's take a swim."

"Sure."

They padded down the stairway and out the back door. "Watch out for glass," she said. "One of the kids broke a bottle around here the other day."

"Where are the kids?"

"At their grandmother's for the weekend."

"Which one?"

"My mother. She figures I'm screwing somebody, but she aids and abets. I'm doing what she always wanted to do."

"I take back what I said about getting married. Adultery must run in your family."

"It runs in all families. You just don't find out about your parents until you're grown up."

He paused. "It's a nice swimming pool, anyway."

"Yes. Some things I don't mind small, like houses or cars, but you can just forget about your tiny swimming pools or itsy-bitsy telescreens. I'd rather not have one at all than be bumping my head against a pool wall every time I take three strokes or have to be squinting down at some dwarf TV."

"I'll remember that," he said, and dove in. "Lovely."

"Shhh. The neighbors."

"Okay. I'll swim quietly."

They swam until a late breeze came and they figured the room had cooled down, but by that time they were heavy-lidded and sleepy, and there was no compulsion to make love, so they waited until morning.

Bell had never slept better, never. Sally was almost as old as he was and, with her children, had lived more. She was richer than he and knew politics just as well. Suddenly he felt the weight of trying to impress her slip away. She was past all impressing. For the first time in his life he was totally relaxed with a woman, and at a time and place when he least expected it, Bell discovered something he suspected was love.

Edwards read the long list of figures, smiling as he went on. The list was a computer printout of post-convention preferences in the southern and midwestern states. My kind of computer, Edwards thought. It would be hard to stop Levine now. Rose might try something, but there was nothing he could do but stir up nastiness. Edwards was was used to nastiness—he knew there was no such thing as a gentlemanly campaign any more than there was a friendly game of real poker, but he knew that Rose was smart. Rose would see soon enough he was beaten and hold back on anything really dirty.

He wondered what Rose's first move would be. Levine was free from any scandal. The party had checked him out with the usual detailed investigation and, just to be sure, Edwards had hired a good private detective agency, listing its cost under "Research." He did this on every major candidate, never mentioning it to anyone else in the party. It wouldn't be good for his assistants—Bell, for example—to get the idea that their word wasn't their bond.

Levine checked out just fine. No family scandals, though he did have a nasty-looking, nasty-talking twenty-six-year-old kid. Who didn't, Edward thought? Levine's money was clean, and in the years he had worked for the party and advised presidents there had never been a hint of using the influence for money or power. Of course, the early part of A.L.'s career was a little vague, but there was little way of checking out a sales representative's life. Edwards remembered the old days and the jokes about traveling salesmen. There probably wasn't a person left in the country who called himself a traveling salesman. "Sales engineers" were what they were now, and they rarely traveled. The computers and the video conference calls did their traveling for them. Rose could crack wise about "traveling salesmen" all he wanted, and half the country wouldn't even understand what he was talking about. And that half would be Rose's own constituency, the hairs and the Westmoreland League, clumped together in their walled cities in Arizona and Florida. The golden oldies would understand, but they wouldn't take it as an insult. Lots of them had made some sales themselves.

Whatever Rose's move, it would be different, and it would have to come soon.

"I've been listening for weeks now," Rose said, "and I say we've got to go at this thing head on."

Elsworth Palmer shook his head. "I don't think the people will go for it. They still remember the quota years. You start attacking Levine as a Jew, and you'll get the Poles and the Irish and the Greeks and god-knows-what all bunched up together again, just like they were in 'seventy-six. They're just beginning to get over that, and you'd scare the shit out of them again. You'd bunch them up and bunch 'em for Levine."

"Maybe, but not necessarily. I still don't see all that love between the Irish and the Jews. What we can do is isolate Levine, put him off in a rowboat all by himself, then take away the oars."

"You're kidding yourself, Rose," Palmer said. "You've been talking to those fucking kids too long. They think you're God, and maybe you are, but you've got to listen to me about some things. And I'm going telling you that if you start shouting 'Jew, Jew,' all those hunkies are going to see themselves next in line. You maybe could do it in another country or against another candidate, but Levine wouldn't let you out of it. He'd remind all those Bronskis and di Napolis of what happened when the spooks went on the Black Power kick."

"Okay, Els, I'll give you that. But there are two other points. First, my own people, the hairs, the Westies, they're not going to be happy with a Jewish president.

And second, neither am I. Goddammit, I just don't like it. So I've got to go along on my personal convictions."

"A lot of people are going to call you anti-Semitic," Palmer said.

"Of course I am. Always have been. I'm not Hitler or anything like that, but I'm entitled to my likes and dislikes. And I'm no redneck. I know my history and economics and sociology. What I respect is a man who works with his hands, a man who's a producer. Name me any Jew who got rich any way besides buying something cheap and selling it more expensive and I'll respect him. And my people are the same way. We're not ignorant. We just know how this country was built and who built it."

"Okay," said Palmer. He guessed that it hadn't helped Rose's outlook on American history to have a childhood among the beautiful media people in Chicago where everyone named Rose was automatically considered Jewish.

———————

James Minifee was the president of the Westmoreland League. Like most of his group, he looked like a haunting throwback to the 1950s. His hair was aggressively short and he wore a pink button-down shirt with a simple black knit tie. It was just this side of being a string tie, and it had obvious appeal to the Westerners and Southerners who were the backbone of the league.

Minifee limped as he was shown into Rose's study. He had lost a leg as a navy pilot during the Vietnam war, and his stirring speeches in defense of the bombing of New Delhi had given him national fame during the brief scuffle with India in '80.

Palmer introduced the two men and then left.

"I'll be brief," Minifee said. "We haven't met before because I have no hesitation in saying I have no regard for most of your supporters. The League may be against the selling out of America, just as you are, but we have no intention of handing it over to a group of wild-eyed polygamous bandits. However, right now we have a common cause and a common enemy."

"Levine," Rose said.

"Correct, Minifee said. "I want to assure you of one thing, Mr. Rose. I can't speak for all my followers, but I have no personal feeling against the Jewish people. As you may know, I graduated from Harvard in 1965. A third of my class was Jewish. One of my roommates was. Two of the ushers at my wedding were Jewish. My sister's married name is Friedenberg. My opposition to Mr. Levine is based on his politics. It has nothing to do with his religion."

"That's your prerogative," Rose answered.

There was a small pause while Minifee pondered Rose's answer. He decided not to pursue the matter any further.

"The league needs someone who can stop Levine and his people. They're the same people who gave away China, Vietnam, the Philippines. Now they want to give away Mexico. You know our motto, Mr. Rose?"

"'Win the Next One,'" Rose answered. His voice was flat.

"That's correct. We're tired of seeing America's power evaporate. In fact, we won't allow it."

"Let's talk money," Rose said, and they did.

"That's the mayor!" Fingers pointed, eyes turned. Jessington's fat 1958 Cadillac, tail fins chromed, pulled to the curb.

"Hey, Jess!"

"Hey, Mayor!"

"Hey, fat man!"

Jessington bestowed a languid wave of his right hand. His diamonds sparkled. The crowd murmured. Jessington waved again. He had seen the old Pope do something like that in a newsreel. They loved it in Chicago too.

"How you been doing, Ty-Ty?" Jessington asked.

"No major problems, Mr. Mayor, no major problems."

"Peace with you and to you."

"You tell 'em Jess."

"That I'll do, that I'll do." Jessington darted into the lobby, followed by Arthurson. An elevator was waiting. They went to the sixth floor. The conference room was filled. Everyone was waiting. Nothing beats being the mayor, Jessington thought.

"Let's hear it," Jessington said. His little introduction had become a trademark—his lieutenants, to impress their precinct workers, started off *their* meetings with "Let's hear it."

Ward by ward the leaders gave their weekly reports. Garbage collection was still the big problem in the Near North. There had been a little numbers violence in Calumet—two runners killed. Captain Willis of the Eighth Precinct had gotten drunk again and started arresting braless teen-agers for indecent exposure.

Jessington tried to figure out how many times he had heard about Captain Willis and how many times people

284

had complained to him about garbage collection. In his first few years as mayor he had enjoyed going to cocktail parties, but he had stopped when he found that every conversation, once the simplest pleasantries were over, slid into a complaint about garbage. He was a man of no little culture, and it offended him to go to a reception for the Civic Opera and have the opera's managing director whisper in his ear for fifteen minutes about poor trash pickup on his block. After a few years he returned to socializing with old friends.

When Jim Goins finished reciting the woes of Back of the Yards, Jessington grunted, and said, "Well, nothing new there. I'll get after all that. Now we're going to get into the heavy part. The fun. You know how we've worked this before. We've got an election coming up. You've been out on the streets. I want to know what people are thinking. I don't want to know what *you're* thinking. I can tell the difference. Let's go."

There was silence, then a confusion of voices. Jessington did not interrupt or try to restore order. He liked seeing how the men sorted themselves out, who commanded the floor by mere bullying, who held back but came through with the winning points. Meetings were like the mile run—the ones out in front right at the start almost never showed anything worthwhile. They were there to bring the others out.

Blevins, an old-timey mortician, was up talking right away and had kept on talking as the others jumped to their feet. He never wavered a moment in his recital, and the others, embarrassed by the inane persistence, gradually quieted down. Blevins kept talking and, when he at last had the floor to himself, did not retrace his words or make any acknowledgment that Jessington might have missed a word or two of his oration.

"...thanks to your fine leadership," he was saying, as the waters stilled. "No, sir, we have no trouble in our ward, and that, I tell you, is due entirely and completely to the fine example of Maceo Jessington. So I can tell you that the citizens of Ward Three are one hundred percent enthusiastic about Mr. Al Epstein."

"Levine," someone whispered.

"That one too," Blevins said.

"Thanks. Next."

Next were Kelly and Johnston, two more unctuous toads, Jessington liked them, of course—he needed a daily quota of praise, something he'd never get from his mother.

Finally Goins was speaking again. "Jess, I think we've got trouble. First of all, ain't nobody thinking about elections anyway. All they think about is the Roller Derby."

"There's nothing new about that. In the fall it's football and in the spring it's Roller Derby. If someone told me that the black folk of Chicago were worked up about a presidential election, I'd be afraid for the country."

"No, sir, you're right, but this ain't no ordinary not caring. This is *deep* not caring. And when I spring the name of your man on them, Jess, I tell you frankly they don't know 'im, and them that does know 'im, they don't like 'im. That's the truth."

"I believe you, Jim. What do they say about him?"

"Frankly, Mayor, they say they ain't gonna vote for no Jew. That's about the long and short of it."

"Anyone else hear the same thing?"

There was a murmur of agreement.

"What do you say when they say they won't vote for Levine?"

"Why, I do what you always told us to do. I don't argue them, never. I says I respects their judgment and it's been interesting talking to them."

"That's right. You'll never get anywhere arguing with a voter. Still, we've got to do something about this. Let's go out and get a shave. Meeting's over, men. Next week, right?"

One of Jessington's early heroes had been Harun al-Rashid. If, however, you are the three-hundred-pound mayor of the nation's third largest city it is hard to travel unbeknownst among your subjects. Jessington solved the problem by dropping unannounced into various Turkish baths and barber shops and, draped in towels, listening carefully as newcomers plopped down to get their hair trimmed and deliver themselves of political wisdom. The barber shop remained a solid point of the black community, a home away from home. Choice of a particular shop was important for Jessington. It had to be a place that encouraged political talk, and the prices had to be high enough to discourage the drifters and winos. Jessington had no interest in sitting two hours under hot towels as his neighbors discussed fancy whores.

Goins knew the kind of place Jessington wanted. Raffles Hair Styling for Men on E. Wabash had a solid neighborhood clientele of tradesmen, laborers, and older professional men. Jessington slipped into an empty chair and told the barber, "I want a long facial and a manicure. I'll tell you when to take off the towels."

Goins sat waiting as a new group of customers filled the shop.

"Hey there, Goins," a trim gray-haired man said, "why ain't you out in the streets doing something for the *people*."

"'Cause the people ain't never done anything for me 'cept break my windows and steal my hubcaps."

"Whooo-eee. Got a nasty tongue on you, Jim Goins."

"His lady friend, she says the same thing," someone chimed in.

More laughter.

Goins's voice came back. "Now seriously, Lawyer Welliford, what do you think about the situation?"

"It's bad and it's getting worse."

"You know what situation I'm referring to?"

"*No,* but that's the same for all of them—bad and getting worse."

"I'm talking politics."

"There's no politics in this city. First we had Daley and there was no politics, white style. Now we have Jessington and we have no politics, black style."

"I'm talking about presidential politics."

"You still trying to push that little fellow off on us?"

"What little fellow you mean?"

"Levine, the Jew."

"I'm not trying to push nothing on nobody."

"Well then, you stay away from me, because I suspect you of pushing that Levine and I'm not having any of it."

Jessington's voice, muffled by towels, rumbled forth. "Welliford, what do you have against Levine?"

"I have nothing personal. I've been put upon by Jews my long life and I'm not going to be electing one president if I can help it."

"Lawyer Welliford, if your wife were sick and you had to bring her to the doctor, where would you bring her?" An unfair question, since Jessington knew that Ortis Welliford's wife had spent four weeks in Michael Reese Hospital under Irv Goldberg's care.

"Depends on what you mean, mister."

"I mean would you take her to Michael Reese or to Lincoln."

"Well, I'd take her to Michael Reese."

"And if you had a little legal trouble yourself, say a problem with back taxes and disbarment, who would you get to represent you?"

Another unfair question, since Jessington knew that Alan Stone had counseled Welliford in his mercifully short troubles with the IRS.

"I'd find the best man regardless of race or creed."

"And might that man or woman be Jewish?"

Another pause.

"He might."

"And don't you see the connection between what you said before about the situation being bad and getting worse, between that and Mr. Levine? You're an educated man, Mr. Welliford. I'm surprised that you can't see that if you stick by race pride or some such slogan, pretty soon you'll be holding on to your slogan and nothing else. When the ship is sinking, Lawyer Welliford, you find the best pilot and you don't ask what church he goes to. You just pray he knows the way and he gets you back safe and sound."

"That man's talking sense," someone waiting said.

"Fact is," Goins broke in, "I was going to ask Lawyer Welliford here to head up a Lawyer's committee for Mr.

A. L. Levine. I wasn't going to argue him myself, because I figured that, soon as he thought about it some, he'd come to ask me to head up that committee."

"I was just thinking of doing that," Welliford said.

"'Course, this will be for Ward Three. You will be on the committee for the whole city of Chicago."

"That would be fine."

Jessington motioned the barber to pull off the towels. "I've always said you're a man of common sense, Lawyer Welliford."

"Hey, Jess. I knew it was you all of the time, under all them towels."

"Never thought I could fool a homebody like you, Ortis."

They kissed cheeks the way all the young blood back from Africa were doing, slapped hands, and laughed. Jessington tipped heavily and talked to the barbers. Then he and Goins and the others got back in the car and headed toward the mansion on Lake Shore Drive.

"That's the way, right?" said Goins.

"Right. You lead people to where they see that it's in their own best interest to elect Levine. You tell them it's no different if it's Levine or Epstein or whatever—we need someone used to troubles. Troubles, you tell them. We need someone set for changes. You don't have to give them all that business about 'historic friendship between blacks and Jews' that the people in Washington sent out. Stay away from that unless they bring it up. Hell, there's no more a historic friendship than there is a historic hostility. People aren't interested in that. Go the way I did. And don't push people's noses in it—make them think it's their own idea. Tell the people. Tell the other leaders. We got to make Chicago come in first, we got to show those other cities that Levine can make it big with the blacks. But if we're there first, you and I, we're right there on top. And I'll tell you one thing that's certain—A. L. Levine is not a man to forget a favor. You hear me?"

"I hear, I hear," said Goins.

"You're the quickest I have, Jim, the quickest," Jessington whispered.

Goins was happy. Fat as Jessington was, he couldn't live forever. He'd need to bring forward some of the younger men in the city. Goins wasn't educated like Jessington, but he figured he'd do just as well as the old guy politically. He'd have the swimming pool torn out—he didn't swim.

The old man slammed the front door behind him and stood on the porch. They could sit hunched over the air conditioner like chickens over a pan of seed, but by Jesus he wasn't gonna do it. No, indeed. If a man didn't have sense enough to get cool in summer and warm in winter, he hadn't the natural sense of a baby. Sheila Jo and her son—they were all right, but they had no grit.

Grit. That was a word he hadn't thought of for a long time. People didn't talk about it any more. But it was what the country could use. His family inside, now. They were nice enough, but they wouldn't strike out on their own. 'Course, he had an advantage. He had lived through the Depression, the real one, and he had lived when there hadn't been any air conditioning at all. My Jesus, to hear them shout and carry on when the city gave them their one hour a day, you'd think people couldn't live without the conditioner. Like the guppy fish the bank had had in the window before the War. One of the wars, anyway. Guppy fish that couldn't live without someone bubbling air into their water.

He smiled to himself and peeled some of the paint off the porch pillar. It might as well be all one color instead of half white and half gray. The boy ought to get out and scrape it, but he wouldn't. But the old man could smile, just the same. Lord, they thought these were bad times. They didn't know. He was comfortable with bad times. For most of his life he hadn't known anything else.

In the Depression—the real Depression—he had done most everything a man could to keep alive. Left his wife and his own boy—the girl wasn't born then—and traveled. Done roofing in Valdosta, worked in a sawmill a half year in Blytheville, over in Arkansas, done common labor at the TV and A dam at Muscle Shoals. Painted

white lines down most of Route 441 between Milledge-
ville and Dublin. None of them fancy paint machines,
neither. The gang boss just laid out the strip between
strings, like, and the crew bent their almighty backs and
just painted. By hand. Jesus, it had been hard! He'd done
labor in Texas all one spring along the Rio Grande,
working right alongside the Mexes that were the enemy
today, and the Mexes thought they could out-bend a
white man, but they couldn't. That was long-staple
cotton, ten cents a sack they were paying, but he
outpicked them all. The Mexes was picking with their
families. He was picking *for* his family. It made a
difference. But it was never as hard as those white lines.
Picking, at least you moved from side to side, stood up at
the end of the rows. The white lines, you never looked up
for two hours until they called a piss break.

That was hard, all through the thirties. It was hot then,
a kind of hot that the country lost for a while, until the
Arabs came along and took all the oil. Hot, sweat,
flies—all that went away after the Second War. By the
time Sheila Jo came along there wasn't anyone sweating
in the whole U. S. of A.

Which was what made it easier. Like being a widower.
For a long time after the wife died so young he didn't feel
lonely so much as foolish. Living alone, trying to raise the
girl, he stuck out like a pig in a coal bin. Everyone else was
married and he wasn't. Time went on, though, and other
people's husbands and wives started to die out, and there
were lots more folks by themselves. They kind of came to
him for help—he'd had more experience at being alone. It
made him feel a lot easier, too. It wasn't that misery loved
company. It was that when everyone else was in the same
boat—well, it wasn't misery any more.

Same with bad times. No one was starving nowadays,
and he'd seen some close to that in Roosevelt's times. And
if people were out of work, they didn't seem too desperate
about it like before. The government checks, for one
thing. What was new, what was nasty, was the way people
carried on against each other. Times were hard in the
Depression, but people didn't go around kidnapping each

other. Oh, sure, they was some people like the Barkers
and all that, but they didn't amount to much. Not like the
computer bandits they had now, gangs coming out of the
hills with their Eyetalian words and their crazy ideas.
Common thieving bastards was what they were. Wood
rustlers, mostly, when they weren't kidnapping. They
were young, too, which was the disgrace of it all. You
could think of men with families getting desperate, but if
any of this bunch had ever tried to support himself, he'd
never heard of it. The same packs of bums that never
finished college and wouldn't fight for the U. S. of A.
never got around to getting jobs either. They could do
what they wanted among themselves, but they'd damn
well better leave him alone. Which was a fool thought
coming from a man near eighty.

It was strange, but the only other people who seemed to
be worked up about the bandits were the nigras. Them
and their Patrols were the only ones who were trying to
get rid of dirty books and drugs and crime. Funny, he
never thought he'd end up voting for a nigra sheriff, but
even in the old days the blacks had been churchgoing
people. Maybe ol' Carter had been right about integration
helping the white folks too.

He looked up and down the street to make sure there
weren't any bandits hanging around. Sometimes they
slept in the alleys and came out toward noon. Nothing. He
walked to the corner and waited for the bus, which was a
nice thing, something the Arabs had brought back. You
had to thank them for that. Just wait ten minutes or so
and the bus'd be long. No fare, either. When he was a kid,
everyone paid except the motorman's son, Jamie Mundy.
How he'd envied that boy. Jamie'd die now, knowing that
everyone got on free. 'Course Jamie'd been dead a right
along while anyway.

On the bus he nodded to Miz Sellers and Miz Barber.
Sellers was looking poorly. She'd be dying one of these
days.

"Morning, ladies."

"Morning, Mr. Ledbetter."

"Going to do some shopping?"

"Most likely. Sheila Jo's real tired by the time she gets finished her job."

"Works hard, that girl."

"Isn't it the truth."

He knew just about everyone on the bus. That was a nice thing about hard times. People got together again. Shirley Temple singing "The Good Ship Lollipop." When you're out of work, you've got time to be friendly. Wasn't anyone on a bus at high noon in Macon who'd be going to work. Being out of work was like being old. And he had a lot of experience at 'em both.

He got off at Five Corners. He had some errands to do—buy lettuce and get some Pet milk—but mostly he'd hang around the store and see if Walt or Lacey came in. He hated to let on how much he needed them. Hated to let on, because if either of them died then there'd be that many fewer of them. The Lord taking His people all the time.

He took his time choosing the lettuce. No use in getting stuck. Sheila Jo, now, she never *could* buy right. Grew up with all them supermarkets, everything wrapped in six kinds of plastic, she'd toss things into that ol' basket like a kid snatching toys. Not much of that any more. People looked. They had to. Besides, they had the time.

He tested the lettuce, weighed some, checked for rot and bad leaves. Finally, he couldn't stall much longer. The manager, some new lady who had replaced the fellow with the bad teeth, kept staring at him. The store had its air on and she probably figured him for some feeblie who'd come in to cool off. The bad-tooth man, he never hurried you. Probably had died. He hadn't asked. Afraid to. He paid for the lettuce and Pet in hard cash, no stamps for him, and went outside. He waited in the little park. Back in the old days it had been a filling station. It wasn't much of a park, no trees, but there were benches and a water faucet. The Exxon sign hadn't been taken down.

After a while, Walt came along. He had a nice light step for a man his age. He had a newspaper, too. Usually he picked up a copy on the bus, read it, and saved it.

"Sit down, stranger." He motioned Walt over.

"Don' mind if I do. How's yours?"

"Not bad. Back acting up some. Much new?"

"Not in the paper," Walt said. "But I heard they wrecked up another one of them fancy houses out in the subdivision."

"The bandits?"

"Who else?"

"Lord, Walt, they ought to do something about those demons. They surely ought to do something."

"Why, mister, you talk as though no one ever thought on that. Like no one ever spoke against them or wrote against them."

"If everyone speaks against them, how come they flourish? They're in the hills everywhere from Maine to Florida. Why do the heathen rage? The Lord ought to give a sign. Or the state police ought to come in and shoot the bastards all down."

"State police! Those mangy old bastards don't have squat, and you know it. Had to sell the motor-sicles. Why, hell, the state had to fire most of them. The state's broke, stranger, and you know it. Besides, you could have a thousand troopers, and they couldn't protect all those big ol' houses scattered in them hills. Hunting lodges, fish camps, fancy places—why, they're all sitting ducks. You notice there wasn't anything in the paper about the place they wrecked in the subdivision."

"You mentioned. How come?"

Walt slammed the paper against the bench. "They're afraid, that's how come. They're afraid all those folks in the other suburbs are gonna panic and head to town. Hell, the city's filling up with 'em anyway. Closer you get to downtown and the police station, the harder it is to find a place to rent or buy. My sister Ethel's boy, the nice one, he tells me that they're gonna stop all that construction in Fairview next week. Can't sell the ones they already built."

"Look there, now," the old man said.

An old blue pickup truck, a Ford, pulled up in front of the store. Two young men with mustaches came out of the cab. They wore jeans and had red bandannas tied around their necks. Two women dressed in shawls waited in the back of the truck. One was suckling a baby. The men swaggered to the store. Quiet settled over the little park.

"Look at that," the old man said, pointing to the women. "Like gypsies."

"Never thought I'd see the day," Walt said. "Looks like that first one went in the store is ol' Sam Asperson's kid. Used to be a right smart boy."

"I do believe you're right. How come he's hanging around with those computer people?"

"Shoo," Walt said, "it's not computer, it's Caputo. Some fellow's name. They're a bad bunch no matter what you call 'em. Police ought to do something about them."

"What can you do? They ain't done nothing wrong, so far as we know. Yet. If the Patrols check 'em, they won't find beans. When those computer folks or whatever you call 'em come to town like this, you can bet they leave their pistols and their knives back under some rock. The drugs, too. State police won't be any help. What we need is the government, a president who's just as smart and mean as they are. Mean in a nice way, you know. Someone who'll know an abomination when he sees one."

The men came out of the store, put some groceries in the back of the pickup, and laughed with the women. The laughs were loud and evil, sprung not from humor but from defiance. The laughs were meant to be heard by the old people huddling in the park under the faded Exxon sign.

Part V

MASSACHUSETTS, SPRING, 1982

In May of 1982 Peter Caputo was a graduate student in Behavioral Psychology at Harvard. He was in fact a great graduate student, which is almost a contradiction in terms. Graduate students can be brilliant—in Behavioral Psychology they are expected to be—but their terms are too brief, their influence too fleeting to warrant the word great. It was more natural for people around Harvard Square to speak of great ice cream cones or great lays than great graduate students.

But Peter Caputo was often called great. He was handsome and rich and normal. He had played varsity tennis and A-ladder squash. He was not Jewish, either, and in a field where the average graduate student was ugly, Semitic, and fucked up, he somehow validated the whole area of Behavioral Psychology. He was B.P.'s Jung, the golden gentile whom father Freud loved first among his children. And Caputo was very smart, so brilliant it was almost unfair. Using Skinner's principles, Lorenz's observations, and Delgado's microsensors, he had devised a whole sequence of patterning experiments, experiments using human babies. Not only had there been no outcry against the use of children but Caputo's experiments were so ingeniously constructed, so clearly nonexperimental, that parents pleaded to have their babies enrolled. Of course, Caputo had to factor this kind of bias out, but still, the initial publications were so successful that the Caputo Paradigm was instantly adopted by researchers all over the country. Like the electron microscope, it was a better tool for looking at things. People joked that Caputo's infants were going to be following ducks and dogs around when they grew up, but Caputo didn't laugh. His was a long term study, and his extrapolation was that 12 percent of his subjects would be doing exactly that—mentally.

Caputo enjoyed his work with the same grace that he enjoyed tournament class doubles. Driving back from Newton—where he had left off a girl who had spent the weekend with him—he suddenly realized that he now preferred doubles to singles. In prep school and college he had played doubles because the coaches expected it. For himself, he was bored by a game where you got to hit the ball so seldom. You might just as well be playing baseball. In graduate school, with the tournament pressure off, he found that he liked doubles more and more. With good partners it became so fast, so instinctive, that it was almost a model for simple reflex-arc experiments. Too, there was the fun of working with another person and exploiting the weaknesses of two opponents instead of one. He began to think of experiments that could crystallize the personality traits that a good doubles team needed.

Caputo had decided that it might be a good idea to take some of the air force work on small groups and two-man crews and correlate it with Sheldon's anthropomorphic data—you couldn't ignore the physical characteristics of tennis players, after all—when he noted the car at the side of Memorial Drive with the three black kids waving frantically. A flare light was set in the road. Steam was pouring out of the radiator. It was 2:00 A.M. and he was almost back in Cambridge and he was teaching a ten-o'clock lab session that morning, but the kids looked desperate. Blacks were about the only people you ever saw in trouble like this, because they were the only people whose cars were always held together with wire and hope. Peter Caputo pulled up ahead out of the steaming Chevy.

"Mistah, can you help us?"

Peter nodded. Part of being Peter Caputo was to be uneasy doing anything you did not understand. A car was important enough to understand, and he had worked in his uncle's repair shop at fifteen until he understood cars. He didn't exactly despise intellectuals who said they had no idea of how their cars worked, but he pitied them.

"Let me take a look."

The hood was open and he leaned over to check the radiator cap. The first boy hit him with the jack, breaking his sixth and seventh cervical vertebrae, and when Caputo's head banged against the engine block (smashing his maxilla, ruining his face, and giving him a contra-coup brain hemorrhage), the others pulled him of the hood, stomped him a bit (breaking both radii and seven fingers), went through his pockets, rolled him into a ditch, and drove off in his Mercedes.

The car was found four days later near Ware Beach. An attempt had been made to set it on fire by soaking the upholstery with gasoline, but apparently the doors had swung shut, the windows had been left closed, and the German construction was so thorough that little fresh air seeped into the car. Without oxygen the fire smoldered some in the back seat and went out. Along with stains, letters to various women in Greenville, North Carolina, filled with maudlin, stolen poetry ("Baby, you make me feel like a man, so soon I'll come back and take my stand"), were three complete sets of fingerprints.

Caputo was comatose for three months on Mass General's neurosurgical service. His mother and father maintained a vigil around the clock for the first month, but faced with the same speechless, motionless, shrouded figure, day after day, they drifted back to Connecticut, continuing to visit on weekends. Dr. Atlas had explained that, even though the subdural clot had been removed, there clearly had been bleeding into the cortex. Peter might still improve, he said. When? said Mr. Caputo. We don't know, said Dr. Atlas. All we can do is keep him alive, keep his lungs clear, his skin normal, his nutrition good, and his fractures set so that, if his brain does start to recover, his body will be ready for it. And if it doesn't? Mr. Caputo wanted to know. The doctor raised his eyebrows. Mrs. Caputo cried again and Mr. Caputo thought about euthanasia.

The night practical nurse, Ada Scarborough, was the first to notice the change.

"He's watching me," she told Reynolds, the night supervisor.

Scarborough was always claiming that comatose

patients were watching or trying to speak or moving. She was a big, motherly woman who hated to see anyone die.

Every night for three nights Scarborough reported at shift change that Caputo was watching her. On the fourth time she dragged Reynolds with her.

"You look at that, Reynolds, look right there."

Caputo's eyes followed Scarborough into the room, and Reynolds personally told the neurosurgical resident, who told Dr. Atlas. There was no doubt: Caputo was not a vegetable. He was recognizing people. Two days later he lifted his eyebrows slightly when his own name was spoken. There was joy.

Ellen Friedman was visiting him when he said his first word. Ellen was the girl he had left off in Newton the night he was attacked. She was a graduate student in Biology. Like all the visitors, she had been told to talk to Peter, to bring language back to him, and she was talking about a mutual friend when Peter's lips moved. Ellen looked again. There was no doubt at all: Peter was trying to talk. She leaned closer.

"Peter, dear, say it. What are you saying?"

She bent closer. His lips moved again. "Niggers," he said. It was all he said for the next two weeks.

At staff conference Miss Angevine, the speech therapist, said she had never seen a case just like this one. Of course, there were lots of post-stroke patients, poor things, who repeated the same phrase over and over again or who strung unrelated words together in parodies of sentences, all just to hear themselves speak, to believe they could do it, but Mr. Caputo was different.

"Try to define what you mean by 'different,'" said Dr. Altas, who ran the conference and retained traces of chauvinistic hauteur.

"It's as though he were aphonic instead of aphasic," Miss Angevine said. "That is, we know he can speak and, since he recognizes people, we know that his cortex is working pretty well. He's beginning to obey simple commands very rapidly now: open your mouth, stick out your tongue, all that sort. But he can't speak." She paused. "Except for that word."

Angevine blushed. She was used to obscenities and indeed had once collaborated on a paper with her speech pathology professor on "The Use of Obscenities in Speech Retraining." Their work indicated that some patients relearned language by beginning with simple, basic obscenities and, once the elemental vulgarities had been spoken, progressed rapidly to a normal vocabulary. Angevine had spent three days repeating "motherfucker" endlesslessly to a young white accident victim before his lips moved and the first syllables emerged. After that, Easy Street. Still, it was one thing to say "motherfucker" and another to say "nigger." Especially with Scarborough and the other black health personnel present. You would think that patients would have more consideration for the people trying to help them.

Dr. Atlas was in a hurry. There were four more patients to be staffed. He wanted closure. "I don't think we should make too much of this, Miss Angevine," he said. "I'm sure you're familiar with what Quadfassel called the 'stuck-needle syndrome.' That is, one phrase sticks in the phasic patient's mind, one set of neuronal connections remains to allow him to pronounce it, and the phrase, meaningless in itself, becomes terribly important to the patient. The phrase itself becomes a kind of password to normality. The very fact that the patient can say something, no matter how meaningless, reestablishes his identity as a human."

Angevine was annoyed. "I know Quadfassel's work, Dr. Atlas. What I'm trying to make clear is that Mr. Caputo seems to *mean* what he's saying."

Then the other words began to come back, at first slowly, then in a torrent, and they were the old words, used in a new way. Fascinated, horror-struck, Ellen Friedman heard most of them.

"Don't make excuses, please," Peter said. "They weren't black or Negro or anything like that. They were niggers and they did a nigger thing. We—you and I and our friends—we've let them do that sort of thing too long. Don't tell me about deprivation and poverty. I've read the same studies you have. Now," and he gestured to the bandage that still wrapped his head, keeping the Crutchfield tongs steady, "now I'm reading with my eyes open. It's not because of their color or because they're inferior. I don't think they are. It's because we've let them slip their culture into ours, and we haven't fought for ours, and everything they have to offer is violence. Violent music, violent sport, violent art. There is no discipline. The twentieth century is the product of discipline. When we refuse to teach discipline, we become barbarians again."

"My God, Peter, twentieth-century civilization! Bergen-Belsen, Hiroshima, My Lai! What's come over you?"

"Ellen, listen. Listen. You can understand if you want. Hobbes said, 'The life of man is solitary, poor, nasty, brutish and short.' That was in 1651. You know enough history to see that the only thing different about today is that most people—in America, anyway—don't live like animals any more. People used to be oxen. Now we're out of that. There's hope, but it's hope through learning and discipline. And that's what we're afraid to teach the blacks. The kids who attacked me weren't blacks—they were niggers. They'll stay niggers as long as we pretend they're not."

"Peter, people used to say that about my people. They used to say it about ... about yours."

"Don't stutter, Ellen. You're a big girl. You can say Jew and Italian or kike and dago. Especially if I say nigger. Sure, people said that about us. But it was different. First of all, there was nothing aimless about it. I don't know all that much about the Mafia, but when it killed, it killed for a reason. It was limited to Italians, to other mobsters. You could walk down the North End in the middle of the night, and if you were a Jew or a black, you'd be safe. People might not like you, but they wouldn't kill you. But if you were another Mafioso, and someone had a contract out on you, you weren't safe at high noon in the Ritz Barber Shop. The other thing was that nobody said it was okay or that it was colorful or that it was the nature of Italians. They put them in jail. You know what I mean?"

Ellen saw, in a way. Besides, it was impossible to argue with Peter. He was, she thought, a different person than before the accident. His charm was gone, and in its place was a driven intensity. You couldn't argue with a sick man, someone who had come so close to death, and you couldn't argue with someone who seemed to take everything so seriously. It wasn't like the old days, arguing with Peter about war with India or nuclear power or the Mexicans. Peter had cared about those things, but you could at least talk to him, just like you could the other people in Cambridge. People pretty much agreed that the country was rotten and that it would be only a matter of time before the system collapsed. People pretty much agreed on this. The important thing was to be able to say something new or funny about it. She remembered when she was back in high school and they had started calling Nixon "the Cox-sacker." That was the sort of thing that people enjoyed. The trouble with Peter was he seemed to take everything so seriously. And besides, some of what he said *did* make a kind of crazy sense.

The car was loaded with fingerprints, of course, but when the three kids were brought down to Precinct Four they all had lawyers and solid alibis. Sure, they had been in the car. You would have gotten in the car, too, if some slick with a solid foxy lady had said, "Hop in, brothers, we gonna see some sights."

The name of the slick?

"Hey, man, who knows?" Louis Mantoo said. The dude looked familiar, he thought maybe people called him Stingray, but he wasn't sure. He figured maybe Ellis or Winfry *knew* the dude.

Strangely, it turned out that Ellis and Winfry didn't know him either. They thought he was a friend of Mantoo's. Winfry said, "Look, Mr. Policeman, when someone ax you, real friendly, to come along in a nice car like that, you don't get his driver's license and all that shit. You don't turn it down. Can you catch that?"

The police hung some informers around Roxbury, but not one had seen the three of them together in the car. There were no witnesses from the night of the accident.

When Caputo was able to walk, he was brought to headquarters for a lineup.

It had been a dark night when he had stopped to help the three kids in their old Chevy, but the flare had been bright. Once the post-traumatic amnesia cleared it was very hard to forget the face connected to the foot that broke your jaw or the nose that was the last thing you remembered for three months.

Caputo looked at three separate lineups and shook his head regretfully. There was no one, he explained to Lieutenant Byrne, who resembled the youths who had attacked him. It had been a dark night and his memory of the whole event was blurred.

Lieutenant Byrne was disappointed. The case was going out the window and he was sure—absolutely sure—that he had the kids. But it was no crime to go for a joy ride in a friend's car, and with no further evidence Ellis, Winfry, and Mantoo were released.

Caputo's recovery went well. His speech was normal, though he had some hesitations and idiosyncracies in his vocabulary that had not been present before the accident. He began many sentences with the phrase "From my point of view." He didn't like this, but he couldn't work it out of his speech.

His back still hurt and he would never be able to make a complete fist with his left hand, but his bones otherwise were mending well. Methodically he did quadriceps exercises daily in the physiotherapy room, and to overcome the hospital-induced shoulder atrophy he began weight lifting.

He also read a great deal.

When he was discharged from MGH six months after the accident, Caputo went to stay with his parents in Bridgeport for a couple of months. He continued his exercises, played with his cousins, and talked to his father.

Ralph Caputo owned a construction company which had been built on his own sweat and that of a hundred other Italians, the others not quite so smart as he was. He had only half understood Peter in graduate school, but he had been proud of him. Now he understood his son, and the pride was tinged with fear.

"Why bother?" he asked.

"What must be done, must be done. There is no way around it."

"Think of your career."

"*This* is my career."

"There's no arguing with you, is there?"

"No. Now tell me about my great-uncle."

Who could get to be a rich contractor in Connecticut without knowing someone in the Mob? What Italian didn't have one relative he was half proud, half ashamed of? If you looked around, every family had someone like that. In the Caputo family there was a great-uncle who had married a Genovese, who had been taken into the family business, and whose son, the age of Peter's father, was a man of great influence. He lived in Ridgewood, New Jersey.

Peter went to this Alan Damato and explained his problem. He talked to Damato about Behavioral Psychology. Damato had gone to Rutgers and majored in Business Administration. Still, he knew a good deal about abnormal psychology.

Peter stayed three months with the Damatos. He wrote Ellen and his family brief notes and spent a couple of weekends with Ellen in New York. He explained to her that Mr. Damato's wife was ill, and that the family thus did not welcome visitors.

In the winter Peter went back to Boston. He moved from his apartment in Cambridge to a high-rise in Boston. The high-rise had a shopping complex on the first floor and there was a constant stream of people in and out of the lobby. He used the last name Gregg. He was working on a research project that had to be done anonymously. Ellen Friedman, who stayed with him on weekends, understood.

Three months after Peter arrived in Boston, Louis

Mantoo disappeared on a trip to the liquor store for his
mother. He was gone a week. At the end of that time his
body, slightly rotting, was rolled from a car into the
playground where he usually played pickup basketball.
His penis was stuffed in his mouth and a large Roman
numeral I was carved on his chest.

There was a flurry of police activity, and Lieutenant
Byrne himself checked into the whereabouts of Peter
Caputo. Peter was traveling in Europe and on no certain
schedule, but since his family had received postcards in
what was definitely his handwriting from the Calabrian
hill towns all during the time of the presumed murder, the
investigation was dropped.

Clyde Ellis went low after Mantoo's murder, but, with
Caputo overseas and time passing, he gradually resur-
faced. It is difficult for a pleasant young man, friendly to
both sexes, to lead a monastic life for very long,
particularly if he has a substantial cocaine habit. A month
after Mantoo's death Ellis got a call from a priest who
needed periodic loosening from his vows. He was a vain
and foolish priest, susceptible to blackmail and patheti-
cally eager to please. Ellis had been with him twice before
and, listening to the pleading voice over the phone, he
bounced with delight. He was going to score again and
score big. Besides, the priest wasn't a bad lay. The priest
suggested the usual room at the In-Town Motel.

Ellis wasn't killed. He wasn't even knocked uncon-
scious. He was, in fact, completely conscious during the
time the cautery was held to his eyes. The blindness that
follows this kind of treatment is permanent and not
susceptible to corneal transplants. It differs from other
forms of blindness in the constant pain from the
heaped-up granulation tissue.

The Roman numeral II on Ellis's chest was carved
while he was alive.

Leroy Winfry disappeared instantly, and Lieutenant
Byrne went back to his investigation. There were
postcards again, but Byrne was getting suspicious. He
sent an Italian-speaking detective to Rome by jet and to
Calabria by chartered private plane. Peter Caputo was

there in the mountain village of Saracenia, just as the postcards said he was. His passport had not been stamped since he had entered Italy six months before. The priest, the *polizia,* and the family with whom he lived were astounded by Sergeant Rossi's questions. Signore Caputo had not left the village for a month, not since they had all gone to the *fésta* in Naples together. Rossi stayed a few extra days to check out the locals and look up some relatives and came back to Byrne emply-handed. Caputo hadn't done it, and Rossi couldn't figure out how he had ordered it done. Neither could Byrne.

It didn't take Caputo long to track down Winfry. He knew everything about Winfry, just as he had known everything about Ellis and Mantoo. Unlike the others, Winfry had been born in the South and brought to Boston by his mother when he was a child. He had a sister in New York and a half-brother in Indianapolis, but Caputo figured him to head straight for grandma. Alan Damato's friends in the trucking business made a few inquiries in the town of Snow Hill, North Carolina, and discovered that Eterna Simpson's grandson was back in town.

The Manhattan Cafe in Snow Hill is not often frequented by anyone from outside of town, even though it is right on South 13. It is certainly not often visited by white people; white Southerners are not partial to Manhattan Cafes or Lincoln Schools. The Manhattan Cafe in Snow Hill is run by Tom Johnson, who spent a decade drifting in Harlem before admitting defeat and coming home.

The jukebox works, but the neon sign has been out of commission since 1952, a year after the café opened. The regulars were surprised to see the two white men and the white girl come in the café that night, and Tom Johnson was about to explain (politely) that the kitchen was closed and they had just run out of beer, when the girl started calling out Leroy Winfry. She called him a cocksucker and a motherfucker and a pud-puller and a sister-sucker, most of which was true. The two white men stayed at the door and listened. The girl moved up to Winfry and started calling him out right in his ear. Nasty names. He couldn't take it, not in front of his friends, and started to hit her. She cut his face so fast no one could see where the knife came from. Then one of the men, the handsome one, came over from the door and smiled at Winfry, and said, "Remember me?" Winfry must have remembered, because he started begging and saying it was a mistake, but the man started slashing him. He cut his face some more and his throat, and before Winfry died the man made sure to put three slashes in his chest.

There were ten men and two women from Snow Hill watching all this. No one moved, least of all Tom Johnson, after one of the white men had said, softly, "Everyone else stay still, and no one gets hurt. Tom, I know you've got a thirty-eight in the cash drawer. Leave it there. Sylvester Watkins, I know you carry a little derringer. You keep it there. I don't want to have to use this." He had an Israeli-made burp gun that could get off fifty shots in twenty seconds.

After Winfry had died, the woman put an alarm clock on the bar. It was ticking loudly. "In fifteen minutes the alarm will go off," she said. "When that happens, you can phone the police, leave, get drunk, whatever you want. Until it rings, you stay right here. Don't touch the alarm, don't try to go out the door, don't pick up the phone. Just stay here until the alarm rings." There was no argument about this, and when the alarm finally rang and they tried to phone the state police, the phone line was cut and the Snow Hill sheriff was out of town and the deputy's wife had, as usual, borrowed his car and the deputy didn't want to come to just another nigger stabbing—well, no trace of the two men and the woman was ever found.

Peter Caputo's Manifesto, delivered to four major newspapers simultaneously, appeared the next day, however, ending whatever mystery remained about the killings. From the opening sentence when he wrote, "Yes, we reject senseless violence, but we glory in Right Violence, God's Violence, Justice's Violence," Caputo established himself as a semilegendary figure. The

photographs of him at Ellis's and Mantoo's deaths when
he was supposed to be in Italy, the clarity of his
Manifesto, the bleakness of his prophecy set him apart
from the crazies who had come and gone before.

"We are not revolutionaries," he proclaimed. "We are
reactionaries. We believe in order, honor, learning,
dignity. These are beautiful ideas, too beautiful to defend
themselves. We take upon ourselves that task. Some will
shun us because they see us as racists. Others will flock to
us for the same misguided reason. We are not racist. We
will fight the enemies of civilization, not because they are
black, but *if* they are black. We do not seek recruits. We
operate by the code of *omerta*. Recruits will come to us,
and they will come not because they believe in what we
believe but because they have done what we have done.
Words without deeds are the prattle of schoolchildren:
deeds without words are the acts of barbarians. We shall
keep our words brief and our deeds effective. The
Republic lives!"

That afternoon Lieutenant Francis Byrne of the
Boston police received a telegram from Brattleboro,
Vermont. The telegram read in its entirety: MORTE ALLA
COMMUNISTI. Because of the foreign spelling the message
had not been phoned in but sent from the Brattleboro
station. The clerk had no difficulty identifying pictures of
Peter Caputo and Ellen Friedman.

Three weeks later a young white Demerol smuggler
was deliberately electrocuted while trying to walk across
the border from Canada at night near Norton, Vermont.
The 150 vials of Demerol were left in his knapsack as
evidence, but a cc of $0.1\frac{7}{8}$ hydrochloric acid had been
injected into each one, precluding any reuse. The number
IV was pinned to his lapel. When, under FBI instructions,
the press withheld word of the execution, Caputo sent a
note with photographs and names of the dealer's
Montreal contacts to the *New York Times*. The note read,
"We do not kill for pleasure, but to eliminate evil and to
instruct. If only the evildoer knows of his own death, the
lesson is lost. Use these to teach your readers." The *Times*
headline ran, "Caputo's People Kill in Vermont."

From then on the moving bands of bandits and murderers who lived in the mountains from Vermont to Georgia to California were known as Caputo's people.

PETWORTH CENTER, JULY 21, 1988

Saturday market had been held at Petworth Center, Vermont, since 1786 or 1787. The records were unclear. For some two hundred years, farmers had sold apples and squash in the fall, garden vegetables and baled hay in the summer. The pulse of the town depended on the market until 1945, but even in the postwar years families drove over from Burlington and Barre to get fresh produce. In 1958 someone wrote an article about the market for the Travel Section of the *New York Times,* and it became quaint. In the next five years summer people, autumn foliage pilgrims, and skiers pushed their way down the narrow streets. Instead of Bibb lettuce or Country Gentleman corn, they bought handicraft carvings, salad bowls, and antiques, some of them genuine.

The first marijuana was traded in Petworth Center in 1966, and by 1972 the town had become a focal point for Vermont's newest wave of immigration. Great Victorian houses which in succession had been private homes, funeral parlors, convents, and private schools were transformed into Awareness Centers, Therapy Milieus, and ashrams. In the countryside farms long ago abandoned as unproductive were bought by bands of young people who wanted to be self-sufficient. The farms were still unproductive, and their new owners turned to subsistence labor to keep solvent. There weren't enough waitressing jobs in the entire state to employ each year's dropouts from Smith and Mount Holyoke. As one batch of disillusioned ex-farmers and ex-housepainters stumbled back to the safety of Boston or New York, another took their place. Each month, though, a few more stayed for good, a few more farmhouses were restored, and by 1980 the young people and their camp followers—"hairs" was the local word for them—found themselves with the balance of political power.

The natives were indifferent to them as they had been indifferent to the previous migrations of socialist Yale men in the 1920s and avant-garde Jews in the 1940s, indifferent as long as they paid good prices for crumbling houses nobody else wanted. The summer people, called that whether they came up for July and August only or stayed all year round, lived off the good graces of the natives. They traded the names of reliable carpenters, attended town meetings regularly, paid their taxes without complaint, and praised the flinty wisdom of their neighbors. The natives considered them assholes.

The hairs were different. They were romantic about Vermont, but they were used to making a fuss and to getting their own way. There were too many of them to ignore. When in the summer of 1979 the governor reintroduced the Green Mountain Highway bill, Franklin Roosevelt's old dream of a superhighway cutting the length of the state alongside the Green Mountains themselves, the state split instantly in two. Not since the Civil War were families so bitterly divided. The appeal of more jobs and more tourists was met by a horrified fear of more pollution and less scenery. As the natives tore each other to bits, the hairs found themselves courted by both sides. The pro-highway people appealed to concern about Vermont's own youth, unable to find jobs or decent educations in their own state. The anti-highway people produced enviromental impact surveys which proved that the road would kill all the beaver, all of the bear, and most of the people left in the state.

It was no contest. Whatever little the hairs felt in common about Vermont, they did not want to share the state with anyone else. Handsome young Willard Rose, despite his history of militarism, was infinitely preferable to an opponent who talked endlessly about the expanding economy. If the hairs had wanted an expanding economy, they would have stayed in New York. Rose sensed this, courted them brilliantly, always keeping some distance, and won easily. He was one of the first "no-growth" politicians. Once elected to Congress, he paid the hairs the honor of taking them seriously. He visited their farms and commune and listened to their earnest ideas on the meaning of life. He usually wished he were back at Yale. Still, the kids weren't all bad. He began to build a constituency of old people trying to preserve a Vermont they half remembered and young people looking for a Vermont they had never known. He was crazy, people said, but not crazy enough to lose his following.

Now, running for president, Rose was back among his own people in Petworth Center. The hairs were older than when he had first visited them, their long braids beginning to be streaked with gray, but the faces were familiar. In the back of the crowd, along with the drunks and the wood rustlers, lounged some of the Caputo people, the crazies of the crazies. They did not vote, but they listened and were listened to.

"I want your votes," Rose told the people in the market square, "not because I'm a Vermonter but because I'm an American. We stopped the speculators and the parasites here in Vermont, but our work won't mean anything if the same people take over Washington. You know the people I mean: the buy-cheap, sell-high crowd, the ones who can't look at a sunset without thinking of how to make a profit out of it. They're the same people who want to see America weak, who'll trade us off to any third-rate country like Mexico that wants to frighten us. We've become strong because we've gone back to the land. We're strong in ourselves, not because we depend on allies or alliances. We're strong because we worked for what we have ourselves, not like the welfare hordes of the cities."

The crowd of young people whooped and shouted. A few held up their hands with their second and third fingers spread apart. Once this had been called V for victory, once it had been called the peace sign, but those meanings were forgotten. Among Rose's followers it meant "vanquish." There was a theory that it had come from a television program. It referred, though Rose denied it, to the blacks.

"Come on upstairs," Jones said. "I've got something for you."

"You can't show it to me down here?" Levine said. "I'm back in Washington just a couple of days, I'd like to talk to people."

Jones gestured impatiently. "Talk. If you find anything worth hearing, wiggle your ears. I'll listen over your shoulder."

Levine edged through the crowd. There was always something to learn. Two startlingly pretty middle-aged women were talking intently: "But Bloodwirth is so much more powerful! Not that Freund didn't *feel* for the constitution, but Bloodwirth makes *you* feel it." One gray-haired man was gesturing vigorously at another: "So by tearing down that false front I'll be able to open the whole kitchen area."

Levine came back to Jones. "You win. It's the same Washington stuff: women talking about their careers, men talking about restoring houses. Where shall we go?"

"Up to my bedroom. It's quiet there. I invited these people, I feel responsible for their conversation."

"Don't be guilty. For someone in town just a month you've got friends that are the same as anyone else's."

"Dull."

"That, I didn't say. Which is your bedroom?"

"To the right."

Jones closed the door, locked it, and put a cassette of tape into the recorder that lay on the bedside table. "A friend of ours in Vermont sent this along. As a favor. There weren't any reporters there—which was no coincidence."

As he played the tape of Rose's speech, Jones watched Levine closely. Levine smiled once or twice, grimaced a couple of times, but stayed silent. When the crowd cheered, he winced. At the end Jones kept the tape going until the cheering had died away and there was only the sound of the tape slapping against the reel.

Levine shook his head. "That prick. That prick! I didn't think he'd do it. I told Bell and I told you, 'He won't do it.' You remember, I told you he wouldn't do it?"

Levine sounded like someone triumphant in his own foresight.

"Sure, I remember. You told us he wouldn't do it. You were wrong."

"It's amazing how wrong I was. I must remember. That prick! How could he go back like that, work the Jewish thing? I would never have believed it."

"What do we do about it?"

"Nothing, right now. We didn't hear this tape, remember. There were no reporters there. What he's said at the big rallies you couldn't object to. Who could object to being for nature? My own father—God rest—was for nature. Not that he ever saw much of it. There's no use in leaking this now, telling the press people that Rose is working anti-Semitism, anti-black. I'll talk it over with Bell, Jessington, the others. In the meantime, two things. First, no one else hears this tape. No one. Second, we send someone up to Burlington to find out about Rose."

"That's all been checked out."

"No, it hasn't."

"It has. We—"

"Listen carefully so I do not have to explain again. It hasn't been checked out properly because we don't have anything on him. And, perhaps you remember, I did some business up there. I know a little about land law. A person like Rose doesn't get the kind of land he has the way he says he got it. What was it that piece in the *Times* said, he 'developed an old family estate?' In Vermont, believe me, no one had old family estates of five thousand acres, not even Rose or his wife. Arthur, trust me. Something isn't kosher in all that. In fact, I'll tell you how to prove it. Get me one of those nice young lawyers that works for the National Committee, someone who knows some real-estate law. We need somebody a little crude, not one of those pretty Ivy League types. And no Jews. Send Fabrio—they're used to Italians around Barre. He's smart but not slick. Tell him to check out the land deeds in Rose's county. He might even look into the guy who was probate judge there when Rose was buying up his land."

Jones nodded. "He'll be there tomorrow. If we can get him a reservation."

These people have it made, Fabrio thought. Trouble is, they know it. The air's clean, the politics are almost honest, and there's still some money around. The people were polite, too. He'd spent two days in Burlington, checking out Vermont land law, which had some funny old quirks in it, and gassing with a classmate in practice there. He told the classmate that he had made some money in Brazilian oil and wanted to invest it. The classmate didn't believe it and figured Fabrio to be spending Mafia money. That was okay with Fabrio. Anything, so long as the locals thought he had money and was serious about buying. There was a lot of mob money in Vermont already.

The people in Churchill were helpful, too. They'd seen too many young men in blue jeans buy up hundred-thousand-dollar farms to dismiss quiet, well-dressed Mr. Fabrio. The clerk of the court happily trotted out the land records and registers as Fabrio spent two days pretending to be interested in nineteenth-century transactions before asking for the records of the 1960s. "I'm thinking of assembling some land for a new kind of recreational development," he told the clerk. The clerk, who had seen outsiders assemble land for every kind of recreation from skiing to screwing, wasn't surprised. One never knew what they'd be up to next.

The records were lovely. Fabrio spent three days pouring over them, enchanted by the fine Spencerian handwriting that Vermont apparently required of its registrars of deeds and probate right until IBM came along in 1972. The story of greed and corruption was almost as captivating. Right here in Yankeeland, Fabrio thought!

He called headquarters from a pay phone off the

Interstate after three more days. "I want to speak directly to Levine," he told Bell.

"He's busy. He's in conference."

"Tell him to come out. I need to talk to him now. I need some instructions. Tell him it's important."

In a moment Levine was on the phone. "So?"

"So? So I have everything. All of it. Documented. I didn't even have to use the Minox. They let you photocopy the records right in the courthouse."

"Okay, good, that's good. Listen a minute. Don't get too excited. Did you talk to the guy who used to be probate clerk back then?"

"Welch?"

"That's the one."

"No, I figured to see him tomorrow, show him the stuff—"

"Forget it. Take what you have, whatever it is, and bring it back to me. Don't leave abruptly. Spend another day looking at records from a different township altogether. Then get yourself back here. Don't talk to Welch. Don't ask anyone about him. People get curious, you know."

"Right. I'll be back on Wednesday. You wouldn't believe what I got, Mr. Levine."

"I would, I would."

VERMONT, SUMMER, 1964

Vermont in 1964 was not at all Levine's home court. Unlike the South, this area had seen plenty of short New Yorkers named Levine, and it did not particularly relish them. There was no glamour, no mystery that Levine could work in Rutland or Montpelier. Still, visiting Sam in summer camp, he could no more avoid thinking of real estate than an accountant could avoid rechecking a waiter's addition. What he saw astonished him. It was there, all around him, and it had been wasted. What was wrong with people that they couldn't see what they were sitting on? In the South maybe you could excuse it because the money wasn't there or because there was no tradition of doing anything in the summer except going back to grandpa's farm, but here? Here, where the *Auslanders* had been coming for 150 years, where Abe Lincoln had plopped down for the summers, where even today they thought they were making money if they sold a $20,000 place for $40,000—what was wrong with people?

He learned. He learned after he had set Helen up in a motel and told her that he wanted to stay a few extra days to watch Sam in the canoeing races. He roared up and down the valleys, looking at the ski areas, barren of snow but crowded with summer tourists anxious to ride a chair lift to the top of a mountain, look around, and ride down again. Safer than skiing, Levine thought. He talked to the lift operators and guesthouse owners. Where did people stay in the winter, was it easy to buy a house, how much would a place like that (over there, across the road) go for if it were for sale?

The pattern was clear. The locals thought they were taking the skiers for big money if they sold a farmhouse for double what it sold locally. The people who had come up from New York to make money and semi-retire running ski lodges weren't doing much either. They were working like hell four months a year and barely breaking even. The big-money people, the ones who developed the ski areas, thought their responsibilities ended if they bought another snow packer and added a Poma lift. No one had apparently heard of a recreational development, or, if they had heard, they hadn't believed. Levine believed.

Finally he found what looked to be an ideal site. Five hundred acres of upland meadow, a stream running along the back side, not farmed, off the main road to Mad River, but not very far off. He got out of the car and walked the land. He'd check with the soil engineers, but so far as he could tell—and by now he was an expert in telling—the land was fine for building. There were a couple of old stone foundations with lilacs growing around them. The foundations were deep, and the houses must have stayed a long time. There were no marshy spots, not that he'd expect any so high, and no granite outcroppings.

He checked out the plats in the county courthouse. The registrar of deeds, a seedy, dreamy little fellow named Welch, was interested.

"You looking at any particular piece, mister?"

"No. Just browsing."

"Yup. Glad to be of help."

Levine looked around the countryside some more but found nothing to compare with the first five hundred acres. The name of the little stream was the Wink River. He liked that; it would sell. He circled through the other plat blocks for the county and came back again to the five hundred acres. It was owned by someone named Stallings. As he staggered back to the clerk's desk with the heavy volumes (would that Sheila Jo Williams worked in Vermont!), Welch watched intently.

"You figuring on buying that Stallings property, Mr. Levine?"

Shit!

"No. Just looking."

"You're not looking, Mr. Levine. You don't know me, but I know you. Being in the kind of work I am, you'd be bored if you didn't stay interested in land. Land, Mr. Levine, land! That was a nice little piece they had on you in *Business Week*."

Two years ago and two lousy paragraphs, marking the sale of his Atlanta parcel and mentioning his name just once. He could ignore Welch, but it wouldn't work. The game was over.

"You have a remarkable memory, Mr. Welch. And you're clearly a man of education. Would you care to have a drink with me?"

"Courthouse closes at five o'clock," Welch made to reply, and at five fifteen they squeezed into a back booth in the Green Mountain Arms.

Welch sat down, shifted his weight, and said, "Stallings would never sell to you."

"How come? Does he have children? Is he going to use it himself?"

"Sure he's got kids. Hates their guts. He'd sell his best dog if he thought he'd turn two dollars on it. But not to a Jew. He'd never sell to a Jew." Welch paused and smiled triumphantly. "What d'you think of that?"

Levine shrugged. "It's happened before. Actually, I sympathize. It makes me angry, but I still see it."

"See what?"

"That what Stallings wants to hold on to is his childhood. We all do. Jews in New York, you ought to hear them talking about going back to the neighborhoods they grew up in: 'Negroes here, Puerto Ricans there, the place has gone to hell, you'd never recognize the old place now.' My God, you'd think they were talking of Bar Harbor instead of some crappy little tenement building on the Lower East Side. No, what they're angry about is that there aren't any little *thems* back where they grew up, little Jewish kids running around and making them think, Things haven't changed, I'm still young, the world has stayed still.

"The more different the people are, the less you can

keep that illusion. So for someone like Stallings, selling to a Jew means the end of the kind of life he remembered. Still, that makes him a kind of prick."

Welch nodded. "He is, but he's a likable prick. Kind of like you, if you know what I mean."

"Not exactly. Have another drink."

They drank until seven when Welch, a bachelor, had to report home for dinner at his mother's house. They drank again the next evening and then, just before seven, Welch turned to Levine and said, "Maybe I can do something for you with Stallings."

Maybe he could, Levine thought. As if I hadn't felt him setting me up for this. But it wouldn't wash; there'd be no phony corporations and no straw men. He'd bought land in the middle of Klan Kountry (as the road signs called it) under his own name, and he wasn't going to start using a straw man in Vermont. If he couldn't get the land as himself, fuck it. Not from moral scruples, he told himself, but because he was a hardheaded businessman. A straw man could always turn on you, leave you with a lawsuit or a bad reputation. Forget it.

"I'd be much obliged if you'd see if he'd sell, but, you understand, it would have to be directly to me. The way my corporation is structured—"

"I know that, Mr. Levine. As I said, I know your dealings. No, I was just thinking of doing you a favor. Stallings, the son of a bitch, might enjoy meeting you. He's a lonely old man most of the time. I'll talk to him."

And so a week later (Helen had long since returned obediently to Long Island) Levine found himself drinking hard cider and telling old Stallings about women.

"Pussy," the old man said. "That's all that keeps me going. And there's damn little of it around here. If it weren't for Leavesque's wife, I'd still be beating off in the milking machine. Here's to Leavesque's wife." He raised his glass.

"Here's to Leavesque," echoed Welch.

"Here's to pussy," said Levine, as the other chortled and chuckled. They drank some more, and abruptly

Stallings was no longer playing games but was serious.

"Welch says you're interested in the land along the Wink River. Says you've got plans for it."

"That I do," said Levine. "Let me show you actual pictures of some of the other places I've developed. But let me show you something else first." He pulled an architect's sketch from his pocket.

"Jesus, that's old Uncle Nate's place just as sure as shitting," Stallings said. "Where the hell did you get that? What the hell does it mean?"

"Mr. Stallings, Welch here told me that that property on Wink River used to belong to your great-uncle, that you visited it when you were just a kid. I took some pictures of that foundation and the land around it and showed them to an architect in Burlington I've heard of. He specializes in historical restorations. It's a trade all in itself—they know so much about the past they can guess what a building looked like if you just give then a couple foundation stones. Most all houses built in a certain area at a certain time looked the same. Well, I could give the man in Burlington more than that—the Registry of Deeds had all the records on the house going back to 1830, including the additions the family made on it. So, along with the foundation pictures, he could get a pretty good idea of what the house looked like."

"God damn, that's it, all right. 'Cept that window should be over a bit, and they never had that little entranceway."

"Mr. Aldrich said he couldn't be exactly sure about the portico."

"What do you want with it anyway?"

"Mr. Stallings, if you sell me that land at a reasonable figure, I'm going to restore that house—rebuild it from the foundation up. I'll deed it to you for as long as you live. After your death the house will revert back to the development, but it will be called Stallings House in perpetuity and will be covenanted against any change in design. Inside there will be a plaque—"

"Done, you smart Jew bastard, done. You know

goddam well that I'm seventy-eight years old, Mr. Levine, but I want to see that goddam thing built even if it's only for a day. Done!"

They shook and the deal was complete. Levine bought the land for $100,000, spent another $50,000 rebuilding the Stallings house, and then built a swimming pool and ten houses for $100,000 each. He heard that Mt. Furey, a new ski area five miles away, needed capital. He gave them a $100,000 long-term loan on the condition that all families buying homes at Wink River Landing would have a lifetime pass to the area. Then he sold the remaining thirty building lots for $20,000 each. A cool million on a handshake. Welch never asked for anything, but Levine sent his mother a gift membership in the Fruit-of-the-Month Club. She loved fresh fruit, Welch had said. He brooded about what to get Welch and worried about the appearance of bribing a public official. Welch had done nothing wrong; he had, in fact, done everything right and had shown no self-interest at all, and he deserved to be thanked the way one businessman thanks another. Finally, in an antiques shop in Sheffield Levine saw a small painting of the Hudson River School. He sent it off to Welch and liked to think that the only people who would ever know it was worth $5,000 were Welch and himself.

Welch wrote him a proper note and stayed quiet—for two years. Then Levine received a brief note. "I'd appreciate it if you could come back up here. There is a possibility of a sale that might interest you." Back in the Green Mountain Arms Welch outlined the deal, stunning in its simplicity. There was land, "of owners unknown" according to the real-estate statutes, which had lain on the county tax roles for years. Most of it was valueless, including a large tract in Parrish Valley which was a morass of dead pines poking out from marshy subsoil. The land was no good because of beaver dams that had kept it waterlogged for a hundred years. Welch produced a clipping from a Montreal paper about "Reclaiming Land from Nature." Canadian engineers had devised a way to drain the land, using enormous networks of plastic tubing as wicks to draw off the water.

"Sounds interesting," said Levine.

"It is," Welch said.

"This land must be more valuable now than it was," Levine said.

"It would be," Welch said, "if the county knew about what the Canadians are doing."

"You are the county," Levine said.

Welch shrugged. It was a shrug he had not had before, Levine thought.

"I am the county, yes," Welch said. "I have been on the payroll for twenty years. I earn $14,750 a year. I cannot buy land in the county. I lived with my mother twenty-five years. She died last year. I want to live like a grown-up now, if you know what I mean. I am tired of being a small-town bachelor. I would like to visit some of the places I read about."

"I understand," Levine said.

"The sale of this land is perfectly legal," Welch said. "Right now it is legal to sell it for back taxes, if the Registrar of Deeds certifies it as 'land of owners unknown.' Of course, the county has the option of paying the back taxes itself and then auctioning off the land. But there would be no point in paying the back taxes on an old swamp that has no market value. The smart thing for the county to do would be to sell it for taxes."

"How much do you want for yourself?" Levine said.

"The back taxes are fifteen thousand dollars. There's a lot of acreage. If the county happened to know of its potential value and had to sell it at auction, it would go for around a hundred thousand. You wouldn't be hooking into a sure thing at that price, because that drainage technology is expensive. I think that ten thousand dollars for my help would be about right. That's not a lot of money for a man like you."

Levine was silent.

For the first time since they had known each other, Welch became plaintive, almost begging. "You wouldn't have to worry about me, A.L. If I went off on vacation or spent some money, people would think I was spending some of the money Mom left me. I wouldn't get you in any trouble."

"I know that. It's a most interesting idea, Mr. Welch. The only problem is, I've been concentrating my development in the South and in Texas the last couple of years. Things have gotten so big that I'm reluctant to take on any more developments."

"You came up here when I wrote," Welch said reproachfully.

"Yes, certainly. I'm always looking, and I'd like to help you. But let me think about it overnight."

There was nothing to think about. He would save Welch's face by pretending interest, but he would pay no bribes. When he had tried to do the construction himself on that plot outside of Knoxville, he had ended up bribing the surveyor's office, the public health department, the building inspector, the sewage commission, and the Environmental Protection officer. When the Knoxville development was over, he had vowed never again to do the building himself. He'd buy the raw land, draw up the specs, and subcontract the work to local firms. Let them do the bribing, if there was any. He never again would give some redneck eighth-grader the chance to take $500 in cash and go home patting his wallet and telling himself, "Just like them Jews!"

So in the morning he told Welch that he was sorry that he couldn't go ahead with any more land development in New England. He offered Welch a high-paying job as his agent in the South, just to let him know that he did not consider him morally tainted. Welch refused, as Levine expected he would. Levine went back to New York and kept a weather eye on New England events. The next winter he took a trip to look at the snow-locked Wink River settlement. At the courthouse he was told that Mr. Welch was on vacation in the Caribbean. Because people might remember him, he didn't ask that the registry books be brought to him, but turned and walked out the front door. When he saw Welch's secretary go for lunch, he sauntered back into the courthouse, and, reading the transaction book upside down, noticed that the Parrish Valley land had been sold for back taxes to a young lawyer named Rose.

Els gave him a slow, blank stare.

"Why in hell would you want to bike the length of Route Seven?"

"Not the entire length, just between Burlington and Bennington," Rose said.

"Still, that's a hundred and twenty miles, give or take. Who the hell do you think you are, Johnny Appleseed?"

"I know what I'm doing, Els. There's only so much money they'll let us spend on advertising, and we need to get people talking."

"People have done that before. It's an old gimmick. That guy in Florida, the one in Illinois—"

"Jesus Christ, Els, I know. If you want to talk about that, so did Mao Tse-tung."

"Who?"

"Forget it. What I mean is, I'm not claiming it's original with me."

"Then why do it, for Christ's sake? It's a gimmick and an old one."

"It's not a gimmick. Levine would think it's a gimmick, but I'm surprised you would. It's my state, for Christ's sake."

"So what?"

"So, bicycle down Route Seven and show how they've ruined it. The farms are gone, the mountains are blocked off by high-rises, anyplace where you don't have a retirement community you've got a franchise restaurant. It's all the bad things that ever happened to America. We sold out our heritage, and we sold it to people like Levine. The bike thing will show that. It's my state—the rest of the country knows that I know what I'm talking about. You can't show it from a car window. Cars are what helped kill it. Anyway, you go too fast in a car. You can't stop to talk to people the way you can on a bike. We'll have a couple of landscape architects and historians along. We'll have a set of old photographs, blown up, comparing what the country used to look like with what it looks like now. You know, the sort of thing they run in the papers: 'A Snapshot of the Corner of Broad and Main Fifty Years Ago.'"

"Are you set on this?"

"Yes. I want you to help me, not nitpick."

"Okay. You've been right before. You've been wrong too, remember?"

"I remember. If this goes wrong, I'll take the blame."

"Agreed. First off, I don't like you tied up away from the rest of the campaign like that. Jesus, a hundred and twenty miles! You'll be out a week. Cut the distance. Make it Burlington to Vergennes. That will take an afternoon. Then you'll be able to get back to the rest of the campaign."

"I've got it figured, Els. I can do it in three days, easily. I could do it in two, but we're going to want the press along."

"Hell, the press could do it in two hours in the bus."

"There won't be a bus except for TV equipment. There'll be no press. Of course, anyone who wants to bike along with me can. They'll have to begin at the beginning with me, in Burlington."

"It's still too far," Els said.

"Okay, I'll compromise. We'll end in Danby—there's an inn there I like."

"Then there won't be any coverage."

"Yes, there will."

"What reporter is going to bust his ass biking forty miles a day up and down mountains?"

"They'll find someone, Els, I promise you. Besides, on Route Seven there are hills, not mountains."

Sturgis Hale hung back from the pack awhile and enjoyed the scenery. He slipped the five-speed Cortez-Omega into low and coasted. Off on the right he could see a faint shimmer from what might have been Lake George. The land between the highway and the lake was flat and covered with houses. Hale could remember when there had been nothing for miles but green fields and one or two prosperous dairy farms. The Champlain Valley had been as rich as Wisconsin once.

Coudert glided alongside. He was tanned and healthy and pumping effortlessly. After the first night's stopover in Vergennes, when most of the press had dropped out, Coudert had decided to be nice to Hale. Coudert knew little about Hale except that he had a New England name and worked for the *Times*. Under the frontier conditions of the bike trip, that was enough. Coudert had taken Hale into his court.

"Beautiful, isn't it?" Coudert said.

"Yup."

"I used to drive up here when I was in school, hell-bent for skiing. God, when I think back on it now I wonder we weren't ever killed. Half in the bag to begin with, crazy eager to get on the slopes, always driving in snow or ice. We were nuts. You do much skiing?"

"Not much."

"But you grew up around here."

"Maine, actually. Not many hills there."

"Well, there's Sugarloaf."

"We were on the coast."

Fuck him, Hale thought to himself. We've been on the tour three weeks now and all of a sudden he decides I'm his soul brother. We Wasps gotta stick together. Fuck him.

Coudert sensed he was working an empty field. "Look at us," he said. "It's like Napoleon's retreat from Moscow."

Hale looked behind them and laughed. It was a motley group, a movable disaster area. Spread out for two miles behind them were twenty or so other journalists, most of them coated with sweat and red in the face. Instead of riding their bikes they were struggling against them. The media had had a week's notice of Rose's Bike-a-thon and had gone into a frenzy preparing their reporters. Most papers had gone to their younger political writers, handed them a bike, and told them to start getting in shape—now. Four or five of the regulars on the press bus had decided that they weren't going to get aced out by younger reporters and had gone into intensive training themselves. Strosnider of Los Angeles, a massive ex-football player whose main reportorial talent was his intimidating size, had started doing push-ups in his room twice a day.

The most interesting bunch had been the columnists. As soon as the trip was announced, they had started swapping stories of their athletic feats. Pincus, the frail economist who worked for Canadian Broadcasting, claimed that he had been a vicious hockey player as a boy in Edmonton. Friedman and O'Rourke, the Golddust twins from the *New York Post,* talked endlessly of gang fights in Queens. Paige, a supercilious writer from San Francisco who had never once mentioned his childhood, boasted to everyone that he had made third-string all-Scholastic all-State basketball as a senior. "That was in Indiana, damn it," Paige said, "where people know how to play basketball." This precipitated a vehement argument about Indiana, Texas, New York, and Washington as breeding places for athletes in which every participant, at one time or another, obliquely admitted to his own athletic ability. ("Let me tell you once when I was playing tennis for Reed I got in a tournament and in the first round I drew some kid I had never heard of—he was a black, the first one I ever played against. Figured I couldn't lose. I lost, double zeros. Turned out the kid's name was Arthur Ashe.")

The trip had weeded the talkers from the doers, Hale thought. He had hiked with Rose, and he knew that Rose took a malicious pleasure in seeing writers he despised literally fall by the wayside. There was a ten-minute rest period every hour, and Rose, never shortwinded or sweaty, would wait languidly as the reporters straggled up to the rest stop. On the road Rose was usually flanked by some of the architects, lawyers, and conservationists who had been part of the tour from the start. They were backpackers, day trippers, rock climbers, ski jumpers, kayak tippers, river runners, and bike racers, and they, too, were gently condescending toward the reporters. The Red Cross van complete with cardiograph machine and oxygen that trailed the caravan had been dubbed the "Rose Hilton," and several reporters had spent more time in the van than on the trail. There had been no heart attacks the first day, but three wire-service reporters had collapsed from the heat, and most of the press-bus regulars had simply quit. As a precaution, the *Times,* the *Post,* the news magazines, and Reuters had accredited to the Bike-a-thon not only their regular political reporters but a ragtag of general assignment writers chosen solely for their physical fitness. All these, including a robust lady from *Paris Match,* were still in the caravan.

At the checkpoint Rose was displaying a blown-up picture of Wallingford Valley as it had been in 1950 against the reality of 1988. The TV cameras moved in on him.

"I really don't have to denounce anything," Rose was saying. "I just have to show you America today and America in 1950 and let you decide what went wrong—if you think it went wrong, as I do. Ugliness, cheapness, commercialism everywhere. We couldn't even celebrate our Bicentennial without turning it into the kind of modern Christmas that begins before Thanksgiving and ends in a department store. Just as we have desecrated Christmas, we have desecrated our land. It's not too late to stop." He smiled evenly and got back on his bike.

"Let's stay up with him," Coudert suggested.

"Okay." Most of the time they had lagged a bit off the pace, ahead of the regular press corps but behind Rose. Rose was usually surrounded by the deep breathers and conservationists. When Hale had pulled alongside the lead group he had heard Rose lecturing on Vermont history or geologic formations. It was interesting stuff but no news story.

"Let's get him alone," Hale said.

"Sure."

They moved into high gear and pedaled toward the lead group. Hale cut alongside Rose, leaned over, and yelled, "Coudert and I will race you to Danby!"

"Done." Rose turned to his assistant on the Bike-a-thon and said, "Keep up the regular pace with everyone else." Then he leaned over toward Hale, thumbed his nose at him, and took off in a burst.

"Sonofabitch," Coudert said, and they were off.

"Pace yourself," Hale said. Rose was already out of sight around the bend.

"How far is it?"

"Fifteen miles."

"Jesus. I don't think I can keep this up five miles, much less fifteen."

"That's what I say. Pace yourself. I've walked with him. He's strong, but not that strong. And he's older than we are. Keep your meter at around fifteen miles per hour. He can sprint to twenty-five, but not for long. Hold it at fifteen."

They bent over their bars, kept the bikes in high, blessed the downhills, cursed the hills, and prayed for even a slight following wind. Hale was in good shape and had been training for the bike caravan, and so far as he knew Coudert hadn't ridden a bike in ten years. But Coudert was up ahead, whippetlike, breezing steadily along. Hale pulled himself alongside Coudert.

"Fun!" Coudert shouted. His eyes were shining.

"I don't think we can catch him."

"I think I can."

"Don't wait for me, then."

"I'll hang with you another couple miles. Then I'll sprint."

They moved along together and Hale began to marvel at Rose's insight. This was what men should be doing, taxing their bodies, racing for no good reason except the thrill of racing. Any creep could look up obituaries or pound on a typewriter. He and Coudert and Rose, suddenly released from the sticky indoor world of politics and the press, had thrown themselves into America.

The TV bus passed them on a straightaway.

"They want to film Rose sprinting into Danby," Coudert said.

"Get in their wake!" Hale shouted.

"What?"

"Get behind the bus. Let it be the wind-breaker for you. Stay with it as long as you can. It's what the six-day racers used to do."

"Okay."

Coudert sped off twenty feet behind the bus, while cameramen waved idly from the windows. Idiots, Hale thought. They think it's just a campaign stunt. It's a real race.

He pumped along. His legs hurt and his left ankle was rubbing raw against the pedal clamp. He wouldn't let Coudert beat him by that much. On the last hill outside of Danby, dizzy from exhaustion, hands fastened on the handlebars in a death grip that any amateur knew enough to avoid, he raised his head from the road for the first time. Ahead a half mile he saw Coudert and Rose pedaling beautifully together. They were going uphill and going rapidly and yet there was no sense of effort and they were talking together. The TV van was right in front of them, filming. Someone in the van must have said something, for Rose looked back over his shoulder, saw Hale, and motioned him forward.

Hale thought to himself, Look good, look good, finish smoothly, and he sprinted forward on energy that came from pride and finished closely behind the other two. The caravan was scheduled to stay at the Danby Inn, and as Hale biked up to be grabbed and pummeled by Coudert and Rose, the staff of the inn was out on the lawn, clapping.

"You liked that," Rose said later on the porch. It was an old-fashioned porch with a hammock and rocking chairs, and Hale was in a rocker that was the most comfortable piece of furniture in the western hemisphere.

"Yes, I liked it," Hale said.

"You see what I mean," Rose said. "America isn't for weaklings. It's not for city people. America is the land. Jefferson knew that, Lincoln knew it. People make fun of Theodore Roosevelt, but he was the last real intellectual we had in the White House. Maybe the only one. Wilson was a professor, but Roosevelt was an intellectual. He knew about the land, the strenuous life. You two guys are in on it. You can have the story first. You deserve it."

"What story?" Hale asked.

"I'm making a speech in Denver next week. It's going to be the theme for the last part of the campaign. It's my plan for America. I'm going to call it 'The Old Deal.'"

"The what?"

"That's right. The Old Deal. This country's frightened of new deals and new frontiers and new freedoms. For good reason. I want people to go back to the old deal, the old ideals. Christ, today you can't tell America from Japan from Russia from Germany. We're all the same. Thirty years ago you could go into an airport or a train station and you could tell people of one country from another. I mean, goddam it, Germans dressed like Germans and combed their hair like Germans and walked like Germans, and Americans swung their arms when they walked and parted their hair on the side and had shirts with button-down collars, and now it's all the goddam same. And the same thing has happened to our ideals. They've gotten mixed up, confused. We've got to go back to basics. To the Constitution. To the Old Deal."

Levine and Bell watched the Bike-a-thon on the evening news.

"What do you think?" Bell asked.

"He's a good athlete, that Coudert. Notice how smooth he is. Rose is good, too. It's pretty, isn't it?"

"I mean, seriously."

"I'm talking seriously. That's what I think when I look at it, that's what most people will think. The commercials he puts in, the business about despoiling the land and all that, that will wash off most people the same way the regular ads do. Some of it will stick, I grant you, but mostly it washes off. What they remember will be how smooth he rides. That will be a problem. It takes people back into the past, and when people are worried they like to think about the past. I ought to know."

NEW YORK, AUTUMN, 1936

When he was in the eighth grade, Mr. Slutzky, the director of the Home, called him into his office.

"Levine, how would you like to live in a private home?

"I like it here."

"I'm serious. How would you like to live with a very fine family. A *fine* family. Well-to-do. Outstanding members of the Jewish community."

Levine knew all the tricks. Slutzky was always trying to trap kids into squealing on each other. Now he was trying to get Levine to say he didn't like the Home. He held fast.

"I like it here."

"Look, boy, I'm glad you like it here. I believe you. But, putting aside foolishness, I'm asking you if you'd like to live in a private home."

"Mr. Slutzky, thank you, but I like it here."

"You'll be leaving in two days. Mrs. Grutstein will be here to talk to you tomorrow." Slutzky leaned across the table. "Look good, Levine, look good. Don't try to cross me or I'll break your ass. *Vershteyt?*"

"Yes, sir."

The Home had a program of Domestic Placement. It was a desultory effort, run by Miss Cohen, the history teacher, in her spare time. It was desultory since no one would be at the Home in the first place in any Jewish social service agency had been able to come up with a home placement. Nonetheless, every once in a while, someone went shopping for a grown Jewish child, and when they did they eventually came to the Home.

"The doctor and I have always wanted a child of our own," Mrs. Grutstein explained in the rec room the next day, "but God was not willing. But he has blessed us in many other ways, and now we would like to repay Him. We are looking for a fine Jewish boy like you to raise in our own home."

Mrs. Grutstein was small and blond and very clean. Levine couldn't remember when he had seen anyone as clean as she was. He would have gone with her if her home had been in Hitler's Germany.

"If I may say, Dr. Grutstein and I have many intellectual interests. We are looking for a young man with whom we can share these interests and who, if God is willing, might learn what little we have to teach. Dr. Grutstein is a podiatrist. I have my own career as a music educator for the city of New York. I am working on my Ph.D. as well. Soon perhaps you might call us Dr. and Dr. Grutstein." She laughed.

Levine laughed, too. He had no idea what a podiatrist or a Ph.D. was, but he was ready to go.

"You're going to adopt me?" he asked. He wasn't exactly sure about adoption, but it had something to do with inheriting money. The other orphans talked about it, when they weren't talking about screwing.

Mrs. Grutstein was flustered. "No, not exactly. Not that we *wouldn't* adopt you. By no means. That is, Dr. Grutstein and I have discussed the possibility. Our friends say we both have a way with children"—she laughed again—"but we haven't lived with a child in the home. It would be wrong to commit ourselves prematurely. The possibility exists. When we spoke to Mr. Slutzky we specifically asked for a young man who was polite and whose grades showed that he might benefit from a Jewish home in which culture is important. He recommended you highly. You have excellent references."

The Grutsteins lived in unimagined splendor in an enormous apartment house called the Kingsbridge on the Grand Concourse. Dr. Grutstein had his own bedroom. Mrs. Grutstein had a separate bedroom. Levine had a separate bedroom. Pearl, the maid, had a separate bedroom. Each bedroom had its own radio—Stromberg Carlsons for everyone except Pearl, who had a Philco. For the first time in his life Levine had his own bathroom, with a tub he shared with no one else.

"So this is the boy," Dr. Grutstein said, when his wife marched Levine home for the first time. "Turn around, Alfred."

"My friends call me A.L."

"Ah, but we're not your friends. We're your guardians, which is different. To us you shall be Alfred. Turn around, please, Alfred." Levine turned. Dr. Grutstein stared. "We have a number of things to do, but the first is to buy you some new clothes. These are a trifle small for you."

Years later Levine would remember this meeting and would recognize that Irv Grutstein—pompous, foolish, a perennial schmuck—had had some substance to him after all. He had liked Grutstein at first, admired him even, but with time developed an easy contempt for him. Yet there had been something to that first impression. Grutstein was a fool, but not without perception and never without feeling. Levine's clothes hadn't been "a trifle small." They had been dirty and smelly and ragged at every edge that could be ragged. No two buttons matched. They were awful clothes. But, in addition to everything else, they *were* a trifle small. Somehow Grutstein sensed that Levine, despising the orphanage, would not allow anyone else to share his contempt. To the outside world Levine would insist that the Home was a fine place, clean and well-run, an orphan's Exeter.

Grutstein loaded the boy on the subway and they rocketed to Fordham Road. Levine had never chosen his own clothes before. Grutstein guided him as one man of the world would another. "I don't think that's quite your style, Alfred." Levine had never realized that he *had* a style.

Clothed, fed, introduced to the neighbors on the sixth floor, Levine the next morning found his way to a new school. P.S. 70 was a "junior high school" and, as an experiment, was regarded by the inhabitants of the Bronx as next step to the Torah. Science was the new religion of the Bronx, Einstein was its Moses, and "experiments" were its Way. The seediest nursery school could label itself "an experimental school" or "a laboratory for learning" and be beseiged by parents offering up their children.

"You're lucky to be going to P.S. 70," Mrs. Grutstein said as he hurried out the door. "It's an experimental school. There are lots of children right now begging to be let in."

Levine did not appreciate his luck. P.S. 70 was like most of the other schools he had been in and out of, though it was newer than the school near the Home. The teachers were mostly Irish and American, but there were some Jews. As at the Home, the students were all Jewish. There the resemblance ended.

Introduced to his new classmates Levine set off a wave of whispering in the class and was promptly forgotten. He then sat in amazement as a new world unfolded. The teacher, Miss Bentley, asked if anyone had read what had happened in Europe. A dozen hands shot up in the air. A boy near Levine half leaped from his seat and, crouching, flapped both arms like a wounded condor. A girl whimpered, "Me, me." Miss Bentley pointed a magisterial finger at a gawky boy in short pants. "Ira."

"He quit, Miss Bentley."

"Who quit, Ira?" she asked.

"The King of England."

"Very good. Does anyone know another word—a special word—for what the King did?"

More hands shot up. Excitement swept the class. Children spoke without being called on.

"He weft," a little girl said.

"It's left, Ellen," Miss Bentley said.

"Resigned," a tiny red-haired boy suggested.

"No, no . . ."

It was time to end the farce. "Abdicated," Levine said. Miss Bentley was his from that moment on.

———————

At the Home Levine had done good work in school, and the Home prided itself on the excellence of its academic preparation. It was, after all, a *Jewish* orphanage. The code under which the boys themselves lived, however, was more suitable for a second-rate prep school than a yeshiva. If anyone was smart, he kept quiet about it. No one volunteered answers. No extra work was done. If a boy liked to read books, he crept into the bathroom stalls and read while his dorm mates grunted alongside him. Ultimately, the Home did not believe in the excellence of its academic work. After all, why bother? *These* Jewish kids weren't going to college.

At P.S. 70 Levine found himself in the pressure cooker of the Bronx, a borough which had voted to turn all its first-born sons into doctors, its second sons into lawyers, and its daughters into psychiatric social workers. The Bronx was an enormous refinery, taking raw youth and distilling it into professional men. P.S. 70, defiantly experimental, solidly middle-class, was the cutting edge of the system. No school had more eager students. No school had more dedicated teachers. And no school had more ambitious parents.

The Grutsteins looked down on all the other parents at P.S. 70 and almost all the other parents in the Bronx. Both Grutsteins had been born in the United States and, though they cautioned Levine never to mimic another person's manner of speech or dress, they themselves were not above imitating neighbors who spoke of buying "a nize piece chicken." Irv Grutstein was deferential in the presence of the M.D.s who occasionally referred him patients with stubborn corns, but he was withering if Miss Bentley forgot to address him as "doctor."

Superior in their accents, their nativity, and their professions, the Grutsteins nonetheless plunged with immigrant vigor into the academic competition at P.S. 70. Their whole lives had been a prelude to entering a "parfit gentil knight" in the lists of junior high school, and they took to it like fish to water.

"Tonight we're going to work on vocabulary," Irv Grutstein said after Pearl's pot roast had been polished off (Rose Grutstein was too tired from teaching to cook, except on weekends). Levine sat at the living room table and Irv handed him a list of twenty words: "Arcane, bountiful, epitome, calumny..." Levine tried to define the ones he knew and looked up the ones he didn't. The definitions had to be written out, "so you'll remember them better." He enjoyed the exercise, but after a month Levine discovered that Grutstein was cadging most of the words from "How to Increase Your Word Power" in the *Reader's Digest*. Levine felt the same resentment he did years later when he learned that the great jokes one of his salesmen had been telling him came from a new magazine called *Playboy*. The jokes were still new to Levine, but they were never that funny again.

After vocabulary came music appreciation, with Rose leaping back and forth from the victrola, playing part of one piece, a snatch of another, and pointing out key changes, solo instruments, and rhythm shifts as the music progressed. Levine never heard a piece all the way through. Not until he was thirty and reencountered Mozart did he ever enjoy classical music.

It took all the Grutsteins' combined willpower to keep their hands off his homework. The honor system prevailed, however, and it was not unless Levine was genuinely stumped that he was allowed to invoke adult assistance. The Grutsteins huddled over his penciled, lined notebook and lectured him on the methods of getting the proper answer. They never gave him the answer. If he couldn't think of anything else George Eliot wrote besides *Silas Marner,* he was referred to the *Encyclopedia Britannica*. Unsure of Roosevelt's first vice-president, he was sent to the *World Almanac*. If he fumbled a math problem, a small check mark would be placed beside the step where he had gone wrong, and he would be left to figure out the mistake and rework the problem himself.

The Grutsteins believed in recreation. "We don't want you to become a bookworm," Irv said jovially. After a week's heated debate Levine was granted a half hour of radio before supper, fifteen minutes less than most of the other kids. He chose Jack Armstrong and Tom Mix and regretfully said good-bye to Little Orphan Annie. Uncle Don was kid stuff. He was allowed selected programs after supper, once he had finished his homework. The high point of the week was Sunday, when they listened to *Information Please* together. Rose Grutstein kept score. Levine was over his head most of the time, but stayed in contention by knowing some of the sports questions that

FPA and Kieran did. The Grutsteins did not consider sports knowledge in the same category as opera dates, but, since Mr. Fadiman awarded encyclopedias to sports questioners as well as music lovers, there had to be some value in it.

Reading, if not ordered, was encouraged. There was always a Current Events Discussion at dinner (Levine thought of it in capital letters), and a working knowledge of *PM* and the *Post* was a prerequisite. Levine liked the comics in *PM*, but the sports page was awful. One day on the way home from school he bought a paper himself, instead of waiting for Dr. Grutstein to bring one in from the office or the subway. He was curled up on the sofa reading Dick Tracy when Rose saw him and let out a little peal of horror.

"Alfred, no. No! Never bring that paper in this house. Please, put it in the trash chute right now."

"How come?"

"It's fascist propaganda. Every time you buy that paper you kill a Jew. Besides, it's trash. Gossip and sports and sex. Not clean sex, but dirty sex."

Levine hadn't learned the distinction. He wasn't going to argue on the basis of classifications of sex. There was a weak spot, however.

"Pearl reads the *News*." Pearl was never criticized in the Grutstein family.

"Pearl is a member of an oppressed race. She hasn't had the advantages you have. We believe in tolerance. There are many other things Pearl does that we do not expect of you. Not because you are better—all races are equal—but because you have had more education."

He had lost and he knew it. He gave up Dick Tracy and the pretty girls in bathing suits enjoying the Miami Beach winter ("Hot Enough for You?" was the way the *News* labeled these pictures), and from then on he read the paper in the trash room. The Bluestones' maid got it daily and threw it out untouched except for the racing results.

Culture was not neglected on weekends. Sunday for the Grutsteins was an orgy of museums, folk music concerts, grainy French movies, and, as a treat for Levine, educational puppet shows. Packed in among hundreds of children, most of them between the ages of nine and nine and a half, Levine watched educational puppets perform *Tom Sawyer, War and Peace,* and *The Wind in the Willows.* He sullenly picked at early acne while, afraid he might miss a political nuance, Rose Grutstein jabbed him with her elbow.

From a faltering start at P.S. 70, Levine caught on rapidly. Slutzky had been right. Levine rampaged through the Grutsteins' library (including a half-concealed volume on *Sex and the Modern Child*—the Grutsteins had noticed the acne too). He listened to Walter Damrosch on Saturdays and Gabriel Heater nightly. He read *PM* each evening and occasionally even ventured into the gray pages of the *Times.* At P.S. 70 he cut a swath through Literature and blazed ahead in Current Events.

His deeds were not ignored. Academic achievement did not exist in a vacuum at P.S. 70 and the Kingsbridge, any more than batting averages did in the rest of America. Comparison was universal, constant, and well-informed. One did not have to have children of school age to know who had scored how much on the Age-Adjusted Reading Levels or the Math Aptitudes. The little old ladies who, bundled in furs, regularly sat in the plaza in front of the building, faces pointed toward the flinty winter sun like so many ocean voyagers in their deck chairs, knew the test scores. They were not mothers but maiden aunts or grandmothers, and their English was often an embarrassment to the sons and daughters with whom they lived, but they kept score and they did not forget.

"That's the one the Grutsteins took in."

"A lovely couple!"

"The boy has a real *yiddishe kopf!*"

"Him and Bernie Nathanson, they're both in college already."

"So young?"

"No, not actual college. College *reading.* On the test they all took, this boy and Bernie should be in college already."

"Sonny, come over."

Obedient, Levine went. The old ladies questioned him, touched their dry, blue hands to his, ran their fingers through his hair, pinched his cheeks. He was their good-luck charm, proof that the Jews would survive and survive smart.

The actual parents of the little scholars at P.S. 70 were not so much mothers and fathers as handlers. Some of them were handlers like the ones at the dog show, the ones you saw on Movietone News who trotted their perfectly groomed charges around the ring on a leash, smiled at the judges, and disappeared. Others were handlers like those at the fights, feisty little men who leaped out at their protégés between rounds, wiped off sweat, closed gashes, dashed on some cold water, and kept up a steady stream of encouragement.

Floreat Levine! The Grutsteins could afford an aloof attitude toward "Alfred," could accept their neighbors' congratulations with poise. No need for them to complain to the principal that Miss Bentley wasn't calling on their boy in class. No need to yell him home early from his hour's play each afternoon to get a head start on his homework. Levine was proof of their benign liberal belief that all men, all boys—even orphan boys!—could someday get a Ph.D. and a home in Mt. Vernon.

All went well through the fall and into the winter. As spring came to the Bronx, however, Levine developed signs of restlessness. Whatever the faults of the Home, it had its own baseball field and its own gymnasium. In the gym Levine, prized for this quickness and his deadly two-handed set shot (was there any other kind?), had developed a reputation as a basketball player. The older kids asked him to play. There were hints that, as a senior, he might play for the Home itself. On the baseball field he had developed respectable skills, despite an overwhelming fear that a ground ball might bounce up and break his glasses.

At the Home spring meant baseball, marbles, tops, and renewed efforts to make friends with the local girls. At the Kingsbridge spring meant a redoubling of academic effort. Final report cards came out the first week in June. Oblivious to Levine's restlessness, the Grutsteins continued force-feeding him knowledge. Slowly it was dawning on Levine that what was worst about Irv and Rose was their conviction that they knew what was best for everyone, not merely for him but for Pearl (they kept trying to make her listen to Paul Robeson instead of the church music she preferred) and all America. It was clear, too, that despite their belief in the unity of man they despised all Catholics, hated all Southerners ("Just listen to that accent!" Rose would exclaim when they watched Carter Glass at the Trans-Lux), and feared all parts of the country outside the morning circulation zone of the *New York Times.* There was something a little funny about their love for Franklin Roosevelt, too. Levine loved the president—everyone in the Bronx loved the president— but he didn't like it at the newsreels when Irv would whisper to him, "Clap!" as soon as the president's face was shown.

Still, these were the irritations that a man could accept, the sort that would later make marriage difficult but not impossible. The impossible grew from a discussion in early May. Levine had finished his homework, Irv Grutstein was reading *The New Republic,* and Rose was marking her pupils' papers. When the clock rang nine o'clock, Irv looked at Rose, cleared his throat, and said, "Alfred, we've been thinking about what you'd like to do this summer."

Levine had been thinking about it too. The other kids at P.S. 70 had begun to talk of their summer plans. Each, apparently, went to a camp of Olympian splendor or retreated to an elaborate summer home with his mother (fathers visited on weekends, plus two weeks in August). The Grutsteins, Levine knew, had a cottage in the mountains. He wasn't wild about spending a couple of months cooped up with Rose in a four-room house, but he figured that there'd be other kids to play with. Maybe he'd be able to go fishing, the way he had with his father.

Rose chimed in. "We thought you'd like to go to camp this summer."

"I would, please."

Irv picked up the thread. "We've found a most fitting place, Alfred. Camp Freiheit is run by Phil and Alice Sanzer, friends of ours. It's a new place, very experimental, with a whole new concept. The idea is to teach children about Judaism and do it in Hebrew. You have all the wonderful things of summer, and you'll be learning Hebrew at the same time. And some of your friends from the building will be there, Ira Rosenfeld and—what was the other boy's name, Irv?"

"No."

"No? No *what?*"

"No, thank you."

"What do you mean, 'No, thank you?'"

"I don't want to go. I'd like to stay here. I like it here."

Irv was furious. "How do you know you don't want to go when you don't know anything about the camp?"

Levine knew. He knew that any camp that Ira Rosenfeld would be going to was a shit camp, a camp for creeps and fat kids and kids who stuttered. He knew that he was tired of learning things, that he didn't want to learn anything at all that summer, except possibly not to be afraid of hard-hit ground balls. He knew that he didn't want the Grutsteins running his life any more, but he couldn't say that.

"So? Why don't you want to go?"

"I like it here. I'll be homesick."

"We're both going to be away for the summer," Rose said. "You can't stay here by yourself. Camp will be ideal for you. Why don't you think about it? We don't have to decide now."

"Rose, dear, we have to send in the deposit soon."

"So send. Twenty-five dollars. What can happen?" She turned to Levine again. "Think about it, Alfred. We don't want to force you."

No other camps were mentioned. Levine timidly hinted that Arthur Bluestone was going to a camp in Connecticut where they had four diving boards. No response. Again the matter of Camp Freiheit was raised.

"You see, Alfred"—Irv lumbered on—"we want you to appreciate your ancient cultural heritage."

"What?"

"Your Jewishness."

"I appreciate it." He knew kids who tried to deny they were Jewish when the Irish from Gun Hill Road caught them. The Irish beat them up anyway.

"Not in the sense that will be important. We want you to be ready for the Jewish world of the future, the Zionist state where a Jew can be whatever he wants."

Levine had noted that the Grutsteins, who never spoke Yiddish and who went to synagogue just twice a year, were always talking about Zionism and Palestine.

"I like it here," he said defiantly.

Irv Grutstein misunderstood. "Don't get me wrong. We love America, Rose and I. But, let's face it, we're strangers here too. There's got to be a place where the Jews can control their own country, where other people can be the strangers. At Camp Freiheit you can learn everyday Hebrew, so you can be ready for that country."

At the Home Levine had been taught Hebrew in a system designed to make one forget what had just been taught. It was as though there were a giant slate marked "Hebrew," and as one hand wrote down the words, another erased all that had gone before. Teitelbaum, the Hebrew teacher, had come straight from Poland to the Home. Three was nothing experimental about his teaching method, which deviated as little as possible from the way Teitelbaum had been taught Hebrew in Heder in 1880. The pupils memorized a section of Torah, learning it letter perfect, and went on to the next section, forgetting the previous one. No questions were asked. None were needed. The idea was to memorize, not to understand. Understanding would come later, in ten or fifteen years. The method did permanently to Hebrew what Rose Grutstein's music appreciation method did for twenty years to Mozart.

Levine wouldn't yield. As June approached, he stayed out later and later with Lefty Applebaum and Philip Garanalli, the pariahs of the Kingsbridge. Lefty was feared because he was big and violent, Philip because he was Italian. The little ladies in the plaza, still wrapped in furs though the days were becoming hot, shook their heads. They knew that you couldn't pick a boy out of the gutter and put him at a prince's table. Blood was blood. The verdict was ordained.

When Rose and Irv told him that they didn't want him any longer, he cried a bit to make them feel better. They weren't bad people, he was sure, and it would have been cruel to let them know how eager he was to get back to an orphanage. The Grutsteins explained that they had misestimated themselves, that raising a child was too much after all, that they felt sorry about letting him go but hoped he would understand.

Slutzky was disappointed but, surprisingly, not angry. The Grutsteins had sent in a big contribution—"Five hundred dollars," he confided, awestruck—at the same time that they had returned Levine. *We are thankful for the joy he brought us,* their note read. Slutzky figured that if the yield was that good, he could farm Levine out again. The subject came up a couple of times in the next two years, but by then Levine was too good a basketball player to be forced out of the Home against his will. Besides, he was adamant. He had read *Tom Sawyer.* He knew that he had been civilized, but it didn't take.

"It's nice to have you home for a couple of days," his wife said.

"Me too. After all, I miss the family, just like you miss me."

There was silence. Levine looked around the table. Eli had already started his melon. Helen was checking the silverware to see if the maid had gotten the spoons clean. Laura was examining her nails. Only Samuel seemed to be paying any attention.

"We don't get together as a family very much these days," Levine said.

"Or those days either," Eli remarked, holding his spoon in the air.

"What do you mean by that, Mr. Smarty?" Helen said.

"Now, dear, don't get all upset. Eli didn't mean anything by that."

"If I didn't mean anything by it, I wouldn't have said it."

"Okay, okay," Levine said. "What did you mean by it?"

"I meant that this family goes by some kind of legend of the old old days when everyone was gathered around the table, like a bunch of grape pickers or something. The only time I can ever remember all of us together was on my birthday and on your anniversary."

"And the high holidays, don't forget them, my brilliant son," Helen broke in.

"Yeah, Passover too. I can remember that. But that's what I mean—we can remember the times we were all together. They were something special. Most families, it's ordinary that they're together. Why pretend something that didn't exist?"

Helen started to interrupt, but Levine came in. "You're right. I regret I had so little time with the family when you were young. But if you must travel, you travel. Thank God, we're at least in good health except for Laura's colitis and your mother's hay fever, and thank God we're all together."

"I don't know how you can say that most families are together, Eli," his brother said thoughtfully. "Think of all the people we know who're divorced or separated. Dad's right—we have a lot to be thankful for."

"My God, I came in for dinner, not a lecture."

"You're happy enough to eat your meals here, instead of going back to school or getting—"

"Stop, already," Levine said.

And it almost stopped. Eli ate his roast in elaborate silence, grunting when someone asked him to pass the salt. Helen muttered under her breath that "Some people don't know the meaning of the word gratitude. If they went to school, maybe they could even spell it." Laura tried to talk to Samuel about her youngest, who might possibly have a new kind of disease which accounted for his difficulty in doing artwork at school. As she talked to Samuel, she alternately smiled sweetly at her father and gave Eli the look she reserved for when she leash-walked the dog and he did his duty in a public place. She was with Eli, the look implied, but only by coincidence.

"How do you think the campaign's going, Dad?" Samuel asked.

"Not bad, really. We're picking up support all the time, and I think we're going to do well in New England. So far, no big problems."

"What about anti-Semitism?"

"There's some, just like we expected. When isn't there some? But it's not bad, not much more than the other kind of labels that candidates have to fight their way through—if you're Catholic or a black or a woman or whatever, people say it's a handicap. What you are will always lose you a few votes and bring in a few. Mostly, it's a matter of what sort of person you are."

"Jesus!" Eli said, slamming his fist against the table and knocking over a candlestick that crashed to the floor.

"The candlestick," Helen cried, jumping to her feet.

"Eli, that was my mother's. We had it when we still lived on the East Side, when we just got married. God forbid, anything should happen...." She was on her knees, fondling the candlestick.

Levine ground his teeth. "Eli, what kind of person are you? What kind of person would do that to his mother?"

Eli was almost apologetic. "I didn't mean to knock it over, Dad. Of course I didn't. I mean...but that's just what's the matter with all of you. You're all sitting and turning pale about the candlestick, and you aren't even interested in what's so awful."

"When we finish the candlestick, we'll find out about your precious feelings," Laura chimed in.

"That's it, that's it. Candlesticks first, people second. I always knew."

"Just a minute, young man. No one said candlesticks first." Levine turned to his wife, still on her knees, slightly pale. "Is it all right?"

"Yes. There's a small dent, but I know a little—"

"Good. Now we can hear Mr. Eli Levine tell us what evoked his outrage today. Today's outrage."

"Sure, be sarcastic. But you'll remember someday. I know you don't want to hear, but I'll say it anyway. Dad goes on about how people get elected on their merit and how being a Jewish candidate is just the same thing as being a black or a woman, and everyone tries to forget that we contributed a hundred times more to this country than the blacks or women ever did and no Jew's ever been elected president. It's not the same thing. They've kept you out, Mr. Levine, and they've kept you out because you're a Jew. There's your great system for you. It's as simple as that. If you're a Jew, you're perfectly welcome to give money or give advice or do motivation studies or address envelopes or clean the toilets. Just don't run for office."

"So what is it that I've been doing the past months—cleaning toilets, perhaps?"

"You're a freak. You slipped by. The system doesn't want you, but they had to take you. They sure as hell don't want you elected."

"You mean my friends, my gentile friends, are tossing in their money and their time in hopes that I'll lose? Young man, I know those men: Jessington, Edwards, the others. They're not saints, but they want me elected. Maybe they want me elected only so they will be more powerful—I'm not going to examine their motives—but they still want me elected."

"Sure, some of them do. A few. But the others hate your guts. You're a token, a little sop to democracy. They can all go around patting themselves on how broad-minded they are, but behind your back they're hoping you'll lose."

"Some poeple in your own party always hope you'll lose. You know enough about politics to know that, Eli. The fact I'm a candidate at all is progress."

"Progress! My God, the Republicans ran Goldwater in 1964, for God's sake. The Republicans! They didn't owe anything to the Jews, but no one made a fuss about Goldwater being Jewish."

"The situation was different. That was before your time. Actually, Goldwater—"

"I know about politics. I used to, anyway. I know about Goldwater and Shapp and Lehman and Thalmann. Just because it was before my time doesn't mean anything. I can read. There was a time when I could give you the percentages in any national race back to Roosevelt's first time."

"That's right," Helen broke in. "He was so quick with the election figures. Remember, A.L., when Lyndon Johnson visited us back in the other apartment, and Eli gave him the exact figures on that election for something or other back in 1948?"

"I remember," Levine said. "Mr. Johnson wasn't overjoyed being reminded of that election."

"The Democratic primary for the Senate," Eli said softly. "'Landslide Lyndon.' He hated that."

"It used to be fun, Eli, going over the campaigns with you. Of course, I know you've got more important things on your mind now."

"More sarcasm. I *do* have more important things on

my mind. It's not enough to get elected. It's the kind of society you get elected by. This society stinks. It isn't sick, it's dead and it doesn't know it. It kisses the ass of perverts and loafers and blacks when it should be turning them out, making them work on their own."

"It's not as simple as that, Eli. God knows, I'm in favor of people working. I've never been that friendly with the gays—"

"Fags," Eli interrupted.

"With the gays," his father continued. "But people have rights. The government exists to protect those rights."

"You don't see, you don't see," Eli said.

"Eli, stop arguing with your father," Helen said.

"That's right," Laura said.

"He taught us to argue with him. He told us that we should be interested in politics. He told us to think for ourselves. Now, if I happen to do that, everyone says shut up."

"Eli is right," his father said. "If I had wanted puppets, I would have ordered puppets. Still, I think you're all wrong. Today you seem outraged that people who are on my side are not one hundred percent with me. You would like things to be black and white. They are not. They are usually gray. If you knew your Freud as well as you knew your Caputo, you would know about ambivalence. Politics are an extension of personal life, and in personal life, too, you never get one hundred percent devotion. At least, as a Jew, you should know better than to expect it. We are the masters of ambivalence."

"Sure, politics are an extension of personal life, and for Jews personal life has been one accommodation after another. Be nice to the goyim and they'll be nice to us. Don't raise your voice or people will think we're kikes. Be nice to people, slap the Schwartzer on the back and maybe he'll buy the four-hundred-dollar suit. Jesus Christ, Dad, you kissed asses so long selling radios that you've forgotten that—"

"Enough, enough!" shouted Levine.

"No, it's not enough, it's the truth. That's what you did, that's what you're still doing. Kissing—"

Levine reached over and pushed against his son's chest. Eli, teetering in his chair, toppled backward onto the floor. Levine stood over him, shouting. "Enough, I said! I taught you to think for yourself, not to call your parents names. Out of here. Back to your room. When you apologize you can be with civilized people. No, no, don't do your karate thing here. Not here." Eli had raised back his arm.

Eli stood up.

"Apologize!"

"Like hell."

"Then get out of here until you do."

"With pleasure. Don't wait up for me."

He put his napkin back on the table—his mother had taught him always to do that when he left the table—turned, and walked out. Five minutes later they heard the front door close. Levine started up from the table.

"Sit down, dear," Helen said.

"He's leaving. I'll talk to him."

She was quietly forceful. "You can't talk to him now. He meant what he said. No one like him, no young man worth anything, could be talked back into his house now, by his mother or his father, anyway. Let him go. Sometime he'll be back."

She was right again, he thought. This boy, this arrogant, difficult, brilliant boy. He had felt it coming for years, and yet he had always thought that somehow he would be able to hold onto Eli, as he had held onto the others. He remembered back in the last campaign, when the newspapers had first started paying attention to him, *Time* had run a long feature on him, mentioning Eli's fascination with politics and his work organizing the college voters. *Time* had run a picture of him at his desk, with Eli leaning over to hand him some papers, and the caption had been, "Levine & Son: A New Dynasty?" Eli and he had laughed about it, but he had thought about it for a long time, thought that someday Eli, with his brilliance, his good looks, his height ("My basketball player,") Helen had called him when he reached six feet two inches), Eli with his fascination with politics and the lore he had picked up at his own dinner table, Eli, his lost son, could run for president some day. Was that such a foolish dream for an ugly little Jew?

Tears welled.

"Look, Dad, don't take it so hard. It had to happen someday. He'll come back soon." Samuel, always the comforter.

"No, Sam, only two things *have* to happen and those are death and taxes. Somehow, I could have prevented that. And I am not sure he will be back soon. He might be back, but it would be crazy to say soon."

Helen was silent. Levine patted her on the back.

"Come, dear, there's nothing we can do right now. Ask the girl to bring in dessert."

Laura cried, but finished her rum cake. The others ate little. The children said good-bye tearfully, and Levine and Helen went to bed immediately. They each took a Seconal. Even so, Levine slept poorly. He dreamed that Eli was nine years old, sitting at the table and rattling off the batting averages of the old Brooklyn Dodgers. It was a crazy dream, because Eli had never been interested in baseball at all, and, besides, the Dodgers had moved to Los Angeles long before he was born.

Part **VI**

PETWORTH CENTER, AUGUST 17, 1988

Eli Levine biked the 450 miles from Washington to Vermont. He doubted if his father had put out a Missing Persons notice for him and he doubted if the Patrols would actually issue a warrant, but there was no use taking chances on public transportation. "Apprehended in Bus Station" was too familiar an end to his friends' careers in politics. The highways were filled with bikers, heavy with their knapsacks, churning north toward the New England summer. The youth hostels were busy and anonymous. On the road there was a steady stream of Raleighs, Suzukis, Jacksons, Peugeots. With the energy problem, even the reserved bike lanes on the Interstates were crowded. Unless you were traveling with a girl or a group, all you ever saw of your traveling companions was the back of their necks as you approached. It was the longest solo trip he had ever taken, but the miles went easily.

Eli delighted in his own strength. Twice he turned off the Interstate to visit friends along the way. He came into Poughkeepsie just as the rush-hour traffic was letting out, and, barreling down between the two lanes of creeping cars, he turned his head and smiled at the old people trapped behind the wheels. On the road, too, the thrill of power would come to him when he saw another good cyclist up ahead, some guy really making time despite a heavy pack and a long way to go. Eli would pull up alongside him, and, in desperate, unspoken rivalry, the two would sprint two miles, three, five—until one or the other tired and fell behind. Sometimes it was Eli, sometimes it was his unknown, never-to-be-seen-again, never-acknowledged opponent, but even when he lost Eli was exhilarated by the beauty of the challenge.

He had no idea where Caputo was, but he had an idea

of how to find him. He crossed the New York–Vermont broder at night, a little south of Whitehall, carrying his bike on his back. The official border inspection at Whitehall was perfunctory for young people going into Vermont, nowhere near the hassle that the New York State police gave you when you crossed the other way into their fair state, carrying what they imagined to be packets of assorted drugs or homemade fire bombs in your knapsack. Still, they *did* ask for your registration papers on the Vermont side, and Eli wanted his presence in Vermont to be, at the least, unofficial. There wasn't much trouble in finding a good crossover point; kids talked about them in the hostels the way tourists used to talk about good places to find bargain luggage. New York had 150 miles of border with Vermont to patrol, and, from their side of the border, the Vermonters didn't give one damn to help out. Massachusetts wasn't much better.

He slept a night in a field near Rutland and hurried on to Petworth Center. He stayed away from the franchise restaurants and condominiums. He hung around town a day, watched people come and go, found a place that served good food, and struck up a conversation with some kids who lived in town. One was named Ted and the other they called Bear. Eli said his own name was Jomo. There were no last names. They chatted awhile, and he asked about places to stay. Ted and Bear argued between themselves, and out of their talk Eli got a clear idea of the place he wanted.

Norton's Tourist Home was ideal, just as he thought it would be. Old Mrs. Norton had accepted the coming of bearded young people just as she had accepted the people who used to drive up every fall from Boston to look at the leaves. Ted and Bear had been a little contemptuous of her place, just the same—she attracted the deep breathers, the kids who were into pure hiking and biking. There wasn't much getting together at her place, not much politics, and no grass, even though it was legal in Vermont. It was just what Eli wanted.

He stayed there a week, getting up to jog an hour every morning, eating at the same few little restaurants, talking to people. Even in Vermont, where the legislature had legalized the growing of dope and done away with compulsory education for children, it was unwise to show too direct an interest in Caputo's people. Undercover federal agents still worked the state. Every black, no matter how youthfully cool or defiantly middle-class, was a possible undercover Patrol. People still talked about the elderly black couple who had come up to see their boy graduate from Putney. They had stayed at the inn and everyone in town had loved them—such a nice combination of old-fashioned humbleness and dignity. Lots of the kids had confided in them. And everyone knew their son, Machsmillian, as a solid boy who had transferred from New York, and been at Putney for two years. Max wasn't afraid of dope or hard-porn movies. And so when twenty-two kids from school, plus five teachers and eighteen townspeople, were arrested the day after graduation by a group of Patrols, it took people a long time to realize that Max had been a plant, a two-year plant at that, and that the nice black couple were not only truly his parents but two of the FBI's finest operatives. Experiences like that lingered in people's minds.

So Eli hung low and exercised and listened. He found a street-fighting bar and hung around there. He did not go out of his way to meet people or to start anything. He was smart enough to remember his father talking about his days on the road, and he had humor enough to realize that he was following all his father's old rules about success in a new town: keep your strengths in reserve and let people become accustomed to you, let them come to you. It was only a matter of time.

The man who spilled beer on him was small and semi-drunk. He waved his hands as he talked, sloshing beer back and forth onto the floor. He was next to Eli at the bar.

"Hey, watch out with that beer," Eli said.

"What's the matter, I get any on you?"

"No, but you might. Try to be careful, okay?"

"Okay."

The little guy turned to the person on his other side.

"Fucking punk tells me to be careful. I'll be careful." He splashed the beer into Eli's face. Eli grabbed his arm and forced it against the bar.

The bartender came over. "Do what you want. Outside. In the back." He gestured toward the rear, to the hall leading past the men's room.

"Sure."

A cluster of drinkers followed them. The light was okay. There was no parking lot—parking lots were dangerous; you could never tell who might pop up from between a couple of cars—but just a cleared dirt space, uneven, smelling of garbage. The little guy was no longer semi-drunk. He was quick and his movements were precise. He used a classic Tai Kwan Do style, lots of head weaving and beautiful back kicks. He sent two quick kicks whistling by Eli's head—if either had connected, Eli would have ended up with the flat nose that was the street fighter's dueling scar. Eli did not want a flat nose or the concussion that might accompany it. He kept on his toes, danced away from the little guy's feet, tried to read his style. The guy used a lot of back kicks and hand chops, not much defense in front. His movements were perfect; there were no individual hitches in them. Fighting was something he had learned from a master, not from the streets. You could not make many mistakes with him.

Eli went into his own Tai Kwan Do style. He spun out a couple of back kicks, hit the little guy a glancing blow on the shoulder, and went into a forward crouch. The two faced each other. Eli feinted and whirled twice more. The rhythm of the match was set and he knew that the little guy was too good for him, that the little guy could move beautifully into the classic helicopter moves of Korean attack and that, therefore, the time had come.

Eli feinted backward as the little guy moved forward. Moved forward just a bit, just enough so that Eli's forward kick, a leaping kick out of Thai boxing, landed almost squarely on his chest. The kick had nothing to do with the Korean style they had been using, and it was a good kick, not perfect, but quick and strong enough to send the little guy reeling, and then Eli was on him with both feet until someone pulled him off. Eli struggled with whoever was holding him—you were supposed to try to kill your opponent, and the onlookers were supposed to prevent you.

"Take it easy," someone said.

"Figlio di cane," Eli said.

"Calm down."

"Lascia mi ripicchiarlo."

"Easy, easy."

"Piu facile dire che fare."

"What's he saying?" someone asked.

"Italian, I think," a girl said.

He was back at the bar the next night. He had been there about an hour when the little guy came back in, sat next to him, and nodded, as though nothing had happened.

"That was a good match," the little guy said. "You're quick. I don't think anyone can take me in Tai Kwan Do, but I never saw anyone switch so fast into that Thai kick. Who did you learn from?"

"I spent a summer in Bangkok. I had a friend at the embassy. He got me in with Panit Charavoo. You're good yourself. I knew I couldn't beat you at Tai Kwan Do. Were you in the service?"

The other guy nodded. "Seals. Then, when they were disbanded, I got out of the navy. No use staying. It wasn't that you got in the brig for killing people—shit, they could put you away for just hurting them. It was the women and the fags taking over, if you know what I mean."

Eli nodded.

"And the spades. I mean, I'm not prejudiced, see. Fact is, that's what turned me against them. When I was first with Seals, I was sort of an outsider. A lot of them, they'd been to college—athletic stars, rich families, great swimmers. Shit, nobody gets to be a great swimmer unless the family's got enough money to keep 'em in a pool all winter, drag 'em from one meet to another. I'm an okay swimmer, but I got in because I had what they called 'special skills,' ya know what I mean?"

Eli nodded.

"So I was sort of lonely and the Seals don't make it easy for new people. But the guys who were friendly to me were two black guys, Kelly and Delmar. Sweet people. City guys, like me. People used to kid Kelly about being Irish, and he'd kid back. The both of them, they were so good, so much fun, that you couldn't help like 'em. We hung around a lot together. Not that the other guys were so much prejudiced against spades as they didn't like me. So I drifted to Kelly and Delmar. And we were real friends. Nothing phony about it. Nothing conscious about me being white and them being black. More like it is when you're in the hospital and you're sick and whoever is in the next bed to you, you're suddenly more together with him than your own family, because you're both sick together, and that ties you more than even being the same family."

"I know."

"But then this Black Power thing came to the base. There were a lot more black officers and ABS's and Seals, and they started hitting on Kelly and Delmar for being buddies with me. Like, 'Your own ain't good enough for you, Kelly?' That kind of shit. And Kelly and Delmar, they were in a tough spot. Like the same way it would be in that hospital—when your own family starts to call in the bets, lays it on the line, says, 'Who's more important, your own father or someone you never knew until last summer?' then you have to go with your own people."

There was something familiar about this, Eli thought.

"So Kelly and Delmar stopped eating with me at mess. And we couldn't drink together at night—the blacks all went to their own place. And I didn't have any real friends in the outfit. Basically, I'm a loner, but not that much of a loner. So after a while I quit. You understand?"

"I understand."

The small guy leaned closer.

"*Parla Italiano?*"

"*Si.*"

"*Sei ebreo?*"

"*Si.*"

"What's your name?"

"My real name or what I call myself?"

"Your real name. I know you call yourself Jomo. That's a good name, by the way. Easy for your friends to remember. No, I'm interested in your real name."

"That's my own business for the time being. Why do you want to know?"

"My friends and I are interested in you."

"That's nice, but, you see, I wouldn't ask you the names of *your* friends. I would be glad to meet them, however."

"Perhaps that can be arranged."

The next evening the short guy, whose name was Brian, stopped at Norton's and picked him up. They went to a farmhouse in a narrow valley west of Barre. There were six or seven other people there. People came casually, drank, ate, talked. Everyone spoke English, but most of the swearing and joking was in Italian. People talked about sports and hunting and history. They were good on history, heavy on Pareto and Spengler. Eli felt at home.

"You're welcome to move in," Brian said on the way home. It was more a request than an invitation. Eli accepted. He did his assigned jobs around the house, chopped wood ("There's no such thing as too much kindling," Brian said), and listened. The political talk was familiar to him: the weakness of mass man, the corruption of society by barbarism and pornography, the need for limitations, the symbiosis of physical strength and intellectual development. He kept quiet as the others argued. Brian's crudeness, he decided, was part genuine (he had indeed been born in Jersey City) and part affected. In the farmhouse he was bright, articulate. His speech was like his fighting.

"You don't understand," Brian told a girl named Robin. "It's not at all similar to Maoism."

"Why not? Didn't Mao make the intellectuals and the parasites go out and work with the people?"

"Mao sent the thinkers in the field to humble them, make them part of the state. We get out of the city, do things ourselves, so we can be independent of the state. We're not trying to break intellectuals, we're trying to make them stronger."

"Well, the process is still pretty much the same thing."

"If the object is different, then the process is different. It's one thing to be out on a prison gang, chopping wood for the warden's fireplace. Chop the same wood to keep your own place warm all winter, and it's different."

Eli had heard it before, but he liked the way Brian made things concrete. He had some things he would like to add to what Brian had said, but they could wait. In the farmhouse he could sense that the less he said, the more he would be respected. No one had mentioned Caputo. No one had even talked of a leader.

A few nights later Brian came over to him. "There's a man over in New York State—Plattsburgh—who's corrupting the young. He owns a movie theater in the old section of town, not out near the drive-ins. During the spring and summer he shows dirty movies after the regular shows. Fuck pics. Lesbians, animals—everything. He gets away with it because he buys off the police. Also, people are afraid of him. They say he has gangster friends. What do you think should be done with this person?"

"He should be warned privately that he should stop."

"That has been done twice, and the warning was ignored. What should be done next?"

"Is the man married? Does he have any children?"

"He is married. There are two children."

"Then he should not be killed, now. His theater should be destroyed."

"You will come with us, then?"

"Of course."

"In fact, my friends will let you plan it."

"That would be fine. I'll need some information."

"We'll be glad to supply you what you need. You look at what we have, think about it, and then talk to me."

Over the next couple of days Eli studied the case report. The man's name was Fletcher. He owned a chain of small movie houses in northern New York and had gone heavy into drive-ins. He'd done well until rationing started. Towns were far apart in the Adirondacks; with coupons scarce, teen-agers couldn't drive 60 miles just to watch a movie and pet. Fletcher was overexpanded. He started importing dirty flicks from Canada after the state assembly had outlawed them and the courts had backed it up. When he received the warning letters, he had hired a couple of new ticket takers. One was named Caniglia and the other Guiterrez. They were both from the city, and they both carried guns.

The information folder was up to date within the week. It had Fletcher's schedule from his home to his different theaters to his office. It had descriptions of Caniglia's and Guiterrez's work days, hour by hour. There were photographs of everyone who worked for Fletcher. There were a couple of pictures of the downtown theater and a crystal-clear aerial photo of Plattsburgh itself.

Eli looked at the maps and restudied the folder. He went over to Brian in the field one afternoon.

"Plattsburgh's not an easy place to hit and run."

"We noticed that. What do you think?"

"We ought to hit and stay?"

"We thought of that, but Fletcher's people keep a lookout for strangers in town. Besides, he's got the police in his pocket, and they're not bad, when they're working for him."

"The aerial photo shows that the marina's already crowded. Boats going up and down Lake Champlain. Most of them put in just overnight, but some of them stay a week or more. They get supplies, they go sightseeing. Someone should tie up at the marina—a couple people should come and go from the boat, a couple should stay hidden. Wednesday night, after Caniglia and the other guy are gone, the movie should be burned. No one will get hurt; there's a vacant lot on one side of the movie, and the grocery store on the other side has been shut down for years. On Wednesday nights, Caniglia's over in Burlington shacked up with a nurse. That's clockwork. Even if she cancels, he still won't be able to do much," Eli said.

"A boat? Four or five people? Don't you think that's a lot just to knock out one dirty-movie man?"

"The people who got this folder together, the ones who

got these pictures—they must have thought it was pretty important."

"Where are you going to get the boat?"

"I'm not sure yet. Maybe we could ask the person who got the plane for the aerial photos."

Brian nodded. "We might, we might. What sort of boat would someone want? A cabin cruiser?"

"No, no. A sailboat. A nice one. Thirty-forty feet. The sort of thing some silly rich kids would sail around Lake Champlain after final exams."

Within forty-eight hours four more young people had drifted into the farmhouse. They were tanned and short-haired and they smiled guilelessly. They looked as though they had been sailing all their lives, and they had. One of them, Holcombe, was an expert arsonist. The girl, Sophie, played the guitar and banjo. Another of the boys had worked in a Hyannis boatyard for three years and could repair anything that floated.

"Do you sail?" Holcombe asked Eli languidly.

"A little."

"'A little' to a sailor means you've crewed on the Bermuda race. If you really don't know anything about it, you say 'not very much.' If someone asked you if you knew any karate, you'd say 'a little,' right?"

"Right. I don't know very much about sailing."

"Fine. We'll teach you."

It was actually a lot of fun. The boat was a North Star, so everyone had to take turns sleeping topside, but things were so well organized that Eli never minded. He was learning all the time. They picked up the boat in Fort Ti and sailed it leisurely up the lake. They made a lot of stops, so people would remember them. When they got to Plattsburgh, they tied up at the marina, and Sophie and the other two guys went into town and bought food at the open-air market and some paregoric at the drugstore. At night Sophie played her guitar gently. She and the guys got invited over to a couple of other boats. Eli and Holcombe stayed out of sight. On the third evening, at 2:00 A.M., Eli and Holcombe drifted into town. They stayed out of alleys, but they made sure to avoid the few streets that might have someone on them. Holcombe didn't didn't conceal his gasoline can, but he didn't flaunt it. In case someone stopped them and asked questions, the can was half filled—their auxiliary motor was low and they were trying to find a gas station that was still open.

They broke in the back door of the theater. While Holcombe spread the gas, Eli waited outside on lookout. Guiterrez wasn't likely to show up, but Eli wished he would. In ten minutes Holcombe came sauntering out.

"Nice and easy back to the boat. We've got about half an hour, maybe an hour, before anyone notices anything."

Guiterrez didn't show up. Nothing bothered them. Back on the boat they heard, an hour later, the sound of sirens. Some police came by the marina the next day, asking questions. They stopped by the boat, where Sophie was playing the guitar and one of the boys was polishing the rails. The police asked if they had seen anyone suspicious the previous night and Sophie smiled and said no, she had been on the boat playing her guitar. The police smiled and left.

"That was very nice," Brian said when they got back. "Suppose the police had looked in the boat and found you and Holcombe. How come you hadn't been around?"

"We were sick," Eli said, smiling at Holcombe.

"The paregoric, man, the paregoric," Holcombe said. He looked as though he had been sailing boats and burning down buildings all his life.

After supper that night Brian took Eli aside. "I'd like you to meet a friend of mine. Do you have tomorrow free?"

"Whatever you say." He figured Caputo was looking forward to the meeting almost as much as he was.

Brian said, "I would like you to meet a friend of mine, Peter Caputo."

Eli nodded. "I am honored." Caputo was as handsome as people had said. There was a kind of golden ease to him which make Eli nervous until he identified it as "the Yacht Club Thing." The Yacht Club Thing appeared at East Hampton one summer, a summer the Levine family had spent in a great house, totally ignored by the neighbors up and down the shore drive. They had come for quiet, but not isolation. The Yacht Club Thing was a man of about forty, deeply tanned, straight-featured, wearing solid red pants and a dark blue Lacoste shirt, whose Volvo broke down in front of their house one day. Eli went down to look, found that the alternator had been banged loose on the graveled back roads, and started the car. The man said, "Thanks."

Eli said, "I'm Eli Levine. We live over there." He pointed to their lovely house, half hidden by the carefully clipped ramblers.

"Oh," the man said, barely opening his mouth. "That's interesting," and drove off.

When Eli explained the incident to his father, A.L. had said, "Forget it—that's the Yacht Club Thing." Two days later, in the village, Eli had seen the same man in the same pants in the same Volvo. "Dad, there's the Yacht Club Thing." They both laughed, but the name and the idea had stuck.

Caputo had the Yacht Club Thing: his looks, his movement, his voice, even his clothes. There was nothing tough or revolutionary about him.

"Look, it was terribly good of you to come," Caputo said. "I've heard good things about you, and I wanted to have a little chat."

Eli was wary. Everything underground was a possible test. He had not expected Caputo to be a street fighter, but neither had he expected one of those languid young men who had interviewed him at Exeter.

"E un grande onore," he said.

"E, bene—I'm pleased to hear you speak Italian. It's a formality, but one I like to observe."

"I wasn't sure, particularly when your English was so—how should we say?"

"Cultivated?"

"Yes, that's it."

"I'm a cultivated person. Why pretend? Your own Italian, by the way, is excellent. It has a Roman hint, but it's not effete. It doesn't sound like the kind of Italian you learn in New York or New Haven. How did you get it?"

"I studied. I had some tapes and I went over there. Besides, my parents speak some Italian. My father, anyway."

"Your father? How interesting. I know a good deal about him, but I didn't know he spoke Italian. Where'd he learn it?"

"He was in Italy in the army. But mostly the same place he learned everything else. First from books and tapes, then from trying it out on people. He did it with Spanish, French; he even tried it with Chinese."

"Let's speak English now. I'm convinced of your credentials, if you're convinced of mine."

"I was never in doubt."

"You should have been. In our work there is always doubt."

"Of course you are correct."

For a moment the formality of Italian, uncontaminated by slang or contractions, held their English in check, and then they began to relax.

"I was delighted by your work over on the New York side," Caputo said. "It must have been fun."

"Fun?"

"Sure—cops-and-robbers sort of thing."

"Yeah, I guess so. I did it because it was our mission."

"From my point of view I mentioned fun because I'm a

psychologist by training. I'm still interested, not only in what people do but why they do it. You have to be able to sort out your own motives, just as you have to be able to spot other people's. I know that when I went after the people who tried to kill me, part of the motive was pure excitement. I had to question myself on how much of it was just the fun, the plotting, the hiding. We all like that sort of thing, if we're normal. I made sure that my main motive was revenge and instruction—I was convinced that there was no use preaching to murderers. I am still convinced. Once I was sure of what I had to do, then I felt free to enjoy the enjoyable parts. I'm not sadistic—I would have preferred to hire someone to do the actual killing. With my heritage that's a perfectly honorable, normal thing to do. But at the time there wasn't anyone else around to do that sort of thing—at least when it wasn't a matter of money or direct Syndicate business. So I had to improvise."

"You did well," Eli said. "You started a movement."

"No, the movement was already there. I just released the brake and gave it a little push. Come on and eat."

A woman whom Eli recognized as Ellen Friedman came in, smiled, and said, "Welcome. Peter's the kind of revolutionary who believes a woman's place is in the kitchen. He lets me out just often enough to say hello to the guests."

"And to carry out a little bomb job or two," Caputo added.

"A woman's place is *almost* in the home," she said. Eli was envious. They had a relationship of respect, but one where the woman was more than just a breeder of children. He could never go for the old Mustache Pete thing himself.

Supper was quietly elegant, with chicken in casserole and a good Bordeaux. There were linen napkins and homemade bread.

"I understand our neighbor up the pike, candidate Rose, likes to lead a rustic life," Caputo said. "If my grandfather had liked a rustic life, he wouldn't have left Italy. It was a rustic carnival there—if you didn't have to live it yourself. Mascagni could write *Cavalleria Rusticana* and Mozart could put a lot of dancing peasants into *The Marriage of Figaro* because they didn't have to sleep next to those people. Or if they did, they had them scrubbed up first. They stank. People confuse rustic with simple or dirty. Jefferson was a rustic, Washington was a rustic. You don't have to be a slob to live in the country. If Rose wants to gnaw on a haunch of venison, let him. It's good for votes anyway."

"Don't you think it's going to be hard to start a revolutionary movement with an antirevolutionary bias?"

"Not antirevolutionary. Antipopulist. That's different. Yes, it will be difficult, but not half so difficult as for those idiots who tried it in the sixties. My God, when I think that people listened to them! Assholes! I remember reading about one of them—Hoffman or Rubin, the one who was supposed to be educated—saying that he had believed in the American way until he got to college and found out about Sacco and Vanzetti and racism. College! So this genius, this intellectual, reads two books in college about his own country, discovers that it isn't exactly what they told him it was in second grade, and becomes a communist. Sometimes I wonder what will happen when he reads a book about Russia."

"Or France," Ellen Friedman said.

"Or England," Eli said, and they laughed together.

"Drugstore revolutionaries. No wonder everyone ended up despising them. You see, they wanted to set the people free. We want to free ourselves, and we will help those who want help. We reject a mass movement. I myself am ambivalent about the masses. Sometimes I feel contempt, sometimes great admiration. From my point of view, it really doesn't matter what they do. 'Freedom First' is a very good slogan. I disagree with Rose's methods—or at least what his methods have been up until now—but I suspect that we may agree on the ultimate goals."

"I have trouble with the blacks," Eli said. "It seems as though we're the only ones really fighting them, and yet we're fighting them on the opposite ends of the seesaw.

We fight the Patrols because they interfere with what we read and what we do and claim they're for law and order, and we're fighting the street dudes because they're criminals."

"There's nothing dichotomous about our position. We're for freedom. What *is* schizophrenic is the position of the black community. I've been working on a long paper on the subject the past few months, and I think I've got it conceptualized. You see, the blacks are the Irish of our time—at least, they've taken the position in society that the Irish held between 1880 and, say, 1932."

"Those are funny dates."

"They're arbitrary. It's roughly the period from the time they first elected an Irish mayor in New York until Roosevelt started making federal jobs more important than municipal ones. In between those years the Irish were both the major criminal element and the backbone of the civil service, at the same time. Irish crooks were arrested by Irish police and hauled before Irish judges. Before 1880 the Irish were a minority on the police force in New York. If they were visible at all, it was as the criminal element. When people in New York in 1880 talked about how the streets weren't safe—and they did talk that way and the streets in Hell's Kitchen *weren't* safe—they were talking about the Irish. On a comparable time scale, the blacks are at about 1900."

"You mean that they've become the biggest group of police?"

"Not just the police. The clerks in the municipal buildings, the sanitation unions, even the schoolteachers. The civil service is the first step up from the ghetto, and the blacks are making that step. The trouble is, there's nothing so repressive as someone who's just one step away from crime. Ask any Italian who lived in Brooklyn in the 1920s. It wasn't the Yankees they were afraid of so much as the Irish. The whole history of the cities between 1900 and 1940 is a struggle between American values on one side and Irish peasant values on the other."

"Aren't the blacks different?"

"No, if anything they're worse. I've puzzled about it a

lot and I'm sure it's linked to the basic slogan, Freedom First. That is, they just haven't had enough experience as free men. Their model was slave. You've read Mannix, Williamson, Genovese, right? It was a world in which there were only two models, slave and master. A master is not the same thing as a free, independent man. A master is himself contaminated by slaveholding. When the slaves were freed, they were only technically free. They're right about that. They continued as spiritual slaves—most of them, not all—right until the Civil Rights Act, until they could vote. Then they started acting like masters."

"You mean, they can't be independent men?" Eli asked.

"Oh, no," Ellen Friedman interrupted. "That's a totally racist concept. Peter thinks there's something to race— maybe a ten-point spread on IQs, though he doubts even that—but it's nothing compared to environment and history."

"My work was in behavioralism, after all," Caputo added. "No, I think blacks can become independent free men. But it takes time. It took the Irish from 1848 to 1960 to come up with John Kennedy. It might take longer for the blacks because of what we've done to them—first slavery, then the refusal to admit that they could assume moral responsibility. The racists said they couldn't assume it because they were inherently inferior. The liberals said they couldn't assume it because they had undergone two hundred years of repression. Either way, it kept them in the slavery mentality and delayed their development. The problem is that now the country can't wait any longer. Black criminals are poisoning our society and the Patrols are destroying our liberties. They're just part of society's problem, but they're a big part. And since no one else seems willing to teach them, that's our job."

"Did the beating bring you to all this?"

"It crystallized it. Remember, I was a very good graduate student. I read a lot and I thought a lot. The simplest fact about crime was that, when the penalties were extreme, there was no crime. The criminologists in Cambridge—the Gluecks and all those—argued that severe sentences weren't deterrents. They had all sorts of statistics and studies proving it. The problem was that the studies were all done in the United States, where criminals knew that the punishment was only theoretical; the books said life imprisonment for first-degree murder, but even if they could convict you, you were eligible for parole in ten years in most states. But in places where they meant what they said about punishment—Russia, China, Saudi Arabia—there weren't any significant crimes. You could get drunk in Moscow, because that wasn't much of a deal. But if you imported heroin or just had it in your possession, you were gone: Siberia, the camps. They meant it. They did it. So there wasn't any heroin. It was as automatic as a trip to the jailhouse used to be in this country if you exposed yourself to a little kid. But in America punishment was becoming theoretical, not real. So we were being taught one thing, but the evidence pointed the other way. The professors knew it or suspected it, but they didn't want to face the contradiction. Somebody once said that the function of graduate students is to say the unsayable. I did it."

He paused and sipped his coffee. "The beating made things jell. You must remember that there's a streak of violence, of vigilantism, in all of us. The movies during the sixties and seventies began to play with that primitive feeling and let some of our fantasies out in the open. Liberals have sex fantasies and they have revenge fantasies, too. They're more ashamed of their revenge fantasies than they are of the sex. They can talk for hours about screwing their mothers, but if you ask them if they'd like to get back at the kid who stole their favorite silverware, they blush and say that they're upset but that they understand the pressures of poverty. A part of them would like to kill the little bastard. That's what those movies—*Joe, The Killer Elite,* the others—did. The creeps at *The New Yorker* were upset by the movies because they were upset by the ultimate truth behind them. The first truth was that the movies pandered to our violent fantasies. The critics were right about that. The ultimate truth was that our violent instincts were ready to flare up because of street crime and, simply, the blacks. *The New Yorker* couldn't see that."

"Then you're not anti-black?"

"God, no." Caputo paused. "Though I guess not many of my best friends are black." He smiled and touched the scar on his forehead. "I've had my troubles with them, you see. What about you?"

"I went to an integrated school."

"Oh. That'll do it every time."

———————

Eli was eight when his father persuaded his mother to move down to Washington. He heard the conversations going on for weeks. She had lots of objections: the climate, her hay fever, and, in the end, "the children." "What about their friends," she said. "What about their schools?"

The schools weren't any problem, Levine assured his wife. Samuel was about to start high school; he'd have to be changing schools anyway. His friends in the party said there wouldn't be much trouble getting Laura into Cathedral. As for Eli, they could try the public school in the neighborhood.

They did. The neighborhood, with its security-obsessed apartment complexes and quaint little town-houses, was almost all white, but the students at Stanton were not. Eli was not frightened—he had gone to school with blacks before. The ones at Stanton were different, though. They talked in a way he had trouble understanding, and, besides, there were so many of them. There were only ten other white kids in his third-grade class of thirty-five, and most of the white ones were really Chinese or Korean or something. There was a very blond little boy who came from Sweden and who cried every day.

Eli's parents asked him how he liked his new school and he said it was okay, but he didn't really have any friends and he felt a lot of the kids didn't like him. He was bigger than most of the boys in his grade, though, and the blacks left him alone. They tried to force the little kid from Sweden to give them his lunch every noon. Usually he did. Eli thought it was wrong, but he sensed it wouldn't be a good idea to interfere.

After a while one of the black kids in the class seemed

to stand out from the others. His name was Telford
Brewington. For one thing, he spoke normally, and you
could understand what he said in class. He looked nice
and he dressed somehow more like a regular kid. He was
good in school—he knew the answers in English class and
he was good at kickball. Some of the orientals were good
in class, but you couldn't talk to them. Telford and Eli
began eating together at lunch. His mother was a nurse
and his father worked for the government. He liked *The
Munsters* and basketball and model trains.

Eli took him home after school one day. Old Barnes at
the desk looked a little surprised, but they went right up
and played with Eli's AXX track racer. His mother was
home and made them some chocolate. Telford came by a
lot after that. They used to race cars and talk about
school. They talked about the teachers and the girls.
Berthelle Jones was the one they talked about the most.
She was in the sixth grade, and she was taller than any
teacher in school and she had great big tits. They giggled
about Berthelle's tits.

His parents liked Telford and were happy Eli had a
friend. He overheard them talking at their parties. "No,
the school has worked out well. Actually, Eli's best friend
is an adorable little black boy named Telford. They play
together all the time and Telford feels right at home here."

Which was true, except that Telford wasn't his best
friend, he was his only friend. And Telford wanted to have
Eli over to his house, but he lived all the way over in
northeast; his mother had given the school system an
address that was really his aunt's apartment, but it was in
the Stanton district. She didn't want her son going to the
low-rent school in her own neighborhood.

Still, school wasn't bad, but Eli noticed that the
friendlier he was with Telford, the nastier Berthelle and
her friends got. Most of the black girls were bigger than
the boys, and they used to laugh in school and point to
between the boys' legs. In the hallways Berthelle started
pushing Eli. "Hey, little boy, you stop bumping me or I
have your little white ass." Her friends, Denise and
Brenda, would laugh and push Eli, too. One day Berthelle

and Denise found Eli on the playground, and in the line
waiting for recess bell to ring Denise got in front of him
and Berthelle in back.

"Now, all you children in a straight line and no talking
and no pushing, please," Mrs. Schaus said.

Berthelle pushed Eli into Denise and said, "Hey,
Levine, what you do with your lover boy, Telford? You
take him up to your place, right?"

Eli said nothing.

"Answer me, boy. What you do with your lover boy,
Telford? You play sticky-dicky with him? That nigger
thinks he's too good for the rest of us. Tell me, Jewboy, his
shit smell just like anyone's, right?"

Mrs. Schaus said, "No talking in line."

"Answer me, you little motherfucker."

Berthelle gave him a vicious punch in his back.

"Answer me or I break your back."

"No."

"No what?"

"No, we don't do anything wrong."

Berthelle pushed him into Denise again. Denise
whispered over her shoulder, "Hey, white boy, you stop
feeling up my ass. You ain't got no right to feel my ass. I'm
gonna tell my mama on you. And I'm gonna tell Brenda.
We gonna whip your ass."

They filed into the school. "That's much better," Mrs.
Schaus said.

Eli lived in terror for the next few days. He knew
something would happen, and he knew that there would
be nothing he could do about it. Three days later, at the
end of lunch break, he went back into the school and
headed for the boys' room. Brenda, Denise, Berthelle, and
another big girl were waiting in the corridor.

"Here he come now," Berthelle said. The girls moved to
block him from the boys' room. He turned as if to run
back, and when they came toward him he spun around,
dodged underneath and around Brenda, and ran into the
boys' room. Safe!

The girls came into the boys' room! Eli was speechless
with horror and fear. Two little oriental boys looked up

and ran out. Telford came out of one of the stalls and
stared.

"We got you now, you little white fairy boy," Brenda
said. "We find out if you got a real dick on you or just
some pussy hair." The other girls laughed wildly. Eli
stared at Telford. Telford looked back.

"Don't look for your little lover boy to save your white
ass," Berthelle said. And then, turning to Telford, "Get
out of this room, nigger, and keep your nigger mouth
shut. Hear?"

Telford fled. Denise clamped her hand over Eli's
mouth. Berthelle gripped both his wrists in her one hand,
her thick wrists and big, big arms bulging with power.
Brenda unbuckled his belt and slipped down his pants.

And his underpants.

They played with him. Brenda said, "Shit, he ain't got
nothing. My baby brother got a bigger dick on him than
that. Denise, you ever see anything like that? This boy's a
maphrodite. He ain't normal."

"No wonder he play suck-dick with that sissy nigger
boy."

"Ain't anything he can ever do for a lady."

Someone pulled on his penis. Someone—someone!—
was touching his ass, trying to put a finger in.

"That the only way he ever get to fuck, some sissy boy
come stick it up his ass."

Berthelle let his hands go. Denise took her hand off his
mouth. Eli couldn't move. He couldn't cry. He couldn't
shout. He was ashamed to be alive.

Berthelle said, "Okay, boy, you lucky for now. Lucky
we don't really hurt you. But if you say anything, we—"

Denise interrupted. "Don't worry, B-B. This boy ain't
gonna say nothing."

And he didn't. What could he say? The teachers
wouldn't believe him. His best friend had deserted him.
The dream of happiness that his parents had built for him
had been destroyed. If he told them, he sensed they would
be shattered. But even if he felt they could help him, how
could he describe the awful things they had done. They
had touched him—there. They had kissed him—there.

They had put their fingers inside him—there. He couldn't describe it to himself, much less a grown-up.

He went home that afternoon and stayed in his room. He didn't eat supper. He didn't get out of bed the next day, and complained of a stomachache. He didn't eat the next day either. When his parents realized something was wrong, his father asked, "Did something bad happen at school?"

"Yes."

"What?"

"They keep calling me a dirty Jew."

They kept him home and after pulling some strings transferred him to Friends School the next week.

————————

Caputo nodded. "That's a bitch."

"It's hard to forget."

"Of course, bad as it is, it's not that unusual. In fact, it's pretty much run-of-the-mill. That age, that situation. It's usually the black girls who are the aggressors. They mature faster, and they're not subject to any social control. Two or three years later they'll be all having babies. Knowland did a study on aggression in public schools, but the Title Two people who funded it never bothered to release it. The same thing, over and over. It's as classic for a white kid in the situation you were then as the rape of a black woman used to be in the old South. There's no one worth complaining to—the people who can do something about it won't listen to you, and the people who listen to you won't do anything."

"I think I got over it. I don't think I exactly hate them. I hate Berthelle Jones, though. If I could find her today, I'd stomp her face in."

"You got over it, but you got over your illusions, too. You got over the white-guilt shit. You got over putting your energy into saving blacks instead of saving yourself and your own people. You got over being ashamed of your own body, and into training it. Now I've got some real work for you. No more little raids. This is something big. Do you think you're ready?"

"I think so."

"Let me tell you, it may hurt your father. I can't tell you the details now—we'll have to start planning and training—but it might hurt your father."

"You mean if he gets elected?"

"Either way."

"Would it destroy him? Harm him physically? If it were that, I couldn't do it."

"We wouldn't ask you for something like that. No, it would not hurt him physically. It might embarrass him, humiliate him, hurt him politically."

Eli thought for a moment. "I'd have to think about it," he said, "but I could do it."

"I still don't understand it," Bell said to Sally. "He'd never made a speech before in his life except in front of some synagogue men's club. He'd never met crowds or campaigned before—hell, he'd never run for anything—and he does it like he's been at it all his life."

"You try too hard," she said. They were in his apartment, watching the news on television, and she was beginning to be a little annoyed by his intensity. "Ding Dong Bell," the reporter called him, but she was no longer amused.

"Try what too hard?"

"To understand things. Can't you ever accept anything? Just say to yourself, 'He's a natural politician,' and let it go at that. Why do you have to try to break everything down?"

"Because that's what they taught me. When I was at Indiana and got hooked up with a bunch of intellectuals they taught me there was no such thing as a natural, nothing that couldn't be analyzed."

"Well, they certainly got their hooks into you. You're going to study it so hard that it's going to disappear. It'll be like repeating one word over and over again—luggage, luggage, luggage, luggage—until it stops meaning anything and becomes just a sound."

"I still think it's important to pin it down, because if we knew what made Levine go, then—"

"Sure. You could bottle it and make a couple hundred others go every two years."

"Not exactly."

"But close. I'll tell you what. What's your candidate doing the day after tomorrow?"

"He's got a tour of some shopping centers and markets in Baltimore. He's got to be back in Washington at eight for a speech to some labor people."

"Get me in the press bus and let me follow him all day. Then let me have a quick interview with him. I'll tell you what his secret is."

"Woman's intuition?"

She smiled. "They outlawed that back with the ERA. No, I'll tell you because I've been following Spence around for God knows how many years, and because my father was a state senator—and besides, I have woman's intuition."

"You can go on the press bus, but it won't be through me. There's enough gossip as it is. You'll have to lean on Arthur Jones."

"My Lord, what people won't do! He's got to be the least seducible person since Calvin Coolidge."

"Your husband's a senator. He'll listen to you. He may not give in, but he'll listen."

She grinned and reached over to muss his hair. Intensity and all, he cared for her, took her ideas seriously, and had nothing to gain from her but love and companionship. She had been courted so long for her connections—first her father's, then her husband's—that she reveled in simple affection.

———

She saw Arthur Jones the next afternoon. He was seducible. In the past very few women had tried. He was not seducible in a sexual sense and never would be, for his manner had been fixed by Methodist Sunday school in 1935, but he was, in an old-fashioned way, attractive. He knew that women could climb telephone poles and deliver hot pizza door to door, but he knew it in the same abstract way that he knew that his parents must have copulated to produce him. In his own mind women were gentle, soft creatures whose mission was to bring integrity and comfort to men. Thirty years of marriage to a rasping bitch whose moods swung wildly between deep depression and manic anxiety had not changed his mind on this, though it did account for his devotion to his job.

Sally Cunningham was natural womanhood personified. Her smile was open, her giggle infectious, and her legs memorable.

"Of course we can arrange that, Mrs. Cunningham. We always have a couple of places open in the press bus for observers. Just the other day we had five Chinese reporters. All looked exactly alike and, would you believe it, they all wore exactly the same clothes. They kept wandering off in all directions, and we never could tell except by counting if we hadn't left one behind. Just like back in kindergarten. Of course, we're a little short of space, with the energy thing. I remember how Bobby Kennedy came through Indiana back in 'sixty-eight. God, there must have been five busloads of them. And the planes! Just for a primary. Well, they didn't have to worry about oil. That was campaigning!"

His eyes rolled and he gazed at the ceiling and she thought, That's what the energy thing is to Arthur Jones, five press buses instead of two. He doesn't mind the sweating or the walking; he thinks two press buses are a personal affront. And all of us, we've all got our days of five press buses and the glory that went with them.

"Be at the Hilton at seven thirty sharp. He starts on time."

At the bus the next morning she recognized most of the reporters by face, if not by name. They had formed a permanent part of Spence's background for years, but he had never truly liked any of them, except for a few old friends of friends like Blaine Coudert. Even Frieda Kraft-Lawrence, whose grandmother had been his mother's bridesmaid, was too much for him to take.

Still, Sally knew that they knew her and that they would be both curious and resentful about her presence on the bus. She attached herself to Arthur Jones and flirted with him awkwardly but steadily. Let them make something of that, she thought. Hale from the *Times* nodded to her pleasantly, and Merlin, the television person whom Spence detested, looked at her quizzically. She tried to think if she had been seen with Bell in public recently. He was stuck in Washington today, which was just as well.

But as the morning wore on, she forgot about the other reporters and concentrated on Levine. It was easy to concentrate on him, because with each stop he grew more and more enthusiastic, more and more compelling, until the reporters themselves stopped trying to top him and sat back to listen.

They descended upon the Lexington Market in Baltimore like ants on a picnic. The market was an endless series of food stalls under one roof, a library of smells, sounds, and tastes, and Levine crashed up and down the aisles, tasting fruit, shaking hands, speaking Italian, talking to a pretty woman, a benevolent Attila the Hun. People were bored with politicians, the commentators said, but they did not appear to be bored with Levine. Sally Cunningham kept her eyes focused one or two aisles ahead of Levine's entourage. She saw the shoppers, women hefting honeydews and squeezing tomatoes, become aware of the commotion. She saw them stop, look up, look around, catch the hubbub as the tour approached, and then suddenly recognize Levine. They smiled, dropped the honeydews, and headed toward Levine. They were not diffident, they were not playing hard to get. A star had entered their life, and they wanted part of it.

Levine, Sally saw, juggled four or five roles simultaneously. He saw the women bearing down on him and waved. He darted over to the next stall, the one bearing the sign "D. Gueraldi and Sons, Green-grocers," and shouted, "Hey, Angie, got any fresh dill?" The greengrocer, who until then had apparently been composing an angry mental letter about the effect of political rallies on the sale of artichokes, suddenly leaped to life.

"Levine, sonofabitch, why didn't you tell me you were coming? We're just out of dill. Maybe you want some watercress?"

"One bunch, right away. Wash it so I can nibble on the way. Angie," Levine said, turning to the man next to him, "You know the mayor? Bob Muller, Angie Gueraldi. Bob, you may be the mayor, but if you don't have Angie on your side, it's not worth it. Angie's the only man in Baltimore who can get you fresh dill in October. He's the only man who can get you enough basil to feed fifty people *gnocchi al pesto.*"

"Hey, and don't forget the mint. We don't do just guinea food, you know."

"And if you've got a Derby Day party and you need mint for a couple hundred juleps or some frozen Southsides, Angie will get it for you—the same day."

"Here's your watercress, Mr. Levine. *Buona fortuna!*"

"*Mille graz',* friend."

And the troop stormed down the aisle, Levine introducing the mayor of Baltimore to his constituents, shoppers to storekeepers, storekeepers to reporters. At each new aisle the candidate lifted his head in the air, sniffed, and murmured, "I'm hungry." Like a beagle after a rabbit, he gave a short yelp and disappeared down the aisle, emerging with strawberries, tartar steak, cracklings, crab cakes. Reporters were pushed forward to sample the fresh apple pie at Garland's, the coffee at Dickinson's.

"Let's go now," Levine said. "Time for clams." They descended upon a section of the market where, at a circular command post, four blacks opened clams for hungry shoppers. Levine looked around a moment and focused on one of the men behind the counter, a middle-aged black whose cigar ash dangled dangerously close to each clam he opened.

"That's the one, Mr. Mayor," Levine said. "That's the one. Board of Health violation if I ever saw one. If it isn't illegal in Baltimore to smoke cheap cigars while opening clams, it should be."

The black did not look up. "Man, I smoke cheap cigars, like I say, because the cheap Irishman I work for don't pay no more than six bucks an hour for skilled labor"—a grunt as he forced open a stubborn Cherrystone—"and because that wise-ass Jew that done sent me the *good* cigars—'scuse me if I offend anyone—hasn't been around"—another grunt—"since he got so high and goddam mighty. Levine!"

"Jefferson!"

The black tipped the ash off his cigar, threw off the protective gloves he wore, and reached across the counter to touch Levine's hand. Flashlights popped. Levine grabbed his fist in a conventional handshake, held it a moment, and then released it.

"Mr. Jefferson, even though I don't need your clams for a while, you clearly need my cigars. There'll be a box on the way next week."

"Appreciate that, Mr. Levine. My customers will, too."

Levine ordered a dozen clams for the group, and Jefferson and the others grunted, sweated, and squeezed and the clams were ready. Not all the reporters were enthusiastic about the snack—"I'm from Maine and by God if we eat clams on the half shell at eleven A.M.," said Hale—but Levine finished off the leftovers and with the rest of the group went looking for something called a Polack Johnny sausage.

Sally Cunningham lingered. "Mr. Jefferson, I'm Ms. Cunningham of the press. I wonder, did you know Mr. Levine was coming today?"

"Hell, no, ma'am. I heard he was mixed up in politics and all, but I ain't seen him for a couple years or so, and I like to forget him altogether."

"How'd you get to know him?"

"Must have been ten years or so ago, 'cause my boy was in high school then. This man Levine, he used to come around on Saturdays. He'd come in, usually with his wife, after they'd be shopping, and he'd have clams or oysters, whatever. She didn't eat no seafood. He'd be like a lot of them regulars from the country or Washington, coming in on Saturday. And he'd get to joking with me about that cigar, 'cause I always keeps one going. And then he had some big party in Washington, something for the politicians, and he wanted clams and oysters on the half shell, so he asked me if I could work out in the evenings, and I could, and so he got me that job and some others came along. Then one day, like I say, he was here in the market, just jawing with me, and I was feeling low, and I just felt like talking to someone, and seems like he was the right person. So I just takes off my gloves and my apron and I asks the other guys to cover for me, and I ask him if I could buy him a drink. He says sure, so we go across to the Sportsman Bar and I have some beers and he has the Mexican drink and I tell him my problems—like I'm not earning enough and my boy won't listen—you know. And he asks me how much I'm earning an hour and tells me I'm the best at the market and the market shuckers is the best shuckers in Baltimore and Baltimore shuckers is the best in America, all of which I knew, but hearing it from him makes it clear. And he figures out how much an hour I can make shucking at private parties, like the ones in Washington. So he tells me to go back to Mr. Keane—that's the owner—and tell him the same thing I told him. Which I did, and Mr. Keane didn't say nothing but just raised me to what I wanted."

He paused and looked at Sally Cunningham. "You really a reporter?"

"Not exactly. I—"

"I figured so. The reporters, they never let you say as much as I said without butting in. But you do know politicians, don't you?"

"Oh, I do. My husband—"

"Well, I don't care none about your husband. But let me tell you one thing to tell him. You know what the best thing Levine ever did for me?"

"What?"

"He didn't raise one finger to help me. Not one finger. He told me what to do and I done it. Lots of white men like him, having a job where they could put some business the way of the market, they would of called Mr. Keane and told him he had a fine man, Mr. Jefferson, working for him, and why didn't he pay him some more, because if he did, then they'd send Jefferson more business for them cook-outs and the wholesale business. You know. And Mr. Keane, he'd of given me that raise if Levine called him like that, but he would of, you see, *resented* me from that time on, and to tell you the truth I would of resented Levine. Because I would have more money, but I would think Levine got it for me, and Keane would be paying me more, and he'd be angry at me for that too. So Levine never said a word. But later, after I told him I got the raise, he wrote Mr. Keane a real nice note, saying he was glad talent was recognized and that I was the Johnny Unitas of shuckers, and saying he might put some business Mr. Keane's way. Which he then did."

She understood. She understood back on the bus, when they stopped at a suburban supermarket and the women and the men house-sitters crowded around, and when they went for lunch—lunch!—at Sabatini's, where Levine ate clams linguine and spoke to the owner in Italian. Sally Cunningham's junior year in Florence had been long ago, and yet she was sure that it was Italian Italian, conversational Italian, that Levine was speaking.

In the afternoon, accompanied by Jessington, who had materialized at the restaurant in time to eat two full orders of crabs and white sauce, they went into the black districts. Sally Cunningham dreaded this. She had done it with her father and she had done it with Spence and she had done it in school with Bobby Kennedy, and no matter how fine the motive there was in the end a horror to it, not a horror of the living conditions, which were bad enough, but a horror in the way, as at the asylum at Bedlam, the conditions were used to amuse and instruct. She knew that her husband and the Kennedys were sensitive enough to realize that they were exploiting misery, as TV cameras and dozens of reporters trailed them into roach-infested tenements with "fuck" scrawled on the doors and orange peels in the halls; and she knew—because she had heard them say it—that the only way to overcome the poverty was to exploit it, to drag it before America on the six o'clock news and scream, "This is the way it is!"

It was a horror to her because she remembered the sullen stares of the people whose apartments and schools they visited, and because she knew in her soul that the smarter and more sensitive the people were, the more they would resent their misery's exploitation for a politician, even a good one, and the more they doubted that a visit from anyone—even Bobby Kennedy, even the president—would make their houses one bit better. It was only the lame and the foolish who were quickly cooperative.

But Levine's tour was different. They stopped in some real slums and Levine shooed the photographers away and talked to people. Mostly guided by two black city councilmen, they chatted with black people who were making it—proud in their white-walled cars, washed every Wednesday night and Saturday morning, secure in trim apartments with pictures of John Kennedy and Jim Rackey and Martin Luther King over the mantel. Levine's walk slowed; he no longer darted, he ambled. His voice slurred. There was nothing consciously black about him, he shook hands instead of giving the blood handshake that had been taken up as quickly by the politicians as it had arrived from Africa, and yet, Sally Cunningham saw, he seemed more at ease than any of the people around him, even the black reporters.

They finished up with a reception at a synagogue. "The frosting on the linguine," Jones whispered to her as they

filed in, and indeed it was. From his opening remark—
"People have complained that I'm not Jewish enough"
(pause); "am I Jewish enough for you?" (wild cheering)—
to his rabbinical intonation as he rolled into his answers
to "What are 'Jewish ethics'?" and "Is there a Jewish
politics?" to his final star-spangled gallop to the summit
about the convergence of Jewish ethics and American
democracy, it was a triumph. He did not make the
mistake of giving them a quick flash of his face and
assuming they were in the bag. They had voted for
Mandel a couple times and they had turned down some
hotshot young Ivy League Jew. They were a Las Vegas
audience—they wanted the act to succeed, but they had to
be shown. Levine showed them.

They fought their way back on the buses.

"Is he always like this?" she asked Hale.

"I hate to say this, Sally, but I think my cool reportorial
detachment is cracking. He's not always like this, but he's
always good and he keeps getting better. I've never had so
much fun on a campaign in my life."

"Don't bother about dinner," Sally told Bell over the
phone. "I've been eating all day. I'll come over for a drink
later."

Bell's place was in an overgrown apartment complex,
available through basement parking. Because Sally had a
key that would activate the basement elevator, no one,
not even the desk clerk and closed-circuit TV, could see
her come and go, much less speak to her. Of course,
someone she knew might get on the elevator on the way to
the fifth floor, but she always carried a gift-wrapped
package. She had it all worked out: "I'm on the way to a
little going-away party for one of my friends in the State
Department." It sounded very convincing, she thought.
She was a novice to adultery.

"How was it?" Bell asked.

"I've got the secret," she said.

"Which is?"

"That Levine likes what he's doing. Hell, he loves it. As
Spence used to say, he's like a pig in shit."

"That's no secret. They all love campaigning. At least, lots of them do."

"No, the secret is that some people love campaigning. Levine loves meeting people, learning things. He doesn't think of it as campaigning. As soon as you do, you're not as good at it any more. He's a man who's been listening all his life in politics, who's been getting money and doing the technical stuff, and now he's out there saying what he thinks, and he loves it. People sense it."

"That's not all. He—"

"Of course it's not all. But what's different about him is he put in the apprenticeship. It's not just theory and it's not just plain emotion. It's a combination. He's paid his dues."

"As a politician? He's never even run for dog warden before."

"Don't you understand? Not as a politician—as a human being."

"It's the same thing."

"I've lived with politicians all my life, and I'm beginning to think you're wrong."

"Sure, I'd be glad to see Mrs. Cunningham. Send her right in. Tell the others I'll be late. No, I have no idea. Maybe an hour or so."

He sure as hell hoped Spence Cunningham hadn't caught on to Sally and Bell. He sure as hell hoped she wasn't about to leave her husband. He sure as hell hoped that his right-hand man would keep his pecker in his pants.

"Come on in, Sally. Always a pleasure to see you. How's things? How's Spence?"

She gave him a quick look and winked. "Things are fine, Mr. Levine. You can relax. Spence isn't going to find out on his own and I'm not going to tell him. It's just a crazy thing I've got with your friend, and I don't think it's going to go much longer. No, you can relax."

"I'm glad. I don't like to see people hurt. Then why the big rush to see me?"

"I was with you yesterday campaigning—"

"I thought I recognized you."

"—and I need to get some things straight in my own mind. Do you know you're an actor? Do you think of yourself as an actor?"

It was a strange interview, he thought.

"No, really, I want you to think seriously about it," she said. "Up before all those people, do you feel like an actor?"

He thought and then smiled. "No, never. When I thought about it, I wasn't sure what you meant, and then I wanted to be sure I was telling the truth. I never wanted to be an actor, but does an actor *feel* like an actor? Maybe I was feeling like an actor and not recognizing it. Or not admitting it. But no—I'm sure I don't. Because, and this is the truth, sometimes I *do* feel like a comedian. I never wanted to be an actor, but as a kid, listening to Jack Benny and Fred Allen and then listening to the comics in the mountains, I thought, I can do that. I thought, I can do that, and I half wanted to do it."

"The mountains?"

"The Catskills. We used to go there when we were first married. The hotels always had comedians, Jewish comedians, and I always admired them. An actor speaks what other people write, but a comedian, if he's a good one, thinks it up himself. And sometimes, like when I was talking before that synagogue group yesterday, I think of something funny and I say it and I think, I knew it, I knew I could be a comedian! But an actor—never. Why do you ask?"

"Because I saw you change so much in one day. When you were talking to Mr. Jefferson you were part black and when you were talking to Mr. Gueraldi you were Italian, and when you were at the synagogue you were totally Jewish."

He looked puzzled. "You think I'm insincere?"

"I'm not saying that. I just wonder why you do it."

He looked at his desk. "Helen tells me I do that sometimes. But it's not acting. It's—responding. That's the word. If you're with people you like and they have different ways, you pick up their ways. Have you ever visited Ireland?"

She nodded.

"Then you know that after two days you're speaking a whole new language. Different rhythms, different accents. You're not imitating, you're not pretending to be Irish, but it just seeps into you."

"But you do it so quickly, so many times in one day. Where's the real Levine?"

"That's a metaphysical question, and I don't answer metaphysical questions before lunch."

"Try."

"I've tried before. The best I can come up with is that the essential is a quick responder. Part of it comes from being Jewish, I'm sure, but God knows I've seen plenty of Jews who lived a lifetime in Atlanta and felt every minute of it was an exile from New York. So part of it has to be me."

"Doesn't it bother you? Don't you worry what part is really you?"

"I'll tell you a story about that. One night back in 'sixty-two I was driving from Knoxville to Cincinnati. You know I used to do a lot of traveling. It wasn't my favorite trip, even though I met Hollins that time, when he was still a lieutenant. Anyway, I was driving and it was late at night and the sky was clear and I had a good radio that was getting Opry music from Nashville. I like country music. I always have and I always will. I don't need anyone to explain it to me and I don't have to apologize for it. The words come right out of real people, they're not afraid to care. There—that's a country song right there—'I'm Not Afraid to Care.' I've got a sentimental streak in me, and when people start singing about dying mothers and orphaned children and cheating husbands, then I start crying in my car if the time is right.

"And I was listening in the car to George Jones singing something about 'Billy Doesn't Live Here Every Day,' and I was all choked up with tears, and all of a sudden the radio starts to fade. Well, I'm moving north at a pretty fast pace, and old WMS is getting weak. And pretty soon, right over George Jones, comes Mozart. One of the horn concertos. The one that sounds a little bit like 'Columbia, the Gem of the Ocean,' I guess it's the Second. Anyway, it's Dennis Brain on the horn. I'm no hillbilly. I started listening to Mozart in graduate school. But you know, I drove thirty miles or so with the one moving in and out of the other, the Opry and the Mozart, and I couldn't tell which one I wanted to hear more. I wasn't trying to impress anyone. There wasn't anyone to impress. I couldn't decide. Both of them made me cry, maybe in different ways, because I thought of Mozart dead so many years and still the best there ever was, and I thought of that little kid visiting his father on weekends and how Jones had picked up exactly the right phrase that drove a hole in my heart, and the only conclusion was that if the real A. L. Levine stood up, the car would be too crowded to park. What about the A. L. Levine who wants to go out dancing on tabletops when he hears Manos Hadjiakos? What about the A. L. Levine who wants to go out and beat up Jews when he hears those goddam Nazi marches? They were all stuffed into that little car, and each was as real as the other."

"I guess that says it, all right."

"Are you going to print it? I noticed you had press credentials."

"No, I'm not going to print it. I'm going to see if I can get it over to your friend Bell. He still thinks of you as a natural politician. I think it's more than that."

"So, tell me."

"I think you're a natural man. There are some around, but not in politics. Bell's been in politics so long he sees everything as an act."

"You've found a secret thought of mine. The people who started this country and the Old Testament prophets had one similar idea."

"What's that?"

"That leaders did not come from a full-time leadership caste. The idea of a priest or a rabbi who does nothing but be a priest or a rabbi is a new one. Even a hundred years ago, most rabbis in Europe were workers or tradesmen of one kind or another who became chief religious officers because they knew more Talmud and were more honorable than the people around them. But they kept their jobs as goldsmiths or cobblers or whatever. And the Founders, the people who signed the Constitution and wrote the Federalist Papers, were afraid of professional politicians. Their ideal was the cultivated man—a farmer in those days—who had enough learning so that he could leave his occupation for a few months and decide problems of state. They never anticipated someone like Nixon who got a law degree and immediately started running for office."

"Kennedy too, don't forget."

"Kennedy too, but he had more of a war than Nixon did. The PT boat—he really was a hero. That's quick on-the-job training for being a genuine human being. But more and more you see people who get out of law school, run for local office, and four years later are in Congress.

That's not what we were meant to have."

"Don't we need experienced politicians?"

"No, we need experienced human beings. I'm not saying a life in politics is an automatic disqualification, but, Christ knows, it certainly destroys people's spontaneity. The only thing I ever respected George McGovern for was when he told some heckler, 'Kiss my ass.' The campaign was going so bad then I suggested to Hart that they print it on a hundred thousand bumper stickers. It couldn't have made things any worse."

"But aren't the good ones able to pick up what the people are thinking and translate it into laws? That's what Spence tries to do."

"Yeah, but picking up what people are thinking isn't what it used to be. You don't sit around a hot stove and listen to the old men bitch. You hire a pollster and give him a list of issues and ask him to find out what people are thinking. That's how being a politician destroys you."

"How?"

"Because the only questions you put on the questionnaire are the kind of questions that politicians ask about. You're already limited by your own horizon. Some congressmen say, 'I look over my mail very carefully—I can scent what's bothering people from my mail and see if there's an issue in it.' And I think the best of them can do that, but even there they're limited by what people write them. There are some things that people just don't write to senators about, and maybe those are the very things that senators should be thinking about. Not necessarily making laws about, but thinking about.

"The Congress talks about leadership. But it's instructed only to respond. They're like reporters—they respond to events, they don't make them. Oh, I know they have wives and children like everyone else. *Almost* like everyone else. But they spend twelve hours a day most of their working lives in that atmosphere of trading, lobbying, jockeying. All of it gets further from reality."

She looked at him. "I'm convinced. I think I'll vote for you."

"That sounded so good I think I'll vote for myself. Take care now."

WASHINGTON, SEPTEMBER 15, 1988

Edwards set the requisition forms in front of him and began checking through them as he dialed McKelvin's office. He had approved publicity and travel expenses of $425,000 when, on the twelfth ring, someone in McKelvin's office picked up the phone.

"This is Edwards. I'd like to speak to the senator, please."

McKelvin was on immediately. "Hey, what's up?"

"I've got to speak to you for a while, Senator. Today. In private. Your office, preferably."

"God damn, George, I didn't chop cotton for ten years and walk five miles to school in old army boots to eat lunch out of some crappy paper bag at my desk. I'm a Senator of the Realm, goddammit. We'll eat at An Lap's."

Which they did. Edwards couldn't argue—he was always uneasy when McKelvin talked about "chopping" cotton. He had no idea what it was, but the phrase alone bound the Southerners in a web he couldn't penetrate. McKelvin called the reservation over the phone and got answered on the second ring. Goddammit, the Viets really worked instead of sitting around on their fat asses waiting for the coffee break. Fucking gooks were *good* for America. They'd about taken over the whole dental profession, and in Washington they'd forced the Greeks and Corsicans out of the French restaurant business because the Corsicans were too busy sucking up to last year's congressmen to bother with their food, and since everyone knew that the best French food in the world had been in Saigon and since everyone knew that the best food of any kind in Paris had been Vietnamese, then it was only right and proper that the slopes were running Maxim's and Pierre's and Le Quatrième Etat and a dozen places like that. The only thing different about An Lap's was that

399

ol' An Lap had gotten tired of running the Le Plat d'Or for
a bunch of absentee Corsicans and had bought the
goddam place himself and had really made it work.

"So good to see you, Senator. And you too, Mr.
Edwards. Here, we have a table ready for you." An Lap
himself showed them to their place.

Son of a bitch, McKelvin thought, I'm pleased that An
Lap is here showing us the way. I came to this town a
jug-eared country boy and I swore to myself I'd never put
on Washington airs, and I still fool myself that I haven't,
but here I am sucking up to some goddam waiter. A gook,
at that. Wouldn't Momma hate to see me now!

"Here you are, gentlemen. Have a pleasant time."

McKelvin ignored him. He wouldn't give An Lap the
final ass kiss. He'd damn well better have a good table
next time, too.

"What's the big mystery?" he asked Edwards.

Edwards leaned over the table, looked at the
banquettes and tables on either side of them, and
whispered, "There's no big mystery."

"Shit, yes, of course there's a big mystery. You don't
come calling up for little *genoux-à-genoux* chats every
afternoon."

"What chats?"

"Genoux-à-genoux. It's French. Means knee-to-knee.
This place always brings out my cultured side."

"Oh. Anyway. I just wanted to ask you a question."

"Go ahead."

Edwards leaned over the table again. "Have you ever
heard anything about Levine and . . . women?"

"Why, shit, yes. Ol' Levine would screw a snake if you
tied it down."

"What!" Edwards felt his palms getting cold.

"You heard me. I said Levine would screw—"

"You're right. I did hear you. What do you mean?"

"I mean that ol' A.L. had some just about every place
he ever went. And he went a lot of places. Of course, he
was sly about it—he never was one of them boasters. How
come you're interested?"

"How come? My God! He's our candidate. He'll be

president unless that prick Rose knocks him off. And Rose will, if this gets out."

"If what gets out? Hell, no one's going to bother about some candidate knocking off a little pussy here and there. Not if it's female pussy. You get yourself caught with some fag kid in a hotel, like ol' Springer, and you might as well hang up your jock, never you mind what they've been saying all these years about Gay Liberation. But hell, Levine ain't got any problems like that. I can swear to that." He chuckled to himself.

"Oh, for God's sake, Curly. This—"

"Don't get yourself all excited, now. Time to order." McKelvin motioned the waiter over. He was looking forward to a complete meal with a double portion of the fresh asparagus, and listened while Edwards requested scrambled eggs. The waiter made a small moue of displeasure. The waiter, at least, was French.

"I'm sorry, M'sieur, this is the luncheon menu. We do not serve breakfast. Perhaps you would like an omelette?"

"I don't want an omelette. The cheese is bad for me. I'm not hungry. I want scrambled eggs. If you can make an omelette, you can make scrambled eggs."

The waiter shrugged and looked reproachfully at McKelvin. McKelvin was furious—furious at Edwards for ordering such a hick piss-ant lunch, furious at the waiter for trying to embarrass Edwards, furious at himself for being embarrassed by Edwards.

"And you, M'sieur McKelvin?"

Goddammit, they wouldn't win everything.

McKelvin stared back at the waiter. "I'll have the scrambled eggs. Don't make them too dry." Take that, you candy-ass waiter. We won it for the Gipper! Ain't no one back home going to say that Curly McKelvin has sold out to the frogs.

"You on a diet?" Edwards asked politely.

"As of now. You were telling me about your problems."

"Our problems, Curly, ours. We've got some bad soundings on this."

"Who's been whispering in your ear? I've known A.L.

for a long, long time, and he's as careful about his chasing
as any man I know. Somebody from the other side?"

"No, nothing like that."

"Hell, there are letters in every campaign."

"Not dozens of letters. I mean literally dozens: women
all over the country claiming Levine used to screw them.
Four women who claim they have his kids."

"Why, that little devil! God damn, he sure got around!"

"Look, Curly, this isn't any joke. It's not like the
sixties, when everyone was shacked up with everyone else.
The country's sick of that sort of thing. You remember the
polls—one of the strongest things A.L.'s got going for him
is the image of a devoted family man, the Jewish father.
Christ, look what happend to Carter. If this gets out,
we're in real trouble."

McKelvin picked angrily at his scrambled eggs. The
waiter had lost the battle but won the war. The scrambled
eggs were awful, and they were especially bad compared
to the venison he might have had.

"You understand, don't you?" Edwards added.

He understood. Edwards was right. They wouldn't be
able to shrug this off with some reference to Kennedy or
Grover Cleveland or whatever. If it got out, it would cause
hell with the campaign. And it was going to get out. It
always did.

'You're right, George. We got to get ready to anticipate
trouble. People aren't going to take any too kindly to this,
not when we got them all hot and bothered with Levine
like some kind of plaster saint. Hey, do the Jews have
plaster saints?"

"Damned if I know. I don't think so."

"Neither do I. Well, at least they won't be able to call
him that. They'll call him something, though."

"What do you think we should do?"

"The same thing you do. Call in our tiger and get the
story from him."

"As soon as possible, right? With Bell and the others
there?"

"Bell, yes, and Jessington, and Brandon. Jones, too, I
guess. Forget the rest. Let's go."

WASHINGTON, SEPTEMBER 16, 1988

They were all sitting around the table and all exactly on time, which by itself was a bad sign. Levine nodded to them and sat down. There wasn't much conversation to quiet down when he came in, but whatever there was died.

"What's up?" he asked.

The others turned toward Edwards.

"It's this woman thing."

Oh, Christ, he knew something like that would come up sooner or later. He had tried to tell them. He had tried to tell his family. Not very hard, but he had tried.

"What woman thing?" he asked.

Edwards shrugged. "This." He pushed a pile of letters and telegrams over to Levine. Levine glanced through them. Jesus God, talk of your voices out of the past! He saw one neatly typed letter, with the return address square in the left-hand corner, just like they told her in typing school—Jolene Lewis! Jolene, the one who used to laugh like a maniac when she started to come, laugh so hard he had to take her out of the motel for fear he'd get kicked out. Good old Jolene! Funny thing, she never knew she was laughing and she always denied it afterwards. He'd planned on getting a tape recorder to prove it to her, but he'd never made it back. Jolene!

And Doris. And Mrs. Myerson. And Vivian. And others who were half-remembered names. Who in the world was Sharlette?

"If you're through reminiscing, we need some information," Edwards said. "In the past two weeks we've received approximately fifty-five of these letters. I say approximately, because some don't come right out and say you've been their lover, but ask if you are the Mr. Levine who came to Mobile in 1959 or Albuquerque in 1964 or whatever. Most of them, however, come out and say that you screwed them or lived with them or used to see them or whatever, and they just want us to send their regards to you. The letters were sent to the National Committee, by the way."

"That's interesting. I don't know much about all this. After all, Levine is a common name. I used to chat with people all the time when I was traveling, but these names don't sound very familiar. Maybe it was someone else."

Edwards grunted and slid over the photographs. There was one with Jolene, taken—now he remembered—by her mother, who'd been so thrilled that a real nice man had been courting her daughter. There was another one, a Polaroid, with a forty-year-old Levine alongside a rabbity-looking blonde at the beach. The forty-year-old Levine had his hand possessively on the blonde's ass. Levine recognized the Levine but could not, for the life of him, remember the girl. And there was one with Sheila Jo and the boy. The old man must have taken that one, he thought.

"Well, that's me all right," he said, somewhat proudly. "I had more hair then. And that's a woman I used to know. Sheila Jo Williams. And this one's name was Jolene. I can't remember her last name offhand. And this other one I've clean forgotten. I think that was at Litchfield Beach, but I'm not sure."

"Goddamn it, A.L., we're not trying to recapture your youth. Do you understand what's happening? We've got calls from our people in twelve different states. Twelve. In every one the big newspaper has some woman who says that you and she used to "date," that she was your mistress, that you took her out, that you were married at the time. In twelve states they've got their best reporters checking out every motel record for the past twenty years, talking to neighbors, trying to pin things down. They've got people up trying to get the salesmen's records from that company you used to work for—what's its name?"

"Arco."

"Yeah, Arco, trying to find out what cities you visited and when."

"That won't work. I took those records with me when I left. It was part of the agreement."

"How come?"

"Who knows? I just felt better having them in my possession."

Jessington interrupted. "A.L., we're not so much interested in the details as what we do next. Can we assume that all these accusations are true?"

There was another pause.

"Yes."

Edwards pushed in. "I want to make it clear that the word 'accusation' isn't really precise. None of these women are accusing you of anything. The letters, in fact, are quite pleasant. They all want to know if you're the same man they used to know, and, if you are, they wish you luck. They don't say anything about talking to the press, though apparently some of the women who are being tracked down in the twelve states are among the ones who've written to us. What's happened, apparently, is that they've told their neighbors that they used to go out with you and the neighbors have told their neighbors and it's gotten to the newspapers and the papers are trying to track it down. The papers are scared shitless to print a word unless they can prove it, but it looks like some of them will be able to prove it pretty soon. Jones here has been getting calls from reporters..."

Jones nodded solemnly.

"...and there are hints that there are some other photos around."

"I doubt it. I was pretty careful about pictures."

"Jesus," Brandon said, "why weren't you careful about women?"

"My God, Gar, in 1954 I was just a little yid electronics salesman out of New York. So I have some fun with a woman fifteen hundred miles from home. Who's to hurt?"

"Maybe in 1954 you were just a little... electronics salesman, but in 1964 you'd already been invited to the White House. We've got letters from 1964."

"Oh."

"And 1968."

"Oh."

"And we've got some from the McGovern campaign."

"Really?"

"Yes, really. And we've got some from this campaign, and you've got to get rid of that Kathy."

"Oh."

There was another pause.

Levine shrugged his shoulders. "Well, it's a strong man's weakness."

"Goddammit," Sweeney said, "that's an Irish saying and it's another weakness."

"Well, this one's mine. Now, what's all the excitement about? I'm running for president, not Pope. People don't expect a celibate any more. I never messed with married women. I was always very careful about that. In fact, as soon as I suspected that there might be a chance one of these ladies would get back together with her husband—if she was one of the ones that was separated—I would do everything I could to get them together. I remember one time I paid for a psychiatrist, because I thought the woman really might make it if she had a little professional help."

Edwards nodded. "The woman you got the psychiatrist for was one of the ones who wrote us. She says it all worked out okay."

"That's nice. I'm relieved. I always wanted to know."

The others smiled. The tension began to seep out of the room.

Bell wasn't happy. "Christ, this isn't some social services agency, it's a presidential campaign. Levine isn't running on how many people he can help. He's part of a family-morality campaign. Besides, don't we have one letter saying he paid for an abortion?"

Edwards nodded.

"Well, Christ almighty, wait till *that* hits the fan. I can see the headlines just as well as you guys can. Come on. Let's get on with this."

"Just a minute," Levine said. "I never paid for an abortion. I do remember once a woman claiming that she was pregnant. Who knows? It's a wise father, right? Even in your own family. Anyway, she wrote me at work—the only address I ever gave—and told me this. I phoned her, spoke to her. She was a nice girl, separated, already had one child. Frankly, I don't like abortion. The rabbis were always against it, and for good reason. But it's one thing to be against it in theory, another to say to girl that she has to have a baby. So I told this woman I was sorry for her, I wouldn't acknowledge that she was pregnant by me, but that I personally would like her to have the baby. At the least, she could put it up for adoption—she was a beautiful girl, smart, the baby would give joy to some couple who couldn't have children. If she wanted to keep the baby herself and the tests proved that it could be mine, then I would support it. If she wanted an abortion, that was her own decision. I sent her money to help her through the pregnancy. What she did with it, I don't know."

"She says she got an abortion," Edwards said.

"Well, I wired her the money and there's no way it can be traced."

"I still think you people have lost sight of what's going on here. We've got a campaign going on. We've got to anticipate." Bell was insistent. And angry.

"Look," Levine said. "There's no big deal. Wait it out, ride it out. Kennedy messed around, Johnson messed around—people loved them for it. Nixon never messed around—people hated him for it. No president ever got hurt by a heterosexual scandal."

"Jesus, A.L., you should have been a Jesuit," Sweeney said. "Those guys were already elected. Kennedy was dead when most of it came out. You're still another fucking candidate, and you're running against the hairs and the Karate duels and the communes and the breakdown of the family. That was one thing you had going for you, the idea that Jews are good family men."

"That's not all I'm running against. Besides, my own family's intact."

"So far," McKelvin muttered.

"Okay, I see your point. Actually, I've seen it since you showed me the letters. We'll have to get something out before they get to us. I'll go home with Bell here and work on a speech. We'll meet tomorrow morning, check out the speech, and set it up for nationwide the next evening. Okay?"

There was nothing left to say. The others filed out

silently, leaving Levine behind with the letters and pictures. He stared at his hands and shuffled through the letters. Names, faces, positions began to reassemble themselves in his mind. Jesus, what memories! They had been nice women, and they had taught him about life and about America, but in the end the screwing itself seemed as important as anything to him, and in the dark-paneled conference room, with the portraits of Roosevelt and Truman and the others looking down, he began to remember the women and was filled with the first gentle pulsations of developing lust.

He had to tell Helen, of course. She was strangely silent and accepting, even when he told her that he wanted her to be on the television program with him. She nodded, said she understood, and told him she'd talk to the children. They worked together on his speech—the first time they'd gone over anything he'd done in years—and then she went to her desk to write out her own talk. Bell came in and talked to them both.

In the morning they checked the speech with the committee. There were no objections. The following night, in prime time, the Party preempted the bullfight for what it called "a message of great importance."

The speech began with a simple shot of Levine and his wife, seated on their apartment couch. Levine began. "Imagine yourself a man, short, unattractive, a thousand miles from home, always traveling, a stranger in a strange city. Imagine that a fine woman smiles at you, talks to you, is kind to you. If you can imagine this, then..."

And so he detailed it. There had been women he had been intimate with, he said. He would not reveal their names, nor would he confirm or deny the claim of any particular person. Some women might claim intimacy merely because he was now a prominent figure. But there had been women—more than one, more than several. Only his wife knew the details. He had told her all (which was almost the truth). Of the actual women involved, he had only kind thoughts. He had never deceived them as to his own status, never interfered with a married woman. Whatever the relationships had been, they had not been exploiting (which was true). Whatever they had been, they were over (which was almost true).

Helen spoke. "My husband and I have been married over thirty-five years. He is a fine man, a passionate man. His work required that he leave home for weeks at a time. I would have wanted him to be faithful but could not expect him to be so. I wanted him to be discreet and honest and loyal to his family, and that he has been."

She had not, she said, questioned him about what he did in other cities, because she did not want to know, did not want to force him into honesty. He had never lied to her. Now, because of politics, the truth had come out. She was not surprised. She was not angry. She was not angry at the other women—she was sure they were fine people, who recognized in her husband the very qualities of excellence that she herself knew. She was hurt, yes; marriage was never easy. Their marriage had survived crises in the past. They had spoken to their rabbi (long distance, to the one who had married Laura and Harvey). They had received counseling. She would stick by her man.

They kissed chastely and the program ended.

———————

"Score one for adultery," said old Tom Ryan, watching in the Towers.

"That's Sheila Jo's little Jew," old man Ledbetter cackled to no one in particular. "He sure is slick. He could talk his way out of a gopher hole and up an eagle's ass."

Why have I been worrying about him? Eli thought, and switched off the set. Peter Caputo and Ellen had walked out in the first moments of their embarrassment. Eli went over to them. "It's okay. I'll do what you want," he said to Caputo.

———————

"That wasn't so bad," Levine said to Helen, later that night. "You know, dear, I'm still amazed at how well you took it. I know you wrote down what you said all by yourself, and it was absolutely perfect, but, still, I would have thought you'd be angrier."

There was no reply from her side of the bed.

"Dear, weren't you the least bit angry?"

"Angry. Angry? What do you think I was doing all those years you were on the road? You think I was fingerfucking myself? You jerk, you conceited ass. I must have screwed everyone who ever came near our house. Now shut up and leave me alone."

He never knew the truth, and he never asked her about it. He was afraid she might tell him.

They held their breath and waited. "Levine Tells All" was the headline, but the headlines were not important. What was important were the comments, the commentators, and, most important, the polls.

Frieda Kraft-Lawrence caught the major theme, the one that was repeated unsaid in editorial after editorial.

> This country dearly loves a sinner come to the bar, and in his television appearance Monday night A.L. Levine turned ashes into gold. There was no fake humility about it, no pandering to "the new morality," whatever that may be. It was a straightforward confession, done from the soul and, in every regard, convincing. Mr. Levine may not have convinced the voters of his essential decency and devotion, but he has convinced me.

The voters, too, appeared convinced. The polls showed a sharp upward rise in Levine's popularity. Bell was puzzled.

"I don't figure it," he said to Jessington. "I mean, I can see where he might be finished by the whole thing, but to jump five percent, that I don't understand."

"How come you thought he'd drop?" Jessington asked. "Morality?"

"No, I thought he'd lose ten percent on pure envy—all

THE WANTING OF LEVINE 411

those guys who've been cheating all their lives, never get anything except the company lay at the Christmas party and even for that they get hell from their wives, and here's this little shit who says he's had how many women, and he's running for president and his wife forgives him. I thought people would go after him the way they went after Adam Powell. It wasn't the absenteeism or the nepotism or the corruption that bugged them, it was the pussy—and the fact that he was getting away with it."

"My son," Jessington said, "your remembering is a little mixed up. Mr. Powell's people reelected him in 1968 after all that fuss. It was the House that took his seniority away; they were the ones who were envious. Of course, the voters finally got rid of him, but that was because he had let things fall apart back in the district. No, the voters never minded Adam's chasing. Maybe the rest of the country's catching up to Harlem."

It seemed that way. Clergymen of all faiths were interviewed at length, and there was more discussion of talmudic strictures against adultery and evocation of ancient Hebraic polygamy than at a rabbinical congress. Rose was tight-lipped about the matter. "I saw Mr. Levine's performance. I hope his confession was sincere. It would appear to me that a life of deceit and deception hardly qualifies one for the presidency. My sympathies, of course, go to Mrs. Levine."

As the clergymen clashed swords, individual women began to emerge from the list of names. Sheila Jo captured the most attention. She had the most documentation of their affair and, as always, there was something engagingly delightful about her interviews. Levine crept away to a private set at the committee to watch Merlin's exclusive half-hour interview with her. She fluffed her hair, grinned, and said, "Oh, no, there was never any deception at all about Mr. Levine. He told me his real name right off—lots of those men never will—and he told me he was married and all. But it didn't matter to me. Lord, I was over twenty-one, divorced three years with a four-year old child; I wasn't a blushing virgin, if you know. And being with Mr. Levine after being with those ordinary men I used to hang with, well, it was like watching TV in color—good color!—after you'd been watching it in black and white all your life. So much fun he was!"

There was reaction, of course. The word "backlash" came out of storage. Preachers who had had fears or hatreds of a Jewish candidate but who had been reluctant to voice them suddenly found themselves a new issue. "The Women Taken in Adultery" blossomed on more Methodist sermon announcements that Levine's Methodist-watcher could count, and the Baptists were right up there too. The South was no longer solid. The Midwest, where he had never been strong, was almost hopeless. The Rocky Mountain states looked bad— "Fucking Mormons," van Dillinham said, "you'd think they'd appreciate some outright adultery."

And it was the end of September, and there wasn't much time to come back. Again they sat at the big table and brooded.

"Let's go with the Vermont land deal thing," Brandon said. "It'll take the press play away from all this screwing for a while."

"It's not enough to get them off the scent," McKelvin said.

"It is if Rose is a man who's supposed to be red hot for protecting our land against developers."

Levine thought. "It was a long time ago and it doesn't sound like much, but it's all we've got. Hold it for a week, though. If we release it now, it will look too obvious. Besides, they're still interviewing those girls. It won't get any play."

They waited a week and released the story. Rose denied, backed off, denied again, explained, and did not look good. He was hurt, but not badly. Levine's attrition in the South stopped. The Rocky Mountain states, where land deals were the staff of life, did not like this one. Levine inched back.

"How does it look?" Farbstein asked one night. One could count on Farbstein not only to have an automatically wrong view of any political situation, but to have a fair sense of human responses. Levine was depressed, and he knew it.

"All right, I guess. The polls are okay. Not spectacular, but okay. The crowds seem good when I speak. The goddam bands keep playing 'Love is Sweeping the Country' every time I get up, like it was 'Hail to the Chief' or something. But some of the fun has gone out."

"I can tell you're depressed. Why not take a little vacation, go down to Miami or the Islands?"

"Jesus, Farbstein, this isn't the garment business. I'm in a campaign. You don't just take off a week and walk on the beach. I've got every hour scheduled for the next four weeks. Not every day, every hour!"

"So go fishing, already."

They canceled a day and trolled for bluefish on Chesapeake Bay. The fish were there and the company—McKelvin, Jessington, and his own son Samuel—was pleasant, but the tackle was heavy and the fish were not so much caught as dragged to the surface. There was something dispiriting about it, a good thing gone wrong. Almost like the campaign.

His wife understood. "I'm sorry, dear. What's done is done. I can see the spark go out of you. You don't even walk the same. What's the matter?"

"I guess I was fooling myself. I didn't think I had the messianic urge—when my name came up I truly thought that I would be as good as any of the others, that it was about time a Jew should run, and that maybe I could be instructive even if I wasn't elected. Now I see that my whole life was a way of positioning myself for this campaign, even back to when I wanted to be president of G.O. in high school. I never thought of myself as much of a Jew, but now I see that I've got as much of the messiah built into me as any other Jew, maybe more. When the campaign started, I felt that surge all the way through me. I wanted to teach, to lead. I was really exalted. I thought that as a Jew I might be able to show people how to live together, to feel things that were just ready to bloom. I thought that because I had lived all over the country, because I knew so many ways of life, I could bring my book knowledge together with my experience. I thought I could do something about getting along with the goddam Mexicans. Instead, I'm destroyed by my own lust. I end up talking about pussy."

She was quiet for a moment, thinking. "You know, I think I have an idea for you. In fact, I know I have an idea for you."

"What's that?"

"You should see a tzaddik."

"A tzaddik?"

"Yes, you know. A sage. A wise man."

"Look, when we had that trouble about the women, we called that rabbi, what's his name, the one who married Laura and Harvey."

"Sure, you called him because you knew that whatever it was, he'd say it's okay. A modern rabbi, what does he know?"

"Okay, maybe he's no Einstein, but why a tzaddik? I don't go to shul, I've forgotten my Hebrew, I don't believe all that stuff—I never *did* believe it."

"A tzaddik because when a wise man like you, whether he's religious or not, can't find the answer to what's bothering him in a book, he goes to the tzaddik."

"Where did you hear that?"

"I read it someplace."

The campaign had many advisers—foreign policy, economic, sociologic—all busy working away on position papers which they hoped would elevate themselves to Levine's attention and, eventually, an assistant secretary-ship in his cabinet. There was even a board of religious advisers, who had kept him informed on what were said to be the "Jewish" aspects of social policy. There was another board of religious advisers working to keep him from offending Christian sensibilities (it had found little precedent for adultery). There was no one, however, who knew of tzaddiks. Probably one of the rabbis on the Jewish board might know a name or two, but Levine was reluctant to use them; intoxicated with power, they were compulsive gossips. Levine could feel them arriving home, hugging their wives, and whispering, "Guess who I put our friend Levine in touch with today?" They might be good at keeping their congregations' secrets, but Levine wasn't a parishioner; he was news, and after years of keeping secrets, a clergyman dearly loves the opportunity to let them out.

Levine thought longer.

"Farbstein, come in a moment."

"So?"

"Farbstein, do you know what a tzaddik is?"

"Certainly—a wise man, a learned man. Jewish, of course."

"Do you know any?"

"Levine, you know me better than that. I'm a socialist. My parents before me were socialists with Hillquit. We rejected superstition when we left Europe."

"Okay, but do you know anyone well who might know a tzaddik?"

"Of course. Have I turned my back on my relatives? I have an uncle Beryl, very religious, a Hasid. He's a follower of Rabbi Moishe Leib Isaacovitch. The rabbi's headquarters are in Williamsburg, so they call him the Williamsburger."

"Does your uncle know you're here in Washington with me?"

"No. He is the kind of relative one loves but rarely sees."

"Would he have read about you in the papers?"

"Not the papers he reads. All he knows are diamond cutting and the Talmud."

"Would he know my name?"

"That he'd know. Even the Hasids talk of worldly things. Not often, but they'd know your name."

"Then please, go to New York. Make a local call to your uncle. Ask him for the name of a great tzaddik, but one who can speak good English. It doesn't have to be the Williamsburger. If he wants to know if it's for you, equivocate as best you can. Explain it's a very personal thing. Then speak to the tzaddik and make an appointment. Say it's for a friend. Don't give your own name, unless you have to."

"It's for you, right?"

"Right."

"It's a good idea. I'm a socialist, but I believe in tzaddiks."

"Thanks."

"By the way, as I remember, they usually charge for their advice. How should I arrange payment?"

"For God's sake, however the tzaddik wants. Just don't use campaign money."

BROOKLYN, OCTOBER 1, 1988

Eminently ordinary, he flew to New York alone and unrecognized. He took a group taxi to the tzaddik's synagogue, a squat brick building in the Williamsburg section of Brooklyn that had not yet been rehabilitated. On the crowded sidewalks blacks, Puerto Ricans, Mexican refugees, and ivory-pale rabbinical students, their hands weaving great theorems in the air, bumped by each other.

In the shul Levine took a deep whiff and was overwhelmed with odors of childhood. There was something so profoundly, uniquely redolent of 1935 in the air that he could not rest until it had been tracked down, identified. A deeper whiff! Roll it around your nostrils! Let it breathe! Of course, it was the boys' closet—the cloakroom, he suddenly remembered they called it—at the Home in 1935. It was the fall of 1935, in fact, and it was a wet fall and what he was smelling was the lost, innocent smell of wet wool. God, those heavy woolen skirts and those hairy woolen pants that kids had worn—how they steamed and smelled when they were wet. And, of course, the last people in America to deck themselves in those identical, scratchy, funky woolens were the Orthodox Jews, forbidden forever to indulge in the glories of polyesters and virgin vinyl.

A somber rabbinical type caught him sniffing.

"Something's the matter?" the rabbinical type wanted to know.

"Not at all, not at all. Just my allergies. Excuse me, my name is ..." He almost forgot the name he had given to Farbstein. "Pinksman. Saul Pinksman. I have an appointment with the rabbi."

The man nodded. "I'm Rabbi Proner. The rebbe's *gabbai*—his secretary. The rebbe is expecting you." He

ushered Levine down a long hallway and off to a
book-lined study.

"Wait," he said. "The rebbe will come."

Levine waited. The books were in Hebrew, most of
them bound in ragged leather with gold lettering, a very
few apparently new. There were no magazines. There was
nothing in English. There was no clock. Levine waited.
He put everything out of his mind except what was
bothering him.

Rabbi Proner came back. "Now," he said, motioning
Levine toward an inner door and opening it for him.

The rebbe sat behind a long table. Hebrew books and
scrolls were strewn over the table. There was, Levine
noted, a Brooklyn telephone book but no telephone.

The rebbe looked—how else to say it?—like a picture
of a rebbe, some bit of pasteurized Chagall that might
grace the walls of a suburban accountant. The dark wool
hat with the upturned brim, the great flowing gray beard
surrounding rosy, rather sensual lips, the lined face and
hawklike nose—Levine had seen them all before. Only the
eyes were surprising. They were not sad or even solemn,
but quick, perhaps merry.

"Mr. Pinksman?" The rebbe gestured.

Levine nodded and sat down. "I'm honored to meet
you, rebbe. I know you are a busy man and you have more
to do than bother with my worldly problems. Here, here is
the *kvitl.*"

Levine shoved a little cloth bundle containing his
mother's name written in Hebrew, a brief Hebrew prayer,
and a check for $5,000. The Hebrew had come from a
scholar on call to the White House.

The rebbe nodded, pushed the *kvitl* aside, and said,
"And so, Mr. Levine."

"I was just about to tell you. I'm sorry I had to make the
appointment under a false name, but under the circumstances. . . . You understand?"

"I understand, but I don't approve. We start out badly.
Do you think I would run to the newspapers to tell them
of my newest client?"

Levine shrugged. "No, of course not, but I couldn't

reach you directly. The people around you might not—"

The Williamsburger interrupted. "You trust the people around *you?*"

Levine nodded. "I apologize."

"Tell me what is bothering you."

"I have been having problems recently. I thought that my private life would not interfere with my campaign. I suppose that's incorrect—I guess I hoped that it would not interfere. Anyway, some of this became public and—"

"I know," the rebbe said dryly.

"I wasn't sure how much you follow things like elections." He did not feel like a presidential candidate.

"We Hasidim live in the world," the rebbe said. "This isn't a monastery. You understand that to us your world is of less importance, but it is there."

"The details of my life have become public. They have hurt my campaign. More, they have hurt me. I see now that I was hypocritical, that I was doing just what I criticized other people for doing. I despised people for compromising their honesty to make money. I felt I never did this, never lied to anyone. Now I see that I didn't lie about money or power because they weren't that important to me. When it came to something important— women—I lied. Probably these other men weren't that interested in women."

The rebbe shrugged and said nothing. He was beginning to remind Levine of the psychiatrist he had gone to when he first had some money: the shrugging, the prolonged silences, the lifted eyebrows. The resemblance was far from coincidental.

"So for the first time I've lost faith in myself. I've lost faith in what I'm doing. I really wonder if politics means anything at all, whether maybe it's just a form of activity to keep us busy until we die, something to ward off loneliness, depression."

The rebbe nodded.

"If that's all there is, why am I destroying my wife, alienating my younger son, growing away from my friends? Why bother?"

He stopped and waited. They locked silences. Finally

the Williamsburger spoke. He hadn't been playing games, merely thinking.

"So, as I gather, you are asking me two questions. One is about the worth of yourself; the other is the worth of what you do. The two are separate, but linked."

"That's right."

The rabbi opened the *kvitl,* slipped the check in a drawer without looking, and read the Hebrew.

"You see the Sages would tell you that your life is worthless already. When my grandfather—*olav shalom* —was rabbi in Sanz, there was much talk one year of who would give the first prayer on Yom Kippur. A man named Brod was expected to, because he was not only a learned Jew but he was rich and had given the Sanzer a large donation. But others expected that the rebbe might call upon Lewisky, who was by far the cleverest of the Jews in the rebbe's court. Lewisky could take a section of Torah and turn it every way, just as a diamond cutter can take a dull stone and make it shine from every dimension. But instead the rebbe called on a man named Khlar, a poor peddler, not very smart, who drove from house to house and village to village selling dry goods.

"All the members of the rebbe's court were astonished, and after services they asked him why he had chosen Khlar. And the rebbe said, 'Lewisky is a good man and he is a smart man, and he takes his brain and applies it to Torah. And Brod is a good man and a rich man, and he takes some of his money and gives it to the Jews. But one day last year I was walking in the streets and I saw Khlar, who was in his little cart. His horse was plodding on and the reins were slack, because Khlar was paying no attention to where he was going. As his cart came by me I could hear Khlar repeating to himself the day's portion of Torah. He couldn't be in shul, so he was doing the whole section by himself. He would come to a place he couldn't remember and stumble, and do it again, and when it came right he would smile. All the time the horse carried him on to his next stop. From that time I made note to watch Khlar when I passed him in the street. Always he was working in his mind a section of Torah. For others in my court, Torah is part of life. For Khlar, it is all of life. So Khlar reads.'"

Levine nodded and motioned as if to leave. The lesson was over. The rebbe gestured for him to stay.

"So you see that while in your world you are an important man, probably a good man, in God's world you are little. What can I say to you? You are a Jew and yet you are not Jewish. When you are in shul, you can't read the prayers. Worse, when your father dies, your friends die, you can't say Kaddish—"

Levine interrupted. "I can say the prayers. I can say Kaddish."

The rebbe lifted his eyebrows. Learned men did not show emotion openly, but it was permissible to indicate mild surprise. He gently lifted a Hebrew volume from the side of his desk and turned it toward Levine. "So read," he said.

It came back. It came back as it had when Rackey was arrested and Merlin had interviewed them on the beach. It came back along with the smell of damp wool and sweat and hot tea. It came back, too, because he had anticipated this and had reviewed the day's section of Torah with the party's expert on Judaism. A little cramming for an exam was permissible, even in the yeshiva.

Levine read the section. He read it not fluently, but not badly, and the rebbe stayed silent.

Levine plowed ahead to the next passage, and the tzaddik lifted his hand, motioning him to stop.

"Enough. So you're not hopeless. This is different."

He closed his eyes and began murmuring to himself. He rose from the table and paced back and forth, occasionally glancing out the window to the world of God outside. He came to the bookshelf, pulled out a volume, searched through it rapidly but gently until he found what he wanted, and laid it back on his desk. Rabbi Proner would replace the books by the next morning.

Levine knew that his own responsibility at this time was to stay silent. It was one thing to present a problem to the tzaddik; it was another—and unacceptable—thing to question him or even to attempt to fill in more details.

Finally the rebbe sat back in his seat and, half looking at Levine, half looking to the bookshelves, began to talk.

"There is no direct precedent for your situation. We were kings in Israel, and the duties of leaders are well established in Torah, but these are for Jewish princes leading Jewish people. But we know that the Almighty blesses 'the righteous of the peoples,' and the rabbis have told us that the plural means that Heaven shall include the righteous gentile as well as the righteous Jew. The Almighty, blessed be He, has laid greater responsibility on the Jew, as well as greater duty to His Word. The Jew who does not follows His Word is far more wretched than the gentile who lives a decent life without knowledge of the Word.

"It is acceptable for you to become a leader of gentiles as well as Jews. It is your *parnosseh*—your livelihood— and it is not forbidden to Jews. But you cannot be a good leader to gentiles if you are not a good Jew, and you cannot be a good Jew if you do not obey the Law. Of the mitzvahs commanded by Almighty, you have kept only a few. The Sages told us that when Jews went out into the world of the Others in Poland and Russia, certain mitzvahs could not be kept. They understood that only the holiest of Jews could keep all six hundred and thirteen mitzvahs, and that in gaining *parnosseh* a Jew might have to forgo one or another of his duties to God. But he must know that he was denying the Almighty, and he must keep the main mitzvahs. True, you have kept the mitzvahs of charity and of learning, and for this the Almighty will not forsake you completely. But your learning has been too far away from His Torah.

"You have allowed yourself to dress like the gentiles, which is permissible under certain circumstances. But you have defiled yourself with forbidden food, even the tortoise, which is an abomination. You have made no place in your life for His Sabbath, and in this you resemble only a clever animal.

"Because of your work, you cannot observe all the mitzvahs. The Sages knew this—'The Law is for man, and not man for the Law.' But these you must do: You must read each day's section of Torah until you complete it on Simchas Torah and begin all over again. You must refrain from forbidden food. You must keep Shabbas holy.

"Do these things and you will be enough of a Jew to help the gentiles. You will not be enough of a Jew for the Jews, but you will have begun, and the Almighty blesses a beginning. After you are elected, then you must keep more of his Commandments. If you become too holy too suddenly, people will say you do it for love of votes rather than love of God. When you are president, then you will show all people how His mitzvahs and His Torah bring the good life."

The tzaddik made a faint upward motion of his hand, gesturing that the session was over. Levine rose, thanked him, and then, overcome, asked, "You spoke of 'when' I am president. Do you think I will be elected?"

A small smile played around the tzaddik's mouth. "I read the Talmud," he said, "but I also read the *Times*. You are not a good Jew—you have not been a good Jew—but you are not a bad man. You have tried, in the manner of the unbeliever. Your mother and father were taken from you young. The Almighty takes that into account. I think He would like a Jewish president."

He ushered Levine out the door.

On the plane back to Washington Levine refused a shrimp salad for the first time in his life. I wonder how he knew about the turtle soup? he thought.

There are superhighways in northern Vermont, but most of the roads are narrow and twisting, not much better than they were in 1935. The locals like them that way. Anyone who has legitimate business in the mountains can take his time. And anyone who runs an illegitimate business in the mountains—like smuggling or kidnapping—prefers the security of half-hidden roads in narrow valleys. The back road from East Enosburg to Hectorville is one of the most tortuous of these, which is why a troop carrier full of Patrols was there in the first place. Stationed at the border stop in Richford, they had been told—by a reliable informant—that a shipment of machine guns had been smuggled over from Canada and was heading, by way of the Hectorville Road, to some of Caputo's people near Craftsbury.

Eli and Caputo watched with pleasure as the carrier, a distant dot in their binoculars, made its steady way toward their bunker. The vehicle would disappear from view for a moment, then pop up farther along the winding road. Enough leaves had already fallen so that the carrier could be tracked any time the distant road didn't duck behind a mountain or curve totally out of sight.

They had had only a day to scout out the location themselves—there was no use lurking around a lonely road and arousing suspicions—but their location was everything that Hoadley said it would be. "Find us a place," Caputo said, "which is within fifty miles of the border, where three men can command the road coming through, where the valley is so narrow that there's a ravine on one side and no escape up the sides of the hills, and where the curve is so tight that the way in and the way out aren't more than three hundred feet apart. Make sure we can't be seen from a helicopter. Make sure no one can get a bead on the spot from any other mountain." Hoadley found the place. He hadn't been an Appalachian Mountain Club member fifteen years for nothing.

As the troop carrier came closer, silently crawling through the mountains like a caterpillar inching in the grass, Eli realized that the plan was going to work. When Peter had outlined it, he had gone along, even with enthusiasm, not because he thought it would succeed but because it was so daring. Never could he refuse an honor offered directly by Caputo himself. Still, as the plan was laid out in the farmhouse, it had seemed suicidal.

Now he felt the noose tighten and the bus get closer, and he realized that it would work. It would work because the planning was so careful, the psychological planning along with the physical planning. It was typical of Peter that he had an expert for every part of the plan. Nothing was hurried. All the options were worked out in advance. They would get away with it.

Brian came over to them. "I figure it would be in another ten minutes," he said.

Caputo looked at his watch. "Right. Better get to your place." Brian slithered off through the woods, the bazooka strapped to his back.

Eli focused the glasses on the carrier as it inched up the last hill before the valley. He could count eighteen Patrols in the car, sitting facing each other, plus the driver. All the Patrols except two were black. The squad leader was Tierney, just as their man in Richford said it would be. Tierney was nineteen years into a twenty-year career, and Caputo figured him unlikely to do anything heroic.

The car disappeared from view, but now they could hear it as it headed downhill, swung around the corner, and popped up in sight below them.

"Away we go!" Caputo said, and pushed the plungers. There was a backup dynamite system in case anything went wrong, but nothing did. The man who had rigged the charges had dynamited daily for five years in a granite quarry. "No amateurs," Caputo had said. "Just home-grown professionals." The charge ahead of the bus was set only fifty feet above the road. It took only three seconds for the blast to dump a truckload of rock across the valley, sealing the forward way out. The rear charge was set higher up on the mountainside, starting a small, well-planned avalanche which closed off all escape fifteen seconds later.

A few boulders were still tumbling down the side of the hill when Tierney, an automatic rifle in his grip, appeared in the door of the bus.

"Captain Tierney," Caputo said into his bullhorn. Tierney looked up, not so much shocked as quizzical. "Captain Tierney—please get back in the bus. You are surrounded and will not be hurt so long as you do not return fire. Tell your men that. We can destroy you in a moment. We are going to fire one warning bazooka shot over your heads to let you know we are not bluffing. Then we want your men to throw their weapons—including the cannons—into the ravine alongside the bus. We will fire now."

Brian sent a shot over the bus.

"I repeat. You are completely surrounded. Please do not cause any unnecessary loss of life. This is Peter Caputo speaking to you. You know my word is good. My lieutenant, Eli Levine, will obtain your freedom so long as you do not try to use your weapons. If you do, we shall have to kill you all."

Tierney stepped inside the bus. Eli could see him explaining the situation to the others. A young black private gestured wildly, grabbed his BAR from the overhead rack, and tried to force open a side window. The window stuck slightly, as bus windows always do. Before the Patrol could poke the barrel of the BAR out the window, Brian's .357 cracked and the man jerked back, dead before he hit the floor of the bus.

"That was regrettable," Peter said into the bullhorn. "We are not kidding. We want those weapons in the ravine—now. We can see every move, so don't make the mistake your private did."

Tierney talked to his troops again. Then he walked to the front door of the bus, held up his arms to show he had no weapons, and turned again to the inside of the bus. The men had formed a bucket brigade and were passing the BARs, rifles, and cannons hand over hand to the front of the bus. As Tierney got each piece, he looked at it briefly and then tossed it into the deep ravine alongside the road. The weapons clattered as they plunged 150 feet to the bottom.

Eli scanned the bus with his binoculars. "The driver's on the short-wave," he said. "He's scared shitless, but he's talking a mile a minute."

"That's fine," Caputo said. "We've got their nuts in a vise. Let's see how long it takes for the signal to travel to the central nervous system."

They stretched out alongside their weapons and turned on the short-wave radio and portable television set, to watch the chaos they had created unfold.

Bell tapped Levine on the shoulder. "The president wants to talk to you."

"Which president?"

"Bigelow. Of the United States."

"I had almost forgotten about him. What's he want, my address book?"

"He says it's urgent."

Levine took the phone and listened. "Oh, shit," he said. "Oh, shit. Yes, I'll be right over."

"What's the matter?" Bell said.

"Eli's in trouble."

He'd been in the Oval Office before and he had just enough composure left to notice that Bigelow had placed some locker-room slogans on the wall. "When the going gets tough...." Bigelow was always about ten years behind the times.

"Let me explain the situation," the president said. "Ten minutes ago the Communications Room received a message from a Vermont border station in Richmond."

"Richford," Levine said.

Bigelow looked puzzled.

"Richmond isn't on the border," Levine said. "Richford is."

"One or the other," Bigelow said. "Anyway, a busload of Patrols, eighteen of them plus the driver, has been trapped in a little valley near there by a group including Peter Caputo and your son."

"Are they sure it's Eli?" Levine asked.

"The kidnappers have a short-wave radio. They've already been in touch with Richford. Voice prints over short-wave aren't a hundred percent reliable, but the FBI says the person who calls himself Eli Levine exactly matches a set of voice prints they have on your son."

"Why did they have prints on my son?"

Bigelow shrugged. "I don't know. I guess they knew something we didn't."

Levine felt a tearing inside. He had known it or felt it all along. He should have been as smart as the FBI.

"What do they want?" Bell asked.

"They want release of eighteen of their associates from prison. One for each of the hostages. They want a commitment to keep all Patrols out of Vermont. And they want you to resign from the campaign in favor of Milwood."

Levine looked at the ceiling and thought. "Does my wife know of this yet?"

"No. The press people don't have it yet, but they will. We thought you'd want to tell her. The . . . ah . . . terrorists want publicity. They're in constant radio communication with Richford. Their demands for the prisoner release are very clever and precise—we'd never be able to work an immediate recapture on any of them." Bigelow paused. "I'm very sorry about this." He looked almost tearful.

"You don't have to be sorry," Levine said. "God knows, we've had everything else. Candidates' sons arrested for dope, for sodomy. Kidnappings—everyone's been kidnapped. Sooner or later, sooner or later. . . . Why shouldn't a man's son turn against him? They must have worked on him. A man's most vulnerable possession. Most valuable."

Bell had never heard him so disjointed. "I think we need time to think this out, sir," he said.

"Sir? I'm not sir. I *am* thinking, Philip. Why do they want me to quit? Have they been in touch with Rose?"

Bigelow shook his head. "The FBI hasn't any thread

between them. We haven't contacted Rose yet. That's another thing we're holding off until we speak to you."

"What plans do you have?"

"We don't have anything yet. The NSC chiefs are just coming in. FBI, CIA, Defense—all of them. From the early reports it's a hell of a situation. Your son and this other fellow are up in some rocks on the hillside. They've got heavy weapons—bazookas, the Patrols say. One man's already been killed by a sniper. We don't have any idea of how many of them are up there. They're all over the hillside. Probably ten or twenty, the Patrol captain estimates."

"Jesus."

"There's no straight line into their hideout. They say that if we put helicopters in the valley, they'll blow up the bus. Those men are sitting ducks. We could put a big federal presence in there on the ground, but we've been trying to avoid that. The people are so hostile to begin with, we figure that would start the Civil War for sure."

"Yeah."

"One thing's been suggested already...."

"What's that?"

"The Needle missile. It's small, silent, heat-activated. You can program it by computer into an area fifty feet square, and then the heat-scenting part takes over and—"

"You're talking about missiles against my son? My son!"

"One of the military aides suggested it. Of course we wouldn't use it without your approval and—"

"My approval!"

"That's right. We're meeting in an hour. The people in Vermont—your son and this Caputo—haven't given us any deadline; in fact, they've told us they're prepared to hole up as long as a week. Just the same, we don't want to waste any time. I've asked Sterling from the National Security Council, Miles of the Joint Chiefs, and Clark from the FBI to be there. As you know, it's policy to notify the major candidates of any crisis situation during a presidential campaign, so we would have cut you in on this even if... you know."

"Yes."

"But in this particular situation we want you right in the Oval Office while we work on it. To the degree I can get it, I want your suggestions and, ultimately, your approval for what we do. I'm not shifting the responsibility off on you—God knows, I'd like to—but I'd like to think that, whatever we do, you concurred. I barely remember your boy. We met once or twice, but..."

"Of course."

"We have a car waiting outside. I'd like you to go home, tell Mrs. Levine of the situation yourself, and bring her back here. If she has any friends or relatives she'd like with her during the waiting period, bring them. Betty will make them welcome."

––––––––––––

Helen cried but didn't panic. Her gift for the concrete came to her help. It not only preserved her calm, it made her valuable in thinking of alternatives.

"What are they going to eat up there? It's getting cold already in New England. Up on a mountain—they're going to freeze."

"No. They've got enough food to last them a week, apparently. And the way they planned the attack, I'm sure they were careful enough to have sleeping bags and some kind of shelter."

Huddled in the back seat of the White House limousine, he put his arm around her and stroked her face.

"Why Eli?" he said. "Why does it have to be my own son?"

Now it was her turn to be sensible. "Why not?" she said. "The fact he's your son made him someone those people would want to be nice to. To lure him into their group. And the fact that he's your son made him more susceptible."

"Why?"

"Because this is America, that's why. Because sons can't follow in their father's footsteps. They've got to be bigger, better."

"I never told him that. I never forced him."

"No, never directly. But you used to be so proud when he was interested in politics, when he'd watch the conventions with you when he was a little kid. You didn't have to tell him anything; he could feel it. So now he's as important as his father."

"God help us all," Levine said.

———————

Inside the White House a tall marine in full uniform gently ushered Helen to a side door. Levine panicked.

"Wait," he told the marine, "It's her decision, too. The president—"·

"No," she said. "In the end, even with Eli, this is politics, and politics is your job. I trust you, but it's your responsibility."

Bigelow met him outside the Oval Office, took his arm, and led him inside. "I'm keeping this group small," he said. "These are people I trust. We don't need anyone else."

"You said the candidates have been informed. Is Rose here?"

Bigelow hesitated. "We informed him. No, he won't be here. We asked him to come to the meeting, in fact, since one of the demands is your dropping out of the race."

"So?"

The president gave a slight sniff of distaste. "Well, he said it wasn't his problem. He said he'd endorse any decision I came to." He paused for a moment and then hurried Levine inside the Oval Office.

"You know these gentlemen, I believe," Bigelow said. "All except General Miles. General, A. L. Levine." They shook hands.

Bigelow was surprisingly efficient. Even though he had never wanted to be a president, he at least acted like one when he had to.

"Cleve, you start."

Cleveland Sterling chaired the National Security Council and was director of the CIA. He had a Ph.D. in Far Eastern History from Harvard and had taught a popular undergraduate course nicknamed "Coolies and Commies" before being named to the CIA post. There was a general feeling in Cambridge that he had been reporting to the agency since the time of his first field trip to Hong Kong, but no one had ever been able to prove it. Both sets of grandparents had been missionaries in China, which gave him the deep-seated conviction that the Far East was his by Divine Right. He was very smart, and he knew it.

"As you know, Mr. President, we have no announced policy on dealing with domestic terrorists. When we signed the Oslo Declaration in 1980 there was a lot of feeling in Congress that we should apply the same rules to domestic hostage-taking that we had agreed to for international crises, but the people just weren't ready for a no-negotiation policy. So we can do what we want with these people.

"We've already put a photo plane over the area," he continued. "We have their direct transmission on video tape. Let me show you some individual frames."

The lights dimmed, and a screen dropped on the far side of the room. Crisp, beautiful color slides, a tourist's dream, followed in rapid succession. Vermont from 80,000 feet, Lake Champlain shimmering in one corner of the slide. Closeup views, focused on the Cold Hollow mountain area, brilliant with autumn red and gold. A marked square within that frame, exploded a hundred times in size, suddenly revealed a twisting road through the mountains and—no doubt of it!—a military bus halted in a curve of the road. Another click of the projector button and two human figures were shown crouching beside a rock. Their faces were indistinguishable but Levine recognized with a start the bright blue jogging shoes that Eli had always worn for his workouts along the Potomac.

An arrow suddenly appeared, pointing at the shoes.

"The people in the basement at Langley tell me that those are Garcia Supers, a kind of jogging shoe. We've checked, Mr. Levine, and I believe your son owns a similar pair, also in blue."

Levine nodded.

"Seems sort of a dumb thing to be wearing for that kind of operation," General Miles said.

"On the contrary," Sterling said. "They're remarkably sensible. Strong, with good support and, what's more, excellent traction. Just right for scrambling uphill. A fair number of the professional guides are using them on short trips instead of hiking boots. Much lighter."

Levine felt unaccountably relieved that his son's choice of terrorist attire had been endorsed by the CIA.

"That's the geographic setting," Sterling concluded.

"Holly," the president said, gesturing toward the chairman of the Joint Chiefs, General Holbrook Miles.

"Mr. President, sir," Miles responded, "we have a number of options. We can put in an attack helicopter with a SLAM group aboard and overpower them. Negatives here are that we have every reason to believe that the two men could—and would—be able to get off their bazooka at least a couple of times and destroy the hostages in the bus.

"We could try to wait them out. We know that in situations like this, even if the hostage-takers are well armed and well supplied, their resolve tends to weaken after forty-eight hours. Our computer print-out on similar incidents suggests that in approximately seventy-eight percent of cases first-time hijackers will eventually give up without killing their hostages just through the process of temporal attrition."

"Temporal attrition?" the president asked.

"Waiting. Just as the hostages tend to identify with their captors, the hijackers begin to see the hostages as real people. Their own goals become fuzzy in their minds. Give them some sort of token recognition and they throw in their cards."

He paused and cleared his throat. "Unfortunately, information we've received from the FBI"—he nodded to Director Clark—"makes us pessimistic about the waiting approach in this particular case. We're then forced to consider the Needle missile. This, of course, is top-secret, but I believe you were briefed on it during the closed budget hearings last spring."

Bigelow nodded. "Refresh my memory."

"Basically it's a laser-aimed strategic antipersonnel rocket. It has a built-in self-correcting computational device that corrects for target movement, et cetera. It was designed for just this kind of situation, say if you want to take off the cockpit of an airplane where the hijackers are without hurting anyone ten feet away. The blast is extremely limited by a container-controlled flash device that has a very rapid fallout from Point Zero. Your average weapon has a blast intensity that decreases exponentially with the cube of the distance from Point Zero. Because of the nature of the explosive force in the Needle, you can set your radius of destruction in advance very precisely, and come up with a gray zone of partial damage which is extremely small."

"Which means what?" the president said.

General Miles was warming to his subject. "Well, you don't have any surrounding blast damage or shrapnel wounds or civilian damage." He suddenly hesitated. "You just...ah...vaporize everything within your predetermined target area."

"Jesus Christ," Levine said. He turned pale and put his head in his hands.

Bigelow got up from his seat and walked around to Levine's chair. Tenderly he touched the man's shoulder.

"That's absolutely ruled out," he said. "Absolutely. I will permit nothing like that to happen." He stared angrily at General Miles.

"I'm sorry," Miles said. "I was just presenting options."

"Well, that's closed. Forget it. You said something about what the FBI had told you. Let's hear from them directly."

The FBI director consulted his briefing book.

"Sir, we have files on both these young men. Begging Mr. Levine's pardon, we've had some information on his son Eli for the past two years. There's been no clandestine surveillance or electronic surveillance, I can assure you of that. We've gotten our data perfectly legally, all within the confines of S-One and the Privacy Act. Of course, if we had required electronic surveillance, we would have obtained the necessary court orders under the—"

"Please get on with your information," the president said wearily. The director of the FBI was a noted civil libertarian.

"Sorry. Our informants indicate that while young Eli Levine had been in direct contact with terrorist groups for the past two months only, he has in that time participated in one violent, nonfatal guerrilla raid in northern New York. Furthermore, he's been in open contact with various aggressive or revolutionary organizations for the past two years. Of the young man Peter Caputo there can be no doubt as to his commitment and willingness to use lethal force. He has been involved in four acts of personal retribution and has participated in at least a dozen episodes where people were executed. He is a hardened revolutionary. We've never been able to infiltrate his inner circle. There is no reason to expect him to become sympathetic with his hostages or otherwise to yield without a direct confrontation."

"What's your plan of action?"

"Sir, we just collect domestic intelligence of this sort. This kind of incident doesn't come under our mandate. We were rather hoping the military might have some sort of contingency—"

"Oh, Christ."

"Sir, we can develop a plan," the FBI director went on. "It's just that this early in the affair I gathered from your staff that you wanted our data and our profiles on these men."

"Okay. It's all right. What sort of psychologic profiles have your people drawn up on the two men?"

"It's very interesting. The first man, Caputo, is a behavioral psychologist himself. In fact, the chief of our Crisis Division worked with him in Cambridge. Amazing—"

"Get on with it," the president said.

"Yes, sir. The profile is very accurate. The subject took most of the standard tests while a graduate student and took others after his accident. Caputo is totally controlled. Scores almost zero on the Impulsiveness scale. He's also very high on Creativity, Detail, and Aggression.

It goes without saying that his Intelligence and Knowledge scores are on the far edge of the chart. It's a very interesting profile—creativity without impulsiveness. There's also a lot of aggression, but again, much control. There aren't many weak spots."

"What about the other subject, the Levine boy?"

Director Clark shrugged. "We have almost nothing on him, Mr. President. It's almost the exact opposite of Caputo. He's never been in any official trouble with the law before, and we've never had him under direct personal surveillance."

"What about the tests he took in high school, in college?"

Clark looked over at Levine. "It turns out, sir, that when he was in public school here in Washington psychologic profiling had been stopped because of complaints from various racial groups. Then, when he went to private school, his, ah, parents refused to let him take the MMPI and other standard tests in use at that time. It was optional."

The president looked at Levine, who remembered vaguely his irritation when Eli had brought home a request slip, couched in the prideful jargon to the trade, asking that Eli be excused one afternoon for "psychometric testing." The testing, parents were assured, "is designed to bring the young person more completely in tune with himself and to develop areas of strength which might otherwise be overlooked." Results of the testing, the request continued, "would, of course, remain strictly confidential."

Unless the FBI needed them in a hurry.

Well, Levine thought, he had been irritated by testing then, and he was irritated with it now. Why should Eli waste a beautiful afternoon out of his life answering hypothetical questions along the lines of "Most other people consider me——"when he could be out learning to field ground balls? It wasn't so much that he had feared that the psychologic testing would be worthless as that he had disliked the idea that it might, after all, be accurate. He did not want his son's personality wrapped up in a dozen or so well-chosen phrases, like a scientific version of "Your Stars Today."

"And at college?" the president asked, breaking the silence.

"He went to a college which did not permit psychologic testing."

Bigelow rounded the table. "So we know nothing about him?"

"That's right," said Clark. General Miles nodded. Levine nodded.

Levine nodded?

"Just a minute," he said. "We know a fair amount about this boy. My God, he's my own son. Maybe I've screwed up somewhere and maybe I don't have perfect insight, but I know something about him."

"Of course," said the president. "I want you to get your chief psychologist over here right away. You'll cooperate with him, won't you, Mr. Levine? Fine. If Mrs. Levine can talk to him, if she's up to it, he'll see her too. There's no use planning without any information. It's eleven thirty now. Let's reconvene at two o'clock. I want you all to have contingency plans by then—have your goddam psychologists come up with something practical. We know fifty percent of the givens in the equation—have them play around with a bunch of possible Eli Levines. Have them try to figure what any weaknesses would be in this situation. Have them figure which possible personalities might play off against what we know of Caputo. Then, when the FBI boys are through with Mr. Levine here and we have some idea of what sort of person his son is, we've already got a leg up. Thank you all for coming."

He headed out the door, flanked by his press aide, Maiwald.

Levine gestured. "Just a moment, Mr. President."

Bigelow wheeled about and stopped.

"Sir, what does the press know of this? Are we going to be able to keep it a secret?"

Bigelow grunted. "Are you kidding? You couldn't keep the . . . the . . . secret around here." His imagination having failed him, Bigelow went back to the facts he felt more familiar with. "The hijackers or whatever we call them haven't made any public demands and haven't gotten in touch with the press, but you can't keep a bus and nineteen men hidden. The word leaked out to Burlington about a half hour after we first got it. The networks should be full of it by now."

———

"...and presidential press secretary Charles Maiwald deferred any further comment, saying only that the White House was in full command of the situation and that a special task force had already been mobilized to deal with the crisis. Maiwald would not comment on the members of the task force, but CIA Director Sterling, FBI Director Clark, and Chairman of the Joint Chiefs General Miles were seen entering the White House earlier today. It is believed that young Eli Levine's father, A. L. Levine, is also directly involved in the crisis group. And now we resume our regular programming."

"Jesus," said Levine.

"Do you want to rest a bit?" said Dr. Logrillo of the FBI.

"No, let's get on with it."

"Fine. Now, I was asking about his feeling toward authority figures. I don't mean merely you and Mrs. Levine, but teachers, policemen, guards, people like that. Can you remember any incidents when he deliberately provoked a confrontation with people like that?"

And again Levine plunged into the rubble of his son's childhood, raking over half-forgotten incidents, stirring regrets and hopes that brought the past back all too vividly. He had made "Never look back" an unspoken rule, and Logrillo's questioning eroded the very basis of his optimism, raising as it did the possibility that things might have turned out better if he had done this in 1965 or that in 1970. He had had no illusions about raising children. Children were necessary, not for enjoyment but to complete the life cycle. During the height of discontent in 1968 when half his friends' children were in Canada or in jail, he had said, "All I expect of my kids is that, if they get arrested, they do it without getting their names in the paper." Now even that hope was gone.

———————

". . . that young Eli Levine's father, A. L. Levine, is also directly involved in the crisis group. And now we resume our regular programming."

The Mexican ambassador watched the announcement on his set and sat staring at it as *General Hospital* returned to the screen. He watched silently another five minutes and then went to the Communications Room, where he put in a direct, scrambled call to the president in Mexico City.

"I think it is now time to announce your birthday," the ambassador said.

"I've been watching too, and I agree," said the president. "It shall be done immediately."

———————

The White House had a copy of the Mexican announcement thirty minutes after the Inspector General of the Federales had finished drafting it, a quarter hour before the full cabinet in Mexico City had voted its token approval. The bulletin was terse.

> Because of the continued exploitation of Mexican resources and Mexican workers by imperialist forces from north of the border, on this day all properties, industries, or businesses in which over twenty percent of the capital is North American shall belong to the Federal Government of Mexico, which will assume all rights and responsibilities of ownership. The Federal Government shall be the sole judge of what constitutes North American capital investment. There shall be no restitution— restitution has already been paid in the blood and sweat of the Mexican worker.

———————

There was a light tap on the door and a presidential aide walked into the room, interrupting Levine's attempt to remember if Eli had been a rare or occasional bed wetter.

"Excuse me, sir. The president would like to see Mr. Levine immediately in the Oval Office."

Inside, Bigelow handed Levine a copy of the announcement. "We just picked this up from the palace in Mexico City," he said. "No one else knows about it, not even the Mexican people"

"Jesus," Levine said. "What news! Just like the Japs. Pearl Harbor all over again. Wait for the most vulnerable moment. Vulnerable. Your own son. After all those treaties we've signed with those bastards. When was the last one, the one guaranteeing against expropriation?"

"Eight months ago," the president said. "I signed it myself. My triumph. I gave them the import cut in return. 'The Munich of the Rio Grande' someone called it. I guess they were right. Son of a bitch!"

He straightened himself up. "Sterling, Clark, and the others are on their way back here. We should be organized in about ten minutes or so. We're going to have to put your son on the back burner, for a moment."

"Just what they wanted," Levine said.

"Yes, of course. No coincidence. Just a way to maximize the confusion. Well, we'll show them. Somehow. It's good you're already here. This is the same sort of thing that the hostage situation is—something where I'm bound to keep the candidates informed. Why don't you go to the Communications Center while we're in here? Maiwald will be with you. We'll ring you when we're ready to talk about options."

"Certainly."

He and the press secretary walked silently to the Communications Center, a vast theater of a room where dozens of scanning units displayed and printed out the burdens of the world. Levine watched it all silently and then turned to Maiwald.

"May I use your phone?"

Maiwald laughed. Humor was not his strong suit, but even he found something amusing in the request.

"Be our guest. The White House operators can locate anyone in the world in about five minutes. No busy signals, either."

The Williamsburger rebbe was a match for the White House operators. "I'm sorry, the rebbe's in his study and can't be disturbed," he heard Rabbi Proner tell the operator.

"It is the White House calling," the operator said, his voice rising.

"I don't care if it's the president already, the rebbe can't be disturbed."

"It *is* the president calling," the operator hissed.

"So, like I just told you, I don't care. The rebbe can't be disturbed."

"Tell him to hold a minute," Levine said to the operator. He motioned Maiwald over to the phone. "Tell this man you're the president's press secretary and you're calling for the president. Tell him it's an emergency. Tell him that the FBI will be investigating him and his diamond deals and that if he wants some consideration he'd better get his boss on the phone in a hurry."

Maiwald spoke crisply into the phone. There was a pause and then he handed it back to Levine.

"What did he say?" Levine asked.

"The diamond deal was perfectly legal, he won't do it again, and he's getting the rabbi."

In a moment Levine heard the familiar voice. "So?"

"Rebbe, is that you?"

"Who else?"

"This is A. L. Levine. Look, I have a terrible problem."

"I don't know about it? I don't have a television set?"

"If you know about it, what should I do? The president is giving me power to control what they do. What does the Law say in a case like this?"

"You've got the power, use it. Act like a mensch. If you've got power, be powerful."

"Don't hang up on me. Help me."

"I'm not hanging up. And I am helping you. Do what I said. Stop running to me with your problems."

"Rebbe, I need guidance. I've got to help choose between the life of one person, who has done wrong, and the lives of nineteen innocent men. But the one person is my son. What does a Jew do in a case like this?"

"The Law says it is never justifiable to commit an immoral act."

"So?"

"So whatever you do will be unjustifiable. Perhaps at Yom Kippur you can try to atone for it to the Almighty. But you can't justify it. Whatever choice you make now will be evil."

"So I should choose the lesser evil?"

"I didn't say that. There is no lesser evil."

"That doesn't help me."

"For that, I'm sorry. I have told you to stop thinking about lesser evils and you say it doesn't help. Perhaps in twenty years you will learn. I have to get back to my study. A man is waiting."

Levine knew when he was lost. "Well, thank you, rebbe."

"My pleasure." There was a pause. "By the way, good luck."

He hung up. "What was that?" asked Maiwald.

"A friend of mine in New York," Levine said. "I thought he might have an idea about my son. No use."

———————

There had been no help and yet, walking back toward the Oval Office, Levine felt a solution trying to force its way to consciousness, a solution that somehow grew from the desperation of the twin crises themselves. If the Mexicans timed their move to coincide with a domestic horror, then somehow they must have lacked ultimate faith in their ability to carry it off by themselves. If success was mutual, failure could be mutual.

Joined by Philip Bell, he waited in a side room next to the president's office. Helen had reached Laura by phone, and she, too, was hurrying toward the White House. We are going to have a family reunion on Pennsylvania Avenue, Levine thought bitterly to himself, and then suddenly the pieces fell into place and locked, and he saw a way to lift the yoke.

He motioned to Maiwald. "I must speak to the president now. I think I see a way out of all this. Tell him I must speak to him alone, just for five minutes."

"He's back in there with the National Security Council," Maiwald said.

"I know that. But he'll listen to me. Tell him it's urgent."

A moment later Bigelow appeared, standing outside his own office. Levine silently blessed him for his decency. "The quietest place right now is in the corridor," the president said. "Let's talk there."

Marines like statues stood guard fifty feet away at either end of the long hallway as Levine whispered to the president.

"The most important thing for the plan is knowing when the Mexicans are going to make their move officially. Has anyone found out about it yet? Has there been any official activity down there at all?"

"No. The only people who know about the order are the Mexican cabinet and us. From the signals we're getting they won't be able to make an official announcement for another one or two hours. They haven't even called in their own press secretary yet."

"That saves us. Listen, you and I are going to make an official announcement about the thing in Vermont. How long does it take to set up a national TV announcement from the White House?"

"Ten minutes. We call the networks, explain it's an emergency presidential announcement, and that's it. The broadcast facilities are always on standby."

"God is good. Now, let me explain what must be done. It is a bluff, but then, God save us, it is not a bluff."

Pacing in small steps, Levine explained. The president nodded, asked a few questions, and thought. Then they stood together, alone in the long corridor, both silent.

Bigelow nodded. "Are you sure you are willing to take the chance?"

"I have no choice," Levine said.

"I will tell the people inside," Bigelow said, gesturing toward the Oval Office.

"You're sure that you can get me into short-wave touch with my son?"

"They've got the frequency monitored in the Communications Room. With the equipment there you can talk to a guy on the moon; Vermont is no problem. In fact, you better head back there now. I'll let you know if the NCS has any objections or additions."

Levine returned to the Communications Room with Bell. A duty officer guided him to a transmitting unit. Levine noted in an absently professional way that the equipment seemed Japanese-made, though all manufacturer's marks had been removed. He wondered if Arco and Hersch had ever tried to sell the White House.

An aide handed him a wireless phone. Bigelow's voice was clear. "Go ahead with your transmission as planned," he said. "The NSC has no objections. We called in Logrillo. He confirms that your estimate of your son's probable reaction is a realistic one. You won't back out, will you?"

"How can I? I've given my word. Besides, I know this must be done. There is a saying among the old Jews that 'Jewish thief is twice a thief.' And what is another Jew but a member of one's own family, and thus what is said about Jews is said of one's family."

"I don't understand," the president said.

"You don't have to," Levine answered. "May I broadcast now?"

"I've already told the duty officer to get you on Eli's wavelength."

"Thank you."

He turned to the transmitting deck in front of him, now alive with glowing dials. The duty officer, a navy commander, indicated the built-in microphone. "Any time you're ready, sir," he said.

"Now would be fine."

There was a little crackling noise from the banks of lights and switches, and the duty officer leaned over and said, "Eagle's Nest, Eagle's Nest—this is the White House. Do you read me?"

Eli's voice came in, close and clear. "We read you."

The officer nodded and Levine spoke.

"Eli, this is your father. Is that you?"

"Yes. Hi, Dad, how are you?"

"Eli, I'm fine. We don't have time for pleasantries. Let me tell you—the president has asked me to approve any action they take against you. He won't take any move without my agreeing. So I'm in a dilemma. But I know what must be done. I love you. I'm sorry we haven't been as close as we should have been. Things get in the way. I love you, but I can't let innocent men get killed on your account, and I can't allow murderers to go free. You understand. So far you've been acting under coercion. You haven't committed any serious crime yet. It's not too late to give up, to save yourself. And your friend."

"I'm sorry, Dad, but I'm doing what I think is right. I have my comrades to think of."

"Look, Eli, don't do anything foolish. There is still time. Your mother is very worried. I am going to make an announcement with the president very soon. You have some time. Remember to be just to your fellowman."

"I'm sorry about Mother. I can't talk any more."

"Okay. Good-bye."

"Over and out."

"Yes, over and out."

Eli sounded like he had when he was nine years old, and someone had given him a toy walkie-talkie for his birthday.

Levine walked away from the transmitter and slumped in a chair.

"Is there anything I can do?" Bell asked.

"No. I expected that. Now I have to rest for a moment, and then join the president."

The cameras had been moved into the Oval Office for the occasion. Bigelow was seated behind his desk, Levine a bit behind him and to the left. The voice-over intoned, "The President of the United States," and they were on.

"Fellow Americans," Bigelow began, "as you know, a group of American security forces is being held hostage at this moment in northern Vermont. In return for the safe return of these hostages, the terrorist group holding them has demanded that we release from federal prisons a number of their fellow revolutionaries already convicted and imprisoned. In addition, they are demanding the withdrawal of the presidential candidacy of Mr. A. L. Levine. One of the two active terrorists is Peter Caputo. The other has been positively identified as Eli Levine, the son of the candidate.

"Because it is long-established policy that major presidential candidates shall be informed of governmental crises as they occur, so as to bind the continuity of our government, Mr. Levine would have been kept in touch with this crisis as a matter of course. Since a member of his family is directly involved, the White House and the National Security Council have sought the guidance and concurrence of Mr. Levine. I would now like to introduce Mr. A. L. Levine."

Levine cleared his throat and began. "Terrible times bring terrible decisions, decisions that cannot be avoided. As President Bigelow has said, my son and another young man are holding hostage nineteen innocent men. The terrorists are counting in part on my prominence, my own position in an election campaign, to make demands that would mean either the death of these nineteen men or the unleashing on the public of a band of convicted killers and arsonists, each of whom is more than willing to kill again.

"Your president has humanely asked my advice in this crisis. As a parent, I would be a monster if I consented to the death of my son. Yet I would be infinitely more despicable if I chose to let my son go free while nineteen innocent men—or even one innocent man—were killed in his place. The Lord God says justice must be done. Therefore I have given my consent to demand that my son and his accomplice release the hostages within two hours. After that time, I have given my consent for the president and the military forces under General Miles to act appropriately, up to and including the use of force. God willing, it will not be necessary."

The camera switched back to Bigelow. "We appreciate the agonizing decision Mr. Levine must make. We plead with Peter Caputo and Eli Levine to yield. We will not, however, bargain with terrorists. Thank you."

––––––––––

"Now what do we do?" Bigelow asked. "I know we wait for the Mexicans, but how long?"

Sterling interrupted. "Sir, as Mr. Levine outlined the plan and as we concurred, we make sure that the Burlington television stations carry the Mexican manifesto as soon as it hits the international wires. I have the network presidents on standby. I haven't given the exact details of what's coming, but they say they will consent so long as we can guarantee the Mexican thing's for real."

"No doubt about that," General Miles grumbled.

"As soon as the announcer has finished reading the text of the Mexican bulletin, we're ready to plug you, Mr. President, and Mr. Levine into the Burlington stations."

"Okay. Now, let's get the Mexican ambassador over here."

"Sir, he's on his way."

––––––––––

For the occasion the Mexican ambassador wore a green beret and a black jump suit. He looked like a young, minor-league Fidel Castro.

Bigelow's greeting was curt.

"Please sit down, Mr. Rojas. You know Mr. Levine?" he asked. Levine again was sitting just to the president's left.

"Ye , of course."

"You have been watching television this morning?" Again, the president's manner was less questioning than accusing.

"*Si.*"

"Then you know we are having problems with some hostages in the northern states. Now, Mr. Rojas, we have received some disquieting words from our representatives in Mexico City. We understand that President Sarcasta is about to make a declaration about United States property in Mexico."

"I am afraid I do not understand what you are talking about."

The President tapped a button on his desk. From a wall speaker came Rojas's voice: "I think it is now time to announce your birthday." An anonymous voice from the CIA then read the text of the manifesto, first in Spanish, then in English.

"So we shall play no games, Mr. Rojas. Agreed?"

"I must protest the intrusion—"

"Shut up," Bigelow said. "Now listen, and listen closely. I have not been a great president, but I will not be a bad one. I'm not going to be blackmailed on my way out of office, not by another country, not by a friend's son. Now, if you truly were watching closely this morning, you would have seen that I am willing to kill the son of my old associate here for the sake of national peace. You saw that Mr. Levine here is willing to have his son killed rather than to allow strangers, innocent men, to die. Mr. Levine and I are both old men, Señor Rojas. You are young and perhaps you do not understand. But let me speak clearly so that you and your president understand. You can see that I am fatigued from having worried over this hostage business, can you not?"

Rojas nodded.

"And you can see that, having worried about that and having sat with Mr. Levine here and having decided that we might have to kill his son, I am tired and that things which once seemed horrible to me seem less horrible. You can understand that from the perspective of two men who have had to sit and decide the fate of one man's son, the force of world opinion is less important than it once was, can you not?"

Rojas nodded and started to say something. Bigelow cut him off.

"Please let me continue. I will be brief. You can understand, can you not, that having acceded to the death of a young man I have known for many years, the death of a few thousand or even a few million more seems less important? All are strangers, after all. You understand that?"

Rojas nodded.

"So you will understand that I will not stand for one moment the expropriation of our property and the violation of a treaty that I signed personally, with my own hand—*con mi verdad mano*"—the Spanish startled Levine and Rojas equally—"and that if your government's order is not rescinded within one hour we will bomb the shit out of your whole country? You realize that, too?"

Rojas nodded.

"Because I want to make it clear that I don't give a God damn what anyone else in this country or your country or the whole fucking world thinks about it. After I kill off Levine's son it will not be no problem at all to kill off a few million Mexicans. You will tell that to your president, will you not?"

Rojas nodded.

"And will you be sure to tell him that if I, Stephen Bigelow, am a bloodthirsty bastard, he ought to worry about Mr. A. L. Levine, who is willing that his son die that his honor not be disgraced. And be sure to tell him that if he does not have to worry about us, he should be prepared to worry about Mr. Rose, who believes we should have bombed Mexico City two years ago just for the hell of it. You will tell him that, certainly?"

Rojas nodded. He was sweating very slightly.

"Now, it is very important that he understand that he'll never see that blonde in Callo Vallejo again and that he won't get to use the money he has in Craft's Bank in Nassau and that he'll never get to play with his new fighter planes. Because I'm going to blow them all to pieces, *comprende?*"

Rojas nodded.

"So I want you to pick up that phone over there and tell him just what I've said. Tell him I'm going to be easy on him—he can say that the manifesto was a forgery or the result of a junta or whatever, and we'll back him up. I'm

not going to embarrass him. In fact, it was a bold move.
But it was a mistake. Go ahead. I'll tell you when the line's
open."

Rojas stared.

"Okay. You wait a bit. Think it over. You can't leave
here for a few minutes anyway. We have to wait for the
official announcement of the manifesto from your
government. Sit down. Have a candy."

Eli was tired of monitoring the television. After the
flurry of announcements and special reports, there had
been the joint appearance of his father and Bigelow, and
the networks had resumed their regular programming.
Indeed, like a bad memory of his childhood, *Christmas
Every Day* was on and the same women—and now
men—were leaping and scrambling in that same humiliat-
ing way when, suddenly, the picture faded and a voice
said, "We bring you a special announcement from
Washington, D.C."

He tapped Caputo on the shoulder. "Peter, listen.
They're back to us again."

But instead a crisp voice said. "We interrupt your
regular programming to bring the following bulletin,
released from the presidential palace of the Republic of
Mexico. 'Because of the continued exploitation of
Mexican resources and Mexican workers...'"

The announcer read the rest of the manifesto, paused,
and then said, "We now transfer you to the White House,
where President Stephen Bigelow will again address the
nation, this time regarding the Mexican situation."

Back to the Oval Office. Back to Bigelow, in the same
undistinguished suit, sitting behind his desk. Back again
to Levine, slightly to the left and toward the rear.

"Fellow Americans, you have just heard the text of a
manifesto issued but minutes ago by the Republic of
Mexico. As Commander in Chief of the armed forces, I
have a responsibility to defend our citizens and their
property from this outrageous act, which is not only in
violation of international law but in direct contravention
of the recent treaty of the Rio Grande, signed by myself
and the current president of Mexico. I have called a

special session of Congress to act upon this clear-cut repudiation of decency. In the meantime I have put the nation's military forces on standby and have authorized the use of full and appropriate force, up to and including nuclear weapons, to prevent any forcible interference with American lives or holdings within Mexico. I take this step with the full and solemn knowledge of the possible consequences. Because we are now engaged in our presidential campaign, I have the legal responsibility to notify the candidates of the major parties of any action the consequences of which they may have to deal with after my term is over. The action just outlined meets with the full accord of Mr. A. L. Levine"—a slight nod in the direction of Levine, who nodded back—"and his opponent, who could not be here for this broadcast, Mr. Willard Rose."

"Jesus Christ," Eli said.

Caputo was silent.

"Jesus," he repeated. "What do you think, Peter? What's it mean?"

Caputo smiled wanly. "I think it's the end of the system. I don't much care for the Mexican revolutionaries, but they're doing our work for us."

WASHINGTON, OCTOBER 5, 1988

Levine and Bigelow came out of the Oval Office together. Rojas was sitting in the Fish Room, staring at a television set on which *Christmas Every Day* had abruptly resumed.

"You saw us?" Bigelow asked cheerily.

Rojas nodded. His eyes were now fixed on an ancient blue marlin, the relic of one of FDR's fishing trips, mounted and hung over the far end of the room.

"It is now time to call your president. Most of the world hasn't gotten that announcement yet. If you talk to him right away, you can save him humiliation. You can save millions of your countrymen from death."

Rojas started toward the door.

"I don't think you need to go back to your embassy. Remember the recording I played for you earlier. We hear what happens there, we hear what happens in the Palacio Presidencial. You might as well call from the Communications Center. We'll give you a quiet booth and a couple of quarters. Mr. Maiwald will show you the way."

Rojas left quietly.

"I think we've got him," the president said.

"It looks that way."

"I've convinced the Mexicans that I'm crazy enough to kill your son in Vermont. I've probably convinced your son that I'm crazy enough to kill a million Mexicans. I'm not sure, though, that even that's enough to make Eli back down."

"I know. I'm not absolutely sure, but I think it will work."

"Why?"

"There's nothing more real to those kids than television. Seeing it like that, they feel it. Eli isn't psychotic. He'll feel the forces closing in on him."

"Maybe he'll feel them, but I don't know about the

other one—Caputo. From the profile they gave us this morning, he seems more determined, more fanatical."

"That's true. That's what I'm counting on."

"What?"

"That the two of them will fall apart. I only pray Eli doesn't get killed."

A communications aide walked up to Bigelow.

"Mr. President, sir. That Mexican transmission's beginning now. We have a voice-over translation, if you don't mind."

Bigelow touched a switch. Two Spanish-speaking voices broke out of a speaker on his desk. Over them both droned a slightly affected, mildly Oxonian translator.

"El Presidente wishes ambassador good day. Ambassador reciprocates. Ambassador calling from White House where he believes North American president has become deranged by crisis. Bigelow, usually a man of caution, now speaks and acts like a madman. With him in White House is the Señor Levine, who also lacks judgment. Levine's true son is enemy of the government. Levine has agreed to bomb him. No family feeling. Señor Bigelow insists he will destroy Mexico.

"Now El Presidente says this is empty threat. Ambassador says no, Juan, no, I have seen it in their eyes. They are madmen who will kill us all. Is that all, El Presidente asks? Ambassador says no. Bigelow also says you will never see the blond person in Calle Vallejo and never attain Craft's Bank. El Presidente says, Enough, what does he want? Ambassador says we are to announce that manifesto was illegal, maybe a junta, and he will support us on that. El Presidente says that does not sound like madman. Ambassador says do not take the chance to find out. El Presidente says okay."

NEAR RICHFORD, OCTOBER 5, 1988

In the mountains they heard the news of Mexico's capitulation. "Amazing," Caputo whispered. "They backed off."

"Peter, my father and Bigelow are crazy. They'd have killed the whole world; they're going to kill us. It doesn't matter to them."

"So let them."

"It matters to me. This is suicide. I never signed up for that."

"Be brave."

"Be brave! Of course I'm brave. Could a coward do what we have done? But now it's just craziness. I don't want to kill those men, and I don't want to get blown up. Not by my father."

Caputo was angry. "You talk like a child. Now you're afraid of violence, afraid of death."

"I'm not. I'm not afraid of it, but I don't like it. In your manifesto you talked of sensible violence. This is senseless."

"The manifesto was a long time ago. Now we are here and there is nothing to do but complete our plan."

"Bullshit. You're crazy."

"I knew it." Caputo's face turned purple and his voice squeaked in a new and foolish way. "I knew it. When it comes to the showdown, you're a goddam yellow kike."

"Son of a bitch!" Eli shouted. People had called him that before, but never anyone he had respected. It hurt. "Son of a bitch!" he shouted again, and hit Caputo a straight chop across the back of the neck. Caputo rolled back toward the sleeping bags. Raising his hands high above his head and waving a piece of white cloth, Eli stepped out of the bunker and, gingerly, down the steep mountainside. A few pieces of granite tumbled along in his path.

His valet stepped back a pace and peered at him solemnly.

"I think that does it, sir."

Levine twirled slightly before the full-length mirror. His tails swung with the motion. The pearl buttons on the vest sparkled. He tugged slightly at his jacket sleeves; a bit too much cuff showed. The top hat rested on the dresser shelf.

"That's fine, Walter, that's fine. Tell you what—why don't you wait outside a few minutes while I finish cleaning up? I'll buzz you when I'm ready to join Mrs. Levine and the rest of the family."

"Certainly, Mr. President."

With Walter gone, he stood for a moment staring out the window. Beyond the Ellipse stretching toward the Washington Monument the miliatry units of the Inaugural Parade had finished assembling. Levine scratched his ass gently—his hemorrhoids tended to itch when he was nervous—and slumped down in the armchair facing the monument.

It was awesome, there was no doubt of that. He had heard that during the 1976 transition, when Carter had come up to be briefed by Ford, the new president-elect had been unimpressed by the job. There's not as much to it as I had thought, someone had heard him say. Well, he had learned, but it had been a difficult learning.

I don't see how he wasn't scared, Levine thought to himself. God knows, I've been around presidents on and off for twenty-five years, but I never guessed, never suspected, the scariness of it all. The absolute intimidating fearsomeness. How could Carter have missed it? he wondered. Smart as he was, maybe he lacked imagination. A bit of imagination could throw you off on this job, he thought, looking around the room.

Oh, it wasn't the awesomeness of the past that got him, the ghosts of the great men and the great events that the commentators like to talk about. It has been the ghosts of the future which had come pressing in on him since November, the prefigurements of events that he somehow had never felt but which he knew would be as real to him someday as the shoes on his feet.

Day by day since the election he had been stuffed with the nation's problems, problems that had never seemed important or even real during the campaign. He had thought he knew what it would be like to be briefed on the African situation by the Secretary of State. After all, during the campaign he had sat down with dozens of ex-secretaries of state and ambassadors, and he had even been given an outline of African policies and problems by the incumbent. But, he remembered, he had once thought he had an idea of what it would be like to play professional football, and then a friend had given him a ticket to the sidelines and for the first time he had heard the screams of the players and the smash of helmets and had felt the thunder of feet and had smelled the ammonia and the grass and the fear, and he had known that this was an entirely different form of life.

What was the poem Kennedy had liked so much? Something about everyone shouting suggestions, but only the man in the ring had to face the bull. He would ask Jones about that. Jones would remember. Anyway, the idea was right: it was all posturing until you had to get out—alone—and face the beast. "The buck stops here," Truman had proclaimed, but as a slogan it was too cute, too shallow. Truman said he had never agonized about dropping the atom bomb. He should have, Levine thought. Jesus, I'm not one for retrospection, but I'd at least have looked back a little.

No, there was no way to prepare for the job, and if he had spent years in the Congress or in a statehouse somewhere it wouldn't have been any better. Maybe it would have been worse, because it might have given him the illusion, as it had Carter, that he was somehow ready for the job. Better to know from the start that you weren't.

The problems were out there, and they wouldn't go away. He sensed, if no one else did, that the disunity of the states would have to be his immediate priority, and that he would have to face down the series of tariffs, travel restrictions, and harassments that his predecessors had preferred to let stand rather than chance secession. His attorney general, Basmadjian, was a signal to the states' rights people that their era was over—or that, at least, it would be challenged.

Somehow, too, the bitterness toward the Patrols would have to be diffused. Jessington had been a help already, but even as FBI director he wouldn't be able to take all the burden. The energy problem would not go away, either. He had given his okay to the two fusion plants that Bigelow had stopped work on. The environmentalists were furious, but they'd been even angrier when Carter had cut off their electricity back in 1980.

Something always had to give. In that he felt his strongest hope. If there is anything I can do, he thought, it's to mediate, to intercede, to explain. What the country needs is a middleman, and as a middleman I've had two thousand years' practice. Without a middleman, without someone who genuinely felt for both sides, the country was going to tear itself apart, the young at the throat of the old, the freezing at the throat of the conservationists. The defenders of privacy clashed with the legions of the right-to-know. The right to bear arms collided with the right to avoid being shot to death at a stoplight. The right to bark was inconsistent with the right to sleep-filled nights. Each American had his passion, and each clamored for attention, shouting, "I'm right, I'm right" and demanding, insisting, that the government ensure his claim to the right—while denouncing the spread of government.

Levine listened to the clanging voices and knew the secret, knew that they were all right, and sympathized with their rightness, sympathized totally with one side until the moment he heard the other, when his emotions and his sympathies tended to follow like a shadow.

Was he a man without convictions, he wondered? No,

for his strongest conviction was that convictions were dangerous, general principles unsound, justice fleeting, and error common. In that he felt he offered something that his predecessors, politicians all—yes, even Eisenhower!—had lacked. They had been able to point to a body of positions taken and characterize themselves: yes, I'm a conservative; yes, I'm a liberal; yes, I'm a pragmatist. He could not, would not, do that. The press had been unable to do it. There was a clean slate. There was hope yet.

There was a light tap at the door, and Walter's head appeared. "They're waiting, Mr. President."

He cradled the top hat in his arm and went to join his family.